Jane Hadley

To those glorious fiends who taught me to feel with music.
This is not Jock Jams.

Author's Note

This is a novel set to music.
Footnotes throughout will cue each song.
janehadleywrites.com/oypt

1

The first time Arthur Ohashi put on his obaasan's kimono, he sang feelingly, "I'm Through with Love" in his best imitation of Marilyn Monroe from *Some Like It Hot,* and his mother had walked silently up to him and smacked him in the mouth. In the bathroom afterwards, as he watched the blood bead on his lower lip, he tried to summon up the shame he was supposed to feel, but the only lesson he walked away with was that next time, he wouldn't get caught.

The first time Arthur Ohashi met Eve Clark, it was the fall of junior year, and he'd just managed to convince his mom to let him live in the dormitory. He had his own room in Comstock Hall, and it was *heaven.* He could drape himself in his kimono, enjoy the slip of fine silk over his skin, and let his Velvet Underground records hammer his heart back into shape as he basked in the careful concoction of ephemera that made him thrum with bombshell energy.

On that particular fateful day, he was mindlessly messing around on the ivory keys of the out-of-tune upright nestled in one corner of the Coffman Union commons, wearing his armor of buttoned shirt and tie. The tune wasn't anything special, just a few blues chords while he chewed on a problem he and his group had encountered in their Linear Structural Analysis lab. He'd seen B.B. King at The Depot over the summer, and he couldn't get the rhythm out of his fingers. It was no coincidence that, as he was humming "Ask Me No Questions" over the chord progression, a sparkling vision of a girl dipped her chestnut head into Arthur's line of vision and said, "Can I ask you a question?"

Arthur blinked and had a rude realization that he was indeed perceivable here in the corner. It was a beautiful fall day; everyone was supposed to be out in the quad. It took him a moment to brace himself for an unexpected social interaction before he said, "Yes?"[1]

"Where did you learn to play like that?" the girl asked, her voice carrying a lilt of some kind of British accent. Arthur ducked his chin to hide a blush that was rising, less because of the compliment and more from the horror of having to speak to such a beautiful girl. With his head ducked down, it was impossible to ignore that, in addition to an alluring, symmetrical face, the girl had also been blessed with curves a Renaissance painter would have sold his soul to paint. What on earth had possessed someone like her to speak to him?

"My parent's church," Arthur replied and tried not to grimace. He was a certified loser.

The girl's dark eyes widened, and one slash of eyebrow quirked upwards. "I've never heard of a church playing rock music."

Arthur scooched his glasses up his nose and squirmed. "Well, I just learned how to play the *instrument* at the church. The rock and roll was more of a ... secondary interest."

The girl laughed, her smile wide and beguiling and utterly perfect. Arthur was staring. He really shouldn't stare. The girl reached down and slid her fingers around his hand.

---

1. "Femme Fatale" The Velvet Underground

"You have gorgeous hands, darling," she murmured. Arthur swallowed hard and desperately tried not to snatch his hand back or say something completely weird. Her smile curved into her cheeks and left dimples on either side. "Have you ever thought about playing in a band?"

He couldn't help but furrow his brow in confusion. "A band?" he repeated, flustered.

"Yeah," the girl said casually, as if it were totally normal to chat with a stranger about something as complicated as joining a musical ensemble. "I sing with a combo and the tunes we're working on could really use some of those far out riffs you're laying out."

Far out? No one had ever used that phrase to describe Arthur Ohashi. Not once, not ever—not since that slap in the face. His mother hadn't meant to hurt him that day. She'd imparted a severe but serious lesson to protect him. Arthur had been a novelty in his West St. Paul high school teeming with blue-eyed, blonde-haired teens. Granted, the Ohashis weren't the only Asian family in the area; there was a modest Japanese-American community in St. Paul proper, made up of the families of men and women who'd escaped Minidoka and Manzanar to prove their loyalty at the Military Intelligence Service Language School. But Arthur's penchant for glamor was far too much of a liability to pile on top of looking vaguely like the Vietcong. If he did anything to draw attention to himself in church or school or any number of more public venues, much less dress in a way that made his usually tightly-locked body feel at ease, the reckoning would be so swift and painful it would make his naive little head spin. Precisely the reason why he could never, ever be in a band.

"Oh, um, that's very nice of you but—"

"Come on," she interrupted him, pulling him by his hand towards the center of the commons, "You have to at least come and meet the others before you say no."

Arthur stumbled over the piano bench, darting a hand out for his abandoned bag as the girl dragged him across Coffman Union.

"I'm Eve, by the way," she said, shaking the hand she had seized entirely against his will. "Eve Clark."

"Arthur," he replied awkwardly.

"Really?"

Arthur tried not to roll his eyes. "Yes. After General MacArthur. My father served under him during the Occupation."

Eve frowned thoughtfully. "I hope he named you before that bastard threatened to nuke Korea."

He shouldn't have been surprised that she knew something about international political history just because she was pretty. Just like she shouldn't have been surprised that he had a Scottish name just because he was Asian. "Technically yes. But just barely."

"Well, Mr. Arthur..." she looked at him expectantly. He stared blankly for a moment.

"Oh, Ohashi."

"Well, Mr. Arthur Ohashi, you'll fit right in with the rest of the guys."

Yeah, right.

No one could blame him for being skeptical. She dragged him over to the doors that led out onto the quad and shoved the door open, a shaft of late afternoon sunlight blinding him for a moment.

It occurred to Arthur that he had no idea where she was taking him, but it also occurred to him somewhat more forcefully that he was parading across the quad holding hands with someone who was arguably in the running for the most beautiful girl on campus. Eve drew the eyes of everyone they passed, from the hippies to the Young Republicans and everyone in between. And who could resist looking? Her shining brown hair flowed thick and straight down her back, her breasts and hips swaying more comfortably in a sleeveless top and miniskirt than he had ever managed in his obaasan's kimono (and he had been safe in the dark privacy of his basement).

She caught the eyes of her adoring public too. Caught their gaze and smiled winningly as she held his hand. *His* hand. Arthur Ohashi, the nerd who played piano for the old biddies at his parent's church. It made him feel for a moment that perhaps the social humiliation of trying to play music with strangers might be worthwhile if it meant he could spin in Eve Clark's orbit for a little while longer.

"Here they are. Jim! Deb! Look, I found a piano player! Arthur Ohashi, may I present to you Jim Novak and Deb Gutierrez."

Arthur's eyes darted between The Guys. Nothing about them suggested he would fit right in with them. Jim was tall and willowy, his hair flowing over his shoulders in thick, blonde curls like he was ripped from the picture sleeve of Led Zeppelin II. He was clean-shaven and lounging in the grass in jeans so tight they'd have put Mick Jagger to shame. Deb was not precisely a guy—at least, Arthur didn't think so, given the name—and wore a white t-shirt with a cigarette pack rolled up in the sleeve like she was James Dean or something. As unusually long as Jim's hair was, Deb's was the opposite. Short, and not in a fashionable bubble bob, but pompadoured and slick with pomade. Both of The Guys regarded Arthur with equal skepticism, the cigarette drooping incredulously from Deb's lips. The only way he would fit in with this group was by virtue of the fact that he was as completely different from them as they were from each other.

Deb transferred her skeptical glare onto Eve. "You found a piano player in the ladies toilet? That's a first."

Eve laughed. "No, of course not. I found him in the Commons *after* I went to the loo."

Jim's regard was significantly less hostile than Deb's, but only by virtue of the fact that beyond a brief, unimpressed once over, it seemed he could hardly care less about Arthur's presence. "We don't need a piano player badly enough that you need to abduct poor, unsuspecting CSE students."

Arthur prickled. When he got the chance to enroll in the College of Science and Engineering, no one would blame him for jumping at it. Not only did it present an alternative to the draft that fed the meat-grinder of the Vietnam War, but it meant he could move out of his parents' house and have a bit of privacy of his own, even if it was restricted to a 10 foot square dorm room.

"How do you know he's a CSE student?" Eve challenged, crossing her arms across her chest and pressing her breasts into two perfect swells swathed in burnt-orange polyester. Jim caught Arthur looking and rolled his eyes. Maybe he was Eve's boyfriend. It would make sense with the amount of disdain the man was leveling on him.

"Are you?" Jim asked him.

Arthur pressed his lips together. "Well, yes, but I don't see what difference—"

"Eve," Jim sighed. "There are plenty of bands with only three members."

"Oh, stop being such a wet blanket," Eve chided, her flippancy cutting through the tension with finality. "We need a bigger sound than a guitar, bass, and drums on their own. Besides, we need another voice for harmonies."

"How do you know he can sing?" Deb interrogated.

Eve turned to Arthur. "Can you sing?" she asked sweetly.

"Um, yes, but—"

"See!" Eve crowed, right as Deb crossed her arms and said, "Alright, let's hear it, then."

Arthur shrank, looking awkwardly between the three of them. "Maybe I should let you all work this out..."

Eve reached out and cried, "No, it's fine!" just as Jim said, "Maybe that would be best."

"It's alright," Arthur said. "I don't have a whole lot of time to work on a side project anyway. I've got to prepare for my final design next year, and I usually spend weekends at my parents'..."

Leave it to Arthur to make himself sound significantly more like a loser than he actually was.

"You live on campus, don't you?" Eve said in an all-business tone.

"I do. Do you?"

"Well, not *on* campus, but near enough," she shrugged. "Do you know the Coffeehouse Extempore?"

Arthur tried not to grimace as he reluctantly nodded. That place was for hippies and, well, queers. He'd be lying if he said he'd never peered curiously through the windows while passing by, but Okaasan would be apoplectic if she smelled a place like that on him. She could detect Mary Jane and deviance a mile away.

"We're playing a show there tomorrow night. Come see us play. Let us blow your mind. Then you can decide for yourself." Eve smiled, her eyes alight with mischief that made him insatiably curious. Arthur almost let himself think about it for a moment, standing on a stage, playing piano and singing. A performance of beauty and wonder, otherworldly and beguiling. That person wasn't him, though, at least not the person talking to these band members right now. He was just a nerdy CSE student. The notion of him playing in a rock band was ridiculous.

Jim rolled his eyes while Deb smirked as if they agreed. Arthur's eyes flicked between them. He wondered if they both imagined some claim over Eve. It was entirely possible if they were Extempore aficionados. The last thing a love triangle needed was a fourth corner.

"I'll think about it," Arthur said, readjusting his satchel over his shoulder and scooching his glasses again.

Eve smiled beguilingly and leaned forward to press her lips to his cheek. Her hand was heavy on his shoulder, and her breasts brushed up against his chest. She tipped her chin down, looking up at him beneath her eyelashes as she tucked her hair behind her ear. "I hope you do."

Arthur blushed all the way to the tips of his ears. Jim gave out a long-suffering sigh and flopped back on the grass.

"Okay," Arthur managed, his voice somewhat higher pitched than he'd like. Swallowing hard, he forced himself to turn around and head towards his dormitory.

"Eve, you're incorrigible."

Arthur just heard the words as he walked away, unsure whether it was Deb or Jim who said them. He pushed his glasses up so he could rub his eyes. This was some sort of farce. He didn't know what, but he resolved then and there to forget all about the Coffeehouse Extempore.

2

"Artie, you *have* to go!"

That was Tomiko. She was a political science major whose parents had served with Arthur's at the Military Intelligence Service Language School, and they'd grown up going to church together. It was surreal to hear her bully him into attending a musical performance, because her usual line was bullying him to attend demonstrations with the Student Mobilization Committee for the End of War in Vietnam. Either way, it would be easy to say no, because Arthur already made a habit of avoiding anything Tomiko thought he should do, ever since the Mobe took over Coffman Union and Morrill Hall protesting the Kent State shooting last spring. He wasn't certain how they managed to avoid getting arrested, but he thanked his lucky stars they had because after all his father had been through in World War II, seeing him behind bars would have sent Otosan into cardiac arrest.

"I don't know," Arthur said, pushing ketchup around his plate with a French fry. "They gave me a bad feeling."

"Everyone gives you a bad feeling, Artie. It's called social neurosis."

"I don't have a neurosis."

"Just keep telling yourself that." Tomi muttered.

"Well, have *you* been to Extempore?"

"Of course I have. I'm a hippie," she said primly.

Arthur glanced up at her. "Well, then, what was it like?"

"Like a hippie cafe, Artie. If you don't know what that means, then you definitely need to go. How have you made it to 1970 without ever going to a hippie cafe?"

Arthur shrugged. He wanted to ask her about the other part, the *queer* part, but he couldn't manage the courage to form the words. He didn't want to sound like a square, nor did he want to appear too interested.

"Oh you're so pitiful, just *go*, for fuck's sake. Most bands I know of break up after three weeks anyway, so it's not as if you're committing to anything. Besides, didn't you say she just asked you to hear them play? You don't even have to say yes if you don't like it."

"I don't know, Tomi. Eve is ... different. I'm not sure I can say no to her."

"Is 'different' the new word for hot, now? You poor, pitiful virgin."

Arthur stuck his tongue out at her. He should never have told her that.

Tomiko gave a long sigh as she shoved her chair back from the table. "I don't see how you *can't* go, under the circumstances. I'd be a terrible friend if I let you keep hiding in your dorm doing E=MC^2 until your brain oozes out your ears from lack of human contact."

"Einstein's a theoretical physicist. I'm just studying civil engineering."

Tomiko smacked her hand on the table like she was giving a speech at a rally. "Fact is, Artie, this almost certainly the one and only time in your life a hot girl asks you to be in her band. In fact, I'd put good money on that. So if you don't go, you'll be stuck wondering what might have been for the rest of your life. You only have one life—"

"—Not according to the Buddha—"

"Stop that. You're a Methodist. You know I'm right. I'll walk over there with you, if you want."

"You *really* don't need to do that—"

"—but you *need* to do this, Four-Eyes." Tomiko gathered her books in her arms and gave him the look she usually saved for riot police. Arthur was appropriately chastened.

"I won't say 'I told you so' tomorrow, but I'll be thinking it!" she called as she turned on her heel and pushed the dining hall doors open, heading out into the dusk. Arthur buried his face in his arms.

He should never have told her. She was always right—it was really quite annoying.

Arthur went back up to his room and realized when he looked at his watch that he didn't know what time Eve's band played. So he anxiously tried on all of his button-up shirts, which looked ridiculous without a tie (but who wears a tie to a hippie bar?) and then settled on a short-sleeved paisley polo that was the closest he could manage to psychedelic. At the back of his wardrobe, his kimono beckoned to him. He closed the door with a petulant bang.[1]

He stood quietly for a moment, regarding himself in the mirror. He experienced the odd sensation that he was looking at a stranger. Who was that awkward boy? It certainly wasn't him. It wasn't the boy who'd squeezed onto the rail between screaming Black girls last summer to see B.B. King. Who sang along to every song at the top of his lungs. Who played the Kinks in the basement at home while lounging in Obaasan's kimono, sucking on strawberries to stain his lips red.

This shell of a reflection, with his short, black sheaf of hair, tortoise-shell glasses, and armor of collared shirts and navy blue slacks, wasn't him. He *could* play piano well. He knew that. He *could* play music with other people. He wasn't actually this facsimile of an Asian American stereotype he wore every day.

---

1. "Oh! You Pretty Things" David Bowie

Arthur straightened slightly. He messed up his carefully combed hair. Really, the only thing he was afraid of was not fitting in. That wasn't so scary, was it? It's not like he didn't spend his days feeling on the outside of everything. Maybe a hippie cafe was just the place to be a little strange.

Arthur reached out to his bedside table and snatched his wallet and his omamori, stuffing both in his pockets. He'd need all the luck he could get if he was going to go through with this.

By the time he made his way to Cedar Street on the West Bank of the Mississippi River, it was dark. Students milled about outside the bars, smoking cigarettes and filling the air with the scents of stale beer and tobacco. It was two blocks south to the Coffeehouse Extempore, near the corner of Cedar and River-side. The facade was a brick wall with two large, painted arrows pointing to a nondescript door painted with the word *Music*.

"Hey, man, you got a light?"

Arthur turned and foud himself face to face with a gangly, bearded man with long, stringy hair. He smelled like reefer and body odor. Arthur dug in his pocket for his matchbook, and his fingers brushed his omamori. He hoped the luck rubbed off on him as he struck the match and lit the hippie's cigarette.

"Thanks, man. You want one?" The man flicked a cigarette from the packet in his hand.

Arthur politely declined and reached for the door. There was a hand-drawn poster taped to it with an illustration of what had to be Eve and The Guys. It was in the style of Robert Crumb and whoever had drawn it had taken particular care in the rendering of Eve's bosom. The lettering identified the band as the Tarts. Arthur grimaced. A little on the nose, then.

He pulled the door open. There was a clatter of dishes and voices in the main tea room, but the thump of drums and bass made the pathway to the music gallery clear. He slipped through the door to the left and went through the dark antechamber to find himself in the music gallery the Extemp was known for. The cloud of smoke that puffed into his face as he entered was enough to assure him that he didn't need a cigarette to smoke in this place. Along with the smoke, the thump of drum and bass assaulted his senses as he sidled into the gallery. Eve had been right about one thing. It was *loud*.[2]

"*I wanna see you move*," growled that posh accent, amplified over a crunchy sound system. Eve stood at the front of the stage wearing a scarf as a top, a leather mini-skirt, and suede go-go boots. It was immediately evident from the way the silk draped over her body, the way she twisted as she thrummed the bass strings, why it was so crowded in here. It didn't even matter if the music was good. Eve's magnetism was more than enough to draw a crowd.

The drums and guitar blared as Eve sang. Her hips swayed as she flirted with the microphone, her voice hard and rich with vibrato. Her breath huffed through the sound system. Arthur stood still even as the crowd jumped and danced with the beat, stomping their feet and clapping their hands, letting the music move through them as easy as breathing. Jim's willowy form curled around an electric guitar, his large hands plucking out a desperate riff full of wild longing as his golden hair formed a sort of halo that obscured his face. He was wearing a skirt, made from some kind of Indian patterned silk. Arthur felt his heart skip a beat.

Deb ricocheted behind the drums, sweat and pomade dripping down her face, her eyes squeezed shut. Everyone, the band and the spectators alike, were moving in time, melded together in the web woven by guitar, drum, and a breathy, accented voice that rippled through the room, chanting the most innocuous "hey hey hey" nonsense as though it were an ancient spell. They were good. They were simple musically—blues rock, basic beats, nothing groundbreaking—but the pure sex that oozed

---

2. Feels like "Suffragette City" David Bowie

from Eve, from her voice and her body, and the spectacle of that ... it *was* spell-binding.

Arthur twisted his fingers in his palm. He could be a part of that. He could help Eve make the hippies lose their minds as she moaned into the mic as if the risk of being arrested for public indecency were some distant nuisance as easily shrugged off as an afternoon chill. And she wanted him to be a part of it. *Him*.

The song ended—well, there was no other term for it other than orgasmic. Several girls next to Arthur nearly fell over him giggling with delight. He sidled away and ran into another body on his other side. He looked up at a middle-aged man with high and tight hair shot with silver who peered at him sideways. Arthur felt his fear rise up in his chest. Was this fellow a vet? Could he tell Arthur was Japanese? Did that matter, given that no one could tell Japanese from Korean from Vietnamese anyway? It wouldn't be the first time he got beat up for his face.

Arthur scrambled away and ended up shouldering his way past a table or two, tucking himself into the corner near the PA speaker where it was too loud for most to tolerate. He was close to the far edge of the stage, and as Eve laughed and bowed, her eyes seized upon him. The smile that stretched her perfect, pink lips—hell, even General Curtis LeMay would have cowed to a smile like that. Her hair was curling around her face, and she glistened with sweat over her cheeks and neck. No one would blame him for falling to her charms. No one was strong enough to tell a woman like that no.

After the set, Eve bounded off the stage (what a spectacle *that* was) and seized him by his shoulders.

"Darling, you came!" she gushed and placed kisses on either of his cheeks, both a posh gesture and a lingeringly intimate one. "Deb, you owe me a drink!"

A muffled "Dammit!" resounded from behind the drum kit.

"What did you think?" Eve asked eagerly, her breath still a little shallow from her performance. Arthur glanced around and saw several fellows lurking, hoping to attract Eve's attention. They didn't appear to afford Arthur much credence.

"It was..." he began, bringing his attention back to Eve. "It was incredible. You were incredible."

"Oh, stop, I'd be nowhere without the guys," she preened, basking in his praise. "Jim writes all the words. I'm rubbish with lyrics."

Arthur could honestly say he had no idea what the lyrics to that song were. Wasn't that a characteristic of magic spells? That the words slip away from you like you never heard them? But the feeling stuck with you forever? He was sure he'd read that somewhere...

"I—" Arthur started.

"—But don't you see where a piano would make it all so much better? It's so thin as it is. I want to be able to dance and play hand percussion too, so I can't be strapped to the bass guitar all the time. A piano has the whole range. It could do so much for our sound!"

Her eyes were round, bright with excitement and sparkling gold and brown. Her smile was so eager, so welcoming. Arthur wondered distantly if she was really interested in him, or if she actually had control of that insatiable charm and was using it to get herself a piano player. He didn't want to believe it was the latter. He chose hope over cynicism.

"Okay," he said, and Eve squealed with delight and kissed him again, this time full on the mouth like it was entirely normal for beautiful Englishwomen to thank nerds like him with something most people saved for their spouse behind closed doors.

Arthur was entirely taken aback and his chin dropped in surprise. Which parted his lips. Which made her let out an interested murmur and seize him by the back of the neck. She kissed him for real, with teeth and tongue. Arthur was utterly *mortified*. He'd only ever kissed Tomiko, once in the church choir room, after which they'd laughed and decided it was weird.

The other fellows who'd been hoping to catch Eve's attention scattered, one guy looking at him pointedly with jealous confusion. Maybe it was the knowledge that he was envied, but that was what dropped the whole experience into his groin. He tucked his chin quickly, pulling away from the kiss and shrinking into the wall before she could feel how aroused he'd become.

Eve did not appear to notice at all. She grinned at him, perhaps more coyly than she had before, and said, "Darling, you must come to our place after this. We're having a few people over to listen to some records, have some drinks. Nothing special, just an intimate gathering of friends. You simply must come."

She emphasized this point by letting her fingertips run over his jaw. The only thing he could manage to say was, "Sure."

3

The second set was far out. Eve danced with abandon while Jim made his guitar positively wail. Arthur couldn't decide which was more orgasmic-sounding—Eve's breathy vocals or Jim's guitar. Either way, Arthur stayed to the side, leaning on the wall and trying desperately to puzzle out these people he'd agreed to play music with.

The Tarts was an apt band name. Eve's lips put Mick Jagger's to shame. Full and round and glistening... Was that from kissing him? What the hell was happening? Didn't they say that girls loved a musician? This was why all the boys in high school wanted to learn how to play guitar. But piano wasn't sexy like a guitar. Was it? He supposed it could be, when you were a gorgeous girl in particular need of a pianist. He giggled, and it was about then that he realized he was probably getting a little second-hand high. The smoke permeating the room stank of reefer. He tried to worry about it, but he really couldn't manage it.

"Arthur, darling," Eve cooed in his ear after the show, draping an arm over his shoulders and pressing her very obviously unbound breasts against his arm. Warm silk, soft flesh.

"What was that?"

"I said could you be a doll and help Deb and Jim load out? I have to dash up to the flat and make it presentable before our friends head up."

Arthur looked down the scant few inches between their heights and blinked. He didn't want her to go. In his addled state, he would much rather she drape him in that silk scarf. Those kinds of thoughts were not helpful. "Sure."

"You're a hero, my darling," she simpered and placed a nipping kiss on his jaw that made his breath catch. Then she slid away from him, leaving him cold while she entered the throng and left the Extempore with five or six other people trailing behind her. She was in every way a perfect front-woman for a band. The charisma poured off of her, intoxicating everyone much more effectively than the second-hand reefer. Arthur could see as he followed the group that there were plenty more where he came from, hangers-on and admirers jockeying for acknowledgement from Eve. Except, he reminded himself with a small smile, none of *them* played blues piano.

Jim was none too happy to see Arthur had been assigned to load out in Eve's place.

"Well, she sure got you tied around her finger fast," he muttered, leaning to nestle his Les Paul into its case. His hair cascaded around his face so Arthur couldn't tell if he was being funny or mean. Probably mean.

Deb rolled her eyes and set Arthur to carrying her toms.[1] It turned out that Eve's apartment was just next door, above the New Riverside Cafe, and the gear was all being hauled out the door, round the corner, up the stairs, and into the back bedroom. Arthur tried not to be annoyed when he saw there was already a group of at least ten people mingling as he passed through the living room. Eve was putting the needle on a record and filling the room with something psychedelic he'd never heard before.

"Set 'em there, Smarty Artie," Deb said, gesturing to a corner in the back room. "We'll set everything up again later."

---

1. "I'm A Boy" The Who

"How did *you* learn my intrepid nickname from high school?" Arthur drawled, not entirely meaning to say it aloud.

Deb let out an amused chuckle and ruffled his hair. "You're alright."

She rounded Jim on her way out of the room, who was lugging his amp and glowering at Arthur.

"*You* alright?" Arthur lobbed, unable to keep his annoyance from his brows now that the second-hand reefer had him loosened up.

"Fine," Jim sniffed, setting his amp next to the doorway. "We practice on Tuesdays and Thursdays and try to find a show every weekend. You can use the combo organ for rehearsals."

He gestured to the far wall where a Fender Rhodes electric organ beckoned.

"It's mine so don't break it," he concluded and left the room. Arthur rolled his eyes after him, then turned to regard the organ.

It was lovely and expensive-looking. Arthur ran his fingers over the white keys, feeling them give slightly under the pressure. He felt a tingle of excitement in his chest. He was normally so cautious about not putting himself in harm's way. But Eve's enthusiasm was contagious and the Extempore set seemed to be faring just fine with their flamboyant garb and devil-may-care attitudes. It was very rock and roll. He couldn't help but want to be a part of it. What was the point of setting out on his own, leaving the confines of his family and church behind, if he carried those bonds with him and continually made sure they were securely tied around him? Tomiko was right. He needed to take a chance.

The piano was so lovely. It was a silvertop with an amp beneath. Arthur's hand hovered over the dial, and he realized he was hesitating. He resolutely switched it on, and the tube amp hummed to life. He played a few chords, and the trebly electric notes charged the room. It was like having an amplified wind-up music box beneath his fingertips. He'd never encountered an electric piano before. It was significantly different from a string piano and reminded him of the mod pop music his mother loved when he was a teenager. He wasn't sure how that sound became rock and roll. He felt a tendril of doubt wrap around his chest.

"That's the same kind of piano Billy Preston played on 'Get Back.'"

Arthur's hands recoiled, and he looked up over his shoulder at the door. Jim leaned against the frame with two beers held between his fingers, the same stony expression on his face.[2]

"Do you play?"

"Not very well." Jim shrugged. "Want a beer?" He proffered one.

"Sure."

Jim approached and handed him the Schmidt bottle.

"Thanks." Arthur spun the dewy bottle in his hands. He wasn't sure what to say, and he couldn't stop his eyes from darting to Jim's skirt. It was a golden yellow print silk with a beautiful drape, and it made Jim look even taller than he already was.

"Come on, there's time to play around with this later," Jim said, reaching past Arthur to switch the Rhodes off. His hair smelled like incense. "Let's join the party."

Arthur followed Jim into the main room, which was sparsely furnished with a sofa, chair, and a large console record player. He wasn't sure how this was a small, intimate gathering when there were at least twenty people milling around now with beers and wine glasses. And the group was eclectic indeed. Gender markers seemed to flow like water between these people; long hair, short hair, lipstick, glossy platform heels, flowing skirts, tight jeans. It was a set perfectly suited to flank Eve's glam-

---

2. "Rumble" Link Wray and the Wraymen

orous brand of unconventionality, and they spun around her like planets orbiting a glittering sun.

Arthur tried to resist the urge to shrink against the wall and failed. There were more people than really should fit into such a small room. He busied himself with his beer and watched Jim cross over to the record player. He looked thoughtfully at the sleeve of the single that was playing. Arthur wanted to ask him about his skirt. Did he make it? Did he get harassed when he wore it? Arthur took a swig of beer and resolved to sleep in his kimono when he got home.

"Shake your head." Deb leaned on the wall next to him. "Your eyes are stuck."

"Where did he get that skirt?" Arthur blurted.

Deb shrugged. "Why, you want one?"

Arthur pressed his lips together. Deb rolled her eyes. "You better ask him. He doesn't bite, you know."

"Are you sure about that?"

Deb laughed. "Not unless you like that sort of thing."

Arthur grimaced, wrinkling his nose as he looked down into his beer bottle.

"Oh, don't be a prude," she grumbled and shoved him towards the record player. "Go ask him and stop being such a wiener."

Arthur looked over his shoulder accusingly as he did his best to turn his stumble into a saunter.

"So what's on the turntable?" he asked as he approached Jim, trying to sound casual.

"Some English squawker Eve picked up over the summer."

"How dare you." Eve held a wine glass like a sommelier and took a puff off a joint, holding it in for a moment before she blew it out in a great cloud over Jim's face. "It's Marc Bolan's latest. An early copy, naturally, darling."

"I don't know why you come back here," Jim said as he frowned at the album sleeve and then handed it to Arthur.

"There's an actual music scene in London. Not just touring bands and Top 40 covers."

Eve preened and said, "I know, but my mum has a soft spot for the Midwest. Besides," she leaned towards Arthur conspiratorially, "sometimes it's nice to be a big fish in a small pond."

"Eve, we're out of wine," called a young woman with an outrageously large hat and a beaded crochet poncho.

"Oh, let me dig another bottle out," Eve replied and scampered over, her silk scarf fluttering against her skin and leaving very little to the imagination. Arthur couldn't help but watch her go.

"You know," Jim said, clearing his throat, "these guys aren't half bad."

Arthur looked down at the single's sleeve. Two square-jawed men, one with cascading dark hair and the other with hair just like Jim's but dark, looked back up at him from the picture. *T.Rex* was emblazoned on the top left in bold, red font. "Are they wearing ... makeup?"

"Probably," Jim replied, bemused. "Ever since Mick Jagger started wearing lipstick, Eve has been obsessed with that kind of look for the band."

Arthur turned and looked at the record turning under the needle. There was electric guitar with a string quartet. It bopped like a pop single, but the guitar was crunchy and the vocalist's voice was other-worldly. Nasally, but also rich and deep—masculine—with tight, relentless vibrato.

"How does she find them?"

"Eve's dad is from West London, and her cousin plays drums for some group that plays out with bands who have cut a record or two. She's always coming back from summer vacation with new stuff no one has ever heard of."

"Why come back here then?" Arthur couldn't imagine why one would want to live in Minnesota when one could live in London.

"Her heart is set on a communications degree, I guess." This appeared to be meant as a joke. When Jim smiled, his narrow lips disappeared and his mouth became a stark slash across his sharp-featured face. He looked down as the song ended and flipped the single.[3]

"Have you been playing together long?"

"We've been playing as The Tarts for about a year now, but before Deb came on, Eve and I used to play out just the two of us." Jim laughed. "We used to have this really dorky folk group when we were teenagers called The Children of Stonehenge where I'd play guitar and Eve would sing about fairies and dance around in hippie fringe. We only ever played at the Highland Community Center though. Probably a good thing, in hindsight."

"Oh," Arthur said, glancing over at Eve and then back at Jim. "So you've, uh, known one another for a long time?"

"Yeah, we grew up together." Jim must have noticed Arthur's confusion because he added, "Her mom's from Highland Park."

"But her accent...?"

"She didn't have it when she was ten, I'll tell you that much." Jim leaned against the console and pulled a packet of cigarettes from the breast pocket of his tight t-shirt. "She's also not friends with this Marc Bolan guy, either. Don't let her fool you. He's some friend of her cousin's. Want one?"

"Sure." That seemed to be Arthur's mantra this evening. He didn't really smoke; his mother hated the smell. He wasn't a huge fan of it either, come to think of it, but the room was already hazy with tobacco smoke so what was the point of being particular about it? Jim leaned down and lit the cigarette for Arthur. He took a puff, pulling the smoke into his mouth but didn't inhale for fear he'd cough and look like a square in front

---

3. "Summertime Blues" T. Rex

of this group of sophisticated counter-culture aesthetes. Jim slid the ashtray across the console and flicked some ash into it as he caught Arthur's gaze. His eyes were really blue.

"So, are you and Eve, uh..." Arthur gestured helplessly with the cigarette, "together?"

Jim snorted. "No. I'm not sure Eve is uh..." He mimicked Arthur's gesture, "'together' with anyone."

Arthur found that hard to believe. In the kitchenette, she'd climbed up onto the countertop to reach the top-most cabinet, and two men with Mick-Jagger hair and tight jeans took the opportunity to look up her skirt. Jim sighed exasperatedly.

"Evie, it's not up there, for Chrissakes," he called and pushed off the console to go help her. Arthur puffed on the cigarette and watched Jim sidle between the two offending perverts, reaching up to help a giggling Eve down by her waist.

It was a pity, really. They would make a gorgeous couple.

4

The wine was in the broom closet in the end. Once it began to flow, Arthur noticed the guests getting a little sloppier. Laughing louder, drinking more liberally, dancing with abandon to the records Jim took over selecting.[1]

"You know," Jim said conspiratorially, leaning over to Arthur as they both resumed their lean upon the record console. "I can't ever bring out Jefferson Airplane when Eve's sober. She gets too sour trying to sing along."

"Sour?"

"Jealous, I guess. Grace Slick's just got a rounder tone than Evie. And there's nothing she can do about it. You can't compensate for human variation."

Arthur raised his brows; he couldn't imagine a woman like Eve being jealous of anyone. Eve and several other girls were swaying with their eyes closed to the music. They looked like evangelists at a prayer revival, except the only deity here was Grace Slick.

"But when she's drunk," Jim said, taking a swig of his beer without taking his eyes off Eve, "she doesn't care. She loves them. It's like her nerves disappear, and all she feels is the music."

---

1. "Watch Her Ride" Jefferson Airplane

Eve writhed, her hands sliding up her sides and catching on that damned flimsy excuse for a top. The silk was printed with a large blue circle, with ripples radiating out in purple and black and brown and pink. It had to be china silk, because it draped delicately over her piqued nipples. Her curves were elegantly proportioned, smooth like an hourglass, a gift she clearly had no problem sharing. The female form was so graceful, not sharp and clumsy like men were. And Eve Clark's body was ideal. The silk caught on the back of her left hand, lifting, and he could see she had a pin-prick of a mole over her left ribs. The silk fell back into place before anything more scandalous could be revealed; though given how sheer the silk was, it didn't seem to make much of a difference. The only thing it had going for it was that it was opaque.

"I see you understand what I mean."

Arthur snapped his eyes up to Jim, mortified to be caught staring, but the other man didn't seem annoyed or derisive. His blue eyes seemed distantly amused, one eyebrow lifted.

"You look like a castaway staring down the prospect of a square meal," Jim observed.

"I—" Arthur stammered. "Um, I'm sorry."

"No need," he replied, turning to change the record. "It's the normal human response to Eve."

Arthur gave a nervous laugh, turning away from the female spectacle before his interest became a point of public notice. "I think I might be drunk too, come to think of it."

No time like the present, especially if liquid confidence was already in evidence. "Jim, where did you get your skirt?" Arthur blurted, his fingers gripping the edge of the record player.

Jim stilled, the new record selection halfway to the turntable. A small smile played on his lips as he looked over at Arthur. "I made it. You know, I don't think many people know this, but it is really difficult to find men's skirts these days."

It could have been a sarcastic response, but the way Jim's blue eyes played on Arthur's, he felt in on the joke. Like Jim could see him, just a glimpse inside his shell, and found something he liked.

"I, um," Arthur said. He should have said it made Jim look like an elegant, phlegmatic druid or something else equally as likely to be a lyric on a Led Zeppelin album, with his sweeping skirt that trailed behind him when he walked, golden curls cascading over his shoulders. But all Arthur could muster was, "I like it."

"Good," Jim said, dropping the needle on Janis Joplin's solo record. "Let's dance."[2]

Arthur hesitated, but Jim pulled him into the thick of where the girls were waiting for the next song to play. When the drums dropped in and Janis began to keen, Jim grasped Arthur's two hands in his own. Arthur swallowed hard and looked anxiously at the others. Just because Jim was wearing a skirt didn't all of a sudden make this normal.

"Trust me," Jim said with a sardonic brow. "This is my best party trick. In three ... two ... one—"

And as if on cue, Eve slid herself up in between their arms, so that their linked hands formed a loop around her waist. And as Janis began to wail in earnest, the girl twirled her hips and slid an arm around each of their necks. Jim gave Arthur a look that was the universal nonverbal expression for "I told you so." Arthur let out a relieved laugh and let the alcohol carry his nerves away, closing his eyes to tune in on the music and enjoy the slip of silk against his forearm.

The dancing dominated the party for the entire A-side of the album. When the needle scratched the label, Arthur opened his eyes. Eve's chestnut hair curled slightly at the ends from the heat of the room, and she was grinning like a fox as she disentangled herself from his arms and went to flip the record. Arthur couldn't help but watch her with astonishment. He was

---

2. "Try (Just a Little Bit Harder)" Janis Joplin

not the kind of person who fell in with people like Eve and Jim. Artistic people, non-conformists. Glancing up, he caught Jim regarding him with an inscrutable expression.

The party thinned out after that. Arthur felt like he should have met, well, anyone else, but he'd spent the whole night either wall-flowering with Jim or using the cover of dance to touch Eve. He said as much to Jim as he was putting Janis back in her sleeve. (Well, about the not meeting people part. Not the groping part.)

Jim frowned and looked up at the backs of the last retreating guests Eve was seeing out. "Don't worry, you didn't miss meeting anyone famous. It's not like Jack Baker comes to these parties. They're just some of the folks from FREE."

"I sense that FREE has some sort of meaning that I don't understand," Arthur pointed out, lifting a brow.

Jim hesitated, holding Arthur's gaze for a moment. Then, he swatted Deb's hand away from the record player. "Don't you dare put on Joni Mitchell. Do you want to kill what's left of the party?"

Deb's mouth dropped open. "How dare you. Joni Mitchell weaves a tapestry of the female experience wefted with heartstrings."

"Jim, Karen just told me to tell you she's not doing FREE anymore." Eve sidled herself in between Jim and Deb and resolutely dropped the needle on Joni Mitchell. "And FREE, Arthur, stands for Fight Repression of Erotic Expression, except now that Jack Baker's pulling publicity stunts trying to marry his boyfriend, it's just 'FREE: Gay Liberation of Minnesota'."

"Tell us how you really feel," Deb muttered, rolling her eyes.

Arthur found it a little difficult to swallow for the tension in his neck. Was that his own repression? Best not to interrogate that too deeply, especially after drinking.

"They're suing the District Court over it," Jim pointed out.

"The name change?" scoffed Eve. "They would."

"No—Jack's marriage," Jim corrected, sneering at the folksy lullaby of "Morning Morgantown" drifting out of the console's speakers. "If you're going to make me listen to this, I'm gonna need a joint."

As he stalked off, Eve snatched a bottle of gin hidden inside the console and poured some of it into Arthur's half-empty glass of wine. Apparently it served as both a record player and a bar. "Don't look so shocked, darling. A homosexual is in every way the same as a heterosexual, except they are much more likely to know where your clitoris is."

Arthur choked. Wine and gin was *not* advisable.

"What?" Deb squawked. "There is no way in heaven or on earth Tom knows where a clit is, and he's the gayest person I know."

Arthur swallowed the rest of his glass in spite of his better judgment.

"I mean, in *theory*, he probably does."

"I should probably get going," Arthur said, feeling the heat from Eve's evil cocktail radiating through his stomach.

"Oh no, darling, stay," Eve cooed, wrapping her hand around his wrist. "Did you just drink all that? No, you *must* stay. You'll be a perfect target walking across campus this time of night."

"It's alright, I'll be fine."

"Just sit for a minute," she chided. She pulled his hand to her chest and turned her big, kohl-rimmed eyes up at him. "See how you feel in five minutes."

Well. In that case.

"Jim, does Tom know where a clit is?" Deb asked as Eve led Arthur to the sofa and curled up next to him. Piano softened the room, cooled it and made the room feel larger, looming. Jim was right. *Ladies of the Canyon* was a terrible album to get drunk to.

"How should I know?" Jim replied, folding himself onto the floor and taking a long drag from the joint he'd brought back with him.

Deb laughed. "Well, he's gotten closer to yours than anyone else in this room."

Jim leveled her with an irate expression. "I'm not sure if you've noticed this, Deb, but I do not have a clitoris."

"Ignore them, Arthur," Eve pouted in his ear. "They're terrible deviants."

"Takes one to know one," Jim called, flopping back to sprawl on the floor.

Arthur couldn't help but crack a smile at this. He should leave. He really *should*. But as much as he'd love to bury himself in Japanese silk right now and build his wall of denial ever higher, he wouldn't find The Tarts at the back of his wardrobe. Perhaps he did belong with these people. After all, normal men didn't need to wrap themselves in women's clothes to feel like they had their head screwed on right.

"Are you gonna pass that joint, Jim, or are you going to hog it all to yourself?" Deb chastised.

Jim let out a groan as he sat up like he was twice his age, and held the joint begrudgingly out for Deb to pluck from his fingers. She dragged smoother than a Dead Head and passed it to Eve.

Eve pressed her shoulder into Arthur's as she took a drag. "You want some?"

"I, uh, haven't ever—"

"Oh!" Her eyes lit up predatorily as she passed the joint to him. "Go on. You'll love it."

Arthur set the moistened paper to his lips and sucked in.

"You have to inhale it," she said, eyes intent on him. In his effort to pull the smoke into his lungs, he choked and sent himself into a fit of coughs.

Deb giggled. Eve leveled a glare at her. "Don't be a twat, Deb."

This only made Deb giggle louder and with such abandon that Jim joined in too. Soon they were all laughing like preschool children, in an effervescent fizz fueled by cheap wine, hash, and Joni Mitchell.

5

The next morning, Arthur woke up with the most horrific headache. There was a very real reason gin and wine were not mixed together, and it was pounding at the inside of his skull with an urgent message.[1]

He honestly wasn't sure exactly how he'd ended up back in his own room. He was fairly certain Jim had walked him back, but Eve and Deb might have been with them as well. He could only recall snippets of dark streets and too-bright street lamps, the din of a rowdy fraternity party they passed by, the stitch in his side as he laughed too hard at one of Deb's jokes (ah, yes, she had been there). This meant they all knew where he lived. Had they come in?

Arthur sat up blearily and surveyed his room. Everything was strewn about, but that didn't mean that he had invited them in. He wracked his brain for a moment, trying to put together the pieces from before he fell asleep. He remembered curling into his bed as his head spun. He really didn't think they'd come up. He dragged himself out of bed and checked his watch to discover he'd completely missed breakfast and was in danger now of missing lunch. He was wearing the kimono and it was an awful mess of wrinkles.

---

1. "Hold Your Head Up" Argent

"God dammit," he muttered to himself as he surveyed the damage. He was going to have to borrow Tomiko's iron again.

He hung the kimono carefully over its hanger, then shoved his legs into his pants and pulled on a shirt at random. He tried to smooth his hair into some semblance of order before he blundered down to the dining hall. He had just sat down to soak up the remnants of the previous night's poor choices with a slice of toast when Tomiko took the seat across from him.

"You look like hell."

"I *feel* like hell."

"I take it you went to the show, then?"

"No, I decided to pledge a fraternity," he deadpanned.

"How was it? Are you going to join the band?"

Arthur regarded his toast with queasy hesitation.

"Yeah," he said at length, addressing his food rather than his friend. "I think I will."

Tomiko squealed—and to be clear, she was *not* the kind of girl who squealed. She was more the kind to put a flower in your rifle and then kick you in the crotch. "Oh, this is so exciting! *Arthur!* I can't wait to go to your shows and say, 'I'm with the band.'"

Arthur couldn't help but crack a small smile.

Later that day, he ran into Deb at the record store (she worked at the Electric Fetus and how he never noticed her before, he did not know). She told him to be back at the apartment for a rehearsal that night. Arthur, still reeling from the previous night, wasn't sure how well he'd do with amplified music given the pain already thrumming in his head, but did his best to drink a metric ton of water and pop Excedrin until he felt semi-human again.

He arrived at Cedar and Riverside at 7 pm, carrying a paper sack with a sandwich in it like a horrific nerd worried he'd impose. He spotted Jim through the window of the New Riverside Cafe, sitting at the coffee bar like an Edward Hopper painting.

"Wow, you look worse for wear," Jim said when he saw Arthur.

"Don't mention it."

Jim grinned crookedly. "That's just proof positive that you had a good time last night."

Arthur glowered. "I'm lucky I even woke up this morning at all, much less showed up for this rehearsal so short-notice. If I hadn't run into Deb earlier, I wouldn't have even known about it."

"I told you last night."

"Yeah, I don't remember that. Next time, maybe confirm I'm sober first before relaying time-sensitive information."

"Don't be so salty, Arthur. If you were actually that annoyed, you wouldn't have come." Jim grinned and pushed his chair back, tossing a couple quarters on the table next to his empty mug. He and Arthur proceeded outside to the upstairs entry and went up to the apartment, where Eve and Deb sat on the sofa listening to records and chain-smoking.

"Rehearsal time," Jim announced gruffly as they entered the foyer.

"Wait, we have to finish this side," Eve sang, her languid body sliding down the couch and onto the floor as the longest, most gratuitous drum solo Arthur had ever heard carried on and on and on from the console speakers. "'*In-A-Gadda-Da-Vidaaaa babyyyyy!*'"

Jim regarded the girls with a flat expression. "Deb, what is she on?"

Deb grinned, too lopsided and too long. "Wait—Smartie Artie, did you bring a *sack lunch*?"

"Right," Jim said, shaking his head and rolling his eyes as Arthur tried to hide his sandwich bag behind his back. "Arthur, why don't you help me get the gear set up while these two get their heads screwed back on."

Eve snickered. "I'll screw *your* head." Then she collapsed into guffaws. She wore a jumpsuit with a halter top that looked like it was made of macrame, and as she rolled on the floor, her breasts threatened to slide out of the thing. The play between twisted cotton cord and smooth flesh was captivating. Alarmed at his observation of a woman who was so clearly not in present possession of all her faculties, Arthur followed Jim somewhat ashamedly to the back room and helped put the gear back together so they could play something. The drums by themselves took ten minutes, during which Jim continually grumped about how Deb was going to redo it all anyway, so why fucking bother.

Once everything was more or less set up, Arthur turned the Rhodes on, enjoying the warm hum of the tube amp.

"No point in waiting around for those two," Jim muttered irately as he tuned his guitar. "Let's jam on something. What do you know?"

Arthur twisted his mouth to the side in thought. "I can play pretty much any blues as long as you tell me the key."

"How about the Doors? 'Roadhouse Blues,' maybe?"

"Wait, how does one that go?"

Jim sang him a snippet before Arthur remembered it. He wasn't keen to admit how nervous he was about "jamming." He'd never played rock and roll with anyone else. The only songs he performed in combo were church songs or classical pieces. He looked down at the piano and plunked out a basic blues form in the appointed key. The eerie electric notes rang out through the room.

Jim joined, taking his cues by watching Arthur's hands on the keys. Arthur remembered there being a lot of high, repetitive piano riffs so he tried to throw those in. Once they had the form pretty well established, Jim started to sing.

Jim's voice was reedy, a fine tenor in every respect. He was able to easily hit the higher notes, but when he tried to swing down to "*All night long*," his voice nearly cut out as he reached the low end of his range. This didn't seem to bother him in the least, and he took a solo.

It was unexpected, Arthur realized, to experience how easy it was to feel the rhythm, the ebb and flow, the movement of the music back and forth between them. Suddenly the blues weren't just in his fingers anymore. They were crying out in the room, filling the four corners with wild desperation, thrumming through his body, his head nodding to the beat.

After they exchanged a few solos, they moved back into the A part. Arthur didn't decide to sing. Rather, the words sort of just sprang to his mouth and came out. His voice was a baritone and had a rough high end that was well suited to Jim Morrison. He pushed the lyrics hard, feeling the tension in his throat as his voice strove to be heard above the electrified instruments. When the lyrics swung down at *All night long,* his rich baritone smoothly projected the notes above the guitar and piano.

"Well, shit," Jim said as they felt out the ending. "Guess you can sing."

"I *told* you he could sing!" Eve was at the doorway, hanging off the jam and gaping at Arthur with an absurd caricature of eagerness. "You're just full of surprises, aren't you, my darling?"

"It's nothing," Arthur shrugged self-consciously. "It's not my main..." he gestured helplessly, "...instrument."

"Coulda fooled me," Deb muttered, fixing him with a side-long glare as she sat on her drum throne. "Guess you all *really* don't need me for back-up now."

"Oh, Deb Darling," Eve cooed, crossing to her and draping herself across the drummer's back like a cape. "You are the literal heartbeat of our band."

"I know," Deb said haughtily. "And your tempo was all over the place without me."

"Let's go again," Eve said, clapping her hands, "Only, let's work on something new!"

They fussed with tunings for a moment before Deb counted them into a slower tempo.[2] Eve's bass walked down the form as she stepped to the microphone and started to croon. The lyrics were mostly nonsense, placeholders for something real while she explored what melodies were possible in the form. Her voice was sweet, the notes slightly distorted through her nose, yet cracked with rough authenticity when she pushed. They spent twenty minutes jamming before Jim handed Arthur some chord charts, and they worked on teaching him some of the group's existing covers and original songs.

Trouble was, Arthur sort of had to figure out how to make space for a piano part. This wouldn't have been a problem if Jim hadn't kept stopping to tell him what he was doing wrong.

"You're walking all over the guitar," he said exasperatedly at one point.

"I thought you wanted piano. Not just some clunks between verses." Arthur hungover and running on very little sleep was not the most pleasant of people. He pressed his lips together grimly, knowing he was being a dick, but not so repentant he'd take it back.

"We do want piano," Eve cut in. "There is plenty of space for the guitar solos, Jim. Stop being such a diva."

Jim glowered at her but didn't say anything. They continued playing, and Arthur did back off a bit, just because he felt bad about being such an asshole. It must have been a good balance though, because they were able to move on after that.

They wrapped up the rehearsal with another jam where Arthur was able to find a three part harmony below Jim and Eve that had all of them grinning. There was nothing like the feeling of finding a good harmony, feeling the rightness of it in tension with the other voices.

---

2. Feels like "Hot Love" T. Rex

After the amps were all turned off, Jim made a beeline out to the record console in the living room, muttering about how Arthur needed to take a few albums home for research.

"Are we tied to the Rhodes sound?" Arthur asked, trailing him, "or are we open to acoustic piano?"

"I'm open to acoustic piano," Jim said, "But I don't know how we can haul one if a venue doesn't already have one. The Rhodes is portable."

"I like the Rhodes," Eve put in. "It has this sort of other-worldly quality that I just love."

Jim shrugged noncommittally as he turned and started piling albums into Arthur's arms. "They're two very different sounds, so once we make a decision, we need to stick to it. Tell me if you already have any of these."

Arthur nodded.

"Now, I need these back in *pristine* condition, you understand? Don't store them on top of one another either. They need to sit up sideways so you don't crush the grooves."

"I know, I'm not stupid. I have my own records."

He got Faces, the Doors, Sun Ra and his Arkestra, The Zombies, Steppenwolf, and some group he'd never heard of called Slade.

"I already have the Velvet Underground," he said as Jim deposited a white album with a large, pop art banana on the sleeve.

"Oh, yeah," Jim said, lifting his eyebrows appreciatively, and tucked the album back into the console.

"Oh, I saw them play at the Factory a few years ago," Eve said excitedly.

"How the *hell* did you get into the Factory?" Deb demanded, her long face dripping with skepticism.

Eve gave a self-satisfied smile and cupped her breasts significantly. Arthur blushed and looked away. She certainly was pretty enough to become one of Warhol's superstars. "We laid over in New York on the way to London last summer, darling. I have some very charming acquaintances there who also happen to be in Andy Warhol's circle."

"Charming," Deb repeated flatly. "So did they make you put out before or after getting you into Studio 54?"

"After. Or rather, I expect that was their intention, but I ended up going home with someone else entirely at the end of the night." Eve made sexual predators sound like a lark.

"Ugh, men are the worst. I don't know how you put up with them."

"Anyone we might have heard of?" Jim inquired, a brow of slight interest raised as he flipped through the mass of records in the console.

"Yes, but I'm sworn to secrecy," Eve winked. "All I can say is that he was a relation of a particularly important political family."

"What, the Kennedys? The Nixons? Oh my god, did you fuck Richard Nixon?" Deb exclaimed. "'A man is not finished when he's defeated, Evelyn,'" she muttered in her best approximation of the president's voice, shaking her face so her cheeks jiggled. Eve shrieked as Deb advanced on her and gyrated on her thigh. "'He's finished when he quits!'"

Eve shook her head helplessly, she was laughing so hard.

"Richard Nixon wouldn't be caught dead at Studio 54," Jim put in skeptically, as though this notion deserved even the slightest consideration.

"That's exactly the reason he *would* be," said Deb conspiratorially. "Those traditional idiots still have *needs*, man. An exclusive place like Studio 54 would be a great place to keep a low profile."

"Can you imagine his Warhol silent film, trying to sit still and his jowls just ... quivering?" Arthur asked, and Eve scream-laughed so hard she fell back on the couch for a minute. It was a horrid sound, really, but that didn't stop it from delivering a sweet rush of satisfaction to Arthur's cheeks.

"*That,*" Jim pointed out, trying to hide a smile, "is ridiculous. And also how rumors get started." He piled on a few singles, and Arthur began to wonder how he was going to carry all this home.

"Do you have a case I can carry these in?" he asked thinly.

"Oh, yeah, of course," Jim replied, realizing how large the pile had grown. He knelt and pulled a record case from under the console.

"You can't forget the Kinks!" Eve exclaimed, reaching into the console and drawing out a white album with psychedelic line art. "You'll love this one. Make sure you listen to track 5 on side A."

Jim rolled his eyes hard. "Eve. Just because he likes to sleep in a silk robe doesn't mean he's going to automatically like 'Lola'."

Arthur froze. Whatever flush he'd had drained from his face. He was lucky the pile of albums didn't fall out of his hands. Fuck. He *had* invited them up. And he'd put on Obaasan's kimono in front of them? Oh god. *Shit.*

"Oh darling, don't look so upset. You were such a doll to tell us all about the, uh," Eve's smile faltered, and she looked imploringly at Deb, "you know, cultural significance of the, uh, garment."

Arthur couldn't make his mouth say anything. He just stared at her, mortified. Jim's eyes darted between the two of them, and he set his mouth in a grim line as he sat on the couch. Deb snorted.

"Evie, of course he doesn't remember," she chortled, smacking Eve's arm. "He fell asleep before he ever even got the whiskey out."

"Sorry, I didn't realize you didn't remember," Jim said quietly, taking the albums from Arthur's arms and setting them on his knees. "I shouldn't have said anything."

Arthur gave him a grim approximation of a smile and pushed his glasses up to rub his face. He *had* told Jim he didn't remember last night. *Fuck.* He should have known when he'd woken up to such a mess in his room. His eyes stung. He wanted to just melt into the floor.

"Well, I for one thought it was stunning," Eve said forcefully, refusing to stop kicking the dead horse. "I know there are lots of people who would be threatened by an elegant man who knows his way around a fine fabric, but as for me, the robe took my breath away. Who knew Japanese silk could be so couture?"

Arthur found his breath. He looked tentatively up at Eve.

"Truly," she said, cupping his cheek and smiling. "Most men don't have the courage to bear their true selves in front of anyone, much less a group of lunatics he just met."

Deb laughed. "Yes, it was hilarious. The only person wearing pants was me!"

Arthur couldn't help but crack a small smile. Eve pulled him in and gave him an affectionate hug. "You are most definitely one of us, darling." She looked up at the others. "See, what did I tell you! I have excellent instincts when it comes to finding the misfits."

"I never said you didn't," Jim said, hiding behind his hair as he put the albums into the carrying case and snapped it shut. When he stood and looked at Arthur, his expression was placid. "Here you go."

"Do you want us to walk you back again?" Eve asked, one arm still around Arthur's shoulders. He looked down and shook his head.

"No. It's not even 11 yet," he said with a belated glance at his watch. He shifted in his shoes for a moment before he continued. "Besides, if you do, you'll just want to get at that whiskey again, and I'm sad to inform you that the whiskey was a lie."

"What!?" Deb huffed, mock-offended. "Well, you're definitely on your own then. What's the point of walking across campus if there isn't whiskey when you're done?"

Arthur gave a half-hearted chuckle and lifted the case. "Well, I'll see you all at the next practice, then."

Eve met his eyes and smiled warmly.

"Tuesday," Jim said gruffly, his eyes on his lighter as he lit a cigarette. "7 pm. Don't be late."

Eve rolled her eyes at him and shook her head conspiratorially at Arthur.

"Let me at least see you out," she said and took his elbow, leading him to the door. In spite of everything, Arthur smiled slightly to himself. Turned out beautiful girls admired beautiful things. And apparently men who appreciated the same.

6

Arthur spent the next two days going to classes, reading entirely too much on the subject of structural physics in wintery climates, and listening to all the records Jim had assigned him. The only record he didn't get to was *Lola versus Powerman and the Moneygoround*, which was silly because he actually liked the Kinks, but he couldn't quite bring himself to face whatever was on track 5 of side A that had reminded Eve and Jim of his kimono. He was prepared Tuesday night to address any finer questions on the topic with a lament that he hadn't had time for it with all his classwork. Besides, he'd had an idea for a song that he was worried "Lola" might potentially taint.

The New Riverside cafe did not contain any of the Tarts that evening, so Arthur headed round the side and pressed the buzzer to be let up to Eve's apartment. He set the record case on the counter when Eve let him in and proffered up the paper bag he'd brought.[1]

"Oh, did you bring me another sandwich?" she asked, peering at the bag questioningly.

"The whiskey I owe you," he said with a sheepish smile.

"Oh, darling, you shouldn't have!" she enthused, accepting the bag eagerly.

---

1. "Looking Out the Window" Faces

"Where are the others?"

"Well, Deb's not here yet, and I'm not going to dare wake Jim up until we're all accounted for."

"Wait—Jim lives here too?"

"Of course, my dear! We're *roomies*." She gave a playful grin and shimmied her shoulders. What was *that* supposed to mean? "Do you want some whiskey while you wait?"

"Sure, thanks," Arthur replied and crossed the living room to sit on the sofa. On the other side of the kitchenette counter, Eve plopped ice cubes into two glasses and poured them a finger each of Hennessy. She wore a cute mod dress whose modest *decolletage* was undermined by the fact that the skirt's hem scarcely covered her rear end. Her legs looked a mile long as she strode across the room to hand Arthur his glass.

"Have you ever tried Japanese whiskey?" Eve asked as she curled up on the couch, a swath of milky thigh turned toward him.

"No. I'm third generation. I don't even speak Japanese."

"Oh, I'm sorry, that was a ratty question," she winced. "My father got a bottle of Suntory once from a client and it was divine. Although," she looked into her glass fondly, "I think just about any whiskey is pretty damn good."

Arthur shifted awkwardly. "Um, Eve, would you maybe ... take a look at something before the others get here?"

Eve pursed her glossy lips and took a sip of whiskey, mischief in her kohl-rimmed eyes. "Oooh, color me intrigued."

Arthur wrinkled his nose as he pulled the piece of notebook paper out of his breast pocket. "I got to thinking about our conversation the other night, and I thought ... well, I thought it might make an interesting song."

He handed her the paper, heart pounding in his throat, and waited. Eve's eyes skimmed across the words, her expression intent and thoughtful. After a moment, she turned her wide eyes up on him. "Are these lyrics?"

He nodded stiltedly. "I've never really written a song before, but I figured it's not so far off from poetry. If they're not right—"

"—Do you have a melody?" Eve asked, her expression becoming eager.

"Um, kind of, but I haven't really—"

"Oh, this is going to be *gorgeous*!" She sprang to her feet. "I'm going to go wake Jim. He's going to be so excited he's not the only one responsible for lyrics!"

She hopped excitedly as she dashed down the hall, Arthur's lyrics still clutched in her hand. He blanched and held onto his whiskey glass too tight. He could hear Jim's groggy, muffled voice just as Deb let herself in the front door.

Her hair was pompadoured higher than Ritchie Valens, and when she caught sight of Arthur, she said, "Oh geez, what happened to you now?"

"What do you mean?"

"You look like you've shit your pants."

"Deb!" Eve squealed, dashing out of the hall. "Guess what? Arthur wrote some *lyrics!*"

Deb's thin eyebrows rose, and she regarded him appreciatively. "Oh. I didn't know you had it in you, man."

Arthur cringed a little and took a long sip of his drink. Jim emerged from the hall with his hair in disarray, looking groggy and mildly irritated at having been woken.

"What time is it?" he asked, running a hand over his face and then through his tousled curls. *That hair is wasted on a man,* Arthur thought. He wondered how often girls said as much to him.

"7:10," Arthur said with a glance at his oversized watch before he wiped his sweaty palms on his trousers.

"Ugh, Eve, why did you let me sleep so long?"

Eve shrugged. "Darling, if you slept that long, you probably needed it. I'm not your housewife. It's not my job to wake you up."

Jim frowned and then his eyes alighted on Arthur's glass. "What are you drinking?"

"Arthur brought us some whiskey!" Eve reported excitedly, scurrying across the room to retrieve her glass.

"To make up for the disappointing host I ended up being the other night," Arthur explained sheepishly.

Jim held his eyes for a moment. "You weren't disappointing."

"Speak for yourself, Jimothan," Deb contradicted as she walked into the kitchenette. "Ooh, Hennessy! Very well, Ohashi. All is forgiven!"

In ten minutes, four glasses of whiskey on the rocks duly drank, they headed to the back room to get down to business. Well, as much as rock and roll could ever be considered business. They tuned up and a chaotic jumble of drums devolved into a pretty spirited jam and to be entirely honest, Arthur was content not to bring up the idea of lyrics again.

Trouble was, Eve still had them. She'd stuffed the paper into her bra strap—a marked novelty to note she was wearing one—while she walked notes down her bass and keened into the mic that had been jerry-rigged through a spare guitar amp and tied to a broken mic stand with a silk scarf.

Jim signaled a *finale* with his guitar. Eve and Deb watched him and began to feel out an end. Arthur was embarrassed to admit it, but he was getting so anxious and avoidant that he slammed out a piano solo. Jim's brows furrowed, his deep-set blue eyes critical for a moment as he backed off his guitar line. Deb held off completely, and the solo ... well, it kind of rocked.

After a few measures, Jim looked at Deb and nodded them all back in, and they slammed out a slow, final walk-down to an ending.

"Damn, Smarty Artie," Deb said, leaning back on her drum throne appreciatively. "That was cool."

Eve bit her lip and sighed, "Yes. I knew you were just the man for the job."

Arthur would anxiously extract fierce solos on the Rhodes all damn day if it meant Eve would look at him like that. She smiled a bit, and slid her hand over her neck before she snatched the paper from her bra and handed it to him. It was warm from her skin. Arthur swallowed under the intimacy of her gaze and glanced up to see Jim glowering at him, his gold hair like some sinister mane leveraged to make him look larger and more intimidating.

"Play us what you've been working on, darling," Eve cooed with a sweet smile, then added louder for the rest to hear, "Let's hear Arthur's song."

"I don't think I would call it a song, persay," Arthur muttered and froze when Eve seized both his hands with hers across the Rhodes.

"An artist never apologizes," she said sagely. She patted the backs of his hands and took a few steps back to her spot near the center of the room.

Arthur swallowed. Deb leaned back on her throne with her arms over her chest, looking both amused and patronizing. Jim was looking at Eve with an irritated expression on his face. It really couldn't have been a less friendly audience. Arthur unfolded the paper and tried not to notice his fingers tremble slightly. They should have brought the whiskey in here with them.

He set his fingertips to the keys and pressed out a few chords. He added some rhythm to them, pumping the keys like a heartbeat. He wanted this to feel like the thrum of life inside. To feel real, to feel as desperate and lonely as it felt when he was writing it. Maybe if he could make them feel the way he did, they wouldn't tear it apart.[2]

He threw caution to the wind and sang. He pushed every scrap of isolation and loneliness he could summon into his

---

2. Feels like "Gimme Shelter" The Rolling Stones

voice, let it scratch and break, focused his eyes on his hands and let his body pulse. It was all or nothing. He could sing this straight, and they'd hate it for being trite and fake, or he could sing it with his shell lying cracked on the floor, and they could hate him for who he really was. His throat closed up and swallowed the next lyrics.

But in the quiet of the next measure, as he drew in a shaky breath, he could hear the other instruments. The pulse of a bass drum. The fiddlings of guitar. And Eve's voice, wailing the lyrics of the last line in desperate repetition, like it were the wild and anguished chorus of "Gimme Shelter".

"*Hammer your heart,*" she cried, gripping her mic with both hands. "*Hammer your heart into shape.*"

And it was becoming real. The song was flying from inside his head, out into the world, and becoming something so much bigger than it could have been in his own hands. And it wasn't the end of him. It was a beginning, shared and growing and real. And it fucking rocked.

They jammed the chorus six ways from Sunday, then Arthur slipped the lyrics to Eve, and she ran roughshod in the best possible way over the second verse. Then Jim stopped playing, and the magic petered out.

"I think the beginning needs to be softer, using the Rhodes in a kind of haunting way," he said and picked out something minor on his guitar absently. "It needs a good riff that we can play with as the song escalates."

Arthur nodded. "Yes." Whatever it took for this validating experience to continue.

"I adore that," Eve replied. "Then I can draw on it in the vocal breakdown when we rock the chorus to the end."

"Yeah," Jim agreed, then hesitated with a glance between Arthur and Eve for a moment before he added, "But I think Arthur should sing the lead part."

Eve was taken aback for a moment.

"You're pissed," Jim said.

"No, I'm not."

"I just think that lyrically, it would make more sense for Arthur to sing it than you. I really like that line about '*You can't be a real man so you dress the fool*' and it wouldn't be the same coming from a female singer."

"I suppose but couldn't we just change 'man' to 'woman'? Or not? It's addressed to 'You,' so it's not like it's me singing about being a man." Eve glanced at Arthur then drew up her lips in a pout. "Besides, does Arthur even want to sing it?"

Arthur found himself being scrutinized by them both.

"I really don't mind Eve singing it. I'm not sure I could manage it in front of an audience, to be honest. Besides, Eve's the better singer."

Jim's brow furrowed incredulously, but he didn't say anything. Eve glowed with the compliment.

"This is riveting, truly, but I haven't had dinner yet, and if I don't eat soon, I'm not going to be responsible for my actions," Deb drawled.

They agreed and flicked their amps off before Eve led the way down to the Extempore for some food. The menu was typical hippie vegetarian nonsense, but it was a relief for Arthur to leave the high pressure first-time song-writing behind and just have some sort of hemp heart salad without having to worry about whether he was doing things right.

As they ate, they were interrupted multiple times by Eve's many acquaintances. For each, she would stand and give them a kiss on each cheek. Arthur remembered the first night he'd come to see the band and the kiss she'd given him, full on the mouth. It had been an accident, but a happy one—for them both as far as he could recall. It felt so good to be sitting at her table, to be in her inner circle while all these different people orbited around her.

"Tom, darling, it's been too long!" Eve cried as she kissed the bearded cheeks of a perfectly average-looking young man who had approached with a few other fellows. "How *are* you?"

Tom shrugged and looked significantly at the other fellows. "Could be better," he grimaced, "Michael got fired from his job."

"What? Why?" Jim said, looking up with a frown.

Tom rolled his eyes extravagantly, turning his hands up. "Why do you think? Apparently talking about his husband in the press is a fireable offense."

"Oh, did they manage to get married?" Eve drawled, as though she were asking after a society wedding.

"Did they think he had a conflict of interest or something?" Jim asked, brows furrowed in confusion.

"No," Tom retorted with an icy glance at Jim before turning his attention pointedly back to Eve. "Turns out coming out of the closet is still anathema among the *hoi polloi* and heaven forbid a gay man be found in the University of Minnesota Library. It's the same shit they put me through at the radio service."

Arthur felt his heart pounding in his chest. When had it started to do that?

"We're going to picket the building this weekend," one of the other guys said, his square jaw set determinately. "Being gay has nothing to do with being qualified for one's job."

"Yeah," Tom said, "you should all come. We'll have extra signs."

His friend handed Jim a flier as Eve repeated her cheek-kissing greeting and said an overly-gushing farewell. When Tom and his friends had moved on to the next table to promote their protest, Eve flopped back into her chair with a sigh.

"Well, that was awkward," said Deb, her mouth half-full of lettuce-tomato sandwich, a BLT wretchedly stripped of its bacon.

"You know I can't bear to see Michael so abused, but I simply can't get away for this protest," Eve said, peering noncommittally at the flier Jim was holding. Jim had been reading it and now looked up, craning his neck to look after Tom.

"Give it up," Deb said to him. "He couldn't have made it any more clear he has no interest in talking to you."

Arthur couldn't help it. He looked at Jim questioningly. Eve noticed and grinned.

"Oh, don't look so surprised, Arthur—"

"—I think I might go to the protest," Jim cut in. "No one should have to deal with losing a job over something that has literally nothing to do with their work."

"Well," Arthur said thoughtfully, "I suppose I can't blame the library for not wanting to condone that kind of—"

"—That kind of *what?*" Jim replied, his lip curling.

"I-I dunno. I guess ... you're right that it doesn't have anything to do with the job. I could see if he was, I dunno, propositioning coworkers—"

"—Michael is *married*." Jim's tone brooked no argument. "Even if the state refuses to recognize it. He and Jack have been together for the better part of a decade."

Eve rolled her eyes and lit a cigarette. "The only men who proposition coworkers are straight. And they're usually the ones who do the hiring and firing, and they wouldn't very well fire themselves, now would they."

Arthur shrank in on himself. Deb shook her head at him. He had suddenly lost his appetite.

They finished out their meals and paid, heading back upstairs to resume their practice. Arthur was happy to let the others workshop Jim's latest lyrical offering. He didn't think his heart could carry more work on his own song. At least not tonight. They played through a few of the Tarts' covers and called it a night.

As Arthur made his way back to Comstock Hall, he thought about the protest. Jim was brave to go to something like that. It seemed like a really good way to get the shit kicked out of you, but then again, after that riot in New York last year, it was worth remembering that gay men were still men, and they had the requisite strength to prove it. Perhaps there were more risky protests to be at, in the end.

Regardless, Arthur had firmly resolved to never protest again after the Kent State debacle. What did it matter, after all? You put yourself in harm's way, risk getting arrested or shot or worse, and then what? The war goes on. No justice is gained. No laws change. The only thing they did was draw up your draft card faster. Now you're dealing with legal fees while the government continues to give zero shits and throw your life away. Arthur was sorry for the pain and suffering being caused overseas, to people who looked like him, who only wished to determine for themselves the destiny of their own country, and ashamed of his cowardice.

He swallowed hard and flinched away from that train of thought. As he approached his dormitory, he bummed a cigarette off one of the people standing outside and went up to his room. He pulled off his clothes, draped himself in his kimono, and lit the cigarette as he dropped the needle masochistically on track 5, side A of the Kinks.[3]

He reclined against his pillow on his spare single bed and puffed on the cigarette. It was classic Kinks, shuffling beat and mellow vocals. The verses unfurled, descriptors of Lola adding up one on top of the other. She sounded sultry and seductive. At first he'd thought maybe Eve had connected him to the naive narrator of the song, but as Ray Davies sang about how she walked like a woman but talked like a man, Arthur started to get the idea.

Eve thought he was Lola. With his feminine kimono and his penchant for fine fabrics. With his gender-bending defects and unnatural desire to smear his mouth with lipstick. What had he said that night? What had he *done*? He shrank inside his kimono, the tobacco tasting stale on his tongue. What kind of

---

3. "Lola" The Kinks

horrid retribution lay in store for Lola at the end of this song? For … someone like him?

The bridge lifted the tension of the rather jolly song, and Ray Davies described what Arthur could only interpret as the moment that the narrator discovered Lola's true nature. He braced himself. He should turn it off. He didn't have to listen to this. The narrator looked at Lola, and she looked back.

Arthur stood up. He was in control of whether he let this into his private headspace.

The verse leveled the tension and in a sweet, soft voice, the narrator declared his devotion to Lola.

Arthur blinked at the record player. Arthur blinked again and realized he was blinking back tears.

Except for Lola. She wasn't mixed up or muddled up.

She was the exception.

The narrator of the song proceeded to lose his virginity to Lola. It was utterly irreverent and thoroughly camp, and Arthur perched on the edge of his bed and wept like he had at *Old Yeller* when he was seven years old. He couldn't even identify why. The song wasn't even dramatic or bittersweet. It was just this feeling that was bubbling up and overflowing like beer foam. But this was the good thing about the kimono. It was a safe place. Or rather, if he was wearing it, he was in a safe place. So he let whatever it was overflow as Ray Davies made him feel like a person.

When the song was over, he played it again. And again and again. He played it till the cigarette burned out of its own accord, and he laid out on his bed, half dozing, half enjoying the mental image he'd conjured up of Lola. As the record spun, she'd acquired Audrey Hepburn's face, Marilyn Monroe's breasts, and, well, Arthur's cock, mostly because it was the only one he'd even seen. And the sweet, vulnerable narrator was on his knees for her.

He wasn't ashamed as he reached inside his shorts to grasp his hardening prick. Because he was in his kimono. And when he was in this safe cocoon, he could entertain whatever fantasies he damn well wanted to.

7

The Tarts rehearsed again on Thursday, and Arthur blessedly fielded no comments and no questions about the missing Kinks album. They played Arthur's song, and Deb worked out a positively gut-pumping drum part that made the song pulse like a racing heartbeat in someone's chest. Friday, they had a show, and Arthur stood in the crowd at the Extemp wondering what it would be like when he was ready to play up there with them.

Jim wore a different skirt at this show, a wool plaid miniskirt that he wore with a large, oversized suit jacket, a mod button-up and narrow tie, and black boots that laced up his muscular, hairy calves. It was ... it was a *look*. A couple of dudes in the back shouted something derogatory until Eve strutted onto the stage in a bell-bottomed jumpsuit zipped down to her navel. Deb wore a white men's undershirt and jeans, which was pretty much the same as her uniform of white t-shirt and jeans, but drummers were able to get away with more muted fashion choices given they were hidden behind the drums. Besides, Deb's choices were markedly more unique given that she was a woman sporting the classic 1950s rebel-boy look and in a gender-bending way, suited the nonconformism of it all.

Arthur nursed his beer and tried to imagine himself on stage with them, playing the Rhodes wearing ... what? His nerdy shell of a button-up and slacks? He'd look like a fool. In his kimono? He couldn't scarcely bear the thought of such intimacy on display for strangers to consume, but it had to be something between the two. What he wanted was something that helped him blend in by standing out just enough. He had nothing like this in his wardrobe.

After the show, they all went up to Eve and Jim's place to get drunk and listen to records. This time, Arthur ended up sleeping on the couch and joined the rest of them for a hot breakfast at the New Riverside cafe before dragging himself back to Comstock the next day.

On Monday morning, Arthur ran into Jim on the Washington Avenue pedestrian bridge that spanned the east and west banks of the Mississippi River.

"Oh hey," Jim said, waving as he slowed to greet Arthur on his way to the East Bank.

"Hi," Arthur replied, rather impressed that Jim had acknowledged him in public. After all, Jim was wearing tight bell-bottom jeans and a fur-trimmed trench coat while Arthur was in his usual shell with a nice wool jacket over top, looking for all intents and purposes insufferably dorky.[1]

"Where you off to?" Jim asked, stuffing his hands into his trench pockets, his hair catching the breeze and making him look like he was posing for an album cover.

Arthur shrugged, shifting from one foot to the other. It was chilly. "Nowhere in particular. I thought I might grab breakfast and do some studying." He flicked his chin to the book bag he had slung over his shoulder.

"Ah, right, engineering," Jim said, his mouth crooking in a boyish half-smile.

"Where you headed?" Arthur asked, not sure why his cheeks felt hot.

Jim opened his mouth and hesitated. "Well," he began slowly, "I'm ... yeah, I'm heading to Tom's protest."

---

1. "Your Wall's Too High" Steppenwolf

"Tom?"

"Tom Boroughs? You met him—sort of—a couple practices ago? His friend, Michael, got fired from his job, so he and some other folks from FREE are picketing Morrill Hall."

Arthur remembered. Fired for being gay, Tom had said. Just the idea of a protest made him involuntarily cringe. Jim noticed.

"Sorry," Arthur said quickly, "I think it's great you're going. I do. I just ... I was at the student takeover last year, and it ... well, it sort of ruined me for protests forever."

"Oh shit, did you get arrested?"

"No, but almost." Arthur opened his arms. "As you can see, I'm not really the kind of guy who gets arrested for a cause."

"No," Jim agreed, his eyes flickering over Arthur's shell thoughtfully, "but you could be."

"I'd really rather not," Arthur said with a wince, crossing his arms. "My dad would murder me."

Jim nodded, digging his hands deeper into his pockets. "Well," he said, looking out over the river. "Would you, uh, want to walk over with me? It's right across from Walter Library, which is, after all, a very appropriate study location."

Arthur was momentarily alarmed. Was Jim purposefully trying to hang out with him? One on one? The critical guitarist was Arthur's most significant obstacle to becoming a full member of the band. Not to mention getting Eve to go on a date with him. This could be a golden opportunity to smooth that obstacle into a clear pathway.

"Ah, you're freaked out, nevermind—" Jim started, but Arthur interrupted.

"—Yeah, okay."

"Really?"

"Well, yeah. Libraries are the prime real estate for studying, like you said. And I have a sandwich in my bag so I don't really need to eat out. In fact, I probably shouldn't, given how much I've been eating at the Extemp lately."

Jim blinked at him. "Okay. Great. Okay. Uh, let's go."

Arthur turned around and fell into step next to Jim. For a long moment, they were both silent. They were reaching the end of the bridge when Jim said, "I really don't expect you to go to the protest. No pressure on that front."

"Thanks," Arthur said sheepishly. "Kent State really did ruin me for protests."

Jim sighed heavily. "Fair."

As they turned onto the quad, Arthur craned his neck to see if the protest had started yet. There were plenty of students around, moving from one building to another. It was a bit too cold for hanging out on the quad, but the drum circle hippies were giving it their old college try in front of the Chemistry building.

"Are you, uh, worried folks might ... draw the wrong conclusions about you if you're at this particular protest?" Arthur saw Jim's eyes darken as he asked the question and realized it was probably a rude one.

"No."

"Sorry, I didn't mean to suggest anything," Arthur backtracked placatingly. "I just—it doesn't seem like your thing really."

"Being gay?"

"Well, no, I meant protesting, but I guess that too."

Jim kept his gaze straight ahead and made his Grim Jim face. (Actually, that would be a cool name for a song...)

"I..." he started. Arthur could see his Adam's apple bob in his throat. Was he nervous? In front of Arthur? For ... *why*? "I—I just ... have known Tom for a long time. And I, uh ... well, I don't think Mike deserves how they're treating him."

Arthur began to nod, but then Jim quickly added, "And Eve and Deb are the worst and would never be caught dead at a rally, so I figured it was up to me to save our reputation with the FREE crowd."

"Really?" Arthur asked. He'd sort of imagined Deb and Eve being eager bra-burning types, but he supposed that just because neither of them seemed particularly interested in wearing bras didn't mean they liked to symbolically burn them.

"Oh yeah," Jim laughed as he fished his cigarettes out of his pocket. "Deb's like you—she got burned after a rally that went too far—and Eve? Well, she's just a nihilist and doesn't think any advocacy is worth a damn anyway so what's the point."

"What about you?"

Jim inhaled and grinned, smoke filtering between his teeth. "I guess I'm just here to cancel out my old man."

"He a Republican?"

"One of the 'silent majority,' as he likes to say. Total fucking shithead."

"Fun."

Morrill Hall and the Walter Library were just across the quad from each other. As they approached, a group of maybe 30 people, mostly guys, stood at the base of Morrill's steps with large signs. "Homos are human." "Gay Power." "Evidently, Honesty Doesn't Pay." Tom was at the front of the group, looking beardy and angry with his "End Discrimination Against Gays Now" sign. When he saw Jim, he blinked in surprise. For a second, he looked like he was going to set down his sign and approach them, but then his face closed off and he didn't.

"Oh, look, there's a journalist," Jim laughed, pointing at a fellow off to one side, speaking to one of the protesters and taking diligent notes. "I hope they run a photo in the paper. My dad would shit a brick if he saw me with signs like that." When Jim noticed he was laughing alone, he paused and took a deep drag on his cigarette.

"Well," he said, turning to Arthur all business, "I'll see you at rehearsal tomorrow."

Arthur nodded. "Yeah. Good luck on the protest."

Jim snorted and looked over his shoulder at the tiny group. "Yeah, thanks. He'll need all the luck he can get."

"What makes you say that?"

"Well, how many gay guys do you know that are able to be out at work?"

Arthur shifted uncomfortably. "I don't know any gay guys. Also, I don't have a job."

Jim looked at the ground and laughed. "Fair enough." He pushed a hand through his hair and gave Arthur a small smile, the kind that probably drove the girls wild. "See you later."

And he turned and strode off to the group, where a few of the guys (conspicuously *not* Tom) greeted him gratefully and shook his hand. Arthur blinked back an uneasy feeling (he was probably just hungry) and mounted the steps across the way into Walter Library. He showed his student ID and entered the main room, where long tables and stacks of reference books lined the walls. He took a seat next to the window so he could keep an eye on how the protest progressed.

Jim had acquired an "Honesty doesn't pay" sign and stood near the back, looking very counter-culture with his long hair and coat. Most of the guys there had long hair and beards. It was hard to imagine that these men were ... romantic with other men. They looked like hippies, like the kind of guys who'd show up to any protest because they loved to dissent. They looked strong, resolute, and pissed off. Arthur wasn't sure what he expected. A bunch of men in high heels and minidresses crying hysterically and throwing rocks? It just goes to show being gay had nothing to do with physicality. It was private. No one had to know if you didn't tell them.

So why had Michael talked to the press about it? It seemed like that was his first mistake. Arthur pulled his engineering textbook out of his bag and cracked it open on the table. It did a very poor job of pulling his attention away from the objectively more interesting rally outside. Campus police were lurking across the quad now. Jim's hair fluttered in the wind as one of the bearded fellows said something in his ear that made him laugh. Grim Jim laughing was quite the sight, his lips disappearing as they stretched over his teeth, the corners of his mouth curling up like his hair.

Arthur blinked his eyes back to his textbook. Now was a terrible time to be distracted. Especially not by the smile of the (ex?) boyfriend of the girl he liked, who also similarly liked dresses but had calves like a football player. That was nonsense better left to kimono hour, and besides, he had a report due next week. He picked up his book and bag and sidled over to a different table, one farther away from the window.

There. Now maybe he would focus.

8

Fall fluttered away too quickly. It was always like that in Minnesota. The frost had come, and with it, the cold autumn winds that slaked any remaining leaves off the trees and made walking across campus miserable.

Or at least, it would have normally made Arthur miserable, but today, he had the prospect of his very first show at the Extemp to make his heart race, warming him quite effectively as he made his way across the Washington Avenue pedestrian bridge. The music was good. He was sure of this. And it was Halloween, so if Eve made good on her threat to help him get ready for the show (to "tart" him up a bit, as she had so elegantly put it), his appearance could be attributed to holiday spirit. Regardless, the prospect of dressing up onstage terrified him. He was already wearing jeans, a significant departure from his usual shell, but that wasn't nearly enough, for Eve, nor, if he were being honest, himself.

At the last rehearsal, he'd suggested maybe wearing a suit like Buddy Holly, and Eve had looked so horrified, Deb had jumped in and held her hands over Eve's ears. "How could you say that to her? Evie, it's okay, he didn't mean it."

Eve took the opportunity to crawl into Deb's arms and keen her distress. Arthur was pretty sure they had been kidding, but still. It hadn't helped any.

Trouble was, when he'd been at home last weekend, he'd spent the whole time lying to his parents. Because omitting The Tarts from his response to "What's new at school?" was a lie by omission at best. But he couldn't *tell* them. Because then his mother would set her lips that way she did when she was worried, and his dad would ask what the band was called and then he'd have to say "The Tarts". His parents weren't idiots. They'd known Brits in the war. They knew what that meant. Then they would calmly explain why he needed to quit and move back home and give up his dorm, and he would agree because they'd be right. They were always fucking right.

He had a history of playing fast and loose with his own safety. His mother was lucky she'd intervened early and at least taught him to keep his fashion interests a secret. Fact was and would remain: dressing in women's clothing in public was illegal. He could literally be arrested. Even Jim didn't go so far as to wear skirts outside of the apartment or the Extemp, except apparently for the time they'd all walked Arthur back to Comstock. It certainly didn't help that Arthur was not white. Besides, if he was going to betray his race by refusing to protest the Vietnam War because he was too scared, he couldn't justify getting arrested for being too tarted up.

He was in a much too serious mood when he reached the apartment on Cedar and Riverside. So much so that when Jim answered the door in his eyeliner and crushed velvet bell bottoms (Arthur resolutely clenched his fists to keep from trying to touch them), he said, "Christ, what happened to you?"

Arthur tried to smile. "Nothing. Just getting in my own head."

"Well, it's a good thing you're here now!" Eve exclaimed as she sprang up to greet him. She only had false eyelashes on one eye so far, but she greeted him with a chaste kiss on the mouth anyway, her lips sweet and soft and lingering. "We can help you get your feet back to earth. Or, well, at least back in the vicinity of the Milky Way. I'm not a miracle worker."

Arthur couldn't help but crack a smile. Eve stepped back and took in his clothes. "Oh, hell, Arthur! What are you *wearing*!?" Eve threw her hands up in surrender and stalked off to her bedroom. "I guess I just have to do everything myself!"

Arthur flushed a bit and took off his coat. Jim had gone to help Deb hang up an outrageously gauche false grape vine over the window.

"What on earth is that?" Arthur asked, stepping into the living room and feeling very out of place in his jeans and black t-shirt. (Too small now, but that was the point, wasn't it? Right?)

"Decorations," Deb said around a cigarette pinched between her teeth as she reached beyond her slight height. "For the bacchanal."

"Bacchanal?"

"After the show tonight, Eve decided we're hosting a costume party to celebrate," Jim said, his expression such that Arthur couldn't figure out if he was happy with this development or not. "And she's decided it's a toga party."

Jim's curling lip made it clear what he thought about *that*.

"Don't listen to Jim," Eve said, returning from the hall carrying an armload of clothing. "It's not a toga party, it's a *bacchanal*. It's a celebration of decadence and pleasure. It's not going to be like some idiot frat party. It will be a freak out of immeasurable powers. All demons will be released on the dance floor. Woes of the world and modern living will be meaningless and we shall be free!"

She spun in a whirl of silk and velvet.

"So we don't have to wear togas?" Arthur asked hopefully.

"Oh no, we are definitely all wearing togas," Eve replied resolutely. She tossed the pile of clothes on the sofa and seized Arthur by the shoulders. "Now, let me have a look at you."[1]

---

1. "Star" David Bowie

Eve took a step back and considered him with one critical, eyelashed eye. "Can you play without your glasses?"

Arthur frowned uncomfortably, adjusting the offending frames. "I don't think so. I'm farsighted, so if I don't wear them, I won't be able to see the keyboard."

"Damn," Eve replied. She stepped forward and plucked at his t-shirt with undisguised disgust. "Why don't you just take this off, and we can see what we're working with."

"No!" squeaked Arthur, crossing his arms. Eve tipped her head back and huffed in frustration.

"Fine," she retorted and snatched a brightly patterned garment from her pile. "Try this over it, then."

Arthur held the garment in front of him—light, transparent polyester whose fibers just screamed "PLASTIC!" into his fingers—and fixed a skeptical eye on it. It was a blouse with large, puffed sleeves and a ruffle down either side of the front-fastening buttons. "Whose is this?"

"Hey, that's mine!" Jim cried from his perch balancing precariously on the arm of the sofa while reaching up to sling the fake grape vine over the curtain rod. Eve rolled her eyes.

"Don't get your panties in a twist, darling," she called, tossing the rejected blouse on the pile. "It's Arthur's *debut,* and we have our reputation to uphold. We can't get territorial about ladies' blouses."

She dug through the pile and pulled out a silk scarf as long as her arm. It was crimson red *crepe de chine,* and as soon as Arthur saw it, he wanted it. Eve held it up before him, and when she glanced up from her scrutiny, she smiled.

"Oh, you like this," she murmured and then draped it around his shoulders. "What is it? The color?"

Arthur reached up absently and touched the china silk, then shrugged dismissively. Eve pursed her lips and quirked a brow. Then, she let out an exhale and began fussing with the scarf, trying to decide how to style it on him.

Jim and Deb hopped down from the sofa arm and the dining chair, respectively. Deb had on her James Dean uniform, and Jim seemed completely at ease in his extremely tight velvety trousers. He had a flimsy, sleeveless blouse on that looked like it might be silk, but Arthur couldn't be sure without touching it. (How could he find an excuse to touch it?)

Eve tied the scarf around his neck and then declared, "You need red lipstick."

Arthur's gaze snapped back on to her. "I don't think I feel comfortable—"

"—It's not comfortable, it's rock 'n' roll! They're antithetical!"

"Give it up, Artie," Deb said, picking up a roll of tape and crossing to the kitchenette. "You'll never win."

"Oh, easy for you to say," Arthur retorted. "You get to hide behind the drum kit."

Deb shrugged and took a slug of a Hamms can someone had left on the counter.

Eve stood before Arthur with her hands clasped, and her lips pursed seriously. "Strip everything else away. Forget fear. Forget what other people will think. Forget what *we* think. What do *you* think, darling?"

Arthur's eyes darted away from Eve's, looking across the room for some support. Deb? She only had eyes for the Hamm's bear. Jim? He was lighting a cigarette. When he met Arthur's nervous gaze, he was steady, his eyebrows slanted up and head tilted inquiringly. Arthur shook his head, flustered. "I—I don't know. I don't even know what it looks like."

"Well, I'll show you," Eve said and yanked him back to the hall. "We've got a standing mirror in the bedroom."

There were only two bedrooms in the apartment, and a tiny bathroom with cracking tile. Since the back bedroom had been converted into the practice space, Jim and Eve shared the other room. Arthur hadn't really allowed this to register too seriously, mostly because he hated the entire concept, nor had he been inside the offending sleeping space. When Eve swung the door open, Arthur was both shocked and not at all surprised to find there was only one double bed in their room. The room had a closet built in, but there was also a standing wardrobe and a wide bureau with a vanity mirror as well. If Arthur hadn't been feeling quite green with jealousy already, he would have been worshiping at the altar of costume jewelry bedecked over the vanity, cascading with plastic beads and refracting glass rhinestones. The room was strewn with clothing, the surfaces packed with toiletries and make-up and empty beer bottles.

Yet, none of this could stop Arthur from staring at that bed. The one bed. That Eve slept in. *With Jim*. He shouldn't have been surprised. In fact, all said and done, Jim had been very magnanimous with Arthur trying to flirt with his girlfriend. Or whatever they were to one another, because they clearly didn't prescribe to traditional definitions.

"Here," Eve said and shuffled a resigned Arthur around to face the standing mirror. "Just let me give you a little *zhuzh*."

She fluffed the scarf at his neck, giving the ties a jaunty side angle so they couldn't be mistaken for a necktie. Then she reached up and mussed his hair. He shook her off.

"Wait—"

"Darling, please, let me do something with you. You're so lovely—I just want everyone to see what I see."

How was he supposed to say no to that? He could only press his lips together petulantly.

"I mean it, Arthur," she continued, "What would you do, if no one else were in the room? If you could embody our music, your song, in a ... a vacuum-sealed space capsule? What would you look like?"

Arthur twisted the ends of the scarf in his fingers and stared at his reflection. He knew what he wanted to say, but it was completely weird and insane to say "You" to a beautiful, busty white girl when he was ... well, him.

All he could do was just stare into the mirror. His hair was getting long. Last weekend, in fact, his mother had chided him for neglecting his grooming. But he actually liked it. He liked the way the black locks swept over his face in severe, jagged pieces. But what did it matter what he liked?

"I don't really see how that's relevant," he finally replied.

"You, my dear, are infuriating," Eve said glibly. She ran her fingers down his arm and then took his right hand in hers. "Perhaps we should worry about your hands. That's what will be playing the music. Can we adorn them in a way that might be as excessive as our songs?"

Arthur bit his lip and stared his reflection down in the mirror. "Sure, yeah. I—" he glanced at the reflection of the bed in the mirror and felt his resolve crack a little. "I'm sorry I'm being such a pain. I just—I don't want to be the reason people laugh at you."

Eve seized both his shoulders firmly. "You won't. Arthur, look me in the eye. You *won't*. You play piano so well. That's the only thing that will matter."

"Then why do I have to worry so much about what I look like?"

Eve sighed. "Hell, Arthur, because it's *fun*. Just like the music. It's irreverent, to tart up and push against what we're supposed to wear — a total fuck-you to the status-quo. That's rock and roll, darling."

Arthur nodded. If he was going to play in a band, he had better be ready to perform. "Dammit, I should have asked you to go shopping with me. I really do look miserable." He pushed his glasses up and rubbed his face with his palms.

"Darling, don't fret," she cooed, rubbing her hands up and down his arms. "It's not complicated. In fact, it's very simple. Does it feel good? Then do it. No other criteria necessary."

He grimaced. "Easier said than done, Eve."

"You know what my mother always says?" Eve asked softly, searching for his eyes between his fingers. "'You can face just about anything with a little lipstick.'"

Arthur looked down and nodded, his lips pressed into a thin line.

"And some rhinestone glasses."

Arthur glanced up incredulously. "She doesn't always say *that*."

Eve shot him an unapologetic grin and snatched his glasses off his face. "Don't panic, darling! I'm just going to put a couple rhinestones on the frames. I'll use eyelash glue! It will be utterly temporary, I assure you! Here!"

She tossed him a tube of lipstick and winked, then dashed out the bedroom door, presumably to the tiny card table turned dining table in the kitchen she'd been sitting at when he first arrived. She was still only wearing false eyelashes on one eye.

Arthur turned reluctantly, as though now that he was alone in the room, it was going to rise up and swallow him whole. That fucking bed. It wasn't even big, either. A simple double, strewn with sheets and clothes and certainly not made. Two lumpy pillows. Side by side. Arthur swallowed down whatever feeling that had incited.

He turned resolutely to the mirror. He pulled the cap from the lipstick, turned the tube to raise the crimson stick. It was well-used, half gone. Arthur wondered for a moment if he should pretend that he didn't know how it went on. If they'd be suspicious if he was easily able to line his lips in scarlet paint. But they'd seen the kimono. They wouldn't be surprised, certainly.

He pressed the stick to his lips. Patted the color in layers onto his mouth, pressed his lips together, imagined how his lips were kissing the same tube of color that Eve's did. How he longed for her, for *all* of her—not just her affection, but her confidence, her beauty, the way she drew people to her like a moth to a magnificent, bright flame. He wanted to be that. It was how he'd felt in the basement in his youth. That bombshell energy.

He'd sang, danced, sashayed, pouted, wiggled, and imagined how everyone would fall at his feet like the suited dancers in "Diamonds are a Girl's Best Friend." He wanted Eve—everyone did, it was like Jim had said, it was human nature to want someone like her—but he also wanted what she had. What she was allowed to have.

The lipstick was the right choice. His reflection was fuzzed without his glasses, but the scarf and his lips played beautifully with one another. Arthur found a box of tissues sticking up between some empty beer bottles and grabbed one to blot his mouth. Then, he turned and walked out of the room, letting his impaired vision serve as a shield from any derisive looks. If they didn't like the lipstick, he could always wipe it right off.

"Darling!" Eve clapped her hands together and stood from the dining chair. "Yes, I knew it! You look stunning!"

A crash came from the kitchen.

"Jim, you idiot, pay attention!"

"Sorry, Deb—I'll ..." Jim looked at Arthur with some alarm before turning back into the kitchenette. "I'll clean it up."

"Was that a plate?" Eve asked, turning to investigate.

"Yes," Deb complained, "the one for the grapes, with the grapes on it."

Arthur walked over and craned his neck to try and see what Eve was doing to his glasses.

"Ah ah! Don't touch, it's still wet," she chided, taking his hands and pulling them over her shoulders. Without his glasses, her face was blurred, like a soft filter in a movie. And just like in a movie, she craned her neck up and gave him a soft, chaste kiss on his lips.[2]

"You, my darling," she said quietly, "have gorgeous lips. Where have you been hiding those?"

---

2. "Somebody to Love" Jefferson Airplane

Arthur swallowed, glancing up at Jim, who was bent over the floor with a dustpan sweeping up ceramic shards. Bent as he was, it appeared he was wearing a jockstrap under those tight velvet pants. Arthur looked away quickly, wishing he could unsee that. He already knew too much about Jim after seeing his bedroom. He didn't need to be picturing him in a jockstrap.

He set his forehead against Eve's and banished the thought by whispering to her, "Do you kiss all your friends that way?" His heart fluttered fearfully as a small smile played on her lips.

"At least when they're wearing very nice lipstick, and I don't want to smudge it," Eve replied, reaching up and sweeping her thumb over his jaw. "My god, darling, you don't even have a cupid's bow. Your lips are just full and smooth the whole way round. Like a rose."

He saw her tongue dart out over her own lips for just a moment, so quickly he thought he might have imagined it.

"Eve, are you done yet?"

Jim. Standing there with a broom in one hand like a flamboyant chimney sweep, glowering at them.

Eve bit her lip and grinned at Jim coyly. "I believe I am! Just need to add the finishing touch."

She reached down to the table and set Arthur's glasses back on his nose before he could really even assess what she'd done to them. Eve and Jim slid into sharp focus, both regarding him with some scrutiny.

"They still look pretty nerdy," Eve said, just as Jim said, "I think he's pulling them off."

They looked at each other and giggled, like two people who ... who had grown up together, who shared a bed, who knew one another inside and out and loved one another anyway. Arthur clenched his teeth tightly together and made his face a mask. He remembered, strangely, when his mother had smacked him for wearing Obaasan's kimono. She'd come to the bathroom with a bladder of ice for his lip and explained to Arthur that there were two faces, two versions of oneself. The truth of it all was honne, and it was special. You only showed your honne to people you trusted. The other was tatemae, and that was what you showed to the world.

"Sometimes," she'd said, holding the ice to his mouth, "you have to use the tatemae to keep your honne safe."

Eve and Jim had gone to help Deb put the grapes into a large bucket—certainly not an elegant solution but an effective one.

Arthur had sort of thought that his honne wore lipstick. But right now, he just felt like he was wearing a different type of mask.

JANE HAO LEY

9

Arthur wished he could say that the moment he walked onto the stage in the Extemp music gallery, all his fears fell away. That he'd become the confident, outrageous beauty he'd always wished he was, and that he played that Rhodes with such fucking epic aplomb that the crowd cried for an *encore*. It wasn't that he played badly or anything. He played well. He was just, well, stiff. Stuck in his head. At least that's how he felt when he stepped off the stage after the first set.

He was hot. And tired. And sweating into that perfect china silk scarf, and it was almost certainly ruined. He probably looked like a nerdy idiot with a stick up his ass wearing lipstick. Eve was swept away by her adoring fans, and Arthur walked through the tea room with every intention of hiding in the Chess Room upstairs until he sank into the floor forever.

"Hey," Jim touched his arm. "Good job."

Arthur turned and scratched his sweaty neck under the scarf. "You don't have to say that. I know I was stiff."

Jim frowned. Arthur had never noticed before how long his eyelashes were. Mascara was doing its job, then. "Everyone takes time to find the pocket. It's unreasonable to expect someone to be completely comfortable on stage their first time."

"That's very kind of you," Arthur dutifully replied, looking at the floor.

"Do you want a smoke?"

"No, I don't really think it'll help."

"Not a cigarette..."

Arthur looked up at him. Jim lifted his eyebrows and quirked the corner of his mouth up into this very mischievous, boyish smirk as he pulled a joint halfway out of the breast pocket of his shirt (blouse?). The last time Arthur had shared a joint with Jim, he'd gotten blitzed out of his mind and invited them all up to his dorm to show them his kimono.

"Forgive me if I'm apprehensive after the last time."

"I'm pretty sure that had more to do with drinking a gin and wine cocktail, but that's understandable."

"The Joni Mitchell didn't help either."

Jim snorted. "I like when you're mean." Arthur twisted his lips to one side, holding back a smile. Jim's eyes followed. "But I don't think one hit would do anything except help you relax a little bit."

"Art, darling, care for a drink?" Eve approached, handing Arthur a paper cup and pouring something out of a flask she'd materialized from somewhere. The Extemp didn't have a liquor license (not that that stopped its patrons from drinking on their own). "Oh wait, are we *smoking?*"

Jim led them upstairs, where they hovered in the Collage Room and passed the joint and flask in turn. Arthur smelled the flask and determined it was rum, so he skipped the joint in hopes that he could moderate the chill he required without getting so loaded he couldn't play. Jim seemed to have the same idea, only he kept with the joint and skipped the flask. Eve had no such compunction and indulged happily in both before reapplying lipstick on all three of them.

When they climbed back onstage for the second set, Arthur was feeling a little looser. Which was good because they were playing his song in this set. They kicked off with the not-so-subtle "Do It," which involved a lot of Eve gyrating against Jim's guitar and moaning into the mic. Slowly, Arthur found his body feeling the music. He didn't just stand at the Rhodes—he grooved on it, bobbing his head up and down as he let his hair fall in his eyes and his hands flow over the keys with the driving beat of Deb's bass drum.

By the time they got to "Hammer Your Heart," Arthur had found the pocket. Eve droned the lyrics he had written, her lips caressing the mic during the verses, then jumping up and down at the chorus, her fingers walking lithely over the bass strings. Jim's guitar solo turned heads, and then Arthur had his brief solo, plinking on the Rhodes and capitalizing on its other-worldly electric sound. And it seemed, for a moment, that he turned heads too. For the briefest of moments, the stage, the lights, the crowd, were all fixed on him, hypnotized. It was a dizzyingly powerful feeling.[1]

Lay back and let it ride / Surrender to the beat inside / Hear that voice that cuts you quick / Bleed out the ice that's making you sick

Girls in minidresses and guys with shaggy hair swayed in the crowd, eyes closed and arms swirling above their heads like they were at a religious revival. The guitar buzzed through the room, filling the space with heady frequencies as Deb steadily kicked out the bass drum so that everyone—band and audience together—had their hearts beating as one.

When the song was over, Eve crossed to Arthur and swung her arm around him, pressing a big, wet kiss on his cheek and calling for the crowd to give it up for The Tarts' newest member. And they did. They cheered for him. And he couldn't help but grin.

Arthur was well toasted by the time the show was over. Between the smokey room and the other half of Jim's joint he'd agreed to share in a fit of blind confidence after the second set, he was feeling pretty bubbly when they loaded out and hauled the gear back up to the apartment. He, Jim, and

---

1. Feels like "Life on Mars?" David Bowie

Deb stowed the equipment away and when they emerged, Eve had transformed the living room into a bacchanal, filled with young, attractive, androgynous people draped in bedsheets and drinking wine down like water. And Eve herself—hell, she was stunning swathed in a sheet she'd carefully arranged to display her breasts to their best advantage. She'd tied two corners of the sheet behind her head, let the edges drape to each side leaving a wide swath of skin at the center, and belted it at her waist. When she walked, she flashed a considerable amount of thigh where the edges separated.

"Tsk tsk, my darlings," Eve crowed as they tried to emerge, and she shoved them back into the hall. "There is a dress code, and you are not meeting it!"

She bundled all four of them into her bedroom and tossed them bedsheets. Deb laughed and swigged wine as she draped the sheet right over her jeans and tight t-shirt, tying it over one shoulder.

"Deb, you can't wear your regular clothes underneath it!" Eve cried in protest, but Deb managed to escape and slip out the room, laughing maniacally. Arthur wasn't sure how to proceed as Eve turned on him.

"Arthur, darling, you heard the rules."

"I'm fairly certain the point of Bacchus was that he had no rules."

"No, he had one rule. I told it to you earlier."

"Ah, yes, that's right. 'Does it feel good?'"

"Precisely."

It was at this moment that Arthur caught sight of Jim, reflected in the mirror over Eve's shoulder. He was bending over, in his jockstrap, bare-assed, trying to get his tight pants off over his boots. Eve followed Arthur's gaze and then laughed.

"Jimmy, what on earth? Let me help you, you daft idiot." She darted to his side and pushed him to sit on the edge of the bed as she got to her knees in front of him. Arthur could swear he could feel the air over every inch of his skin it touched.

They were together, and he was just standing there, in their bedroom, watching this intimate moment that contained not nearly enough clothing. (Or maybe too much?) Arthur swallowed hard, pressed down on his half-hard cock as subtly as he could, and slipped out the door. He went and hid in the practice space, clutching the damned sheet Eve had tossed at him, waiting for the image of Eve kneeling for Jim to stop flashing, seared to the inside of his eyelids.

It took maybe five minutes for him to get a hold of himself and drape the sheet tastefully over his shoulders and around his waist such that he was able to skulk into the living room modestly covered. (With his clothes still resolutely *on* underneath.) Jim and Eve emerged from the bedroom minutes later, giggling and stoned. Jim's "toga" wrapped around his waist and draped over one shoulder, exposing the golden blonde hair on his chest. Arthur gulped his wine down and tried not to think about what had just gone on in that bedroom.

The Rolling Stones were on the record player, barking out the opening strains of "Sympathy for the Devil." The guests swilled wine and danced. Others lounged on the sofa and smoked, passing grapes and joints amongst one another. It distantly occurred to Arthur that if his mother could see the scene before him, she would likely faint in a fit of Methodist propriety.

"Hey, I know you!"

Arthur turned around and saw a girl with pink lipstick and blue eyeshadow coming toward him from the kitchenette. She had painted long, spidery eyelashes below her eyes with eyeliner and it made her green eyes appear massive, like a Walter Keane painting. He had never seen her before in his life.

"You were in my communications seminar last semester," she said. "Nancy Webster, do you remember?"

He didn't. Because he'd never taken a communications seminar. Arthur made a grim face. He had a feeling he knew where this was going.

"Choua, wasn't it?"

Arthur set his mouth in an awkward line, realizing he probably still had faded lipstick on his face. He needed to stop this before it went too far.

"Arthur, actually."

"Oh," she replied uncomprehendingly. "Is that your English name?"

"No, it's my actual given name. I don't know Choua, but I think you have me confused for someone else."

She gaped at him for a moment. "I could have sworn you were him. You do go to the U, don't you?"

"Yes, I do. I'm in the College of Science and Engineering—"

"Oh! Do you know Dewey Tran?"

Arthur grimaced. "Never heard of him, unfortunately."

"Oh. Well, he's in the Mobe club too—"

"—I'm not in that club," Arthur said firmly. He looked over her shoulders for some sort of escape.

"Oh," Nancy laughed awkwardly. "Well, it sure is nice to meet you anyway, Arthur. Where are you from?" She seemed to be trying to pronounce his name with some sort of strange accent.

"Here," Arthur ground out. He could have explained and put them both out of their misery, but after the whole bedroom scene, he was feeling vindictive.

Nancy blinked. "Here? Like, America?"

"No, here like here in Minnesota."

"Yes, Nancy, darling! I see you've just met Arthur." Oh thank god, it was Eve. She draped herself over Arthur's shoulder like a second toga. "Isn't he just a dream? His mum and dad were in the Japanese camps during the war—just horrible, isn't it? That they did that to people who were born and raised right here in America? Anyway, they fought in the war, code-breaking Japanese messages and the like. Can you believe it? His parents were basically spies!"

It sounded a whole lot more glamorous when Eve explained it.

"Oh! You're Japanese?" Nancy said, happy to file Arthur away in her ethno-racial social order. Arthur just nodded and hoped she'd go away. "Do you know Yoko Ono?"

"I have to go refill my glass," Arthur said firmly and extricated himself from under Eve's arm to fill his glass to the brim with wine.

"I see you met Nancy," said Jim, leaning against the wall next to the card table laden with wine. Arthur drank deeply from his glass and glared at him.

"It is *so* fascinating," Arthur drawled, swallowing, "to meet all these pretty little white girls, but I confess that I have a hard time telling them all apart."

Jim snorted, his grin a slash across his face, crooked and violent. His pale, blue eyes turned toward Arthur, and he said, "Have you heard the latest from Velvet Underground?"

Arthur shook his head, somewhat pleased Jim had remembered he liked them. He followed Jim to the record player just as side A of *Beggars Banquet* ended. He would allow a great deal for Lou Reed, but cutting an album off in the middle of a side was a bit much. Jim pulled out a record still in its paper record store bag and slipped the disc from the album cover before handing it to Arthur to peruse.

"Hey, wait, we still haven't heard side B!"

Jim ignored that person and replaced the Rolling Stones with the album aptly titled *Loaded*. Arthur watched eagerly as the needle dropped and a clean guitar rang out in the room. It spoke volumes about the musical clout Jim carried that no one protested when a proto early-Beatles vocal rang out across the room. The vocalist started singing about the sun and who makes plants grow. The lyrics were like something out of a 1954 hymnal.

Arthur blinked and flipped the album over. What the hell was this? Where was the experimental viola? Where was the off-pitch, rambling vocals of Lou Reed?

Jim seemed similarly panicked. "Who the fuck is this twit?"

Arthur and Jim leaned in together scouring the back of the album cover for Lou Reed's name. Just as Jim pointed out Doug as the vocalist on the track, the second track began with a tinkling cascade of guitar licks and Reed's voice chanted out his characteristically descriptive lyrics that didn't particularly rhyme. Arthur looked up at Jim, and they exchanged expressions of relief.

Oh, Sweet Jane, crooned Reed.

Two of the girls who had been dancing giggled. "Jane, listen! They're playing your song!"

A third girl whose androgynous pixie haircut left Arthur momentarily entranced looked over at the record player and smiled. "They are!"

The dancing recommenced, and no one except that one guy with the Mick Jagger hair seemed particularly upset that the *Beggar's Banquet* had been cut short.

Arthur and Jim stayed at the record console, consulting the album cover as they listened attentively.

"This is more pop-y than their other stuff," Jim noted. "That's probably why Lou left, don't you think?"

"He left?" Arthur felt his heart drop a little. *No.*

"Yeah, this summer," Jim shrugged sadly, his fingers sliding over the corners of the album.

"Why?" Arthur was moderately concerned his voice would crack. He still hadn't ever seen them live. After discovering their album three years ago, he'd read an old magazine account of the Exploding Plastic Inevitable in Chicago in 1966 and cried in his parents' basement wishing he could have been there. Too little, too late. As always.

Jim shrugged and then regarded Arthur with mild concern.

"Do you..." Jim started, "wanna go jam on some of the old stuff?"

"Like what?"

"I dunno, like 'Waiting for the Man' or 'White Light/White Heat'?"

"Hell yes."

"Ooh, I didn't know you swore," Jim smirked as he led the way through the dancers towards the back room.

"Only when I drink. That's Methodist rules."

"Oh, she's *Methodist*, is she?"

"Only on the weekends I go home."

"I'm not sure Christ is generally down with so many conditions."

"What He doesn't know won't hurt Him."

"You know the point of God is that He's omnipotent, right?"

"Shhh."

10

Jamming on the Velvets was wonderful. Arthur experimented with trying to capture the drones from John Cale's viola on the Rhodes, and it was far out. It filled him up with sound till he was brimming with glittering revolving melodies. Jim sang all of Lou Reed's parts and Arthur did Nico's. They played almost the whole Banana album, though they managed to maneuver around playing "Venus in Furs" without talking about it. Which was sad, because it had been one of Arthur's favorites for a long time, and he wanted to see if he could capture the yelping viola on the Rhodes. But perhaps Jim wasn't keen on singing about kissing anyone's shiny boots of leather. Fair enough.[1]

"How did you find the Velvet Underground?" Jim asked as they took a break for him to smoke a cigarette.

Arthur sat leaning against the Rhodes' amp. His bedsheet toga was rumpled underneath him, and he spread his denimed legs out wide on the floor. "I was in a record shop in San Francisco. We were visiting my grandmother before she died, and I saw the banana and bought it on a whim. I mean, I liked that they had 'velvet' in the name, if I'm being honest."

Jim smiled around his cigarette, one side of his mouth sliding up before the other. "You're like a secret cool guy."

---

1. "Run Run Run" The Velvet Underground

Arthur regarded him incredulously.

"Nah, really," Jim doubled down, pausing to take a drag. "I think you're trying really hard to make sure everyone looks past you. But what I don't get is why."

"Well, for one thing, when I don't put my head down and fade into the background, flighty white girls start asking me if I know Ghenghis Khan or if Chairman Mao is my dad."

Jim snorted and shook his head in his hands. His hair wafted around his face like tufts of golden dandelion fluff. "Fucking Nancy."

"How'd you find them?"

"Who?"

"The Velvets."

"Oh—Eve. Of course. She gets to do everything. Her cousin floats in all sorts of artistic circles so she saw them perform out east. I don't think she was actually at the Factory though. I think she was at a club in Boston or something. She goes off with her family every summer and comes back with all sorts of new music for me." Jim shrugged. "Not as cool as your story."

Arthur considered this somewhat bizarre statement with the ample confusion it deserved. There sat a man with hair like a lion and calves carved of rock, smoking a cigarette and wearing the hell out of a toga, somehow sticking a set of truly remarkable mental gymnastics in order to suggest Arthur was cooler than him.

"It's not a competition," Arthur mumbled. Was he blushing? Stop. Stop it.

"People only say that when they're winning." Jim took another drag from his cigarette, and the smoke hung like a halo around his head. Arthur just stared at him. Winning? Was he fucking serious? "What was San Francisco like?"

"I don't know," Arthur shrugged. He pulled his knees up and wrapped his arms around them. "I didn't see much beyond Japantown."

Jim nodded and picked at a loose thread on the hem of his toga sheet.

"I, uh," he glanced up at Arthur, "I want to go to Castro Street one day."

Arthur had no idea where that was, but if Jim thought he was cool, he'd better strive for casual nonconcern. He shrugged. "Never been."

Jim studied his face for a moment, then nodded, looking down as he tugged the thread free. When he looked up again, he seemed more ... composed somehow?

"New York too," he continued. "But where I really dream to go someday is London. Eve's grandma lives there, and her cousin too, and the music she brings back—shit, Arthur, it's so subversive and innovative and just far out. Music here is so tired. Touring bands and Top 40 covers. There's barely any place a local band can play, much less make a name for themselves. Besides, no one's looking for the next big thing in Minnesota. In London, there's such a big scene that people can get away with all sorts of experimental shit. Like Warhol's Factory, but for songwriters."

Arthur stared at him. "That sounds amazing."

Jim grinned, like it wasn't weird at all that Arthur was looking at him with something like longing. Because they both knew the pull of music in a way other people didn't. And the way he described London; who could resist longing for a place like that? "Yeah. I'll get there some day. Maybe you will too?"

Arthur smiled and shrugged, looking down at the dregs of wine in his glass. It had never even occurred to him, but it warmed him that Jim thought he could be the kind of person who traveled and played experimental music and lived outrageously. "Maybe."

"Looks like you need a refill," Jim said, pointing at Arthur's glass with his cigarette.

Arthur nodded, and they got up and headed back to the living room. As they passed the bedroom door, it cracked open a bit, and a disheveled Deb peeked her head out.

"Hey, Jim," Deb said in a low voice. "You got a couple cigarettes?"

She looked ... suspicious. The lights were dim inside the bedroom.

"Only if you promise to stay off my side of the bed," Jim replied severely, slipping two cigarettes from his pack and handing them to Deb like a father begrudgingly giving his teen some gas money.

Deb nodded and accepted the cigarettes. Then, she blinked. "Which side was that again?"

Arthur strode off to the living room. Deb entertaining a lover was none of his business. Also, he had no interest whatsoever in finding out which side of the bed Jim slept on. By process of elimination, he'd know what side Eve slept on. And then he could determine what direction they would face for optimal spooning. Oh hell, he couldn't unimagine that.

Jefferson Airplane was playing on the record console. "White Rabbit" actually. A group of non-gender-specific people swayed in the center of the room. Two of them, both feminine-presenting, were exploring one another's mouths quite enthusiastically with their tongues. Another couple of people were piled on the sofa. Togas had become significantly ... disheveled. Arthur froze. Eve was reclined on the sofa, and she was kissing pixie Jane. The bedsheet had been pulled askew and a wide swath of Eve's bare skin was exposed on her right side, from clavicle to toes. If it weren't for Jane's hand massaging her breast with not a small amount of gusto, she'd be bare. A third person—a *third* person—was kneeling between her thighs, kissing that guy with the Mick Jagger hair, who was reclined on Eve's lap.

Nope. Arthur looked away. He couldn't. Couldn't. He wasn't supposed to see this.

"Sounds like they're good and loaded if Grace Slick is playing," Jim said as he emerged from the hall. He took one look at Arthur, furrowed his brow, then looked out over the debauched scene playing out in the living room. His expression flattened, but he didn't seem angry, which surprised Arthur. He just looked ... disappointed, maybe? Not even that. It was definitely another of Grim Jim's fatherly expressions, but it was more a "Kids these days" expression than one that portended any imminent fury.

Arthur must have looked devastated, because Jim grabbed his arm and pulled him into the kitchen. "Come on, Pollyanna, let's get you a refill."

Arthur huddled next to the counter and tried not to swivel his head and look back at what was transpiring on the sofa. His arms crossed over his chest of their own accord.

Jim went to the card table where there were more empty wine bottles than full ones and poured some into Arthur's glass. He handed it back to him with a sigh.

"What did you expect from a bacchanal?" he asked resignedly, his voice not unkind. "It's a celebration of pleasure. It's in the name."

Arthur felt supremely stupid. He stared into his glass. He'd heard plenty about free love, but this was pretty extreme. Eve wasn't a hippie. None of The Tarts were particularly hippie-ish. Deb actively bitched about them, for Chrissakes.

Jim ducked his head to catch Arthur's eyes. "Do you wanna go?"

Arthur looked at him. He didn't know what to say.

"I can walk back with you, man. It's not a big deal."

"Don't you have, you know, bacchanalia to do?" Arthur said, unable to keep the bitterness out of his voice.

Jim scoffed, but he was also smiling. "I can do my bacchanalia anytime."

Arthur squirmed under his gaze. Of course he could. He shared a *bed* with Eve. Then, like the fool he was, Arthur slammed his glass of wine, drinking it down in a couple of gulps. With a loud exhale, he wiped his chin and said, "Yeah, let's go."

Jim ducked back into his bedroom to change, resulting in a loud and angry shout from Deb, while Arthur draped his stupid toga over the pony wall by the front door, then hid behind it. He wasn't proud, but he didn't want Eve to notice him. If she tried to talk to him, he was afraid he might yell at her. And that would very much be not cool bandmate behavior. He just had to face the facts: he'd read her attention all wrong. He'd assigned it meaning that wasn't intended. She wasn't interested in him. She just wanted him in her band. Maybe she thought he was cute, a fun distraction to corrupt while she carried on fucking whoever she wanted. Besides, if anyone had a chance of really being with her, it was Jim.

Arthur sighed. She was clearly having a great time, and he was just bitter he was not part of it. Fine. Message received. He didn't want to be a part of that anyway. Jesus. (Especially not now that he had the wine spins.)

Jim returned, wearing a t-shirt and jeans, and threw his coat over his shoulder. He blinked down at Arthur and frowned. "Are you hiding?"

"Yes," Arthur replied petulantly, then stood, grabbing his coat off the pony wall pile and walking out the door that Jim held open for him.

They walked down Cedar Street in the silent darkness. It must have been past midnight. Leaves skittered across the pavement and a cold wind bit at Arthur's cheeks. Nonetheless, the crisp air helped Arthur feel a little less like he'd just gotten off a merry-go-round. They strolled over the Washington Avenue pedestrian bridge, dodging laughing groups of students in Halloween costumes, then took the steps down to East River Road. It was quiet down here, the only sounds the river sloshing steadily downstream. The sky was clear and the stars twinkled like so many thousands of glittering diamonds in the black velvet sky. Jim smoked as they walked, but he didn't say anything. Arthur certainly had no idea what to say. Everything that crossed his mind sounded so stupid, he couldn't manage to convince himself to even say them.

Jim dropped his cigarette butt outside of Comstock Hall's entry, extinguishing it with the tip of his boot.[2]

"Arthur," he said softly, but the night was so quiet that his voice rang clear and velvety smooth. He glanced up at him with one eyebrow raised. "Are you..." He trailed off and furrowed his brow in study. "That is, are you..." Jim shifted awkwardly and scrubbed his hand over his forehead.

"Are you trying to ask if I'm interested in Eve?" Arthur finished for him. Jim looked up at him sharply, but he didn't contradict him. Fuck. He hoped he was drunk enough to have this conversation. "It's only fair for you to ask. You live together, for Chrissakes. Whatever you call it between you, you don't have to worry about me. I'm not ... well, I'd be lying if I said I didn't think Eve was the tops, but ... I think you two are so good together. I don't really understand your arrangement, but you can count on me to not get in the way." Arthur looked at the ground and wished he smoked so he had something to do with his hands. "I think a nice girl who wishes I'd give her my pin would be more my speed, at this point." He laughed wretchedly.

Jim cleared his throat.

"Well, then," he said roughly, as if his voice was suddenly cracked and deep with disuse. "Maybe you should ask Nancy out."

The tension cut clean through the middle and fell aside like shattered boards, and it was an unexpectedly palpable relief. Arthur snort-laughed and shook his head. "Oh my god, no. She'd wonder why I didn't take her to a dim sum restaurant."

---

2. "After Hours" The Velvet Underground

Jim laughed, and the sight of his severe grin felt like relief. Arthur felt loads better having cleared the air.

"Well, I suppose you probably want to get back to the party."

"Yeah, I should probably get my bacchanalia taken care of." Jim pushed his hand through his hair and gave a lecherous grin. Arthur suddenly felt like giggling. His cheeks were hot, but that was the wine.

"That sounds like some sort of awful procedure, like a colonoscopy."

"I mean, technically, a bacchanal *could* include something akin to a colonoscopy."

Arthur was doubled over laughing now. "Jim, stop."

He looked up at Arthur with pale, earnest eyes. "Call me James."

"James?" It suited him and his serious manner much better than the more flippant, funny-sounding Jim. Jim sounded like the guy who stuffed you in a locker in high school and then screeched like a pterodactyl to his flock of football jerks. In fact, Arthur couldn't be certain he *hadn't* been stuffed in a locker by a guy named Jim in high school.

"Yeah. Eve always called me Jim, so now everyone else does too. But I prefer James."

"Oh."

"I mean, it doesn't really matter. Jim is fine too." He scuffed the pavement with his boot. Arthur smiled softly—he really liked this side of James. Unsure, deprecating—it was a trip to see such a good-looking, cool guy like him act like a real human being with fears and wants and imperfections.

"Say," said James, "you, uh, don't have any of that whiskey up there, do you?"

"Fresh out, sorry. Otherwise I'd invite you up." Arthur dug his hands into his pockets. It was pretty chilly outside.

"That's okay."

"Besides, I'd better get to bed. I'm beat after the show, and I had too much wine, and all I wanna do is put on my—" Arthur stopped. He'd been about to say *put on my kimono and pass out.*

"Were you gonna say robe?"

Arthur blushed. "Kimono, yeah."

"Well," James reached out and grasped him manfully by the shoulder. "I'll tell you one thing, man. If I had a kimono like that, I'd wear the shit out of it. It's fucking gorgeous."

It was stupid how much he wanted to hug James. Like, really stupid. Just goes to show how long he'd been keeping that kimono a deep, dark secret. Now that it was out of the wardrobe, as it were, it was like a massive weight had been lifted from his shoulders, one he hadn't even realized he'd been carrying. Three people knew about it, and none of them had disowned him or booted him out of the band. None of them had laughed at him (except maybe Deb, but that was how she showed affection, so it didn't count). None of them had called the police or tried to institutionalize him, either, which played in his irrational fear reel much more frequently than he'd care to admit. Perhaps because it wasn't all that irrational, when it came down to it.

"It is, isn't it," Arthur smiled and looked up at James.

"Heh," James returned the smile and paused for a long moment. Then he touched his own narrow lips lightly with one finger. "Say, you've still got some of Eve's lipstick right ... here."

Arthur grimaced. He didn't want anyone in his dorm seeing him come back after dark with lipstick all over his face. He pulled his coat-sleeve down over his hand and wiped his mouth with it.

"Better?"

James started to reach forward and then snatched his hand back. "Uh, yeah. Yup."

"I'm gonna head up," Arthur said, flicking his head toward the door. "Thanks for walking back with me."

James stuck his hands in his pockets and nodded, his mouth in a grim line. "Yeah, man, no worries. Anytime."

"Cool. See you tomorrow?"

"Yup."

"Don't get too drunk and debauched."

James laughed dolefully. "I'll try."

Arthur turned and headed upstairs. And wondered what difference it made to him whether James got drunk and debauched. The guy deserved to get laid. And not just Eve's sloppy—what was it?—fourths? Arthur shuddered. He couldn't help but recall all the roaming hands snaking across her porcelain skin. He could tell James that he didn't care all the live-long day—he was still jealous. If he hadn't been playing the Velvet Underground with James, things might have gone differently. Maybe it would have been him in the bedroom instead of Deb, and maybe he could have had Eve to himself. None of it bore thinking about. He'd just pledged to give up on any designs on Eve anyway.

Arthur pulled his sweaty clothes off, hanging the crimson silk scarf from the dresser drawer-pulls to air out, and slipped into his kimono. Then he laid down on his bed facedown and groaned into his pillow.

11

The next morning, Arthur woke up and made a very important decision. He was never drinking wine again. Wine was awful. It tasted like acid, it settled poorly in his stomach, and it didn't even make him feel drunk—just dizzy and nauseous and headachey. It was all the drag of having a hangover with none of the benefits.

He ended up at the dining hall for breakfast, where Tomiko found him feeling sorry for himself in a bowl of oatmeal.

"Arthur the *show!* Holy shit, man, it was *amazing!*"

He had entirely forgotten that he'd invited her. "You were there?"

"Yes, you jerk. You didn't even say hi to me. How am I supposed to convince people I'm with the band if you don't even say hello?" She flopped down into the chair across from him.

"Sorry," Arthur stuck his face ashamedly into his coffee cup. "I was so nervous, I was trying not to look at the crowd."

Tomiko leaned back in the chair she'd commandeered. "No kidding. I would have been petrified. Don't take this the wrong way, but I never would have thought you'd be in a band like that. Maybe a nice backup vocalist for some Neil Diamond cover band…"

"Hey, how dare you!" Arthur finally sat up straight, powered entirely by wounded pride. "I wouldn't be caught dead covering Neil Diamond."

"Oh yeah, that's right. You like all that experimental shit no one listens to so you can feel self-important about how obscure they are."

Arthur bristled. "I do not."

"*Anyway*," she continued, giving him a severe look that reminded him of his father, "the band was glorious. That lead singer—holy shit. She looks like a Warhol superstar or something."

"I wouldn't be surprised if he'd offered, and she turned him down."

"Is she from New York?"

Arthur paused. "No, she's from England. Well actually, I think she's from here, but her family's from England?"

"Jeez, what's she doing here, then?"

"I asked the same question."

"That guitar player too. He's *fine*."

Arthur shifted uncomfortably. Leave it to Tomiko to point out exactly all the ways he didn't fit into his own band.

"Like, *wow*, that hair and, honestly, it was a damn shame he had that guitar strapped on the whole show because he had one hell of a bulge—"

"Tomiko!"

"What? He looked like Jimmy Page and Robert Plant had a love child but, you know, in velvet pants."

"Yes, thank you, Tomi, for pointing out how woefully inadequate my looks are for this band."

"Oh, sorry, I didn't mean it that way. You're just, well, a quiet engineering nerd. Or at least, that's what I thought you were. Apparently, though, you're a secret rock star, and you had us all completely fooled."

Arthur shrugged dismissively.

"Hell. What's got you all messed up this morning? You played an objectively rockin' show. I danced till I thought I was going to fall over."

"I'm just hungover."

Tomiko leveled him with a skeptical eyebrow. "Are you?"

"Yes, I feel like shit."

"Is that *all?*"

"Yes, dammit!"

"Fine," Tomiko frowned at him. "But if you need to talk about anything, you know where to find me."

"I don't need to talk about anything."

"Okaaay," Tomiko conceded somewhat unwillingly, standing up. "I'm heading to St. Paul this morning. You wanna come?"

Arthur pressed his fingers into his forehead. "No, I can't. I have band practice tonight."

"I can get you back in time."

Arthur groaned. "I don't want to see my mom when I'm hungover. Are you going next weekend?"

"Yup, but I dunno if I'll have space."

"What, are you bringing home a boyfriend or something?"

"What? No! My dad would murder me. Just hauling laundry."

"But you do have a boyfriend?"

A smile fought for dominance over her lips. "Something like that."

"Tomiko! What? Why didn't you tell me?"

"You were busy being a rock star! Doesn't matter anyway. It's probably nothing. I'll see you around."

She strolled out of the dining hall ripping into a pastry like a wolf to a deer carcass.

Arthur finished what he could of the oatmeal and went back to his room to lick his wounds. He wasn't just hungover. He was, to be entirely honest, a little heartbroken.

When Eve'd looked at him before the show, he thought she saw him. Saw through his shell and saw inside and actually *liked* what she saw. And maybe she did, but just not in a romantic way. And maybe that should have been enough but ... well, hell.

He *wanted* to be seen in a romantic way. That's all he'd wanted — for *years*.

Hopeless romantic wasn't the half of it. He wanted to hypnotize someone, like Louise Brooks or Clara Bow in the old movies. He wanted someone to want him so much, they couldn't help but press him up against the wall and kiss him, damn the consequences. He didn't just want romance—he wanted *passion*. And Eve was like passion personified. When she sang, she lit the entire room on fire. He wanted that, selfishly, for himself. He wanted someone to look at him like that and see something so enticing they couldn't help but claim it.

He'd been such an idiot. He really had. Between James' weird long-term not-relationship with her and then the debauched sofa encounter, it had become pretty obvious that Eve had other interests. She was a shining star and he was some little scrap of space rock spinning around her trying to get her attention.

Damn.

That night, he went to band practice and tried not to act too embarrassed. He thought for sure he'd get the third degree about leaving, but he didn't. He wondered if James had talked to them about it beforehand. Eve seemed like a wrung-out rag and her voice was shot, so they cut the rehearsal short, and Arthur ended up going back to Comstock to spend more time feeling sorry for himself.

Monday brought rain and early morning class, which he was woefully unprepared for after the weekend of preparing for the show and then being a self-indulgent lump afterwards. He had no excuses, and offered none to his professor. He took the disappointed, Don't-make-me-give-up-on-you face in stride and went to the New Riverside Cafe to treat himself for lunch.

And who should he find there at the tables but none other than the source of all his self-pity, Miss Evelyn Clark?

Eve grinned when she saw him, clearly back to her old self, and waved him over to join her.[1]

"Darling, it's so good to run into you!" she gushed as she kissed his cheeks. "Please, sit!"

Arthur did (because who could tell Eve no?) and tried his damndest not to be awkward. He failed spectacularly.

After a moment of silence, Eve lifted one brow and smiled. Her face was like a serene silent movie star, at once enigmatic and mischievous.

"So I understand I gave you a bit of a shock Saturday night?"

Arthur blushed right on cue. "What makes you think that?" he stuttered.

"Jim read me the riot act yesterday. Told me a bacchanal was in woefully poor taste as a celebration of your first show, Halloween or no. I believe his words were something about how it was more a party for me than it was for you."

Arthur shifted uncomfortably in his chair. That was ... apt. Why was she telling him this?

"Oh darling, don't look so out of sorts. I say all this by way of apology. He was right, I wasn't thinking of you when I planned the party. I mean, I think I might have been thinking of you, but only in terms of how *I* wanted you, but anyway," she shrugged adorably, "I digress."

Arthur frowned. She was so confusing. That was flirting. Absolutely outrageous, overt flirting. Wasn't it?

"You're such a dear to be so torn up about it, but as I always say, 'If it feels good, do it.' As long as no one else is getting hurt, there isn't any harm in pleasure, now is there?"

"I suppose not."

"So many people go around heralding their misery like it's some sort of badge of honor but really, pleasure rewards itself,

---

1. "Queen Bitch" David Bowie

doesn't it? It's not a trap. It just feels good. Anyone suspicious of pleasure is overcomplicating things."

Arthur tried not to squirm. In his experience, things that felt good often led to harm. Usually his own harm, at the hands of those who thought the things that made him happy were threatening or unnatural.

"You know," Eve leaned forward conspiratorially, "I think that this whole 'American grit, pull yerself up by yer bootstraps' thing is just a ploy to make everyone buy into the consumer industrial complex. Make us all miserable so we buy things and fool ourselves that consumerism is the pinnacle of happiness."

"Oh?"

"Definitely. We don't need to buy stuff. We have everything we need to make one another happy by merely being together. Talking, laughing, making music, making love—it's all about human connection. And that, my dear, is the real lost city of gold."

"I don't disagree," Arthur said, nodding. "But I will say that some objects do make me very happy, all on their own, because they capture some sort of thought or idea or memory."

Eve grinned. "Yes! I see what you mean. But then, are not the objects no longer commodities, but a sort of art?"

"Maybe? How do you mean?"

"Well, for instance, your robe. I don't think anyone would contend that it isn't art just from a textile perspective, but for you, it isn't just a garment. It's a symbol—"

"—Yes," Arthur cut in eagerly. "That's exactly right. It is a symbol of culture, but even more, of my grandmother, who it belonged to before."

Eve's eyes lit and she leaned forward. "Oh, that's so sweet!"

"Yeah," Arthur said, looking down and pushing crumbs of pastry around his plate. "She was a really strong and beautiful person. She got married in it. When she was sent to Minidoka, she brought the kimono with her. She wouldn't let it get lost with all the other things they had to leave behind. She wasn't afraid that it would, I dunno, incriminate her as a Japanese loyalist or something. So many people my parents knew just threw everything Japanese away. It was dangerous, you know? But my Obaasan, she kept that piece of her life and protected it."

Eve's lips were pressed together. Actual tears gathered in the corners of her eyes. "Arthur," she cried, "that is beautiful! You shouldn't have to hide that. It's the most exquisitely human thing I've ever heard!"

She reached out and took his hand in both of hers. "Oh my god, it's just incredible—how we can enchant an ordinary object with our own meaning. Fuck, Arthur. You have to write a song about her or something. There's so many people who need to hear about something like that."

Arthur couldn't help but be skeptical. "Really?"

"Oh yes. Like Nancy! She's always droning on about how we need to protest for peace in East Asia, but then she went on interrogating you like you were some sort of commodity. Like a piece of cultural ephemera instead of a person."

"Thank you for saving me, by the way."

"Oh, it was my esteemed pleasure, darling." She took a sip from her tea cup and looked at him over its edge in a way he could not fathom as anything other than predatory. She was interested in him. He knew she was. He could feel it hovering in the air between them. So why, then, did she end up piled up with other people the other night? Why did she stay with James? Eve did not seem like the kind of person who played it safe because it was too hard to change.

"Say, all this talk of silk dressing gowns reminds me, my father brought home a new album recently and I think you would just love it."

"Oh, from England?"

"Yes. He went back a few weeks ago because, well, my grand-mother isn't doing too well, and ... oh, now I'm going to cry again!" Arthur reached out and gripped her hand firmly. She sniffled and waved her other hand at him. "Oh don't fuss, she'd hate it if she knew I were talking about her like this. Dad says she'll be fine. But," she cleared her throat, "it meant my father was across the pond and my cousin picked up a few albums for him to bring to me, so I'm flush with new music."

She stood, arranging her features back into confident composure. "Come on, let me show you."

12

Eve led him upstairs, her sleeves billowing and her miniskirt showing a remarkable swath of thigh as she took the steps two at a time. Arthur admired her commitment to the look when it was cold and sleeting outside. But he supposed if one lived above a cafe, one didn't really need to dress for the weather to eat out. When she unlocked the door and slipped off her shoes, Arthur realized this was the first time he'd ever seen the main room empty.

"Where is everyone?"

Eve shrugged. "Deb's at work, I think. Who knows what's become of Jim. Do you want a drink?"

He was alone in the apartment with Eve? "Sure, what have you got?"

Eve cracked a Hamms for each of them and motioned for him to settle onto the sofa.

"After the show the other night," she said, pulling out an album and sliding the record from its sleeve, "I thought you would appreciate this."

She dropped the needle on the record and a wavering, distorted guitar wailed from the speakers. A riff in minor key built up its layers before a reedy voice began slip-sliding around the melody.[1]

"Who is this?" Arthur asked, leaning forward as he sipped the beer.

Eve grinned down at the spinning record, biting her lip, before she looked up at him. "David Bowie. He had one hit in '69. It was a space song and the BBC played it while they broadcast the moon landing. But look."

She handed the album cover to Arthur. Sprawled across the cover was a lithe form in a glossy silk dress and black boots. Long, wavy, gold hair. Flat chest.

"Is this him?" Arthur asked. He kind of floated down to sit on the sofa.

"Yes," Eve breathed, watching him eagerly. Arthur felt the breath go out of him for a moment. The man held a card between his fingers, and it seemed the rest of the deck was strewn across the floor. He was sprawled on a settee draped in electric blue crushed velvet, his silken skirt draping across it. The dress wasn't a woman's dress though. The bodice fit him like a glove and between the clasps, cut-outs emphasized his broad, flat chest. An eerie wail emanated from the speakers, and he felt the hair on his arms stand on end.

"He's beautiful."

Eve nodded. "Isn't he just?" She sat next to him, pressing her thigh against his. "You know, you would be beautiful too, in something like that."

It was utterly terrible of her to say something like that, so sincerely. He blinked hard and shrank a little. "If you say so," he conceded quietly.

"Come now!" she cried indignantly. "I know so. Here, I'll prove it to you. Come on."

---

1. "The Width of a Circle" David Bowie

She stood and took his hand, yanking him back towards the hall. She led him into her and Jim's bedroom, where the clutter was only marginally improved from his last invasion of this very private-feeling room. Eve strode forward and pulled open the wardrobe.

"I don't think you'll fit into my things," she said, giving his body a once over. "Your shoulders are much too broad. But I think Jim might have a few options."

"Don't you think he'd mind me wearing his things?"

"Oh, he minds everything so it won't make a difference," she said, waving her hand.

"I just finally got on his good side. I don't want him to hate me again."

Eve raised a brow skeptically. "He won't hate you."

He regarded her with equal skepticism for a moment before he glanced behind her at the contents of the wardrobe. There was silk in there. Oh, who was he kidding? He was going to let her do this. He let his shoulders fall in resignation and Eve squealed with delight.

"You won't regret it. Oh, this is going to be so fun," she said and began rifling through the contents of the wardrobe. "You like silk, right?"

"Yes," he replied in gross understatement as he sat on the end of the bed with his hands in his lap.

"I think this might have been *his* grandmother's," she said with a grin, pulling out a ladies wool suit in bottle green that had to have been pre-World War II. The shoulders were padded out wide and it had clearly been made for a woman significantly taller and sturdier than Eve. She frowned at it. It would have looked dowdy on an ordinary woman, but when Arthur imagined it on Jim, it had an other-worldly intensity that drew him in. It was incredible how subversion could reenergize a garment. Arthur had to stop himself from reaching out to touch it.

"Jim has a whole bunch of things he never wears in here," Eve said, pulling out a satin peach evening dress. It was rectangular and shapeless with a drop waist and crepe modesty panels beneath plunging v-necklines in both front and back. "This would be stunning on you if we could just remove those panels. It's 1970, for Chrissakes. No one is afraid of a little clavicle."

Eve held the dress up to him and pinched her lips into a perfect little bow. "I don't think it's really your color anyway." Arthur tried not to feel dismayed.

But what she drew out next took Arthur's breath away. It was also from the 1920s, a sweeping silk velvet cocoon wrap that went all the way to the floor with a dramatic collar that unfurled like flower petals at the neck.

"Ooh, you like this one," Eve observed with a smirk and took Arthur's hand to pull him up. She dropped the hanger to the floor and settled the coat over Arthur's shoulders.

"Just look at you," she purred, turning him to face the standing mirror in the corner draped with bras. Arthur looked his reflection in the eye and felt a rush of pleasure blossom in his belly. The coat was dark blue with salmon pink trim, all in exquisite silk velvet. It smelled of mothballs and a carefree glamor that had long been suffocated by economic strife and war, decades before he was even born. Arthur ran his hands down the lapels, velvet pile smoothing under his fingertips.

"What do you think?" Eve prompted.

"I ..." Arthur mumbled, biting his lip and smiling.

"Oh my god, you are so darling, I just love you," she gushed. "Those slacks look positively dreary in comparison. Here, let's find you something to go under it."

She went back to the wardrobe and rifled as though looking for something specific. She emerged with a shiny charmeuse slip in black. On the hanger, it was evident it had been sewn for a large woman, likely dowdy and perhaps aged given the lack of feminine embellishment. "Here, take off your trousers."

Arthur blushed but the temptation of that slippery charmeuse was too strong. He pulled the coat off and set it carefully on the bed before unfastening his pants.

"Oh, don't be bashful," Eve chided and approached, shoving his waistband down. "It's just you and me here, no one to be embarrassed for."

Arthur let out a weak, high pitched laugh and tried not to think about the fact that Eve Clark was crouching down to remove his pants. Thank god his shorts were baggy enough to hide his half hard and very curious prick. He stepped out of the trousers as Eve rose, efficiently unbuttoning the top two buttons on his shirt before pulling that and his undershirt together up over his head. Arthur's shoulders couldn't help but bow around his naked chest as he adjusted his glasses.

"Holy shit," Eve exclaimed, staring at his chest.

"What?"

"How long were you going to keep it a secret from me?"

"...What?"

"That you have such a sexy body," she purred, running her knuckles down the center of his chest.

Arthur snorted. "Since when was skinny sexy?"

"Stop that right now," she commanded and turned them both towards the mirror. "You see how wide your shoulders are? How nipped in your waist? That, my dear boy, is called sex appeal. Your torso, my darling, is a perfect triangle."

She ran her hands up his sides and giggled.

"Oh, Arthur, you're going to wear this so well," she gushed as she snatched the slip from the bed and dropped it over his shoulders. The charmeuse fluttered over him, setting his skin in stark relief against the shiny black fabric. Its drape picked up on every contour of his chest and hips. Eve returned to her position behind him, pinching the side seams snug around his waist. "Damn, boy."

The slip was made of a rectangle of fabric with two triangles sewn at the bust and attached to shoulder straps. Its square angles fell well over his flat chest. The hem went all the way to his shins, obscuring most of his leg hair and making him feel long and lithe and graceful.

"Where does Jim get this stuff?" he asked in astonishment, unable to take his eyes off his reflection as he examined himself from all angles.

"I haven't the faintest," Eve replied as she dug through the haphazard pile of costume jewelry on the bureau. "Actually, I do, I suppose. Some of it was his grandmother's, I'm fairly certain. Others from second-hand stores here and there. He likes to keep it to himself. Which I suppose makes sense, given my penchant for stealing his best finds. And how little privacy we have in this flat." Eve let out a huff of frustration. "Dammit, I don't have any long pearls. That would be the perfect thing." She glanced up. "Oh no, I know that look. What part are you second-guessing now?"

"I wish my shoulders weren't so ... shouldery," Arthur muttered, trying to pull them in.

"Shut your mouth right now, Arthur!" Eve exclaimed, her accent slipping a little in her excitement. "Androgyny is the point! You are the perfect combination of masculine and feminine. Something extra-human, the homo-superior. Hold on—"

She perked her ears toward the door and Arthur immediately shrank as he strained to hear if Jim had returned. Shit. He'd told him he wouldn't stand in his way. This felt like it could definitely be construed as standing in his way.

"Christ, Arthur, side A ended, don't lay an egg. I've just got to flip the record," she said and dashed out into the hall.

Arthur peeked his head furtively round the doorframe she'd just flitted out of. The front door was shut and no one was immediately evident. He hadn't heard anything. Perhaps Eve did just have a sixth sense for when a record required flipping.

13

Arthur spent a few minutes studying his angles in the mirror, tipping his chin and experimenting with the notion that his eyes lent a certain air of mystery to the ensemble. He took his glasses off. At this distance, his reflection was tinged with just a hint of blur, like a soft-lens shot in a Hollywood movie. A relentless polyrhythm and crunchy guitar emanated from the living room.

"Arthur, put on that coat and come out here! I want to see the whole look!"

Arthur bit his lip and then reached for a tube of lipstick on the bureau. He patted a tinge of the coral pigment on his lower lip and pressed them together, then whirled, snatching the coat up and settling it over his shoulders. He took one last look in the mirror and satisfied, he breathed deep and strode out.

Eve was standing by the record player with a cigarette. When she saw him, her glossy bow lips parted and the smoke drifted out of her mouth as she stared.[1]

"You," she murmured, "look *stunning*."

Arthur glanced at the carpet and smiled. She answered his smile with her own.

"Darling, come here, let me get a closer look at you."

---

1. "After All" David Bowie

Arthur approached and she swept her hands over his shoulders and arms.

"Are you wearing my lipstick?" she breathed and he sensed that the truth was also the correct answer.

"Yes," he replied and when he bit his lip, her nostrils flared. The effect fizzed through him, a bolt of bombshell energy striking him electric. He knew it. She wanted him. She was dizzy with it.

"Dance with me," she purred and as the strange, otherworldly guitar suffused the room, she guided his hands to rest on the curve of her hips. She pressed herself to him, sliding her hands up his velvet-clad arms, over his silk-swathed chest. She nuzzled her nose into the crook of his neck, soft lips ghosting along his throat. Her hand at the back of his neck guided his mouth to hers, and she kissed him slow, languid, like the haunting music that hung over them like a mantle. His cock responded. He curled his fingers into a tight ball as she noticed and pressed her hips up into his encouragingly. Her lips parted, and she plied his mouth with tongue and teeth, breath slaking between them.

Arthur could hardly breathe. His cock was hard, and his hands were frozen in tight fists on her waist. She was so relaxed and pliant—he needed to do something. He willed his hands to slide up her sides, his thumbs sweeping tentatively on the sides of her breasts. She moaned into his mouth.

"You love my tits, don't you?" she murmured into his mouth, grasping his wrist with one hand and guiding him to cup her breast. "You're always looking."

Arthur swallowed hard as he felt her nipple harden under her chiffon blouse. She wasn't wearing a bra. Of course she wasn't. Eve tucked her chin playfully and gave him an impish shove. He stepped back, the sofa hitting the back of his knees, and before he knew it, he was seated, looking up at her as she regarded him with a knowing smile. Her eyes flicked to his lap. He followed her gaze and saw his erection pushing against the silk charmeuse. The sight made his breath catch. Fuck, but he wished he didn't have his shorts on. That he could feel that silk directly against his prick.

Eve was biting her lip when he looked back up at her, his brain skipping like a record. Her fingers graced over the frill of her blouse before she began unfastening the buttons, one by one. Her lips curved into a sweet smile as an ever-widening swath of skin was revealed between the edges of red chiffon.

He saw everything through the soft filter of his far-sightedness as she pulled the blouse hem from her miniskirt's waistband and finished unbuttoning. Then, moving her body to the arhythmic cry of the guitar, she let the blouse part to the sides, revealing the most perfect breasts he hadn't the experience to even imagine. They were full, larger than he could hold in his hands, and they undulated as she danced, defying gravity. And her nipples. He couldn't tear his eyes away from them. They were almost lazily pointed, dusky pink, areolas wide and inviting. He licked his lips.

"You can kiss them," Eve whispered, her form diffusing as she moved closer. "If you want."

He wanted. He wanted very much. He rested his hands on her waist as she drew him in by the back of his head. His lips ghosted on velvety skin, and his hands moved to cup around her breasts as he explored her with his mouth. Her nipples were softer than any silk, but they firmed under his attention, eager for his lips and tongue.

"Hitch your slip up," she gasped after several long moments spent thus. "I need to fuck you."

This shook him from his adoring, almost obsessive ministrations. "Oh, I—" he said and then cringed because he sounded so unsure and uncool. (Also, Jim was going to fucking kill him.) "Yeah, okay."

He shifted and pulled the slip up. Impatiently, Eve's hands came down to assist him, and soon the charmeuse was hitched up around his waist, the velvet coat slipped off his shoulders and wedged between him and the couch.[2]

"Fuck, you're so sexy," Eve said under her breath as she drew his cock from his shorts. She gave him a few pumps, and he gasped.

"I—" he stuttered, squeezing his eyes shut, "It's just—I've never—"

She knelt above him. "Don't look so nervous, darling. I have a diaphragm, and I'm on the pill. You have nothing to worry about. Just relax and enjoy yourself. I know I will."

And as she pressed her hips down over his erection, he realized she wasn't wearing anything under her miniskirt, because velvety wet heat consumed him, and he couldn't help but grit out a groan.

"Yes, just like that," she growled and began to move above him, pressing his hand back to her breast as she rode him in time with the music. The guitar wailed, the vocalist trilled, and Arthur tipped his head back against the couch and panted.

This was what he wanted, wasn't it? That kind of passion that could not be resisted? And it was everything he'd hoped it would be. No, it was better, even. For who could have anticipated Eve would so enjoy him in silk? He'd be lying if he said it wasn't doing anything for him as well. The slip of charmeuse against his own nipples sent a shock to his groin where Eve ground into him with such languid skill, he felt a little unmanned by it. The most troubling part of that, however, was how much he *liked* feeling unmanned. The loss of control, the inevitability of it—it was intoxicating. Like bombshell energy in reverse.

Eve's hand slid between her flushed breasts and down her stomach. Her miniskirt was bunched over her waist, and she skimmed over it before settling her fingers into the hair at the apex of her thighs. Arthur watched the blurred scene in fascina-

---

2. "The Man Who Sold the World" David Bowie

tion as she began to massage her fingertips into her cleft, moaning and hitching her hips a little. He couldn't take his eyes off her breasts bouncing as she rocked herself on his cock, pressing her fingertips more firmly and faster as her eyes squeezed shut, and she began to cry out in pleasure. She squeezed around him harder and he gasped, and the door to the apartment opened, and the room snapped back around him in stark, severe reality.

He couldn't see clearly without his glasses, but he was far-sighted and there was no doubt that it was Jim standing in the entry. James. Carrying a six-pack of beer and staring stone-faced at the wanton scene sprawled on the couch before him. The most mortifying part was that Eve didn't seem to notice, or if she did, she didn't care. She carried on as if nothing had happened, pushing herself to her edge. She was gasping and arching her pleasure as she squeezed relentlessly around Arthur, and he was horrified to discover his cock was summarily unaffected by this mortifying turn of events. Quite the opposite, in fact.

James blinked, his expression inscrutable as he walked into the kitchenette and set his six-pack on the counter, the bottles clinking. Arthur trembled with tension as he waited for James to get the fuck out already. He wasn't going to call him out right in the middle of this, was he? What was he thinking, just strolling through like his roommate/bedmate/whomever wasn't fucking someone on the couch right in front of him? They should stop. Arthur glanced up at Eve. Shouldn't they? What the fuck was going on?

Eve continued to show no sign of noticing. She was drawn up tight like a bow and frotting against Arthur in desperation, her mouth gaping as she let out a guttural cry, and he felt her spasm around him.

Arthur should have felt her climax as his own, shouldn't he have? He should have been as enthralled as her. So why was he more fixated on James lurking than on her orgasm? The only way this could possibly get worse was if he couldn't even come when losing his virginity to the most beautiful girl he'd ever met. Of course, that thought didn't help anything at all.

"Oh, fuck yes, Arthur," Eve moaned, collapsing forward onto his shoulder as she rode out her tremors. He tried to focus. You only lost your virginity once, after all. And regardless of how Jim felt, he wasn't in charge of Eve's body or her choices. She was. And she'd chosen Arthur. He was too far gone. He couldn't let some possessive asshole cheat him out of finishing. Arthur grit his teeth and bucked his hips up, embedding his cock fully inside her. This elicited another cry from Eve as Jim sauntered from the kitchen to the record player. Arthur glared as Jim pulled a cigarette out of the pack in his pocket and lit it, watching the record spin in the console, looking as tall and nonplussed as ever in those tight denim jeans. *Get the fuck out of here*, Arthur silently screamed, wishing he had the courage to say it aloud.

Eve had her fingers between her thighs again and was squeezing him, rocking back and forth as she worked to draw another orgasm out. All Arthur could manage was to wonder if she realized James was there across the room, lounging back into the armchair and crossing his legs casually. Meeting Arthur's gaze with steely eyes.

Arthur felt a shiver buzz through him and suddenly, he felt *everything*. Eve's lips on his earlobe, her fingernails pressing into his skin just above his cock, her tight wetness slipping over and over and over him. Under James' gaze, every slide over his cock hummed through his skin, bursting pleasure and shame in equal measure like a psychedelic abstract film and making his lip quiver. He didn't want Eve to stop. Worse, he hoped that James wouldn't leave.

His breath came quick and shallow. James exhaled tobacco smoke and tilted his head. Arthur's vision flashed for a moment, and he felt his edge press insistently against the backs of his eyes. This was not how this was supposed to go, but he didn't care. Let James watch. As long as Arthur got to come. He'd do anything to come.

James blinked, blue eyes icy and relentless, then he lifted a hand to his lips. Arthur heard a roaring in his ears. James plucked a shred of tobacco from his tongue, and the corners of his mouth curved slightly.

Arthur gasped. Eve faded from his awareness. The room tunneled around him and the only thing in focus was James, in his chair. Uncrossing his legs. Splaying his knees wide, a bulge in his jeans. Arthur's mouth dropped open, panting. God, he was so close. James palmed his erection, his grim mouth set provocatively and his eyes never breaking from Arthur's. And *fuck*, it sent Arthur right over the edge and he was coming hard, biting into Eve's shoulder as he shuddered and filled her. She must have liked that, because she came again, squeezing him until he was torturously sensitive and he couldn't take it anymore.

Arthur flopped his head back on the sofa as he tried to catch his breath. He implored the ceiling for some clue as to what to do next, but it offered no assistance. Eve extricated herself from him and pulled her miniskirt down before turning and startling at the sight of James.

"Jesus, Jim, what the fuck are you doing here?" she complained, sounding only marginally miffed, really, despite having had her privacy duly intruded upon.

"Listening to records and having a smoke," James replied nonplussed. "I like this one. What's his name again?"

"David Bowie," she said flippantly. "And that's not the point. Any idiot could see that we were *busy*."

"I did see that," James replied placidly, lifting an eyebrow at Arthur that made him flush to his toes and rush to furtively tuck himself away, feeling like a real grade-A asshole. "I see you took the liberty of going through my wardrobe too."

Fuck, if Arthur didn't know better, he might have thought James was enjoying this. He was still sporting that half-hard bulge.

Eve crossed her arms over her bare breasts. "You are the most selfish, jealous little shit. I'm going to freshen up."

She whirled on her heel and stalked off to the bathroom, leaving Arthur to adjust James' charmeuse slip awkwardly and try to convince himself that his heart was pounding out of fear or embarrassment or anything other than whatever half-aroused, half-humiliated thing he was actually feeling.

Jealous, she'd said. Fuck. There was definitely something between them. He shouldn't be surprised. James had basically all but told him that Saturday night. And when he'd said it, Arthur had genuinely intended to stay out of his way. But ... fuck, come on, it was impossible to say no to Eve.

"Sorry, man," Arthur muttered, standing and wiping sweat from the back of his neck. James glared at him and took a deep drag on his cigarette.

"You should go," James said, his chin working as he looked away and crossed his legs again.

"Yeah." Arthur picked up the coat, whose velvet pile had been a bit crushed beneath him, and tried to smooth it out. He swallowed hard and then turned resolutely, handing the cloak to James. After a minute of James ignoring him, he resignedly set it on the other man's knee. "It's a really beautiful piece."

James looked back at him and his chin worked, like he was trying to hide his disgust.

"Don't ever touch my things again. Not unless I say so."

Arthur nodded obediently, wincing. He wasn't sure if they were talking about the clothes or Eve.

"I'll have the slip too."

Arthur snapped his face up to look at James incredulously.

"Now, please." James held a hand out and set his jaw again, his eyes daring Arthur to object. Fuck, he was so pissed. Arthur grimaced and pulled the slip up over his head, shimmying it over his shoulders. James' eyes stayed on him, nostrils flaring, even as Arthur reduced himself to nothing but his rather damp shorts.

He really hoped James wouldn't lose his composure and punch him.

Curling in on himself, Arthur resignedly handed the slip to James. Sharp, blue eyes scanned intrusively over his bare skin for a moment before James snatched the slip from his hands.

"Well, I guess you're officially one of the Tarts now."

14

Arthur woke up on Tuesday feeling quite a bit worse than he had on Sunday morning. Only, this time it wasn't wine—it was the relentless thump of guilt hammering in his brain. After James had dressed him down—quite literally—he'd dashed back to his dormitory, locked the door, and shrouded himself in his kimono.

But, as he'd proven last night, no amount of records and kimono-languishing could touch this, so Arthur grabbed his book bag and headed out to Washington Avenue to catch a bus back to St. Paul. It was cold and lightly snowing, and he huddled in his wool coat wishing he'd worn a hat until the bus finally arrived. He transferred at Smith Avenue and rode over the high bridge until the 1920s era bungalows gave way to the midcentury prefab ramblers that demarcated the border between St. Paul and West St. Paul.

After disembarking, he walked the few blocks to his parents' house. His father would be at work. When he walked in the front door, his mother stuck her head out from the kitchen and said in her warm Midwest accent, "Arthur? What are you doing here?"

Arthur shrugged and put his book bag on the floor. "Sorry I didn't come last weekend."

Okaasan shrugged back and came over to hug him. "Oh honey, it's good to see you—ugh, you smell like cigarettes. You haven't been to any of those awful fraternity parties, have you?"

Arthur could truthfully shake his head no, although she was a lot closer to the mark than he was comfortable with. "No, I've just been super busy with school work."

"I'm pretty confident that they don't let students smoke in the library," his mother said, putting her hands on her hips. Arthur hadn't noticed until now, but she wasn't in a house dress. Rather, she was dressed to go out. "Letting teenagers with fire near the stacks would be asking for trouble. Gracious!"

"Are you heading somewhere, Okaasan?" Arthur asked.

"Yes, I'm so sorry, honey. I'm off to the church to help set up the fundraiser for tomorrow night. Do you want to come along?"

He really wasn't sure it was a good idea to put a selfish sexual deviant with no respect for his friends in a church, but if he didn't go, he'd just end up in the basement, doing the exact same thing he would have done in his dorm, except he wouldn't have his records so he'd probably have to listen to Earl Hines or something. He did have his old films down there but ... no, he didn't want to be alone.

"Sure."

So he picked his book bag back up and got in the passenger seat of his parents' Chevy Impala. The snow had turned to sleet and the roads were sloppy. As his mother pulled out of the driveway and drove down the street, he watched the bare trees pass by in a relentless flashing gray-brown pulse.[1]

"So," Okaasan said as she signaled to turn north on Smith. "Did something happen?"

"What makes you say that?"

---

1. "God Knows I'm Good" David Bowie

"You just don't usually come to visit on weekdays. Don't you have class today?"

"No, I had a lab but it got canceled," he lied. It was only right, after all, since he'd been lying to her about all sorts of things for years. It was all part of his defects.

"Well, it's good to see you," she said with a smile. "You don't come around so often since you moved into the dorms."

Yup. He was a terrible son. Add it to the growing list of all his sins.

"I know," he said. "I'm sorry."

He wished he could tell her about the band. About the Rhodes piano and jamming and how good it made him feel, to be a part of making the music instead of just listening to it. But then she would ask questions. She always asked a lot of questions—because she loved him and was interested in her only son's life—but it always felt like an interrogation. As much as Fumiko Ohashi meant well, she could be terribly judgmental.

They sailed down the high bridge, a breathtaking view of the Mississippi River flowing steadily past downtown St. Paul, its modest spires reaching toward the leaden clouds that hung low in the late-autumn sky.

Arthur looked out the window and wondered at the people he saw walking on the sidewalk when his mother turned left onto West Seventh Street. He wondered how many of them had lost their virginity by screwing someone else's girlfriend. He wondered how many of them had pledged to stay out of the way beforehand. God, he was such a shit.

He wondered how many of them were caught out and ended up reaching bliss by looking into the eyes of the friend they had betrayed. There was something deeply fucked about that detail. Deeply fucked and yet, somehow, when he revisited the memory, he knew he could do it again. Eve was beautiful, slippery and languid and generous, but kindness apparently wasn't what got his rocks off. Steely blue eyes, a severe mouth, demanding he take off a charmeuse slip while Arthur wondered if he was going to get punched—now that was evidently what really got him going. He choked on his own shame as he acknowledged that moment would live on for quite some time in his jerk bank. Until he did something even worse. Or fucked up so badly that he got kicked out of the band. That might already be happening.

What did it mean, that he got off on being watched, observed by a man who, in spite of all logic and sensibility, appeared to enjoy the spectacle of another man in ladies clothing getting his cock ridden by an actual beautiful woman. It was a farce, a bit of absurd humor for a Robert Crumb cartoon in the back of Rolling Stone.

His mother was just pulling up in front of the Episcopal Methodist church on Portland Avenue and Victoria Street when Arthur was forced to acknowledge that he might be queer. That he might be attracted to both Eve and James and that was why he'd gotten off on the whole situation.

Arthur already knew he was deviant for wanting to adorn himself with elegant and glittering things, to drape himself across a settee like that musician on the album cover Eve had shown him. He was already different enough. He didn't need anything else added to the pile. He bit his trembling lip. He sank into the cushion. His mother yanked the gear shift into park and pushed her door open.

"Sweetheart, are you coming?"

Arthur looked up at his mother and realized he was crying. He blinked and hoped his glasses would obscure the—

"Arthur, honey, what's the matter?" Okaasan slid back into the car, her brows furrowed in concern.

His teeth pressed together tight and his head ached with the effort to control his composure. He looked at his mother for a long time. He wanted to tell her everything. He wanted her to absolve him. But he couldn't. He just ... couldn't do it.

"I don't know," he said. His voice came out cracked and raw. And it was true, he didn't know. His thoughts were a tangle of contradictions, wants and fears—and shame. So much shame.

His mother pressed her lips together in a thin, straight line and pulled him across the bench seat into her arms. Arthur clutched at the shoulders of Okaasan's wool suit jacket and pressed his face into it, smelling the comfort of her perfume and dry-cleaning synthetics.

"You don't have to talk about it, honey," Okaasan said, smoothing his overly long hair that she made no illusions about hating. "It's okay. Shh. I've got you."

Arthur let himself cry into his mother's shoulder. He didn't need to say anything. She knew. She always knew. The way she looked at him with that sideways glance, that look of love and worry and fear—she'd always known he was going to struggle. She'd seen him in the kimono when he was ten, after all. She'd made it clear then that this stuff was not to be discussed. But as much as he scared her, as much as she feared he'd make trouble for himself, it was easy for Arthur to believe she still loved him. Fiercely. And god, was that a relief.

He went to the church for a bit, helped organize silent auction items and answered questions from his mother's friends. They all wanted to know if he was Tomiko's new boyfriend. Christ. How did everyone know about this guy before he did?

After that, his mother drove him back to campus and kissed him on the head before he had a chance to open his door.

"Ki o tsukete ne. Take care, honey," she said and it was both a loving wish and a warning. He dutifully nodded and went up to his dorm room.

Arthur looked at the flip clock at his bedside. He was supposed to be at band practice in an hour.

He swallowed hard against the anxiety this inspired. He had no idea what James would do, what Eve would be like. Were they together now? Were they not-together? Were they *all* together?

He had no idea what to expect and no experience to base his apprehensions on.

It was ten to seven when he finally screwed his courage to the sticking place and grabbed his coat. He walked resolutely out the door before he could change his mind. If James wanted to punch him, he'd let him. He deserved it. If they wanted to boot him from the band, he deserved that too. There was only one way to find out what was going to happen, and that was to let it happen.

He walked across the river in the cold rain (he remembered his hat this time, but the whipping wind made it not really matter much) and buzzed up to the apartment. Eve opened the door and greeted him with a smile and a kiss, like she always did. Like nothing had ever happened. It was both a relief and a disappointment.

"Darling, I'm so glad to see you," she gushed. "Do you want a drink? We're still waiting for Deb."

Arthur glanced over her shoulder and saw James hovering over the record player.[2] That British guy in the dress was playing again. "No thanks, I really shouldn't."

Eve rolled her eyes. "Says who?"

"I have a lot of studying to catch up on tonight," Arthur replied, shrugging awkwardly.

"It's your funeral," Eve shrugged and ushered him into the living room. It was just a turn of phrase, but it felt literal as Arthur stood awkwardly between the two people he'd been thinking about almost constantly for the past 24 hours. After a few seconds of the moaning vocals over crying Les Paul and chaotic drums, Eve glanced furtively between the two of them. "I'm just, ah ... gonna pop down to the Extemp to see if Deb's down there."

---

2. "The Width of a Circle" David Bowie

And she dashed out the door, leaving Arthur to face James alone. Fucking turncoat.

The taller man leaned over the console looking at the back of the album cover between his elbows, hanging between his shoulders with one hip cocked. It was an objective fact that James was a good-looking guy. Arthur furtively tested how he felt about that. It was like peeking through a door, then being too afraid of what was on the other side and slamming it shut before you got a good look. He looked away and decided he'd confront that particular set of urges another day. He wasn't strong enough, especially since he was not out of the woods yet. He walked over to the record player and glanced at James.

"So what do you think of this guy?" Arthur tried, gesturing at the album cover. James ducked his head and exhaled audibly.

"He's too fucking good," he replied tersely. "It's frustrating."

"Makes me wish Eve would take us to London," Arthur agreed. "Then we could at least have more than two choices of where to play."

James scoffed. "She never will. She's too afraid we'd see just how much of her It-girl facade is a fucking lie."

At least he was pissed at Eve too, and not just Arthur. That should have made him feel better, but it didn't. "I'm sure she will, someday. She talks about it all the time."

"No." His voice was flat, emotionless. "She knows it's all I've ever wanted. If she gave it to me, what would she have left to hold over my head?"

He was using his hair like a shield. Arthur wished he could see his face. Then at least he might see what was coming for him. The silence ricocheted between them.

Arthur swallowed hard. He was here, wasn't he? It would be cowardly to show up and pretend like nothing happened, as tempting as the prospect was...

"I'm really sorry about yesterday—"

"You said that yesterday."

"I know. But I really am sorry."

James turned his head sharply, and his expression was so severe, it set off the vulnerability in his eyes in a way that cut Arthur to the quick. "Are you?"

James' glare left no space for bullshit, and Arthur was filled with a shameful intensity that made him both cower and preen. It was heady to be important enough to someone to be able to hurt them.

James shook his head. "You know what the worst part of it all is? It's the part where *you* said you wouldn't try to pick her up. *You* said you'd stay out of her way. I didn't ask you to say that, Arthur. I didn't ask you to say any of that shit. So forgive me if I thought you meant it."

Arthur winced and pushed his glasses onto his forehead to bury his face in his hands. "I know. I know, man. I'm so sorry."

James clenched and unclenched his fist as he stared unseeing out the window spattered with sleet. "Eve is ... Eve. She does what she wants. And if that's you, and she's what you want, then who am I to get in the way? All of that's nothing that hasn't happened before."

"But you live together," Arthur argued. He didn't know why. This conversation had the terrible potential to have them fighting over who would give up Eve to the other, a pitiful race to the bottom.

"That doesn't mean anything. We're not together, I keep trying to tell you."

"I know, you say that, but you keep doing things that make me think that's not true."

"What? Like what?"

"I dunno. Like sharing a bed—"

"—We needed a practice space and there wasn't room for two beds—"

"—or acting jealous or ..."

James regarded him furiously for a moment, and Arthur withered. But then he just turned his glare on the window again.

"You know what?" he ground out after a long pause. "Why don't you take my words at face value for once and stop reading your own melodrama into everything? I'm *telling* you: Do what you want with Eve. I really don't give a shit. Just don't *ever* fucking lie to my face like that again."

Arthur ducked his head. "Yeah, okay. Sorry. Again."

James hung himself over the album cover again. "God, *fuck* this asshole and his fucking dress."

The door to the apartment burst open.

"Guys, hurry!" Eve cried breathlessly, startling the both of them. "Deb has some incredible news you have to hear right now! Stop being neanderthals and get over here."

Deb was behind her with a slick, self-congratulatory smile. Arthur glanced back at James for some sort of—what? Consultation?—before he realized that was fucking weird and walked over to the entry.

"Deb, oh my god, tell them! Hurry!" Eve put her red painted fingernails against her lips in anticipation. In her excitement, she had utterly abandoned her affected accent and sounded just as American as the rest of them. It was like in the Wizard of Oz when the wizard ended up being just a middle-aged man behind a curtain.

Deb shrugged, basking in the anticipation with casual, almost aggressive assurance. "It's not set in stone yet, but my aunts in Madison have a friend who owns a recording studio in Chicago. I wrote to them asking if we could drive down there and record a demo with him. Sounds like he said yes! We can record this weekend!"

Eve squealed and danced on her tiptoes. Arthur's heart hammered in his chest. James gaped.

"Now, we gotta work out the details, like a vehicle and a motel and stuff, but I think if we put out a tip jar this weekend, we can make enough that we'll be able to split the rest."

"Shut up with the details, Deb! This is *fantastic* news! We can send the single with my dad next time he goes to London and ask my cousin to share it round with Marc Bolan and the other fellows he knows."

Arthur gaped now. This was—a lot. Prospects he'd never considered before. Joining the group had been a big enough leap, but trying to record a demo? Trying to attract the attention of working recording artists? Were they hoping to get picked up by a record company?

"Deb!" James cried before Arthur could voice any of his questions. "You wonderful little shit. How long have you been working on this without telling us?"

"Long enough to know it was worth it to not get your hopes up," Deb said roughly as James picked her up and swung her around. Arthur tried to blend into the wall. He couldn't express hesitancy now. He'd already been shitty enough to James, he didn't want to fuck it up any more. A demo wasn't a recording contract. A weekend trip to Chicago wasn't dropping out of school to tour with Steppenwolf. It was a big deal, and worth celebrating certainly, but it wasn't a guarantee. Not by a long shot.

They spent the next hour and a half working out how they were going to fund the trip, when they were going to go, and to wait for Eve to dip down to the New Riverside Cafe to use their pay phone and acquire a vehicle. When she returned, she had a naughty smirk on her face.

"I've got a date on Thursday and a VW van starting Friday."

"This Friday?" Arthur choked. (Also, a date? Jeez. She sure knew how to make a guy feel special...)

"Of course!" Eve exclaimed with large, doleful eyes. "I mean, if you have to study, can't you do that on the drive?"

"No, I don't have anything big I need to prepare for," Arthur sighed. "I just—I told my mom that I'd come out and visit this weekend."

They all stared at him with varying degrees of confusion. Arthur squirmed. "I mean, don't we have a show on Friday?"

Eve sighed. "We do. We said we'd play it and then leave first thing Saturday."

"What's holding you back, Arthur?" James asked levelly. Arthur glanced up at him, worried he'd see that furious expression again, but he didn't. James wasn't even using his stony mask. His brows were furrowed, and his eyes glinted with an openness that made Arthur's toes curl uncomfortably.

"I ... just," Arthur stuttered. For as patient as James appeared, Deb looked like she was going to slap him, and Eve's eyes were wide like he was about to break her heart. "I've been kind of a shit to my family recently."

"Seems like a theme," Deb muttered, glancing at James and earning her a glare in response. This made Arthur fairly confident that there was nothing secret about what happened the other day, and that made him supremely uncomfortable, like he wanted to crawl out of his own skin. He hated the idea that Deb knew about how he'd lost his virginity to Eve. How he'd done it wearing James' clothes, no less, then got caught doing it by none other than the man from whom he'd pilfered said clothes. Oh, hell, that sounded even worse than it actually was, and it was already very, very bad. Like he'd been masquerading as James to seduce Eve. He swallowed hard and looked at the lamp in the corner. At least the lamp couldn't mock him.

"Arthur, darling," Eve pleaded, "you have to come. You fill a gap that we didn't even realize was there."

Deb snorted. James smacked her on the shoulder, and Arthur sank further into the armchair. Maybe it could swallow him up.

"We need you," Eve said simply, her hands open as she shrugged helplessly.

"I mean, I could always sing the—" Deb started, and Eve cut her off with a massive roll of her eyes.

"No, Deb, you can't," Eve's voice was flat and firm. Arthur hadn't ever heard her like that before. "*Arthur* makes the difference between our band feeling like a few kids in their parents' garage and an actual group. The way he plays that Rhodes, and his voice, create that otherworldly feeling I've been looking for for so long! It *completes* our sound."

She turned her wide eyes back on Arthur. "Please, Arthur, this is our chance. How many times will you get the opportunity to play on a record? Even if nothing comes of it, and you go off and become some city engineer or whatever, don't you think your life will have been richer for this experience?"

Arthur pressed his lips together. "Yes, of course it would. I just—I'm, um—I've never done something like this before so I don't want to screw it all up for you."

"None of us have!" Eve exclaimed. "It'll be a glorious, wild adventure! Promise."

Despite Eve's reassuring smile, Deb and James' skeptical glances assured Arthur he certainly could.

15

By the time Saturday morning rolled around, Arthur was feeling like a piece of gum stuck to the bottom of someone's shoe. His mother was pissed at him for bailing on the weekend without even giving a good explanation as to why, because he couldn't very well tell her that he was going to Chicago to record a demo, now could he? *Yes, Okaasan, I'm throwing away the education you worked so hard to acquire for me in order to become a rock star. Yes, I know, almost no one actually succeeds. No, I don't anticipate picking up a heroin habit.*

It was early, and although Arthur had gone home straight after the show last night instead of going up to the usual after-party, he was still exhausted after spending half the night tossing and turning, imagining himself falling apart and seeing the recording technician frown at him and say, "Why don't you get yourself together before we waste any more tape?"

Or worse, what if it went really well? And people liked it, and then he had to figure out how to move to London or New York with the band and break it to his family that he was dropping out of college, or taking a gap year. Because he couldn't very well imagine quitting after this. Not after Eve had spilled her soul insisting that he made the band complete. Christ.

And fine, maybe he loved playing music. Maybe, when he was infused with electric frequencies vibrating in his bones, he felt more like himself than he'd ever managed before. But... one couldn't buy a house or keep food on the table with a feeling.

Suffice to say, he slept fitfully, dreaming of dropping out and then getting immediately drafted, before he pulled himself from his bed and slogged downstairs. He left a note in Tomiko's mailbox letting her know where he was going, with specific directions to not, under any circumstances barring death and dismemberment, tell his parents. Then, with his father's old army duffel slung over his shoulder, he trekked across the Washington Avenue pedestrian bridge.

It was cold that morning, November settling in with icy temperatures and blustering winds. The trees were bare, their naked branches scratching at the leaden sky. Arthur slung the duffel over his head, the strap across his chest, and stuffed his hands into his pockets. He pulled the collar of his wool coat up as he turned south onto Cedar Street. He should have brought a hat.

On the sidewalk outside the New Riverside Cafe, Arthur saw what must have been Deb bearing as many pieces of her drum kit as she could carry out of the door to the apartment and towards a rusty blue VW van parked on the street.

"Oh my god," Arthur said as he got close.

"Yeah," Deb frowned into the back of the van. "It smells like the skunkiest pot on planet earth."

"No, I mean you," Arthur said, gesturing to Deb's dress. She was wearing a knee-length pleated skirt and a sweater vest, with a collared shirt beneath it. A superfine wool coat with a Peter Pan collar. She was wearing fucking saddle shoes, for Chrissake.

Deb glared at him. "Listen, pal, I have no intentions of getting arrested in bum-fuck nowhere Wisconsin for looking too good in men's jeans."

Eve's giggle alerted them to her approach. "Doesn't she look just darling?" Eve wrapped her arms around Deb affectionately, resting her chin on her shoulder and nuzzling Deb's ear. "I love you with your cute little bob."

Deb's hair was indeed styled like a bob. It was too short to really be considered a bob, but it was close enough. It was a bit of a mind fuck, honestly, because she still carried herself with the same swagger and aggressive attitude, just in a skirt. She shrugged Eve off with carefully cultivated grumpiness that made Arthur suspect she might enjoy the attention.

When James emerged from the door, with a guitar case in one hand and an amp in the other, he also looked shockingly normal. He'd pulled his hair back into a ponytail, putting his long, angular face into even sharper focus, and he was wearing a button-up shirt under his shearling denim jacket with jeans that might have actually been the correct size instead of two sizes too small. Upon second glance, Eve looked remarkably staid as well, with a block patterned dress, tall boots, and a princess-cut brown jacket with a fur collar that Arthur would have actually sold his soul to the Devil to own.

"What can I grab from upstairs?" Arthur asked, tossing his duffel between the precariously stacked drums in the carpeted rear of the van.

"That's the last of it, actually," James said, loading his amp and guitar carefully in. "Deb, do you need anything else?"

"Nah, I got all the toms and cymbals in one trip!" Deb proclaimed proudly.

"And the Rhodes?" Arthur asked, treading carefully around the fact that it was James' instrument, but that it was also his to play and sort of his responsibility to account for.

"All taken care of," James replied dismissively as he took the two doors at the back of the van in his hands and stared inside for a moment, taking stock of all the gear. Apparently satisfied, he slammed the doors shut and rounded the van. As he approached the driver's seat, Eve called his name and tossed him the keys, which were attached to a worn gray rabbit's foot keychain.

"Do you wanna sit in the front?" Eve asked Arthur as she climbed into the side door with Deb.

"Sure, thanks," Arthur mumbled and settled himself on the front bench beside James as smoothly as he would if he felt he deserved to be included on this trip in the first place. He should have brought something to study. It would have given him something to pretend to do for the eight-plus hour drive they had ahead of them.

He looked over his shoulder behind them. Whoever owned this van had—well, he'd had a *vision*. It wasn't entirely clear from the tiny disco ball or the polyester faux flowers attached to the brown carpeted walls exactly what that vision was, but whoever it was had pulled out everything besides the front seat to make space for it all. Unfortunately for them, whatever was intended for the van was sort of moot, as the back was filled with their gear. Deb and Eve settled on two bean bag chairs that had been deemed appropriate replacements for the actual rear seats just behind the pony wall that separated the front from the back.

"Who did you get this van from?" Arthur couldn't help but ask.

Deb exchanged a significant look with Eve before the two of them giggled. James turned the keys in the ignition and the engine roared to life.

"His name's Spencer," Eve said coyly.[1]

"Only these days, he's been going by Canyon Flower Fuck," Deb snorted derisively.

"Canyon Roaring Wind," Eve corrected.

"Oh, is he American Indian?" Arthur asked confusedly.

"No!" Deb cry-laughed.

Eve rolled her eyes. "He's a hippie. He was in California all summer, hanging out in Laurel Canyon with Joni Mitchell and CSN."

---

1. "Lean Woman Blues" T. Rex

"Ugh, that asshole doesn't deserve my Joni," Deb grumped. "And neither does Graham Nash, for that matter."

"Hmm, I don't think he really met Joni Mitchell, to be honest. I think he was just flitting about trying to get invited to Mama Cass' house," Eve said, lighting a cigarette as James pulled out onto Cedar Street. "He did end up getting high with Jackson Brown though."

"Are these all the lovely chestnuts you picked up on your date?" Deb asked teasingly.

Eve grinned mischievously. "No, they're what I got out of the pillow talk afterwards."

Arthur slid down in the passenger seat of the van, making himself small. Well, that put the final nail in the coffin he'd built for his hopes that Eve was actually interested in him. He was so fucking glad he'd sacrificed James' good opinion—and his virginity, whatever that was worth—for such paltry regard.

"You are such a little whore," Deb said. Arthur's eyebrows flew up in surprise, and he glanced over the seat, but Eve didn't really seem to care.

"I got a van for the whole weekend, and all I had to do was give a little head and enjoy multiple orgasms," Eve took a little self-satisfied puff on her cigarette. "If that makes me a whore, then so be it. Though, to be clear, darling, I could have gotten it no strings attached. I just *wanted* to fuck him."

Arthur glanced up and caught James looking at him. James looked away before Arthur could get any sense of why.

"Ugh, Evie, really?" Deb groaned. "He's calling himself fucking Canyon for Chrissakes."

"I think Canyon is a lovely name," Eve replied. "Don't you agree, Arthur?"

Arthur felt like a strange voyeur peering over the seat back, but getting called out felt stranger.

"Uh ... sure, I guess."

"Don't ask him. He'll just say whatever he thinks you want to hear," Deb said. "Jim—back me up."

"That Arthur is Eve's Yes-Man or that Canyon is a stupid name?"

"Both."

"Deb, you are very astute," James replied, looking at Arthur side-long as he twisted the knife, "on both counts."

Arthur nodded grimly and turned to look out the window as James turned onto the highway. Maybe he wasn't a James after all. Maybe he'd just been a shove-you-in-your-locker Jimmy all along.

"So what kind of music can we play in this thing?" Deb asked, crawling up on her knees and leaning over the back of the bench seat to peer at the console.

"I dunno, Deb, I'm kinda busy," James said as he signaled to merge east.

"Ah, yeah, doing what," she bantered as she crawled over the back of the seat. "God fucking dammit, these skirts are the Devil's trap! No wonder men thought we were incapable of anything for hundreds of years."

"Is there a radio?" Eve was now draped over the back of the seat, her cigarette hanging from her plump, glossy lips. Her hair cascaded over her shoulders and tickled Arthur's neck.

Deb was craning down to see the radio affixed under the console, her legs on either side of the stick shift James was awkwardly trying to maneuver as he accelerated.

"Ooh, it's AM *and* FM!" she exclaimed, fiddling with the dials. The speakers crackled to life and white noise filled the cab as she tuned through channels searching for an acceptable station.

And then there wasn't any more conversation because Deb had cranked up Steppenwolf so loud that no one could hear one another anyway.[2]

---

2. "Born to be Wild" Steppenwolf (Slade cover)

Soon, they drove out of St. Paul, heading east on Interstate 94 with nothing ahead of them but the sun rising bright behind the leaden clouds and a few trucks starting their daily journeys. The bright sunlight glittered on the frosted grass and fallen leaves lined either side of the road. Songs played through on the radio and after a half hour, James reached down to tune to something that came in clearer. The van sped along over the bridge spanning the St. Croix River and just like that, they were in Wisconsin.

They had passed Eau Claire when Arthur was roused from his window-gazing trance to sounds of snoring in the backseat. He shifted, looking back and saw Deb and Eve snuggled together on the beanbags, sleeping like babes. It made sense. There weren't any good rock and roll stations coming in after they got out of range of Eau Claire— the best James could find was the Carpenters. (The alternative appeared to be nothing but AM evangelists, which wasn't really the mood they were going for. Not that the Carpenters were, exactly, but there was something hypnotic about Karen's voice that allowed her to triumph over the aging World War II vet castigating anti-war protesters.)

And then, beaming in like some sort of incongruous savior, the twanging acoustic guitars of the Kinks piped in and Ray Davies started singing about Cherry Cola.

Arthur leaned forward, blinking. He was so taken aback that he was hearing "Lola" on the radio in the middle of bumfuck Wisconsin that the only thing he could think to say was, "Did they change the words?"

James glanced at him. "What?"

"Lola," Arthur said simply, pointing to the little radio console. "On the record, it was 'Coca Cola' but I just heard 'Cherry Cola.'"

"Really?" James leaned forward to listen but of course, the lyric had passed and there was nothing to hear but L-l-l-l-l-l-l-lola. He sat back again, then glanced sidelong at

Arthur. "I thought you didn't get a chance to listen to that record."

Arthur flushed. "I got around to it."

"Are you planning to return it?"

"Of course I am! Jeez, didn't know it was a favorite."

James shook his head and reached forward to turn the song up.

"I still can't believe this got on the top ten," James said after a moment.

If Arthur had been drinking something, he would have spit it out. "It *what!?*"

James looked at him a little disdainfully. "Yeah. It's been on there for like two months, man. Do you not listen to the radio?"

Arthur shook his head disbelieving. "No, I just listen to records. I only hear the radio in my mom's car, and all she plays is the funk station."

"Your mom likes funk?" James seemed to think this was funny.

Arthur shrugged. "Yeah. And gospel."

"That is so antithetical I can't really even fathom it."

"It's not really from a sound perspective. That's a better description of how I feel about 'Lola' being in the top ten." Arthur looked out the window incredulously, waiting for an explanation from the rolling hills of woods and barren corn fields. "We couldn't even find a rock station around here, but they're playing 'Lola'?"

"Can't argue with Casey Kasem," James shrugged and laughed.

"Who's that?"

James snorted and shook his head. "Damn, man, you really are outta touch."

Arthur frowned. "I am not. I'm very in touch. I like new music. I just don't like to find it on the radio."

There was a long pause, and Ray Davies ripped out the bridge, singing about how Lola was gonna make him a man.

Arthur shifted uncomfortably. He still hadn't returned this record to James because, well, he'd been listening to this song on repeat. It served as, uh, carnal inspiration? See, the thing was, what no one knows can't hurt you, and so maybe Arthur had spent some time draping himself in silk and lipstick while singing along with the song. Maybe he'd imagined himself as Lola. And perhaps, he'd allowed himself to imagine the narrator of the song with long, curly blonde hair. On his knees. And, well, full disclosure, that really did it for Arthur. After all, if a tree fell and no one heard it, did it even happen? Same went for private fantasies. Except, private fantasies could still make him blush unbidden when this song played on the radio because it was on the Top 100 for some fucking insane reason. And he was trapped in a van with the woman he'd lost his virginity to and the man who'd caught him doing it, who was now the one increasingly occupying his most private thoughts. The ones that didn't get a name and weren't acknowledged outside the safe space of his room and his kimono.

"What did you think of it?" James asked.

Arthur flinched. "Of what?"

"*Lola versus Powerman and the Moneygoround.*"

It would be idiotic to admit that he hadn't really listened to the rest of the album. Not after hearing Lola. "It was good."

"Oh. That groundbreaking, then?"

Arthur sighed. "I don't know what you want me to say."

"I want your honest opinion," James scoffed irritatedly.

"Why?" He wasn't the only one who could be derisively defiant. "Because I'm a nancy who likes to dress up in ladies clothes? So I must fucking love this song because it's about a transvestite?"

James blinked and tucked his chin to his neck, frowning. "No, man. Because you're cool, and your opinion matters to me. Jesus."

Arthur curled in on himself. *Bull. Shit.* He flicked his fingers together in an unconscious tick as he glared out the window.

"Besides," James added quietly, "you're not the only one who likes ladies clothes here."

Arthur's chest softened. "Yeah." He sighed and stared at his feet. "I know."

He wasn't about to admit that imagining James in that pink evening gown, with the modesty panels removed and the neckline dipping to his waist in the front and back, was something else that had been occupying the private corners of his mind lately. The human brain should really optimize itself better. The wild, salacious fantasies kicked up while jerking off should be immediately forgotten upon release, just as the percolating sensations and emotions were.

"Deb might be the only one in this vehicle who thinks skirts are the worst," James pointed out, his tone lighter and louder to cut through Arthur's quiet embarrassment.

"And yet, she's gotta wear one to make it through rural Wisconsin."

"The world is particularly cruel, isn't it?"

"Poetically," Arthur agreed with a sad chuckle. "If it were me, though, I don't think I'd have gone for the wool plaid."

"No?"

"It's trying too hard to be normal. She could pull off a miniskirt with her swagger." Arthur glanced up and saw James resisting a smile by pinching his narrow lips together.

"Deb in a miniskirt?" he asked skeptically.

"Yeah," Arthur doubled down. "You could have given her some lessons in how to carry one off before we left."

James snorted. "She'd never let me give her lessons in anything. Besides, Eve is the expert on miniskirts."

Arthur shrugged. "I wouldn't put my money on that."

He stared out the window, watching the barren trees whip by. He could feel James' eyes on him. He glanced up and fell into two pools of responsive blue. James was usually so guarded—it was entirely unfair for him to drop that mask so utterly without warning. Arthur swallowed his heart back down to his chest where it belonged. Shit, he should look away. James raised an eyebrow, just a millimeter of a movement.

"*BWAAAAAAAAAARRRRRRRRR!*" The horn blast of the car passing them was like a gut punch, if such a thing could be delivered through the ears. James startled, gripping the wheel with both hands and focusing on the road diligently as though more attention now could somehow compensate for the fact that he'd started veering into the shoulder.

"What the fuck!?" Deb cried as Eve whined simultaneously, "What the fuck was that!?"

"Just some redneck asshole," James said, making a very good show of being a very alert, not-negligent driver. Arthur curled up against the window and pretended to be invisible, so he could hold the memory of those blue eyes in his mind for a moment. Hold the memory without flagellating himself for increasingly undeniable queerness. Just enjoy it, hold it close, remind himself that he wasn't a complete bastard. He was capable of saying the right thing. Sometimes.

16

They stopped in Madison for lunch. It felt like being back on campus, like they hadn't driven anywhere at all. Except there was a big, white Neoclassical capitol building at the center of everything, towering over the co-eds who walked across the brown grass that was waiting for the first snow to lay it down to sleep for the winter. The temperature was hovering above freezing so as of yet, none had come.

They bought sandwiches at a nearby shop and sat on two benches on the capitol mall to eat them. Well, Deb and Eve sat on one bench. James sat on the other alone, because Arthur had sat on the cold grass rather than sit too near to the man who could make him come with a look. *Christ.*

"I was thinking maybe we shouldn't record 'I've Been Here' after all," James said after everyone had taken a bite and couldn't immediately object. "I think we should record 'Hammer Your Heart.'"

Arthur choked on his ham and cheese. Deb frowned, but Eve cocked her head thoughtfully as she chewed.

"It's lyrically better than anything I've written," James said. He was avoiding looking at Arthur. "And the keys sound better in it because they were actually in the arrangement to start with."

"But it doesn't rock as hard," Deb argued. "It doesn't have that same energy and sex appeal that The Tarts are all about. If we only get one song to say who we are, I don't think that's the one."

Eve frowned. "Yeah, Deb might be right. I'm not sure that's the one that could get radio play. There's so much out there right now that's jam bands and thirty minute guitar solos. We need something *different*."

"I think it is different," James said with a shrug.

"It is different," Deb agreed. "But are we sure it's in a good way? We need to be just different enough to be interesting, but familiar enough that people know how to feel when they hear us. I think 'I've Been Here' does that."

Eve frowned apologetically at Arthur. "I agree."

"So do I," Arthur exclaimed. "My song is fine, but it's not ready to be recorded." His fingers shook on his sandwich. "It's the first one I've written. Give us a chance to figure that out first. It's not worth taking a risk on."

James stared at him with flat eyebrows for a moment. "Well, looks like I'm outvoted."

"Ooh, look at them," Eve said with a grin. She was looking across the mall at two young men walking towards the capitol building. They were tall, in suits, with their hair carefully styled.[1]

James turned and looked after them.

"What about them?" asked Deb, her brow arch with skepticism.

"They look like they want corrupting," Eve grinned around the straw of her fountain drink.

"They're politicians. I'm sure they're already plenty corrupt." James rolled his eyes.

"But they're so young. Do you think they're young Republicans?" Eve started to stand. "I'm gonna go talk to them."

---

1. "Solid Gold Easy Action" T. Rex

"Why?" Deb asked with a roll of her eyes. "If they're young Republicans, they probably don't know a clit from a weenus."

"What's a weenus?" Arthur asked.

"See?" Deb threw a thumb at him like he proved her point, but Eve was already walking over.

James pointed to his elbow. "This is a weenus."

Arthur snorted on his ham and cheese.

"Jesus, she's gonna get herself human trafficked by Nixonites," Deb said, climbing to her feet awkwardly in her skirt and tailing Eve. "At the very least, face-fucked in some marble bathroom." She turned and glared at James and Arthur. "Aren't you coming?"

James shrugged. "I learned a long time ago not to stand in the way of Eve and her notions." He flicked a glance at Arthur. He hung his head shamefacedly, seeking redemption in the crust of his half-eaten ham sandwich. Right. He was a notion. Just a little impulse. Nothing more.

"Well, fuck," Deb replied, her hands on her hips as she stared after Eve.

"Don't go after her," James said tiredly. "She's not gonna go with those assholes. She wants to get to Chicago. She's just trying to stir things up because she's been in a van for five hours and she's bored."

Deb glowered, her knee twitching for a moment. Eve had approached the two men in question by dropping her soft drink on the pavement and squealing as it splashed all over the three of them.

James blinked. "Oh, wait, she's trying to pull the 'I spilled' con. You're right, Deb, she might actually be gunning for the marble bathroom."

"Goddammit," Deb swore and then grabbed a fistful of napkins from the paper sandwich bag before she stalked after Eve, her fists tight at her sides. She looked like a petulant school girl in her pleated skirt and sweater.

Arthur's lips pursed as he tried to work through that exchange. "Wait—what's the 'I spilled' con?"

James let out a long-suffering sigh. "Look, Arthur, there's some things you need to know about Eve."

Arthur blinked. "Like what?"

"She's not available. To like anyone. I tried to tell you that the first night we met. She doesn't want to be together with anyone. She plays games with people."

Arthur remembered the moment he'd shared with her in the bedroom, where she'd grasped his shoulders as he admired his reflection in the velvet coat. When she'd told him he was beautiful. It had been the first time he'd ever been himself in front of anyone else. Had that all been a game? Some flippant seduction? He swallowed dread that was creeping up in his throat like bile.

James looked down at Arthur. What the fuck had he gotten himself into?

"Don't get yourself too wound up about it. She does it to everyone." James looked up after her. Deb was patting Eve dry while the two men snickered. At least one of them had to be named Dick. Eve didn't look too happy about Deb's intervention. "She's a hedonistic nihilist. Sex is her drug."

James shook his head at her, like he'd been put upon for far too long.

"Why do you stay with her then?" Arthur managed to ask. He didn't mean for it to sound like they were *together*, because James would probably pop off at him again for it. But it was still a real question. Whatever their relationship was, it was more complicated than childhood friends. There was resentment in James' eyes. There had been in Eve's too, when she'd seen him sitting in that armchair, watching, smoking. Palming himself for Arthur's eyes only, like some sort of dominance play. God dammit, he tried not to flush, but it was so hard not to.

James shrugged. He was still watching Eve across the mall. "Habit, I guess."

Arthur smirked wistfully. "Maybe she's your drug."

James blinked, his brows furrowing thoughtfully. "Maybe she is."

Deb dragged Eve back to the group as the politicians carried on up the steps to the Capitol, both individually glancing after her. She *was* Eve, after all. Her hair was down, her tits were on display in her scoop-neck sweater, her miniskirt was wet with cola. What warm-blooded man *wouldn't* be doing a double-take?

"Aw, come on Deb! It woulda been fun!" Eve was saying as they returned. She was still dabbing at her miniskirt with a fistful of napkins.

"Not for me it wouldn't," Deb said firmly. She strode right past Arthur and James, making a beeline for the van. She yanked the back door open and climbed right in.

Eve tipped her head back and let out a groan of frustration. "Why the hell does everyone need to get so up in arms about sex?" Her accent was in shambles. It wasn't clear who she was saying this to. A higher power, perhaps? "Sex is sex, for fuck's sake. Cocks can be fun sometimes too."

And she ran after Deb, climbing back into the van too. Arthur and James exchanged a look.

"I guess lunch is over now," Arthur said delicately, folding his sandwich primly back into its paper wrapper.

"Appears so," James replied, then stuffed his remaining turkey sub in his mouth as he gathered up their trash and headed back to the van.

17

Chicago was like nothing Arthur had ever seen. Minneapolis was a big city. It had a solid handful of skyscrapers. But Chicago? Damn. The city went on for miles. They entered traffic shortly after the border between Wisconsin and Illinois and got stuck in it for hours. And for those hours, they passed through thick, urban jungle. Miles and miles of houses built right up next to one another, of three-story shops and apartment buildings and just endless urban sprawl.[1]

Arthur felt like they'd been in Chicago for an eternity but it wasn't until they finally managed to jog over to highway 41, which snaked along the edge of Lake Michigan, that Arthur saw the city proper. The downtown area was a fanfare of towering buildings. One soared higher than the rest, a black block of glass stabbing twin radio towers into the cloudless blue sky. Even Deb and Eve were awestruck, leaning forward over the back of the seat bench to see out the windshield.

Deb grinned. "Have you all ever been to Chicago before?"

Eve shrugged. "I've laid over in O'Hare before, but I never got to go to the city."

James frowned. "Nah, never been out of Minnesota, to be honest."

---

1. "25 or 6 to 4" Chicago

"Oh, yes you have," Eve chided. "Remember when we went to the Black Hills with our families that one summer?"

"Oh, yeah, okay, fine. I've been to South Dakota, too." James rolled his eyes.

"I've never been out of Minnesota except for one trip to San Francisco three years ago," Arthur offered, emboldened by the fact he wasn't the only one who hadn't really traveled. "My parents are not much for the great American road trip. After that, they said never again."

"Ooh California!" Eve gushed. "I've been to LA and San Fran. They're both smashing, though I really prefer LA."

"Oh geez," Deb grinned, rubbing her hands together, "have I got some cool stuff to show all of you."

They found a motel in a neighborhood called Bronzeville, near the lakeside and just south of Record Row. James and Eve were the only White people in sight. Arthur stood out like a sore thumb, too, even though they were apparently just ten blocks southeast of Chinatown. Deb was brown enough to blend in, though, and regardless, she seemed to be in her element.

"First stop, you great ignorant lummoxes, is Meyers Ace Hardware," Deb declared after they'd stowed their bags and gear in their motel room, locking up behind them.

"Please tell me that's a funny name for a bar," Eve pleaded.

"Nope, it's just what it sounds like," Deb said, striding west on 35th Street, paying no heed to the sidelong glances their group was getting from the locals. "Or is it?" she added cryptically, turning around to give them a Bella Lugosi-esque stare.

They were dragged down the street a few blocks until Deb stopped at a shop declaring itself Meyer's Hardware in large melamine signs above the entrance. It had signs in the windows advertising everything from toilet plungers and pipes to paint and paneling.

"Deb, darling, why are we here?" Eve whined. "I'm half-starved."

Deb smirked. "Ever hear of Louis Armstrong?"

Eve rolled her eyes. "Of course I have. What has he got to do with a hardware store?"

Deb pulled the door open and a bell rang. "It wasn't always a hardware store."

Arthur followed the rest inside, eyes roving to understand what on earth was special about this place. Eve crossed her arms next to a display of rat traps.

"Alright, Deb. Get on with it."

"Before this was a humble hardware store," Deb said eagerly, "it was The Grand Terrace Cafe." She waited for recognition, but none came. "One of the best jazz clubs in Chicago."

Arthur looked around the slapdash shop. He tried to imagine it as a cafe. It was difficult.

"So?" Eve said. She was moving from irritated to frustrated.

"So, it was here, in this very room, that people heard Louis Armstrong cut his chops. It's one of the first places where people heard Earl Hines play piano."

"*What?*" That caught Arthur's attention.

"There's the reaction I'm looking for," Deb said, thumbing at Arthur with a glare at Eve and James.

"Cool, but," James shrugged, "it's not a cafe anymore."

"I wish it was," Eve said, "because then maybe we could *get something to eat.*"

"This is our musical birthright, guys," Deb insisted. "Hold on, let's see if we can get them to show us the stage."

Deb hustled over to the cashier and tried to get his attention. After a moment, Deb glowered, then gestured Eve over to join her. Eve rolled her eyes, sighed, and then plastered her most beguiling smile on her glossy lips and sauntered over.

Five minutes later, they were following a short, White Jewish man named Meyer up a steep set of stairs at the back of the shop. He opened the door at the top of the steps and said, "This used to be the stage, so we just closed it up and made it the office."

The office was cluttered and chaotic, but on the back wall, across the burgundy paneling, were paintings. A man playing a saxophone, another facing piano keys cascading like a river over the panels. A truly demonic figure thrashing wildly on a timpani. Giant, black music notes dancing around them. And a massive air duct grate installed right in the middle of it all.

"We coulda painted over it—of course, we have plenty of that around here, right?" Meyer laughed. "But there's not a lot of speak-easies still standing. It's part of music history, you know? So there it is."

Arthur blinked. He was on Earl Hines' stage. A secret place where new music was born, where history was made every night. A thrill played up his spine.

"We had some funny guys in from Europe a few weeks ago. Said this place was their Mecca," Meyer laughed. "They bought toilet plungers to use as mutes for their trumpets, like a souvenir, I guess."

Eve laughed and this time, her smile was warm and bright. She reached up and touched the saxophone painted on the wall. "Alright, fine, Deb. This is pretty cool."

18

They had dinner at Stelzer's Restaurant across the street. It was greasy and filling and delicious. Then Deb bullied them back to the motel, where she changed back into her usual uniform of jeans and tight, white t-shirt and told them all to get tarted up. Eve took the directive very literally and put herself in a sequined minidress and platform Mary Janes that made her look like she'd just walked out of Warhol's factory.

Arthur had no idea what to make of this. He hadn't brought anything more outrageous than his one pair of bell bottom jeans. So he wore those with his usual wool peacoat, looking like a total square next to James, whose hair flowed wild over a brocade ladies wrap-around top he'd brought. He wore no shirt underneath it and it was, well, it wasn't fair for him to just strut around in his tight jeans with his chest hair out for everyone to see.

They hid their most outrageous fashion statements with their coats and followed Deb to a nondescript brick building about ten blocks west. Arthur fit in with them just fine until they entered the club and shucked off their outerwear. Then he was the lone dorky tag-along in a group of pretty young things. The club played recorded music loud, and when they walked into the main room, it became evident that this was a performance venue for female impersonators.[1]

Arthur stood stock still for a moment in the entrance. A woman, for all intents and purposes, danced soulfully on the stage in a billowy white dress, her huge afro spraying glitter on the crowd every time she shook her head. Her immaculately glossed lips mouthed the lyrics to Diana Ross. She looked like she was actually singing, even though Arthur knew she couldn't be—she didn't have a microphone and it was Diana Ross' voice through and through pumping out of the sound system.

Arthur had never seen anything like her. He knew about female impersonators, but only in derision. From newspaper reports of clubs, like Stonewall in New York, being busted up by police. This was supposed to be dangerous. Deviant. But it wasn't. The crowd cheered for Diana, throwing dollar bills at her feet.

"Arthur!" Eve's hand was around his wrist. She glittered in the dark club lights, her sequins sparkling. She grinned at him. "Isn't it wonderful?"

He nodded. It was. It absolutely was.

He joined them at the small table they'd snared. He drank a terrible vodka cocktail. He laughed at Deb's jokes and was mesmerized by the performers.

"Jim, you and Arthur should do this!" Eve exclaimed, two drinks in. "Get dolled up and sing Nico or something!"

Arthur flushed. He couldn't imagine. The only time he'd let anyone see him dolled up, it had been Eve. And that had turned out rather badly, when all was said and done.

James took a deep draught from his glass. "Nah. Like you always say, Eve, the androgyny is the point. The homosapien superior."

And the floor fell out from under Arthur.

---

1. "Ain't No Mountain High Enough" Diana Ross

"I wish my shoulders weren't so ... shouldery."

"Shut your mouth right now, Ohashi! Androgyny is the point! You are the perfect combination of masculine and feminine. Something extra-human, the homosapien superior."

He was such an idiot. She played games with people. That's what James had said. Arthur understood that she wasn't interested in him by now, but she didn't need to pull his soul out first, caress it with assertions that he was something special, before she stomped it all over the floor.

"I'm gonna go back to the motel," Arthur said, standing up. He swilled down the terrible cocktail and turned towards the coat room.

"Arthur, darling, no!" Eve cried, grabbing him by the crook of his arm. "What's wrong?"

He should say it was nothing. That he was just tired. But when he opened his mouth, he said, "Androgyny is the point? Homosapien superior? Are those just *lines* you pull out?"

"I didn't mean anything by it."

Arthur grit his teeth. Maybe it was the cocktail, or maybe it was that he'd lost the last scrap of his goddamn patience. "I know. You've made it abundantly clear you don't mean much of anything you say or do."

And he pulled his arm out of her hands and stalked to the coat room.

"Fucking hell!" he heard her exclaim behind him.

All three of them tailed Arthur back to the motel. It was obnoxious. Every block or so, Eve would shout at him to slow down, to wait for them, and he would ignore her and walk faster.

At one point, he heard her order James to chase after him. Thankfully, James was having none of that bullshit.

"Why should I? This isn't my wild goose chase," James said instead. "You can't tell him what to do. We could have stayed and had a fun time."

"Jim! He's scarcely ever been outside of Minnesota before. We can't just let him wander the streets of Chicago at night!"

"Why not?" Deb. Thanks a lot, Deb.

They caught up to Arthur at the motel. He had to wait for James to unlock the room. Eve stood with her arms crossed, glaring at him, but luckily, she deigned to wait until they were in the room to let loose on him.

"What do you fucking mean calling me fake?"

"I didn't call you fake."

"You did too—"

"No—I said you don't mean anything you say or do."

"If that's not 'fake,' then what is that even supposed to mean?"

Arthur glared at her. She threw her hands up in the air.

"Let me guess. You're upset because for some mysterious reason, your cock hasn't turned me into your little subservient housewife? Is that it?"

"No—" Arthur crossed his arms too. "What I'm pissed about is being set up. You used *lines* on me, Eve. Lines you apparently say all the time, to make me think I was something special for a minute." *You saw me, all of me, and you made me feel like I mattered to you.* "And you did it on purpose."

"I *do* think you're something special, Arthur," Eve insisted. James rolled his eyes and sat in the desk chair in the far corner of the room, pulling out a cigarette.

"Are we all just gonna sit here and fight?" Deb asked. "Because, if so, I would like to get some beer. Or on second thought, something harder."

"Deb, please," Eve chastised, then turned back to Arthur. "I never said anything to you that I didn't mean."

Arthur wanted to scream. "Yes, you did! You said 'androgyny is the point' to me that day. Apparently, according to Jim, you say that all the time. You told me I was—" Sexy? Stunning? Perfect? "—that you needed me."

Eve rolled her eyes. "No, I told you I needed to fuck you. There's a big difference."

Deb's lip curled and her nose wrinkled, dithering awkwardly in the entry. James looked askance out the window and let a cloud of tobacco smoke disperse over its glass surface. Arthur grew increasingly uncomfortable. This wasn't something he wanted to drag them into, but he certainly couldn't just banish them from the room they were all sharing. He sank into the chair next to the bedside and sighed, "You can't just have sex with people under false pretenses."

"Are you fucking *kidding* me?" Eve whirled away in frustration, rubbing her face with both hands. "This is why they tell you not to fuck virgins..." she muttered to herself. Then, she turned back and looked Arthur square in the eye.

"I am not yours," she asserted firmly. "I'm not anybody's. I don't understand why everyone's so invested in the patriarchal monogamy machine." Her accent disappeared as she rolled on. "See, the only purpose of monogamy is to control women's bodies. *My* body. I've lived my entire life in a body that's more commodity than human. So sorry if I don't feel bad for you when you experienced fifteen minutes of feeling like an object."

Arthur cowed under her gaze. *Was* he just another cog in the patriarchal monogamy machine? She took a deep breath through her nose and shook her head. "I belong to myself. And I *like* fucking. If someone wants to fuck me, then I'm on board. It's a good fucking time. For Chrissakes, I've fucked all of you." She swept her arm wide across the room. "And all of you were great! I don't see why anyone needs to be upset or jealous or whatever. We're four fun, sexy people. We share drinks. We share joints. We play music together. We have *fun* together. Why can't we have sex? I *really* don't see what the big deal is."

The room was silent for a moment. James was curled over himself, his fingers on his forehead, his expression as inscrutable as ever. Arthur had no idea what to say or do, even though he had started it.

"You know what I think we need to do?" Eve said, her hands on her hips. "I think we need to clear the air."

"You're doing a great job at that all on your own," James muttered.

"No, I mean sexually. I think we need to just get it all out in the open."

Deb grimaced. "Cool. Yeah. I ... am not drunk enough for this." Before Eve could argue with her, she shrugged her leather jacket on and walked out the motel room door.

Eve pressed her lips together and narrowed her eyes at Deb's back. If looks could kill...

Eve whirled on Arthur. "Come on. Let's free your mind. Let me show you that sex isn't any different than all the other stuff we do together. It's just people making each other feel good. It's not this big devastating sin everyone makes it out to be."

Arthur's eyes widened, and his fingers gripped the arms of the chair. What did she mean? Like, now? He looked at James desperately. Surely he wasn't going to go along with this? (What did Arthur have to do to get him to go along with this?) James looked at him with that damned placid expression, held his eyes with that steely blue gaze for a long moment. Eve sat back on the edge of the bed, a small smile playing on her lips as she watched the two of them consider. Watched them not immediately say no.

"Come on, Arthur," she purred, uncrossing her legs slowly in that damn tiny skirt. "Let me prove it to you."

It was evident that Arthur's cock was interested, but he hesitated, glancing back at James. After a month of dancing around that mercurial man, he had no idea what to expect. And, well, he had questions. Questions, frankly, only James could help him conclusively answer.

But maybe that would be taking advantage of James. After all, as much as James liked ladies clothing too, it didn't automatically mean he was gay. Was he gay? He'd protested with FREE, that one day. But he also clearly had something going on with

Eve. She'd said so just now, when she said she'd had sex with all of them. And if James wasn't hung up on Eve, why had he sat there last week shooting daggers through his eyes at Arthur while she fucked him? But if James wasn't at least a little bit gay, why had he gotten hard? Maybe getting cuckolded turned him on? This was extremely confusing, and a very inopportune time to be trying to parse all this out. When Arthur looked back at Eve, wholly preparing to say no, she had just finished unzipping her dress down the front.[2]

"The rules are," she murmured, "everyone has to say yes. If you, for example," she parted the fabric and unveiled her spectacular breasts, "want to touch my tits, you have to wait for me to say yes."

Fuck, fuck, fuckedy, fuck. He was still at least a little straight. There was no mistaking Arthur's interest now. If James hadn't noticed the tent in his jeans yet, he was fucking blind.

Eve stood with a seductive smile, pressing her advantage. "And if, say, *I* want you to fuck my tits while Jim eats me out, I have to wait for you *both* to say yes."

Arthur let out a soft, involuntary whimper, his lips parting. He didn't even know if he wanted to do that. It just sounded so ... *filthy*. He looked frantically at James, who hadn't moved, who just watched Eve with that same inscrutable look. *Say something*, Arthur wanted to scream. *Say anything. What do you want, you infuriating man???*

Eve rolled her head back and giggled. "Oh come on, you guys. You're so uptight. Admit it! That would be so hot! And *fun*."

James leaned forward and exhaled. "Fine, Eve," he said. "But only if he's in too."

Arthur choked. Holy shit. Was this happening? He wasn't sure how he felt about it. Only that when both their gazes landed on him, waiting for his assent, he felt a surge of bombshell

---

2. "Baby's On Fire" Brian Eno

energy stronger than he'd ever felt before. A power he'd never known.

"Um," he stuttered. "I've never really—"

"Yes, we know, darling," Eve interrupted gently. "That's honestly part of what makes it sexy, at least for me."

Arthur blushed to the tips of his ears.

"We'll take good care of you, darling," she said, perching on the arm of his chair and smoothing his hair aside. "If you don't like something, just say no. No hard feelings, no judgment. And if you don't want anything to do with the idea, you can say no now. Just say the word, darling, I mean it. But," she glanced down at his tented jeans, her false eyelashes fluttering on her cheeks, "you can't blame me for thinking you're interested."

Arthur swallowed hard, tried to breathe normally. And then he let himself nod. Her face lit up, eager and hungry, and she stood, taking both of his hands and leading him to the nearest of the two motel beds. Fuck, even her breasts bounced in excitement.

As for James (apparently the only man on earth who could make communal sex seem like a chore), he stood and casually shrugged his brocade wrap shirt off, letting it land on the prickly green carpet. He was lean and angular, blonde hair thick over his chest and trailing down his stomach from his naval. Arthur's mouth went dry. Not entirely straight either.

"And I'm not eating you out," James informed Eve pointedly as he unbuckled his belt.

Eve exchanged a look with Arthur and shrugged. "It was worth a try."

She laid back on the bed and pulled Arthur over her, her hands slipping under his t-shirt and leaving trails of tingling awareness with her fingertips. She pulled on the hem and looked inquiringly up at Arthur. As good as her word, she was waiting for his permission. He sat back on his knees, straddling her waist, and lifted his arms as she pulled his t-shirt up and over his head. His glasses got tangled in the neck and Eve pulled them off.

"Is this okay?" she murmured as she disappeared into a soft fuzz of light and supple shadow. Arthur nodded, and she set the glasses on the side table before resuming her caresses over his bare skin.

The mattress shifted, and Arthur looked round at James. He sat at the end of the bed cross-legged in his shorts, digging in his discarded jeans pocket for another cigarette. Eve was pressing her lips to Arthur's sternum, but he was too arrested by the sight of James sitting so casually when Arthur felt so simultaneously overwhelmed and aroused that he thought he might just crawl out of his skin.

"You want one?" James asked him, and there was nothing guarded about his eyes when he said it. Just straightforward openness. Arthur watched his lithe fingers flick the lighter to flame and stiltedly shook his head, just as Eve's lips ghosted over his nipple, cutting his breath short. James took a drag and leaned back on one arm, eyes tracking over the pair of them appreciatively. Eve, meanwhile, having taken note of Arthur's response, began to lavish his nipple with devoted attention, her lips and tongue and teeth teasing and testing him. Her big, brown eyes turned up, watching for his reaction. Which was quite vocal, and probably terribly embarrassing.

"I like how responsive you are," she murmured into his skin, placing a chaste kiss on the nipple she'd just accosted. He was already blushing so he couldn't very well blush harder, but when he glanced at James and saw how he studied the two of them, smoking that cigarette just like he had last week while he watched Arthur lose his virginity, well, fuck, it dropped straight to Arthur's groin.

Eve glanced up and smiled. "Do you like to be watched, darling?" she asked Arthur.

Gently, she pushed him off of her. Arthur found his legs unsteady as he slid to his feet at the edge of the bed, watching her breasts perform some sort of hypnotic dance as she shimmied her dress off. No underwear. Just smooth, lightly-curling brown hair between her milky thighs. (Christ, she must have been sitting bare-assed at the club, her skirt was so short.)

"Come on," Eve chided as she pulled one foot up and began unfastening the clasp of her Mary Jane platforms. "Off with those trousers."

Arthur's hands felt miles away, acting of their own accord, or perhaps of Eve's, as they unfastened his belt. "Wait," he found himself saying. Eve glanced up at him, eyes round and warm and eager. "Leave those on."

Her lush lips stretched into a smile, and she very deliberately tucked the ankle strap back into the buckle.

Eve laid back, crossing one foot over her knee to bounce her shoe in his field of vision as Arthur shimmied his jeans down to pool on the floor. He stepped on his toes to pull his socks off too. James seemed content to sit in his shorts and watch, just placidly smoking that cigarette down to a stub. When Arthur made to climb back on the bed again, Eve stopped him.

"Ah ah ah, pants too," she said, looking significantly at his boxer shorts. Arthur felt himself blush, couldn't help glancing at James as though his consent was somehow necessary. James lifted his eyebrows as he exhaled tobacco smoke, and graciously gestured for Arthur to proceed with his cigarette. His slash of a mouth, usually grim, looked soft and pliant when he smoked. *I got down on my knees. I looked at her and she at me.* Arthur glanced down quickly, afraid if he looked at James too long, the other man might see straight past his eyes and into his very thoughts. Which were pretty queer at the moment.

Arthur tried to focus on Eve's inviting nipples, which wasn't difficult because they were rosy pink, pointed, and right in front of him. He dropped his underwear before he could think himself into a corner and knelt back on the bed. Eve pulled him near, coming up to her knees as well as she pressed her warm, soft chest full against his, kissing him deeply. Her hands were in his hair, her tongue in his mouth, her cunt pressed against his erection. It was excellent. Crackling energy pumped through his veins. Arthur tipped his head back to gasp for air.

"Oh, darling," Eve breathed, her hands caressing his shoulders and chest. "You are so fucking sexy, I can't stand it."

She pushed Arthur back towards the headboard, and he reclined against the pillows, pushing his legs out long over the bed as Eve sat back on her knees and admired his erection. And then there was James. Shifting on the bed, crawling over Arthur's legs. Reaching over him until his golden curls tickled Arthur's chest, those steely eyes missing none of Arthur's very involuntary gasp of anticipation as he hovered above him. Arthur's lips parted. His heart raced in his chest. *Yes, please,* he thought, deranged, not really sure what he was hoping for. Something. Everything.

James pressed his stub of a cigarette out in the ashtray that was placed on the bedside table.

"'Scuse me," he murmured, damnably stone-faced as Arthur's mouth went slack with disappointment. Then James fucking retreated back to his perch at the end of the bed like some sort of sadistic watchdog. Where Eve turned to Jim, took him by his hatchet jaw, and kissed him with the same depth and enthusiasm that she'd just kissed Arthur. And to be completely honest, Arthur wasn't sure who he wished he would rather be, him or her.

Once finished with her kiss, Eve laid back against Arthur's chest, pulling his arms around her and encouraging him to fondle her. She opened her legs invitingly to James, but he rolled his eyes.

"I told you I'm not doing that."

She pouted and maneuvered her own hand between her thighs as she placed her other hand firmly around the base of Arthur's cock. An undignified sound escaped his throat. James' eyes flicked between the two of them. He licked his lips. Arthur's brain entirely short-circuited. Eve sighed contentedly, then moaned, her nose turning to nuzzle into Arthur's neck. "Yes, just like that. Harder, Arthur."

He obliged, squeezing her nipples hard between his fingers until there was scarcely any areola left and they were hard and peaked and flushing red.

James looked at Arthur's cock and then back up at his face. Arthur's eyes widened, heart racing. Eve had full round lips, lips that seemed to be made for cocksucking. James' lips were scarcely there at all. And yet, when James leaned forward, hovering with his golden curls ghosting over Arthur's thighs, looking up at him inquiringly, Arthur didn't even hesitate to vigorously nod his assent.

Warm, wet heat enveloped him. Good god. A sob burst out of him. He couldn't help it. Despite the utter overwhelm of his senses, he kept his eyes fixed on the explicit display of naked skin around him, a symphony of sight and sensation. Eve tipped her head back over his shoulder as her breath quickened. Her breasts in his hands, nipples between his fingertips. The heave of his chest matched in time with hers. Her knees up, her platform shoes straining against the mussed bedspread.

And then there was James. His hair spun gold, his nose straight and sharp, tip bobbing towards Eve's hand around the base of Arthur's cock. His eyes were closed and it was both a blessing and a curse. A blessing because he couldn't see Arthur watch him with increasing desperation, a curse because Arthur couldn't see his beautiful eyes. Couldn't look into them, see if this was good for him or if it was ... something else.

Arthur strained to connect the sights with the sensations. The tight suction of James' mouth. Oh fuck, the slip of his tongue. The slight unintentional hint of teeth. How was he breathing? Arthur swallowed hard and gasped as he felt fission build deep in his groin. Eve was gasping into his ear. Arthur imagined for a moment that her body was his, that she had melted into him, that they were one person, tits and cock and cunt, combined into one perfect superhuman. Homosapien superior. Oh hell, that was doing it for him.

Eve lifted her head. Looked down at James' head moving in a slow, torturous rhythm up and down.

"Oh shit," she swore, her voice unaccented and edging on desperate. "I could watch that all damn day."

She pulled her other hand away, where it had gripped the base of Arthur's cock. It was wet from James' mouth. She pushed this hand between her legs to join the other and fucked herself on her own fingers. She slid off Arthur a little, turned her cheek on his chest, and watched as she hummed with pleasure.

James pulled off for a moment, took a shuddering breath, then gripped both of Arthur's hips as he gulped down Arthur's prick. Arthur swore he could feel the back of his throat on the head of his cock. The fission became unstable. Arthur's vision flashed, and he could feel his edge coming on.

"Yes," Eve purred, presumably feeling his stomach muscles tense under her cheek, seeing his hips lift and shake even though he was trying as hard as he could not to thrust and choke James. "Oh my god, yes."

Arthur had no idea what James did then. He just knew that he did something, because Arthur felt like he'd been slammed into a wall of oblivion.

"Shit, wait," Arthur gasped, but it was happening. He tried to pull back, but James gripped his hips tight, pressed his nose into Arthur's belly and oh *fuck,* he opened his eyes and looked straight through Arthur and into his goddamn soul, scraping the insides of him out like a pale blue laser. An intense, brutal orgasm ripped out of Arthur like some sort of exorcism, his voice loud and ragged and utterly beyond his own control.

And James. He held his eyes through it, kept his mouth round him, swallowed around his overly-sensitive cock. When it was over, he pulled off and licked his lips again. And if Arthur had had any questions about himself before that, he didn't any-more. His chest heaved, and he held James' gaze with wild-eyed disbelief. *Oh, God please. Please let that be real. Not some performance for Eve.*

Eve pushed herself up, surveying Arthur's spent cock with a moue on her lips. James pushed himself to his knees as well. His boxer shorts were tented tight across his groin. Arthur bit his lip to see it. He wanted to return the favor, show James how appreciative he was, but he had no idea where to even begin. Eve apparently did. She pulled James in by his neck.

"I want to taste him too," she murmured, and kissed him deep and open-mouthed. Arthur's thoughts glitched. He was scrap metal, piled on the pillows, used and useless. James held Eve delicately on her shoulders, almost tenderly, as he kissed her back. Then his eyes fluttered open and met Arthur's.

"Well, now who's gonna fuck me," Eve complained breathlessly as she broke away from James. She looked up at him expectantly.

James' eyes lingered on Arthur's for a moment longer before he quietly stood and shucked off his shorts, revealing ... well, a frankly enormous cock that was somehow perfectly scaled to his long body. It bobbed out from him with a slight curve, hard and wet at the tip. Arthur laid boneless over the pillows, spent and stupid, and realized his prick was making an exhausted, half-hearted attempt to pay attention to this. Fucking hell. Gay as a maypole? Was his interest in girls actually only limited to a minor obsession with breasts?

"Eeeh! Yay!" Eve squealed, sitting up eagerly. "You know, Jimmy was my first," she confided to Arthur, who had absolutely no idea how he was supposed to respond to that.

"I told you, don't fucking call me that." James somehow managed to look annoyed while giving that magnificent cock a few cursory pumps with his hand. Arthur couldn't stop staring at it. Wondering what it would feel like, what it would taste like...

"It's really too bad that—"

"What? I'm not tied round your little finger anymore?"

"Ha, you wish. No, it's just been too long darling, and I missed your big, long cock." She leaned forward, her ass a perfect curve, as she—Oh, god, as she licked the glistening tip of James' cock. Arthur felt a prick of jealousy. It was a perfectly filthy image. Pornographic, but also artisitic, in its way? Two beautiful people drunk on lust, doing depraved things to one another. Despite the enormous desire to be in Eve's place, Arthur wasn't necessarily angry about the idea of watching the performance unfold.

"You're such a perv." James admonished, his expression still stern.

"You like it." Eve laid back, resting her head on Arthur's stomach as she spread her legs for James, digging the heels of her platform shoes into the edge of the bed.

"Shut up." James gave himself a few more pumps. He hesitated, glanced up at Arthur. Swallowed. Regarded Eve once again. Was he nervous?

"Condom?" he asked.

"Diaphragm," Eve replied.

"When the hell did you put that in??"

"Is now when you really want to ask that question?"

"Fucking hell. Turn over."

Eve eagerly obliged. She turned herself onto her elbows, and presented her full, round ass for James as she grinned at Arthur through a sticky haze of lust. She pressed a few kisses to his chest, so casual and easy and generous that he didn't feel so much like a voyeur.

James bit his lip in concentration. Arthur could tell by how Eve's mouth went slack, how she moaned, that he was pressing in. Fuck. Okay. He was intensely jealous. But how could he ever take her place? He was a man, and she was *Eve*.

"Yes," she breathed. She tossed her long hair out of her face, her body writhing back into James. "All the way."

James lifted his eyes to Arthur's as he complied. His mouth was a dark slash in his face as he gave a sharp intake of breath.

Eve keened, arching. "*Fuck*, I missed this."

Arthur swallowed hard. He shouldn't be hearing this. He wished he could melt away into the mattress. But James held his eyes. Just like before. Steely blue, hard and piercing and slightly wild.

James set the pace, thrusting into Eve. She shifted her weight onto one arm and reached down to take one of his hands from where he gripped her hips and push it between her legs. Arthur wondered if he should do something too. Touch her? Massage her breasts? Could he put his mouth between her legs, kiss her where James was entering her? That thought yanked a sound out of him, one that was observed and duly noted by James, who still watched him with hard, wide eyes. And Arthur was too fascinated to not watch him back. James' chest was flushing, the blonde hair across it beaded with sweat. His nipples were tight and pink. His shoulders were straining, his gold curls cascading over them. And his blue eyes drilled into Arthur's, his chin jutting forward as his breath quickened. God, he was fucking perfect. Just like Eve was. They were both perfect. Perfect for one another. Arthur was extraneous. A novel distraction. Perhaps a little blip that led them back to each other, a funny and fond memory after they'd grown old together.

"Jim!" Eve cried and she shuddered, pushing herself relentlessly back into him. "Yes, fuckfuck*fuck*!"

James didn't slow at all, even as Eve came around him. He grit his teeth and thrust harder. Moved his fingers for her faster. But his eyes didn't lose focus on Arthur's, except to flicker a glance at Arthur's lap.

Arthur followed his gaze. Holy shit. Arthur's cock was half mast, like it was trying desperately to wave a white flag of surrender to the depraved vulgarity it was presented with. James smirked and bit his lip. He pushed Eve harder yet. She cried out, a raw, animal sound. Her thighs shuddered as she came more—or again? James rode her out, splayed a big hand out over her low back. His eyes raked over Arthur as his face twisted, stark and harsh and taut. His thrusts got manic, arhythmic.

"Jim, please," Eve pleaded. Her eyes were squeezed shut and her mouth was slack and gasping. "Come for me, baby. Fill me up."

James swallowed hard. He still held Arthur's eyes. He looked ferocious, golden mane tossing and curls sticking to his forehead. Arthur wanted to believe that this lust had at least a little to do with him. But an insidious notion took hold of him. Was James showing him how much more Eve wanted him than Arthur? Making sure Arthur came so he could present no alternative, then fucking her into next Tuesday with his big cock to prove to Arthur how much of an abberation he'd been? The thought dropped into his gut like a punch, made his breath short. Surely, it was nonsense. What an elaborate way to destroy someone, and Arthur felt sure James didn't want to *destroy* him. But it would be a particularly sweet, if depraved, revenge for how Arthur had betrayed him. Arthur met James' eyes again, a little helplessly, and James grunted and emptied himself into Eve. She cried out, a smile beaming onto her beautiful face.

"Yes, Jim, just like that," she mewled. "Just like you used to."

Eve collapsed onto the mattress, eyes half-lidded and smiling. James' shoulders curled in on themselves as he stepped away. His face fixed itself impassive again, a hard, impenetrable wall. He reached for the tissue box on the console table between the two motel beds to clean himself up. He gave Arthur a furtive glance.

"What did I tell you?" Eve murmured, rolling onto her back like a purring cat and poking Arthur in the arm. "Fun. Easy. Beautiful."

Arthur wasn't sure those were the first adjectives he'd chosen, though he supposed none of them were particularly inaccurate. The first that jumped to his mind was *enlightening. Exquisite torture*, perhaps. No, that was a phrase. *Irresistible inadequacy?* Now he felt like he was writing a song.

James handed Eve a tissue. Though his expression was fixed, the way he held himself seemed ... different. Skulking, unsure, like he was trying to disappear into a black hole. He bent and pulled out his cigarette pack from his discarded jeans.

"Shit," he said. "Eve, can I bum a cigarette?"

Eve looked up at Arthur and giggled, like they were sharing a private joke. "Yes, they're in my purse."

James crossed to the other side of the room and began digging through her bag. Eve turned back to Arthur and nuzzled into him, her warm, sweat-sticky skin enveloping his chest and thigh. "Looks like you could go again, darling."

Her hand snaked down his chest towards his flagging cock. It wanted so badly to be hard, but it was so tired. Wrung out by James' talented tongue. Arthur swallowed hard.

"It's okay," he said, grabbing Eve's hand in his. Once he had it, he wasn't sure what to do with it, so he pulled it to his lips and kissed her knuckles. Eve smiled contentedly up at him and for a moment, it did feel sweet and uncomplicated, just like she said it would be.

James had his shorts on again, and he was perched on the edge of the opposite bed, looking a little frustrated as he tried to get his lighter to flame. Something must have been wrong with it. James was a steady, practiced hand. Eve followed Arthur's gaze and frowned.

"Get that lit and come back here," she demanded. Her accent was back full force. "This isn't a bordello. I insist on languishing in a post-coital embrace."

She reached across the narrow gap and grabbed James' hand as he took his first drag on his cigarette. He pulled so deep, Arthur could hear the paper crackle. James stood and let Eve pull him to the bed. It was just a double, so it was a tight fit. But that seemed to be Eve's desire. She maneuvered herself over Arthur, laying half on top of him and curling her legs around his as she pulled James into the bed on Arthur's other side. It was kind of her. He would have been less surprised if she'd curled into James' embrace, putting her back to Arthur, leaving him to salvage a corner of the bed's edge to perch upon while they whispered sweet nothings to one another. But no. She'd actually made sure to include Arthur.

James pulled the sheets down before climbing onto the mattress. Arthur and Eve both had to shift awkwardly to allow him to get the sheets free. Then, he laid on his back, putting a hand behind his head and yanked the sheets up over all three of them as he took another long drag off his cigarette. He looked at neither of them. The lamp behind him lit up his sharp profile, his furred chest glittering gold, and Arthur felt bittersweet with how beautiful he looked through the prism of Arthur's blurred vision.

Eve nuzzled into the crook of Arthur's arm, watching James with a small smile on her face.

"Let me have that, will you?" she said, reaching out and wiggling her red-polished fingertips. James handed the rapidly disappearing cigarette to her, and she pursed her kiss-swollen lips around it. "Arthur, you want a drag?"

Arthur blinked. He'd been distracted by the strangely beguiling masculine musk that was coming off of James. Wondering if he was allowed to push his fingers through his chest hair.

"Um, no, I'm alright. Thanks."

Eve smiled, then laid a lazy kiss on his mouth. Her lips were sweet and soft, tinged with bitter tobacco. She released him with a light nip to his lower lip, then pushed herself up to lean over Arthur and deliver the same kiss to James' mouth. Her breasts pressed on Arthur's chest. He was hypnotized by the tender eroticism with which she moved.

Eve hummed contentedly as she settled back into the crook of Arthur's shoulder.

"This is perfect," she murmured. Arthur wasn't convinced she was wrong.

19

Arthur woke the next morning tangled up in Eve's naked arms. He turned his head blearily to look at the clock. No glasses. He reached for them on the side table and slipped them on. Ten to seven. Why was he awake this early?

The room was dim, scant light trying to filter in through the curtained window. James was not on Arthur's other side, and the opposite bed was unmade. Arthur wondered if James had slipped over there or if Deb had come back to see the three of them sleeping tangled together and decided to sleep as far away from that as she could get.

He could hear the shower running in the bathroom. Arthur gently extricated himself from Eve's embrace. She was soft and sweet in slumber, her lips blooming gently and her false eyelashes dusting her cheeks. He stood and dressed, pulling on his jeans and a sweater from his duffel.

The door to the bathroom clicked open, and Arthur looked up from buckling his belt. James emerged, a towel around his waist, his hair dripping wet over his shoulders. His head looked strangely small. Rivulets of water trickled down from his hair over the planes of his chest, disappearing into his chest hair. Oh, that's right. Arthur was undeniably still very attracted to him. He tried not to blush and pushed his hand through his shaggy hair as he looked away.

"Morning," James said, tossing a second towel over his head and drying his hair vigorously. "Any sign of Deb?"

Arthur clenched and unclenched his hands, wishing he had something to do with them. "No, I haven't seen her. Was it you who slept in the other bed?"

"Mmhm."

"Oh." *What the hell, Arthur? Don't sound so disappointed. Be normal.* "Cool."

"Sleep okay?" James pulled the towel around his neck.

Arthur blinked at him. Was this a loaded question? Did he mean actual sleep or ... the thing that happened before the sleep? "Yup."

"Eve can be a little cloying," James said, by way of explanation. "She likes to snuggle."

Arthur looked over at her, tucked under the covers, at once both innocent and tawdry. "That's okay," he said. "It was nice." That was true, but he couldn't help but wonder how it might have felt different with James. Gah. He'd opened a veritable Pandora's Box of wants and fears and now he couldn't stuff them back away.

James pressed his lips into a line and nodded. "Yeah." Swallow. His throat bobbing. Christ Almighty. "Good."

Good? What did that mean? Arthur felt a sudden wave of exhaustion overcome him. Eve said it would be simple, that it was just people having fun together. And he had to believe that was true. But he couldn't help but wonder what this meant? What did this make them? How did he act in this situation? He really had no idea how to be normal.

Just then, the door to the motel room swung open.

"Oh, shit, Deb," James said, turning. "You look like hell."

Deb cackled, and Arthur couldn't tell if it was sarcastic or not. "It was worth it, my man!"

"Where were you?" Arthur asked.

Deb bit her lip and giggled. Her pompadour was decidedly askew. Her leather coat was rumpled. "Wouldn' you like to know?"

"I mean, yeah. I did ask you," Arthur said, doing a poor job of not sounding irritated.

"Well, Tweedle Dee and Tweedle Dum, I followed the white rabbit through Bronzeville and got into the Ball."

"The ball?"

"What are you, Cinderella?" James quipped.

"The annual Halloween ball for all the queens. Keep up. It was wild. And I got to compete. Not impersonating a female, 'course. They had male impersonators too. They called me Jimmy Dean, and I placed third! Put that in your pipe and smoke it, Jimmy-boy!"

She stumbled.

"Are you still drunk?" Eve was sitting up in bed, rubbing sleep from her eyes and clutching the sheet absently to her chest.

"Oh, yeah," Deb nodded earnestly. "'Mong other things. Orlando had loads of good shit."

"Fucking hell, Deb!" Eve cried, throwing her hands up and dropping the sheet. Yup, breasts still set to stun. "We're supposed to record today! We can't roll into the studio with a fucked up drummer who can't keep time!"

Deb crossed her arms. "Mebbe you shoulda thought about that before trying to bully everyone into having an orgy, Evie."

"Don't blame *your* bad decisions on *me*," Eve shot back. "Christ."

"If Keith Moon can do it, so can I." Deb rolled her eyes and leaned against the wall, arms still crossed. Her narrowed eyes seemed to keep Eve at bay. "So ... whaddid I miss?"

Arthur flushed as Deb turned a raised brow upon each of them in turn. James chose to ignore her and sidle around Arthur to get at his overnight bag. Wet skin brushed the back of Arthur's hand, catching somehow at the breath in his chest.

Eve smirked, smoothing her hands over the sheets and looking very pleased with herself.

"You fucking fiends," Deb muttered, rolling her eyes again and casting a disparaging look at James in particular. James met her gaze as he pulled his t-shirt on and shook his head slightly. See, this was why Arthur felt like he was missing something important. Because there was something brewing here, under the surface, that he didn't have the first clue about. Deb shook her head and zeroed in on Eve again. "Your tits are out, babe."

Eve looked down and shrugged provocatively. "And what do you propose to do about it?"

Arthur didn't really hear Deb's reply, because James had dropped his towel and was pulling on fresh boxer shorts. And Arthur really could not help but bite the inside of his cheek and stare at his lean thighs and pale ass and ruddy cock, still impressive even when flaccid. A squeal cracked through his reverie, as Deb tackled Eve in the bed and tickled her mercilessly.

"Deb, quit it! I'm still mad at you!"

"No, you're not," Deb cackled with a grin. "You can't stay mad at me."

Deb straddled Eve's lap and smirked as she squeezed Eve's breasts. Eve bit her lip, her eyes lighting up.

"Go get us some coffee, boys," Eve ordered.

What the actual hell was happening? Who were these people and why did they all have sex with each other? Arthur must have been frozen in horror, because James pulled him by the arm, now fully dressed, and led him out the door of the motel room.

When they got outside into the chill November air, Arthur couldn't hold it in any longer. "What the hell was that?"

James shrugged and strode down the sidewalk towards the motel office, lighting himself another cigarette pilfered from Eve's purse. "I think it was kind of obvious."

Arthur dogged him down, and grabbed him by the arm. "Look, maybe you're used to all this free love stuff, but I'm up a creek without a paddle here. Tell me *what is going on.*"

James blinked at him, inscrutable. Then he let out a sigh of tobacco smoke. "I told you. Eve is a hedonist. She believes all that shit she spouts about sex being like a handshake."

Arthur pinched his lips together. He wanted to shout that nothing about last night was like a handshake. Especially not all of the things Eve had said to James. In what insane alternate reality could something so vulnerable be so impersonal? "So she's gonna have sex with Deb now?"

"I guess so." James shrugged, glancing sidelong. "Why? You mad you're missing out?"

Arthur frowned defensively. "No. Though it does beg the question as to why Deb copped out last night, but is suddenly on board this morning."

"Cocaine?" James took another drag and shrugged. "I dunno. She doesn't want anything to do with men. We 'disgust her,' I believe were her words."

"So she's gay?"

"Oh, *extremely*." James flicked ash off the tip of his cigarette, watching it float to the ground before glancing guardedly up at Arthur. "Is that a problem?"

Arthur spluttered. "No! I clearly don't care. I just want to know what's—what's going on. I just—I don't know what to do or how to act."

"Just act like you," James replied, one corner of his mouth twitching up.

If only it were that easy. Arthur looked up into James' eyes. So blue. So clear. He wanted to steal some of that clarity. But all he did was utter something entirely too honest. "I don't know how to do that."

James frowned. His eyes searched Arthur's for a moment. Try as he might to hide it, Arthur saw the pity there. And it spoiled the touch of James' fingers tentatively curling round Arthur's hand. He wasn't going to be pitied. He twitched his hand away.

"Let's just get some coffee," Arthur said, putting his head down and charging towards the motel office.[1]

There was no coffee at the motel office. Whoever was on desk duty that morning had not deigned to brew it. So Arthur walked through the chill lake-effect fog with James to the convenience store down the street and bought four steaming styrofoam cups of coffee and a pack of Marlboros. As they walked back, Arthur desperately tried to think of something to say. Something normal, casual. Cool.

He failed utterly. They spent the entire walk back saying nothing at all.

In the motel room, they found Eve sitting at the desk, applying makeup in nothing but James' discarded brocade wrap top, while Deb snored on the bed.

"Coffee?" Arthur offered Eve as James frowned at Deb.

"Oh thanks," Eve replied with a wide grin. "Sorry about all that. She's just—you know, very good."

"Sorry?"

"She knows where my clit is, Arthur," Eve said as she applied her pink lipstick. "I'll teach you sometime."

Arthur flushed bright red.

"Eve, don't be condescending." James admonished.

"What?" Eve protested, smacking her lips in the mirror. "I'm not being condescending. It makes total sense that he doesn't know where my clit is. He's only just popped his cherry. Besides, she fucking passed out before I could get my legs open anyway. Don't look so horrified."

James shook his head at her. Silence seeped into the spaces between them. Arthur seized the opportunity to use the bathroom, where he could escape the silence's insidious tension.

"Eve, what the hell?" James' voice carried muffled through the bathroom door.

---

1. "It Ain't Easy" David Bowie

"What?"

"You don't need to point out his inadequacies at *every* opportunity." Ouch. Arthur turned away from the mirror. He wasn't sure it was possible to feel smaller.

"I don't do it at 'every opportunity', Jimothy. Only when it's relevant."

"Regardless," James said, "no need to ruin someone who is genuinely nice by insulting his pride and his experience and his intelligence. You're better than that."

"Ruin him I plan to," Eve said lightly, and Arthur could almost hear her smile playing on her pink lipstick.

"Well, you're well on your way."

"Speak for yourself, knob gobbler." Arthur flushed. Pushed his glasses up so he could hide his face in his hands. This was why it was a bad idea to eavesdrop.

"Eve."

"What? Jim, darling." A pause. Arthur imagined her approaching him. Running her hands over his chest. "What you did to him—damn, it was the hottest thing I've seen in a long time."

Silence. Horrible, plummeting silence.

"Jim, darling." Arthur twisted and braced himself on two arms over the sink. Stop listening. Stop. "He's perfect for us."

"Eve..." James' voice was cracked. "No. That's not fair."

"I rather think it's up to him to decide that."

Arthur found the strength of character to turn the shower on and drown out the conversation. As long as Deb was still sleeping, he had time. He smelled like stale sweat and sex. He stepped out of his clothes and into the shower, sloughing his body inch by inch with the complimentary bar of motel soap.

Deb woke up around noon a little worse for wear, but she refused to admit it.

"Nope, I feel great," she insisted with a low, rough voice, drinking down the entire cup of cold coffee in one gulp. "Never better."

They piled into the van, and James drove them up Michigan Avenue to Record Row. The studio Deb had connected them with looked, for all intents and purposes, closed.

"Deb, they know we're coming this weekend, right?"

"Oh, yeah," Deb replied, hopping out of the van. "This is an after hours thing. Guess this guy owed my aunts a big favor."

They followed Deb to the front door, where she rapped and waited confidently, lighting a cigarette as she waited.

The door cracked open and a tall, Black man peeked his head out. "You Debora Gutierrez?"

He addressed the question to Eve.

"Yeah, that's me," Deb said, waving her cigarette.

The guy nodded. "This your combo?"

"Yup," Deb replied, flicking ash onto the street. "We're called The Tarts."

The guy blinked. "Like a fruit tart?"

"Sure."

Eve tried to hide a giggle with her hand.

The guy pulled the door open with a tired sigh, rubbing his hand over his shiny, bald head. "Come on in."

The door opened onto a narrow hallway that smelled like hash. There was thirty-year-old green floral wallpaper hung with framed album covers. A lot of what was hung appeared to be R&B and jazz groups.

"I'm Bill Jackson," the guy said, offering his hand to Deb. "Lupe and I go way back."

Deb shook the proffered hand firmly. "Nice to meet you."

Arthur walked by a framed copy of B.B. King's *Indianola Mississippi Seeds* and felt his heart choke his throat. Talk about high pressure. Jesus.

"We've got about five hours of studio time today," Bill said, leading them into a small room with a sofa and a massive panel of sliders and dials. There was a large tape machine mounted on the far wall and a big glass pane in the wall between a huge control panel and a small sound booth strewn with cables and microphones. "With set-up, we probably won't have time for more than one song. So don't get your hopes up."

"Did you record with B.B. King?" Arthur blurted.

Bill glanced up. "Yeah."

Arthur paled. "That's so cool."

James raised an eyebrow at him. "So where can we load in?"

It took at least an hour to load in the gear and get it set up, mic-ed up, and level. Bill worked fastidiously with different microphones, asking for sound checks and adjusting mics, moving between the room with the control panel and the sound booth where they were set up. He spent the most time with Deb, having her thump out each piece of her drum kit while he ran back and forth, checking mic placement. Eve pulled Arthur down onto the couch in the control room as she dragged on a cigarette.

"Are you ready?" she asked with a smile.

"Yeah, I think so," Arthur replied, his shoulders tight to bear the weight of the pressure. He hoped he was ready.

"Good. I'm so excited," she said with a grin. Then she snaked out a hand and squeezed his. "I'm so glad you're here."

Arthur glanced at her sidelong. "Me too." It came out more guarded than he'd intended.

"Not just in the band. I just..." Eve glanced down coyly and lowered her voice. "Last night was so great, Arthur."

Arthur felt his face heat. "Yeah. It was."

"It felt so right," Eve continued. "I know you felt it too, didn't you?"

Arthur nodded slowly. "Yeah." It was true, but he wasn't sure if that rightness had had as much to do with her as it had with James. He couldn't say that, though. That was awful.

"You know," Eve looked down again. Was she blushing? "Jim and I used to be together."

"I kind of figured."

"We were in love. For years." Eve looked up at him with a wistful expression. "But I don't know. Jim kind of ... drifted away from me. And I guess I did too. But last night, Arthur! Last night, it felt like it used to. And I think it was because of you."

Arthur swallowed.

Eve clutched both of his hands in hers, cigarette hanging between her fingers. "I'm so sorry if I made you feel like a notch on my bedpost. I really do believe you're special, and last night just put that into sharper focus. I hope you ..." she glanced down sheepishly. "Christ, I'm sorry, I don't usually act like this. But I really hope you might want to do it again."

Arthur shifted awkwardly. "With both of you?"

"Yeah," Eve smiled. "I know it's hard to see it sometimes, but Jim really likes you."

"Eve." James was standing in the doorway of the control room. His brows were furrowed and suspicious. "What're you doing?"

Eve looked up at him and grinned. "I was just telling Arthur how special last night was. He's interested in a repeat engagement, right, darling?"

Arthur hadn't exactly said that, but it didn't make it any less true. If it involved James, he couldn't help but be interested. And Eve too. Because even while James had captured his singular interest, Eve was still a fucking goddess. If Arthur was gay, he wasn't like Deb. He wasn't disgusted by the opposite sex. Not at all. If anything, he was enamored. Admiring to the edge of jealousy, really. He nodded, watching James carefully for his response.

James rubbed his temples and shook his head. "Eve..." It sounded like saying her name caused him physical pain. "I told you no. It's not fair."

"But he wants to, Jim!"

"Not to *him*, Eve. Fucking hell! To *me*. I told you, I can't be with you like that anymore."

Eve's face crumpled. Arthur hadn't ever seen anything like it. It was like James had snuffed out her effusive light, somehow. "But, last night—"

"Last night was a mistake," James said firmly. Arthur felt those words crash around them, hurting his ears even though they'd been uttered quietly.

Eve blinked rapidly. An errant tear managed to escape and roll down her cheek. She looked like a different person, younger and older at the same time, somehow.

Bill popped his head into the room. "Alright, we're set to roll tape."

Eve dashed the tear from her cheek and stood up defiantly. "Right. Let's get to it."

She shouldered past James and through the door into the sound booth. James rubbed his face with his hands. When he looked up at Arthur, he looked stricken.

"Arthur, I didn't mean—"

"No, that's okay," Arthur said, standing up. "It's fine. If I were you, I wouldn't want to share her either."

The way James stared at him made him feel like his skin was a size too small, so Arthur slipped past him and went to sit at the Rhodes.

<h1 style="text-align:center">20</h1>

After two practice takes, it became clear that the Tarts were amateurs. It was disappointing, really. The energy and life and magic that happened on stage at the Extemp was sucked up into the vacuum of this tiny space, with only Bill to react to. And Bill was not very reactive.

"That's fine," Bill droned through the two-way comm. "Let's go one more time and then we'll isolate the vocals."

That was the other problem. Eve kept making mistakes. Her usual swagger was cracked and muted. Her voice was strained. Arthur could feel the tension between her and James, permeating like a guitar string pulled too tight, ready to snap at any moment. Eve's face was the same way, tight and sharp.[1]

They played "I've Been Here" once more through. As if Eve's strain weren't enough, Arthur would have been lying if he'd said Deb was in top form. She was also making a lot of careless mistakes. It was kind of embarrassing to give such a poor showing in front of a producer who was used to working with people like B. B. King.

"Well, that'll have to do," Bill commed in. Humiliating. "Let's have the young lady isolate her vocals. Eve, right? Pull

---

1. "She Shook Me Cold" David Bowie

down those headphones, and I'll play the track through there. Sing your parts and give me everything you got."

Eve nodded, setting the large, padded headphones over her head. Her mouth was tight and pinched.

"The rest of y'all get back in the control room for now." Bill added. "Don't want any residual noise in the track."

Arthur nodded and followed James and Deb into the control room. Eve's eyes followed James with a look set to kill. What the hell had Arthur stepped into?

Deb collapsed onto the far side of the sofa and pulled a pillow over her face. Arthur took a seat on the other side, perching on the edge and massaging his forehead with his fingers. What were they going to do if they drove all this way just to blow it?

James hovered nearby, lighting another cigarette.

Bill put his headphones on, adjusted a few sliders, and spoke into the comm mic. "Alright, blow our minds."

And a bright red "Recording" sign flicked to life as the tape machine began to roll. Inside the control room, they couldn't hear but a dulled edge of Eve singing. The play-back track wasn't audible either. But they could hear what the mic was picking up, piped through a pair of speakers pointed at the chair Bill sat in.

"Hey," James whispered. Arthur was startled to find he was perched on the arm of the sofa right next to him. "What did Eve say to you?"

Eve sang the first verse, her voice increasingly tight and raw.

Arthur blinked up at James. "Uh, she said last night was, uh, good, and she wanted to do it again." The way they were talking around this in such polite terms made Arthur feel silly.

James nodded impatiently. "Right. Did she say why?"

Arthur crossed his arms. He really stepped in it now, didn't he? Was this his divine punishment for betraying James to begin with? "She said you two used to be together but drifted apart. And last night felt like it used to and she thought I was the reason."

"'Drifted apart'?" James repeated. He gave a frustrated frown and shook his head, taking an angry drag on his cigarette. "Yeah, Arthur, we didn't 'drift apart,' okay? I broke up with her."

Arthur glanced up, looking into the sound booth, and saw Eve watching him through the glass. Her eyebrows were a slash of mounting concern as her eyes flicked between him and James, but she kept singing.

"Why?" Arthur asked in a hushed voice.

"Because I couldn't give her what she wanted," James replied obtusely. "Listen, Arthur, I love Eve. She is my best friend. But she wants things from me that I can't give her. And I don't want you to get stuck in the middle of it."

Arthur didn't want to get stuck in the middle of it either. But it was kind of too late for that now. "Why?"

James was caught off guard. "Because," he spluttered, "it's not fair to you."

Eve reached for the high note on the chorus.

"No, the other part. If you love her, why can't you give her what she wants?"

Eve's voice cracked and squeaked on a sour note several steps below what she was usually able to reach.

James shook his head and scoffed. "I should think that's pretty obvious by now."

"Fuck!" Her curse was amplified into the room. "I'm—I'm gonna need a minute."

And she pulled the headphones off, dropped them onto the floor, and dashed out of the room.

"Shit," James swore. He stood up and went out into the hall.

"Ugh, what now?" Deb groaned from under her pillow.

Arthur stood up and followed James out into the hall. He was stalking down it toward the entrance, where Eve was swinging out the door.

"Eve, wait, it's gonna be fine," he called. "Come on, Evie, this is our chance! Don't blow it. Please!"

Eve whirled around in the doorway. "Don't. Follow. Me." She slammed the door in his face.

James turned around and looked at Arthur. He looked entirely at a loss, confused and a little scared.

Deb craned her head out the door behind Arthur. "Did she actually just bail?" Deb did not appear to find this amusing.

"Y'all, if you ain't ready to do this right now, you need to let me know before I waste any more tape."

Deb gave Bill a self-deprecating grin. "Sorry, man, just give us one little second here, and we'll be right back on track."

She slipped out the door to the control room and shut it behind her. Then, she turned to Arthur and James and the fury on her face made Arthur feel a fraction of his actual size.

"Whatever the *fuck* is going on between all of you, I'm gonna need you to stick your dicks back in your pants for five fucking minutes so we can actually record the demo that I've been working on getting for *five fucking weeks*."

James glowered at her. "If anyone is dragging their dick all over the place, it's *her*." He threw a thumb at the door Eve had just gone out.

Deb took a step forward and squared her shoulders. James was at least eight inches taller than her, but she was dense and pissed off and looked like she wouldn't hesitate to go straight for the nuts. "I'm gonna need you to shut the fuck up, Jim-boy, before I slap that stupid mouth straight off your face. You know how she is about you. You *know* better."

Arthur startled when Deb then turned her ire on him. "And *you*, new kid. I don't know what all kind of bullshit you've been tossing around, but let me give you a little advice, straight from me to you. Step the *fuck* back. You are here to play piano. Keep your hands and your fucking dick to yourself."

Arthur crossed his arms. He'd fucking had it. "Then why don't you tell me what the hell is going on here? There's clearly more to this than just a bunch of 'friends having fun.'"

"Now is not the time, asshole," Deb declared, and stalked off to the front door. As she opened it, she turned back and pointed at James. "Go tell Bill I'm gonna get Evie back. In the meantime, go lay down some guitar and piano tracks. Don't waste a goddamn second. *God*, I have to do everything."

Her boots squeaked as she turned out the door and slammed it. It rattled in its frame. Arthur stared after her incredulously. What the hell was that all about? What the hell was any of this all about? He'd had it up to here with the obtuse bullshit. He turned to James to say as much, but hesitated. James' throat bobbed as he swallowed, and he buried his face in his hands.

"Hey, man," Arthur said quietly after a long moment. "You okay?"

James took a deep breath in through his fingers and when he looked up, his face had been schooled into his usual, impassive mask. "Yup, I'm good. Let's get these tracks laid down."

Arthur nodded in spite of himself. He wasn't proud of how easily he was put off, but he hadn't ever seen James quite so ... ruffled.

Bill was unamused but cautiously agreeable to the plan. "Fine, but they better get back quick. Last thing I need is to waste an afternoon."

James recorded his guitar first. His solos were superb. Arthur fiddled around with a cigarette that he ultimately didn't barely smoke, watching James' fingers fly over the fretboard through the glass. He'd spent all this time thinking James had been heartsick for Eve, but it had been the other way around, hadn't it? And why? *Isn't it obvious?* What did that mean? Last night, James had been ... well, into it. It didn't make sense that he couldn't give Eve what she wanted, especially if she was the hedonist he claimed her to be. He was in possession of a big prick and he appeared to know how to use it. What could be the problem?

Arthur suspected it had to do with him. Was it that Eve liked having multiple partners and James wasn't interested in that?

Did Arthur present an acceptable, trustworthy alternative for her? But then what about Deb? Fuck, this was so confusing. And the worst part of it was, Arthur had his own agenda. Maybe that was James' issue. Maybe it had been too gay for him? Maybe it wasn't gay enough? Arthur could almost believe it, but he also knew he had a tendency to insert his own desires and fears into situations, drumming up a lot more stress and heartache than was warranted. Besides, he couldn't shake that image in his mind of James driving into Eve, the aggression and defiance in his expression as he looked at Arthur. Wasn't the point of being a gay man that one wasn't interested in women? Wasn't it supposed to make men soft or weak somehow? There had been nothing weak about James last night. Arthur could see it in himself—the fear that closed him off. But not in James. There was nothing cowardly about him.

James finished his guitar lines and the girls still weren't back. So Arthur got up and bashed the shit out of the Rhodes' keyboard. All the confused longing that was trapped inside his chest poured out his fingers and into the piano.

When he looked up at the control room, Arthur felt his heart thump to see Deb muttering to James. As soon as the take was over, he set the headphones down and crossed to the door to find out what was going on.

"Any sign of Eve?" Arthur asked, trying to ignore Bill's annoyed, closed-off posture as he leaned back in his chair waiting for them to get their shit together.

Deb opened her mouth, then paused. "Yes, but … well, I think I made it worse."

James buried his face in his hands again. There was something about it that made Arthur want to gently pat his shoulder. "Fuck, Deb, what did you do?"

Deb pursed her lips and crossed her arms. "I might have pointed out that it was hypocritical of her to expect me to feel bad for her."

James literally gripped his hair in his fists and pulled. "Deb! Fuuuuck."

"I know," Deb replied guiltily. Her pompadour was flagging, strands of greased, black locks springing free. "I just—my head's killing me, and I couldn't think straight. Regardless. She went back to the motel."

"Do you think we should follow her?" Arthur asked.

Bill cleared his throat, calling attention to himself extremely effectively. "I'm sure all this is very important and all, but I'mma need you to figure yourselves out and get something laid down in the next hour or so. I got dinner plans."

Deb swallowed hard. "Yessir."

Bill groaned as he got out of his chair. Arthur got the sense it was less because he was old and struggling to get up, and more because he'd completely run out of patience with their ill-timed dramatic interlude. "I'm gonna step out for a cigarette. When I get back, you're gonna have a plan."

Deb nodded. "Yessir."

Bill walked out the door muttering, probably something about how he was too old for this shit. When the door clicked back into the jam, James finally emerged from his hands.

"We have to do a different song," he said dejectedly.

"I dunno. You could probably sing 'I've Been Here.'" Deb shrugged.

"I can't." James shook his head. "I don't have the range to pull that song off. Christ, it would turn into a Bob Dylan song if I tried, but with shittier lyrics."

"I could try," Arthur said quietly. Deb and James turned to look at him like they'd forgotten he was there. This was awkward. Because Arthur knew he had the range to sing the song. He had a good voice. He'd spent enough hours in his basement singing along with Diva singers when his parents were at church functions. But he certainly didn't have the swagger, nor the simple base-line confidence. What if he fucked it up? Or he was too stiff or stale? And what would happen when Eve heard it, heard his voice singing her song after she got her heart ripped out and threw away her chance to record it?

James' eyes studied him for a moment. "We should do 'Hammer Your Heart.'"

"We don't have time to lay down a whole new song," Deb protested.

"Could we try both?" Arthur asked. "We could try 'Hammer Your Heart' and then double back to try vocals on 'I've Been Here' if there's time?"

"Yeah, that's a good idea," James said. "Besides, bands who need to lay down each track separately don't sound as good as a band that records together. You lose that collective energy."

"Good point, Mr. Producer," Deb raised a brow that dripped with sarcasm. "Besides, Eve will probably murder Ohashi if he sings her song after all this."

James was quiet. Arthur scratched the back of his neck awkwardly.

"Ah fuck it," Deb said finally. "Let's give it a try. If she wants to be pissed, let her. She's the one who walked out."

When Bill came back, they were all at their instruments in the sound booth.

"Y'all ready?" Bill asked over the comm mic.

"Yeah," James said into his mic. "We're gonna try a different song, just all together. Then can I lay down the bass track on top, if there's time?"

Bill fixed a scrutinous eye on them for a moment. "Sure you wanna do that?"

"Yeah," James replied. "If it stinks, just tell us, and we can finish the song we started with."

Bill raised a brow incredulously. "Okay." His tone was high and cynical, but he put a new reel of tape into the machine and asked them to check their tuning. Then, the red "Recording" sign flickered to life, a twin of the one in the control room, and Arthur laid his fingers on the Rhodes keyboard.[2]

In the span of the opening bars, Arthur had a moment of panic. This song wasn't the high energy swagger The Tarts were all about. It wasn't even blues. It was Arthur's, and it felt different. It was heavy on the keys, with a mid-range tempo and a meandering form of verses, pre-choruses, and a bridge that built and mounted and took over the song till the end. In many ways, it didn't even feel done. Too late to worry about that now.

He closed his eyes and sang. He tried to land himself back in his parents' house, looking out the frosty window onto the wintery wasteland of West St. Paul when he was fifteen. Feel that freezing temperature in his church, in his school, in everyone he met regardless of what time of year it was. 'Hammer Your Heart' was an ode to Arthur's shell, his tatemae, hammering out a private space to protect oneself, where it was safe to think your own thoughts, where no one could hurt you.

"What would you do / When the world's so cruel / You can't be a real man / So why not dress the fool?"

James had suggested those lyrics. Arthur had originally had "the world so still," and rhymed it with, of all the ever-loving idiotic things, "might as well chill". Thank god for collaboration with a person who didn't just know how to write lyrics, but also knew him. That thought did something twisty and foreboding in his stomach as he played the final chord of the song.

"Cool, man."

Arthur shook his head. The voice was coming through the headphones clapped over his ears. He looked up at Bill in the control room and the corner of his mouth was turned up, like he might be thinking about smiling.

"Try that again, but tighten it up. Get it in the pocket and you might have something."

---

2. Feels like "Rock 'n' Roll Suicide" David Bowie

Arthur blinked, then nodded. He really wasn't sure he could do it again.

"Don't get in your head, kid," Bill added. "You clearly have something to say. So sing it with conviction. And don't block out your band. They're making the wave your voice is riding."

Arthur nodded again and glanced over at the others. James lifted his eyebrows encouragingly. Arthur let out the breath he'd been holding as everyone took a moment to shift and reset. He couldn't shake that pit in his stomach, though. And when he looked at James, who was watching him with those sharp, blue eyes, the pit bottomed out. Shit, he was going to fuck this all up. Not just the recording, but the music, the performances, the whole band. Since when did Arthur become the kind of person who could set off a powder keg?

The "Recording" sign flicked back on and Arthur had no choice but to push through. He allowed himself to drop into the emptiness that was threatening to flip him inside out, into a vacuumous black hole. Fine. Let it. That's what the song was about anyway.

It hurt. Not physically, but he let that infuse his voice, quiet and raw, as he sang the lyrics from the top.

"Hammer your heart / Hammer your heart / Hammer your heart into shape. Turn it to stone / Plate it with steel / Whatever it takes to stay safe."

Arthur realized he was swaying, riding the force of Deb's beat and James' full, crunchy guitar. He didn't dare let himself imagine what he must look like. He clung to the lyrics with a vice grip, pressing his lips to the hard wire mesh of the mic and wringing all the loneliness he could from the Rhodes.

He didn't understand what had been happening since they left Minneapolis—with Eve, with James, nor with himself. But whatever it was, it was cracking him open, along with his voice. He leaned into the break. He couldn't save this whole thing, couldn't pull them all up with him, but fuck if he wasn't going to try. He pushed harder. Wailed. Let the guitar licks fuel him, felt them in his gut. Slammed his fingers into the keys. Threw everything he had into that microphone.

"*Lay back and let it ride / Surrender to the beat inside / Hear that voice that cuts to the quick / And bleed out that ice that's been making you sick.*"

When it was done, he tried not to slump. He took in a deep, quavering breath.

"*That's* what I'm talking about," Bill crowed. "That'll do it."

Arthur nodded. He looked up at Deb and James. Deb looked mildly approving. James looked ... well. Arthur choked on the thought that flowed out of the crack he'd made in his own resolve. James looked perfect. Completely perfect, sweat beading on his forehead and a grin slashing across his face. And the feeling of it filled Arthur up all the way. Filled in all the spaces, all the cracks till he overflowed. Shit, shit, shit.

Arthur swallowed it down. "Great, thanks."

When the van pulled into the parking lot of the motel, they came upon Eve sitting on the curb outside their room on top of her packed bag. The rest of their bags were piled up next to her. Her makeup was streaked and smudged, like she'd been crying.

"Christ," James muttered as he pulled up in front of her and stomped down on the parking brake. He pushed his car door open as Eve stood.

"No, don't get out," her voice was scratchy and unaccented, her eyes hooded and tired. Still upset, then. "I need you to drive me to the airport."

"What? Why?" James replied incredulously.

"Because my grandma is dying." She let that sink in for a moment while she struggled to keep her expression composed. "While you and Deb were busy blaming me for messing up after all the nasty shit you said to me, my dad was leaving a message at the motel. My grandma is dying, and he's wiring me money to buy a ticket to London. So if you would be so kind, can you please drive me to the airport so I can have the *ghost* of a chance of seeing her," Eve's angry facade cracked, "before she goes?"

James' tight shoulders lowered. "Shit. I thought she was getting better?"

"Apparently not," Eve sniffed. She lifted her bag and rounded the van. Arthur scrambled out of the passenger seat and met her at the rear of the van.

"I'll get that for you," he mumbled, reaching for the bag. She blinked at him a moment, the anger and fear melting from her expression and leaving her features tired and wan. She dropped the bag into his hand, then climbed into the passenger door he'd left open.

Arthur yanked the side door and tossed the bag to Deb. Then, he rounded the van again and gathered up the rest of their bags. He threw the armful into the side door towards the music gear as he climbed in and shut the door behind him. He perched awkwardly on one of the bean bags as James put the van in first gear.[1]

"Do you know how to get to the airport?" James called to Deb over his shoulder.

"There's two," Deb replied. "Evie, which one does your dad want you to go to?"

Eve's eyes widened for a moment, huge and brown and murky, before her face crumpled. "I don't know! I didn't know there was more than one!"

"Hey, it's okay," James said assuringly. He reached out and rubbed his hand over her shoulder as it shook with tears. "We'll just stop at the office and call him."

"He's already gone," Eve snapped, flinching her shoulder away from him.

Deb leaned over the back of the seat. "Evie. Take a deep breath."

"Deb, just leave me alone. Let me think." Eve rubbed her temples and took a deep breath anyway.

Arthur squirmed. He felt like a voyeur, stuck in this van and observing this scene of vulnerable desperation. Which is why it took him a moment before he said, "On our way here, you said you laid over at the airport here once. Was that on your way to London?"

---

1. "Girl" T. Rex

"Right!" Deb added. "At O'Hare!"

"Mmhm," Eve murmured as she swallowed, passing a hand over her face. "Yes. That's right."

"Okay, that makes sense." Deb said. "That's where most of the international flights go out. Go up Michigan Street, Jim, and turn left on 35th. You gotta get back on 94."

They drove in silence for a long time, James navigating the highway traffic and the radio emitting a low fuzz of white noise, tuned to some station they could no longer get in. Arthur wedged himself on the bean bag behind the pony wall, curled around himself. He felt guilty. He should never have let himself get tangled up in between Eve and James. If it weren't for him, they'd all be able to easily swoop in to support Eve, instead of sitting in this awkward liminal space between fighting and helping.

"Eve," James' voice breached the silence. "I'm sorry."

Eve didn't reply.

"I'm really sorry. I led you on. Again. God, I shouldn't have done that. That's what I meant when I said it was a mistake. *I* made a mistake. I fucked up and I'm so sorry."

Arthur shrank inside of himself. He didn't know why that felt so shitty to hear. But it did. It made him feel like a regret, a problem to be covered up and disguised. And it hurt, because for him, last night had been a revelation. He finally felt like he understood what he wanted. But if James thought it was a mistake, if he'd only done it in a moment of weakness for Eve ... well. Never mind then. Arthur looked over at Deb. She was looking up at the front seat, but her eyes flicked to him when she felt his gaze. She put a finger to her lips and shook her head.

"I don't know why, after everything, you can still do this to me," Eve whimpered.

James' hands gripped the steering wheel as he lowered his head.

"I don't mean to," he mumbled helplessly. "I didn't mean for any of this to happen."

That made Eve hiccup on a quiet sob. Arthur stewed, a cruel thought leaping to his mind. It was poetically ironic that all this trouble had started with Eve's own insistence that sex was just a bit of fun that didn't mean anything. How wrong she'd been, for herself more than anyone else. It was a bitter thought, but it soothed his hurt so he let it stay for a while.

Silence seeped into the carpet on the walls of the van, into the woven fabric seats, until it overwhelmed the sour scent of stale hash.

"Evie, you know I love you," James added helplessly.

"You're the only one I've ever wanted," she sniffled. "I don't understand why you're also the only one who doesn't want me."

"I do," James insisted. "I do want you. I love you. You're my best friend."

"You know that's not what I mean."

Silence again. Thick and cloying, fizzing like the white noise from the radio. Arthur hugged his knees as the cracks and potholes of the highway jostled him and Deb about. A deep and abiding bitterness stewed in his gut and he let it. He understood Eve didn't want him. Neither did James, for that matter. These two idiotic, beautiful people had some stupid past that made it impossible for them to be together, even though they loved one another. Arthur was some footnote on their love story, one that was destined to either resolve or end in tragedy and heartbreak. The latter seemed likely, at this point. They'd pulled him into the middle of their schism, and while they were declaring tragic love from either side of the precipice, Arthur was tumbling down the chasm like so much wasted refuse. Sitting in the back of the van, forgotten, forced to listen to two people he'd never belong to try and mend their relationship without him.

Arthur would have done it, too. He would have agreed to try and be with both of them, even though he had no idea what that meant. If it could have helped, he would have tried. He worshipped Eve. And Arthur had never met someone who made him feel like James did—like he was cool. But when all was said and done, James had chosen nothing instead. Was Arthur that detestable?

After hitting a respectable cruising speed for about twenty minutes, James exited on Highway 194. They hit stop and go again. Signs pointed out that the airport was a few miles away. A few miles and an eternity of being trapped in this wretched van.

Eve cleared her throat. "How did the recording end up?"

Deb's eyes met Arthur's. She grimaced silently.

"It was good," James said. "As good as it could be, I mean. Who knows if we'll get anything usable out of it."

Arthur grimaced. God, he wished he could just drop through the floor of the van and dash himself upon the pavement. Deb smacked his knee, and he looked up at her. She shook her head vigorously, mouthed, *He's lying*. Arthur frowned rather pitifully. Deb poked him, her expression severe. She shook her head. She pointed at him. Then she did the gesture of a joyful, satisfied chef kissing the air. It was ridiculous enough to make him crack a wan smile.

"I'm sorry I bailed." Eve mumbled.

"It's okay. It was understandable."

Was it?

Arthur chided himself for being so ungenerous. He didn't know how far back this went. All he knew was that it had been really shitty of her to leave them all hanging after all they'd done—especially Deb—to get them that one chance. It wasn't fair, but he wished she'd had the wherewithal to just get the job done. It put them all in an awkward position, because they'd chosen to proceed without her.

"Even if we just get an instrumental, it's still something," Eve said. "I could sing over the recording for my cousin, see if we've got something we can work with."

Deb's eyes went wide. She pulled out a scrap of paper from her pocket and scratched something on it with a stubby pencil.

Arthur craned his neck to see what she was writing. *Get "I've Been Here" instrumental track.* Wow. Everyone was right back to jumping to Eve's every whim, it seemed. Arthur leaned against the pony wall and tried very hard not to give an exasperated sigh.

"Then maybe," Eve continued, her voice regaining some of her usual verve, "we can all go out to London next summer, like a tour. Play as many of the clubs as we can."

Deb looked up from her note, eyebrows all the way in her pompadour with surprise. "Really?" she blurted.

Eve turned and looked back at the two of them hiding on bean bags in the back. Arthur felt like a little cowering toad.

"Yeah," she said lightly. "Of course, darling."

She reached forward, then, and turned the dial on the radio. A station playing "Raindrops Keep Falling on My Head" crackled into tune. The twangy guitar cut through the acrid silence with such relief, Arthur forgot to be annoyed with how much he hated this song.

It took the rest of the song to get into the airport terminal. Flippity trumpets and back-up singers were "doo-doo-doo"ing as James pulled up along the curb of the terminal drop-off. Eve looked down into her lap, then up at James.

"I hope you get the closure you need," James said, reaching out and pulling her into a half hug. "With your grandma, I mean."

She smiled feebly. "Thanks for the ride."

Then she reached up and cupped James' face with her hand. She kissed him, tenderly on the lips. And he let her. Arthur squeezed his eyes closed. He didn't want to see this. He didn't want any of this. He'd cracked his shell and it kept, well, leaking unwanted feelings all over the place. Big ones—angry, jealous, bitter feelings that he had to find a hiding place for so he could be a functional human being.

Eve cracked the door and slid out of the van. Then she opened the side door, pouring late afternoon sunlight in on top of cowering Arthur.

"Can you toss me my bag, darling?" she asked. Her accent was back, but her face was still so tired. Arthur nodded, not trusting his voice, then reached across the Rhodes amp to yank her bag out. He held it out to her. Eve stared at it for a moment.

"Aren't you going to get in the front?" she asked. Arthur blinked up at her for a moment. Then Deb kicked him.

"It's all yours, Ohashi. I'm taking a nap on the beanbags the rest of the way home."

Arthur half fell out of the van and stood awkwardly before Eve. It took everything he had to stamp down his frustration and bitterness and say graciously, "I hope you get there in time."

She smiled kindly at him.

"Thank you, darling." She pecked a kiss on his cheek. A stark departure from how she'd treated him previously—and how she'd bid farewell to James. "Don't do anything I wouldn't do."

Deb guffawed as Eve smiled wryly and turned to walk into the airport terminal. Even exhausted and heartbroken, she still turned heads in her boots and miniskirt.

Arthur slipped into the front seat. "Do we have to wait and see if she's got the right one?"

James put the van into gear and pulled out. "She'll be fine," he muttered.

And he didn't say another word, apart from "Anyone need to stop for the toilet?" for the rest of the drive back to Minneapo-lis.[2]

It was dark and raining when they got back. Almost midnight. Arthur had dozed on the drive. It had been a blessed relief from the stoney quiet, different radio stations drifting in and out of tune, the intermeaning times filled with fuzz and Deb's soft snores. James pulled up in front of the New Riverside Cafe and stomped the parking brake before climbing out and stretching hugely.

---

2. "Oh Sweet Nuthin'" The Velvet Underground

Arthur pushed his door open as well, felt the blood return to his toes as he stood. He should probably say something, but he didn't. He'd stewed over a hundred things he'd like to say, but he was ashamed to acknowledge he was too scared. He opened the side door and saw Deb laid out over the bean bags, one of them curled up against her chest like a stuffed animal.

"Deb, we're back," he said. His voice sounded scratchy with fatigue.

Deb snorted as she woke. "Ohshit," she mumbled. "I'm up, I'm up."

The three of them quickly loaded all the gear back up to the apartment in the rain. (It should have seemed harder without Eve there to help, but it didn't. Because she didn't usually help.)

Deb set her drum bags on the floor of the back room and said, "Well, that was a shit show." She turned and looked up at Arthur and James. "Are you guys gonna say anything or what?"

"What do you want me to say?" James replied with a resigned shrug.

"I dunno," Deb mirrored his shrug sarcastically. "Maybe 'Thanks for getting us that gig, Deb, even though we fucked it up pretty royally because we can't keep our dicks in our pants.'"

Arthur turned bright red. He could feel the heat burst into his cheeks. He couldn't look at James. Because the blush wasn't as much embarrassment as it was anger. Of any of them, he was the least at fault. The stupid pawn in all their games to manipulate each other.

"Don't act like you weren't contributing your own brand of bullshit," James retorted to Deb. He seemed like he was girding up, and Arthur really couldn't take another minute of this.

"Thanks Deb," Arthur muttered, picking up his duffel bag. "It sure was something."

And he turned out of the room and made a bee-line for the apartment door. He felt like he could breathe again when he got in the hall. When he strode outside, it got even better, until he was back at Comstock, keying into his room and dropping his duffel to the floor with such sweet relief he thought his knees might just crumple beneath him. He scarcely paused to shut the door before he crossed to his wardrobe, shucked his t-shirt and jeans off, and curled into his kimono. He dropped the needle onto The Velvet Underground and laid back onto his pillows until the relentless viola drone buzzed his brain into sweet nothing.

22

There was a loud knocking on the door. Arthur froze. It was way too late for a visitor. Maybe if he pretended the music was too loud and he couldn't hear, whoever it was would go away.

"Arthur, open up, it's me." James' voice. Arthur's heart jumped up into his throat, but he still didn't move.

"Arthur, I know you're in there."

He had no interest in more tangled webs of love quadrangle bullshit. Lou Reed was crying on the record player. Rain was pattering steadily on the windowpane. He looked down at his long kimono sleeves.

"You don't have to hide the kimono. I don't care. Just let me in, it's important."

Arthur found himself standing then. He couldn't imagine what could be so important, James had walked across campus in the middle of the night in the rain. Couldn't it wait until morning? His fractured, tired mind produced ample catastrophes. A plane crash, chief among them. It was absurd, but no one ever expected a horrible tragedy. That's what made it tragic. He crossed the room and unlocked the door, opening it just a crack. He peeked out around the edge. And there he was. James, a little sodden, with the golden hair and the face made of hard planes and slashes, his eyes soft and open and so fucking blue it hurt. Arthur tried to glare at him and failed.

"I need to talk to you," James said quietly. "Can I come in?"

Arthur glanced around the hallway. "It's kind of late."

"I know. I just—uh, it can't wait."

Arthur studied him for a moment. "Fine." Then he opened the door just enough to let James in, hiding himself behind it all the while. James stepped into the room as Arthur shut the door behind him. He had an unlit cigarette in his fingers and he was twisting it to smithereens. Some flakes of tobacco fell to the floor. As James turned around, those eyes regarded Arthur with startled reverence for a moment, sliding up and down the silk enrobing him until they landed on his mouth. It was a look that made Arthur feel simultaneously exposed and powerful.

God, fuck, stop it, he shouted at himself inwardly. *Just stop! It was a mistake! You were a mistake! Give it up already!*

"Do you want a drink or something?" Arthur asked uselessly, unsure if he even had anything to make good on the offer.

"No, thanks," James said, pressing his lips together. He noticed the cigarette in his hands as if for the first time and pocketed it furtively.

"What's wrong?" Arthur asked, pulling the edges of the kimono together self-consciously and crossing his arms over them. "Is Eve okay? I mean, did she get to London okay?"

"I, um," James mumbled, then reached up to scratch his head. "Yeah, I assume so. I haven't heard from her. I need to talk to you about something else."

Arthur's heart was trying to crawl into his mouth now. Stop, stop, *stop.* "Oh?"

"Yeah," James was looking everywhere but at Arthur. He stuffed his hands into his pockets and mumbled something to the floor.

"What's that?" Arthur asked. His voice was tinny and desperate and he hated it.

"Nothing, nothing," James replied. "I—god, fuck. I—" he laughed uselessly "—didn't think this would be so hard."

Arthur felt his shoulders shrink. "I'm out of the band, aren't I?"

"What? Fuck, Arthur, no!" James cut in, shocked into motion. He stepped forward and grabbed Arthur by the arms. "Hell no. I just. I need to…"

The air between them sparked and hissed. Arthur looked the few inches up at James, into his impossible blue eyes. Arthur's brows knit together speculatively. He tipped his chin up slightly. He let his lips part as he inhaled. James' eyes went dark as a tempest, and his head jerked towards Arthur's before he hesitated. *Oh*. Arthur felt a surge of power pulse through him, bombshell energy hissing encouragingly. He looked down at one of James' hands on his shoulder, then back up at James. *Don't do anything I wouldn't do.*[1]

Arthur tentatively moved his hands onto James' t-shirt, feeling the heat and the pound of his heart matching the heightened pace of Arthur's own. He was not making this up. His imagination wasn't conjuring interest where there was none. James had come all the way across campus in the middle of the night in the rain for Arthur. Just for him.

Shit. He'd had this whole thing figured wrong. He'd blinded himself with conventional self-doubt to the point of idiocy.

Arthur tipped his chin up as he pulled James toward him by his coat lapels, which were still studded with raindrops. It was like setting off a perpetual motion machine, because from that slight tug, James' whole body surged towards him. And then all Arthur could see was cumulus sunset curls and gilded eyelashes casting shadows over his cheek as James pressed his lips against Arthur's, and pressed Arthur against the closed door.

Arthur couldn't help but gasp. Clutch at James' lapels. Pull him closer. His lips were hard, insistent, and he grasped Arthur's face with his hands as he sucked in Arthur's air. And Arthur melted against him, tasting tobacco and whiskey and

---

1. "Could I" Slade

pulling, pulling on those lapels like there was somewhere closer James could be.

Arthur pushed his hands up to burrow into James' hair, to clasp the back of his neck. He tipped his chin up to snatch a gasp of breath. James kissed and nibbled along Arthur's jaw.

"You're gay," Arthur murmured and then felt a crash of mortification when he realized he said it aloud.

He felt James' mouth curl into a smile against his neck. "Whatever gave you that idea?"

"I've been a total idiot," Arthur concluded, fingers curling into James' damp hair, holding him close. "All this time, I kept telling myself that it was you and Eve, you and Eve. No place for me, it was you and her. And I'm a fucking idiot. It's not you and her, because you're gay."

James drew away just enough to look at him. "You're seriously just putting this together now?"

Arthur felt so stupid he said, "Well, yes, but to be fair, you—"

"What? Sucked you off?"

"Well, yeah, but—"

"Yeah, but *what??*"

"You had sex with Eve!" Arthur could still see the image of it imprinted on the inside of his eyelids. "There's an equal amount of sex acts in this equation, so don't act like I should have known which one meant something to you."

James stared at him a moment. Then, he sighed and straightened. The inches created in the space between them felt like waking up without a blanket, cold and wanting. "I know. That was a huge mistake. —Having sex with her, not anything between you and I. Up until Saturday, I hadn't done that with her since I came out of the closet but—no, Arthur, I'm telling you now. I'm completely gay."

Arthur remembered James' eyes drilling into him, the fierce, aggressive expression on his face as he fucked Eve. Was that how he looked at people he liked? Arthur tried to be irritated or unsettled, but all he could manage was a bloom of arousal.

"Is that what Eve meant," Arthur spoke to his toes, "when you caught her and I out that first time? Is that what she meant about you being jealous? That you were jealous of her? Not me?"

"Yeah. I was jealous of her," James tilted his head. "I've been interested in you for a while, Arthur. And she knew it."

"Why didn't you say anything earlier?"

"I didn't think I had to!" James seemed exasperated. "You walked me to a gay rights protest. I thought you knew. And when you kept going after Eve, I thought you just weren't interested."

Arthur sighed and tipped his head back against the door. "I have been so confused."

"I tried to talk to you about it. That night I walked you back here, after the Halloween party."

Arthur tried to recall. He'd been wine drunk and downtrodden and—shit, really fucking stupid. Because James had been trying to ask him something, and Arthur had cut him off and made it about Eve. He hadn't given James a chance. He should have fucking known. His insecure distorted thinking had run *circles* around him. God, this was embarrassing.

"I—I'm sorry if I should have picked up on it, but I didn't know."

"What about you?" Furtive blue glance.

"What *about* me?"

"Well, I dunno. I don't want to put words in your mouth, but..." James gestured between the two of them, at his kiss-swollen mouth and the heat that radiated in the canyon of inches between them.

"Am I gay?" Arthur asked quietly. The words felt foreign in his mouth. He bit his lip. "It's a notion that has been increasingly ... persistent. I'm not straight. I can say that with one hundred percent certainty."

James' brows knit together earnestly. "How long have you known?" It felt like there was a right answer to this question, but Arthur didn't know what it was.

"Well..." Probably since he had met James, to be entirely honest. Or since listening to Lola. But he couldn't say a stupid song had flipped a switch in him. "Since you walked in on me and Eve."

James flushed this time. "Yeah, sorry about that. I was really fucking pissed."

"You were really fucking hot."

"No," James took Arthur's face in both his hands. "That was you." James kissed him again, slowly. "In that slip." Another kiss. "I wanted you so fucking bad." Lips and a taste of tongue that made Arthur shudder. "And she had you. And I hated her for it."

"How long?" Arthur whispered into James' mouth.

"Have I known I'm gay?" he clarified.

"No, since you knew you, you know, wanted..." God, this was fishing for compliments. Arthur tried to curb his wince.

"You?" he confirmed quietly. Arthur nodded, shamefaced. "Fuck, since the minute I saw you in this thing." James flipped the edge of the kimono back with his fingers. "I'm glad everyone was so tanked that night we came up here, because my interest was not a secret."

He pressed his hips against Arthur as if in emphasis. His interest certainly wasn't a secret. Any remaining question as to whether or not Arthur was attracted to men disintegrated. This wasn't the slick, enticing pull that Eve had on him when she took her clothes off. The slink of the forbidden laid out for him to feast upon. This felt *different*. This was suffocatingly, achingly hot. It was that desperate pull he'd longed for, vulnerable and powerful at the same time. That sort of animal magnetism that pulled people together, made it impossible for them to do anything except to touch, to kiss, to try and reach some higher state together. He pulled on James' lapels again. He thought he might burst out of his skin wherever James touched him. James' eyes widened, dark and predatory, and Arthur lifted his chin desperately. If James didn't kiss him now, he felt like he might die.

James didn't kiss him. Not as such. He watched Arthur carefully with those limitless eyes and pushed his hands up beneath the edges of the kimono. His calloused fingertips skimmed over Arthur's skin, leaving trails of bright sensation across his ribs. His thumbs rubbed circles on Arthur's nipples, and Arthur could not help the yip of surprised pleasure that escaped his lips. Arthur pulled on the lapels again, pressing the proof of his own need into the hollow at James' hip. His shorts left little to the imagination.

"How do we do this?" Arthur had to ask. It was so awkward, but he didn't know. Felatio? Did they take turns? Was there a way to do it together? To become, you know, one, for a moment? Sodomy was the sin, of course, but it wasn't like folks were walking around with instruction manuals explaining how to do it. After all, he'd only had sex twice before (kind of ... not really); he didn't want to fuck it up. Not now, when everything was out in the open and it felt so fucking good.

"Any way we want," James murmured, and his hand snaked down to palm Arthur's tenting shorts. His voice sounded eager, almost desperate. "I can use my hands. I can use my mouth. You can use me however you fucking want, Arthur. I don't care as long as it's you."

The force of those words could have knocked him to the floor. Arthur's hands squirmed up and snatched James' face. He yanked him into a kiss, one so hard that it kind of hurt. Hurt in the same exquisite, beautiful way that James' words hurt. Something that was so wonderful it hurt to imagine living without it, even though ten minutes ago, he'd had no idea it was his to begin with. The kind of foreboding joy that promised everything and threatened its loss simultaneously.

"Will you stay?" Arthur gasped as James pushed his hand inside his shorts.

"I thought you'd never ask," James growled.

His hard, long fingers pulled on Arthur's cock and light danced inside of Arthur's eyelids. His other hand swirled on Arthur's nipple again, the two hands applying pressure and pleasure such that Arthur had to tip his head back against the door and try not to moan too loudly.

"God, you're so fucking beautiful," James rumbled. "I love seeing you like this."

Arthur could feel the bundle of pleasure deep in his groin, compounding in density like a supernova forming. "Wait," he gasped, grasping James' wrist to hold him still. "I don't want this to be over yet."

"Even if you come, it won't be," James whispered, his chin rough with stubble that scraped below Arthur's ear. "We have all night. And tomorrow. And the next day." Kisses dusted over Arthur's neck. He lost his train of thought for a moment.

James pulled back then, fixing Arthur with an earnest expression. "I'm not Eve," he said plaintively.

"I can see that," Arthur quipped, belied by his breathlessness.

"I'm not like her. I don't want to float from person to person, never getting enough. You're plenty. More than I know what to do with, honestly."

"Same," Arthur rasped, pressing his lips to James'. "Same."

They kissed and kissed. Eventually, Arthur pushed James towards his inadequate narrow dorm bed. James shucked his coat and sat on its edge. Looking up, he pushed the silk off Arthur's shoulders, pressing his lips to his chest and his belly. He didn't sneer either when Arthur dashed away to hang the kimono carefully back in the wardrobe. He just smiled, his eyes clear and open and laughing, the way he had been when they jammed the Velvets together only Arthur was half naked now, and it suddenly felt quite overwhelming. So much so, he fell to his knees in front of James and started yanking his belt open.

"Oh fuck," James choked out.

"What's wrong?"

"Nothing..." James stared at him for a long moment. "Are you sure?"

"Of course." Arthur paused. "Just tell me if I'm doing it wrong."

"I'm not convinced there's much you could do wrong," James gulped, helping to shove his tight jeans down round his thighs. He grasped Arthur's face with both hands, swept a thumb over his lips. "You have perfect lips."

Arthur remembered the night of his first show. When he'd put on Eve's lipstick. James had dropped a plate in the kitchen. Arthur was indeed actually very stupid. "Just tell me what you like, okay? I'm apparently very slow on the uptake."

He released James' heavy cock from his shorts. It was rigid and the tip was glistening. Arthur had no earthly idea where the impulse came from—maybe it had been inspired by Eve's example—but he leaned forward and tasted it. Salty tang spread over his tongue. The firm, taut skin was like velvet against his lips.

"Fuck, Arthur." James watched him with wide eyes, shoulders tight like he was holding his breath. Arthur parted his lips again, pressed them around the head of James' cock.

"Please," James intoned, his voice deep and gravelly and desperate.

The word blanketed over Arthur like a warm mantle. He tipped his head impertinently and his eyes smiled as he obligingly pushed his mouth over James' long prick. It was thicker than he expected, filling his mouth, stretching his lips. Hot and heavy on his tongue. He pressed his tongue up against it, licked as he pulled off till just the head rested inside his lips. He looked up at James.

"Fuck, you're so beautiful," James gasped. "I don't know how—"

He cut off as Arthur pressed his lips up and around his cock again, sliding the head over the roof of his mouth. Arthur surged with power. *This.* This was it, man. The bombshell energy. He was beautiful, beguiling, enigmatic. And James was desperate and gasping in the palm of his hand. Quite literally. This was the stuff of a thousand songs, a thousand nights of lipstick and longing.

Arthur wrapped his fist around the base, pushed his lips up to meet it, then surged his tongue as he pulled back again. It made James grit out a loud groan and fling his head back against the wall. James' hands scrabbled into Arthur's hair, grasping and trembling. Arthur couldn't understand it. He'd scarcely done anything. Nothing like what James had done for him, bobbing and sucking and swirling and—shit, now Arthur's cock was so hard it hurt, and all he wanted was to wrap his other hand around and relieve it.

Arthur pulled off with a harsh gasp. "Is there any way we can do this together?"

James regarded him with hazy, wild eyes. "You mean come together?" His voice was heavy and breathless, his hair wantonly tousled.

"Yes," Arthur whispered. Was this a naive question?

"Definitely," James growled. He stood up and pulled Arthur to his feet. He gripped a hand at the back of Arthur's neck and pulled him in for a kiss. He had to have tasted himself in the kiss, but he didn't seem to care. His hand slid over Arthur's shoulder, down his chest, where his opposite hand met it at Arthur's waistband. He hooked his thumbs in and shoved the shorts down so they pooled at Arthur's feet. Those hands stroked indulgently back up over Arthur's ass, pulling his hips tight against James'. Arthur pushed himself up on his toes so that their cocks shoved against one another.

"Uhn," Arthur said articulately.

"Mm?" James, equally as articulate.

"Off," Arthur gasped into his mouth. He pulled at James' t-shirt. "I want to see you."

James reluctantly released him and stepped out of his disheveled jeans and boxer shorts, yanking his t-shirt over his head. He was too eager to be elegant, but it was a beautiful display regardless. Tight musculature stretched over long limbs, light golden hair dusting chest and arms and stomach and thighs. Arthur shoved James back on the bed, surprising both of them, then climbed over him, straddling his waist. It was the bombshell energy, that feeling of power and sex appeal. It was going to his head.

"Now what?" Arthur demanded breathlessly.

"Got lotion? Or Vaseline?"

"I think so. Why?" His voice sounded like Marilyn's, all breathy and soft. He loved it.

"It's better when it slides." James' head laid back on Arthur's pillow, his hair spread out over the cotton in gold-spun chaos. His lips were delicately sculpted, pink from kissing, and he looked flushed and wanton.

"Okay, yeah." Arthur reached across James to the drawer of his side table, where the record player sat, needle scratching the label of The Velvet Underground. He scrabbled for a jar of Ponds he'd nicked from his mother and proffered it in pathetic offering to James.

"Come here," James said as he unscrewed the lid. Arthur leaned in, pressing their pricks together as he bent for a kiss. James' slicked hands pushed between their bellies as he kissed Arthur back, curling his fingers around both of their cocks, slicking and aligning them together into a channel of his palms.

"Oh, god," Arthur whimpered. After so long with nothing but rough contact, the enclosure of James' hands felt euphoric. The slide of James' cock against his, hot and hard and slick, felt like illicit bliss, something at once both taboo and rapturous (perhaps because it was taboo). Arthur hung his body over James, slung between his shoulders. His hips moved in time with James' hands, sliding inside his tight grip, sending bolts of sensation firing to his every nerve ending. James' hips did this too and there became no need for his hands to do anything except grip them both together. Arthur realized his eyes were closed and he opened them, looking down at James. His gaze was hazy, like a storm of rain-laden clouds, but they saw with a sharpness Arthur couldn't quite comprehend.

"I want to see you come for me," Arthur murmured, then immediately blushed. He couldn't believe he'd uttered something so filthy. He was drunk on power, it wasn't his fault.

"Yeah?" James replied, his sharp chin jutting up as he sighed with delectation. Sweat beaded on his forehead, over his chest, a flush traveling up his neck.

"Yeah," Arthur agreed breathlessly. "I want to watch you."

James groaned, his voice catching in his throat. "Yes."

Arthur pushed himself up on one hand and snaked the other between them, to grasp James' hands tighter around them both. His hips began to thrash, completely of their own accord. He had a distant concern about embarrassing himself or doing something wrong, but it was so far away, he could scarcely hear it for the roaring in his ears.

"I'm close," Arthur gasped. "But I want to see you first."

James' face contorted, teeth gritted and his eyes fierce, boring into Arthur's. "Yes. Whatever you want."

"Come for me, James," Arthur snarled. He was sitting up now, thrusting hard into James' hands.

And, like some sort of erotic charm, James did. His breath hitched and he groaned heavily, hands wringing their pricks tightly together. Arthur could feel his cock spasm alongside James', see the evidence of James' pleasure rope up his chest.

"*Yes*," Arthur moaned, tipping his head back. "Just like that." His voice broke and the tight ball of pleasure coalesced in his gut. He came, bursting in a bright supernova of sensation. It stunned him. Burst after burst, riding it all out into James' hands, watching as James' belly and chest became slick and wet with their shared pleasure. Arthur swore shakily, felt his hips stutter and tremble.

James keened, arching back into the pillow and releasing his grip. His wet hands seized Arthur's sides, pulled him down on top of him. Pressed kisses into Arthur's neck, his shoulder, his cheeks, his ear. Their bellies slicked together, their pricks twitching against one another in the aftershocks of bliss.

"Say it again," James pleaded in Arthur's ear. Arthur had no earthly idea what he'd said, but he was fairly certain he'd say whatever James wanted, no questions asked.

"What?"

"My name," James whispered.

Arthur's breath caught in his throat. "James," he said, his voice deep and harsh and raw. His lips teased at James' ear. "James." He cradled James' head with his hand, pressed their foreheads together. "James."

James' mouth found Arthur's. Their lips slid against one another until Arthur wasn't entirely sure which way was up. James' arms wrapped tightly around Arthur, squeezing with remarkable strength. Arthur thought he might absorb him, that they'd somehow merge into one flesh in a flash of heat and mutual longing.

Arthur pressed their foreheads together again, which parted their lips. His glasses pressed into the bridge of his nose, but he really didn't care. He loved that he could see James up close.

"I'm gonna grab a towel," Arthur murmured and kissed James again before peeling himself up and crossing the small room to snatch his towel off the hook near the door. He rubbed himself dry as he walked back toward James.

"Mmm," James murmured, his eyes hooded and contented. "Stay there. Let me just look at you."

Arthur paused, letting the towel fall away, held in his hand at his side. He wasn't sure what James saw, but what did it really matter, when James was laid out on his bed, naked and sweaty and sated? He lounged with one arm deliciously behind his head, his spent cock flung over his thigh. Fuck, there was no question on heaven and earth that Arthur was attracted to men. At least, this man.

"What do you see?" Arthur heard himself say. Yikes. That sounded like a trick question.

James smiled, a sweet curve across his usually harsh mouth. "Everything I've ever wanted."

The feeling that burst through him was decidedly different from the pleasure that had eviscerated him earlier. This was more dangerous, one that filled his heart to the brim and pricked at his eyes. Turned his stomach in knots. Inspired a sense of impending doom.

Arthur ducked his chin in embarrassment and tossed the towel to James, perching on the edge of the bed and watching him as he swiped his skin and belly hair. "So, I ... um..."

James glanced up at him, his hands stilling.

"I'm pretty sure I'm gay," Arthur said with a self-deprecating smile.

James laughed, an uncharacteristically high titter that cut through whatever awkward tension had overcome him. "Yeah, Arthur. I think that's been established now."

Arthur slid into the bed as James scooched in towards the wall to make space. It was too small for them both unless they laid on their sides, embracing. Arthur didn't mind this at all. They scrambled to yank the blankets out from underneath them, laughing and sinking into one another's eyes as the quilt settled over them.

"Was this what you came here for?" Arthur whispered, nestling himself on his side facing James, resting his cheek on James' bicep. It had to be three in the morning by now and the exhaustion of the day slammed into him. Recording in the studio in Chicago felt years away.

James' mouth ticked up in an endearing half smile. "I mean, I'd hoped, but ... I actually came to say I'm sorry."

Arthur's brow furrowed. "For what?"

"For ... well, for the other night." He tucked his chin sheepishly. Arthur indulged himself and ran his fingers encouragingly through James' long hair.

"The other night was great," Arthur murmured, flipping a curl between his fingers. "I think I needed that, to be able to see what it was I wanted. The part afterwards, though." Arthur gave him a flat look. "That was some bullshit."

James sighed. "I know. I was shitty to both of you. I didn't want to say anything to put you off, but I had no idea what you wanted. And I also didn't want to set off Eve so ... I dunno. I ended up saying all sorts of shit and failed on all counts—god, I'm sorry. I was such an asshole. It wasn't a mistake to be with you. Letting Eve push me was the mistake. I wish it could have been just you and I, but I was chicken shit. I was scared you wouldn't be into that."

"I am indeed 'into that'," Arthur murmured. He pushed his fingers into James' hair at the side of his face, and James nuzzled his cheek into his palm.

"I'm just—I'm sorry if I made you feel that way. Like I regretted you. Because I really, really don't."

Arthur felt his chest rise and fall. He wanted to say that he couldn't bear that kind of thing again. He wanted to ask what might become of them when Eve got back. But he was cocooned in warmth and he didn't want to know the answers, in case they cracked through this floating aberration in space and time to flood them with reality. "It's alright. You're here now."

He pressed a kiss to James' mouth. Tomorrow wasn't here yet. He'd take that as it came.

☯

23

When Arthur woke the next morning, he was stiff from sleeping in the same position all night, but that scarcely registered, because James' arms were around him, holding his back tight to his chest. He could feel the blunt pressure of James' morning wood, and Arthur felt a smile creep onto his lips.[1]

Suffice to say that once James woke up, it took a bit for them to actually get out of bed.

"Shit," Arthur said as he caught a glance of the flip clock set next to his record player. "Is that the time?"

James was still a little breathless. "Do you have somewhere to be?"

"Just my engineering class," Arthur replied as he swung his legs over the edge of the bed. James' hands caught him around the waist, placing kisses on the side of Arthur's hip. "Can't it wait?"

Arthur sighed. "No, as much as I wish I could afford to skip class, I have been a bit behind."

"Booooooo."

"You don't have to get up. You can stay here as long as you like."

---

1. "Sweet Jane" The Velvet Underground

"Nah, it's okay." James pressed kisses to the base of Arthur's spine, in the hollows that formed just above the swell of his backside, and it was not okay. Or rather, it was very okay, except the part that it was a reminder that going to class was the last thing he wanted to do.

"Go on, you lush," James laughed, giving Arthur a playful shove that sent him to his feet. "You know where to find me after class."

Arthur gave a frustrated groan and crossed to the wardrobe to find a pair of pants that would not blatantly give away the erection he was going to get every time he thought about James. Which was going to be a lot.

Arthur did end up making it to class, albeit late. His professor was grumpy about it but whatever. He barely tuned in, and as soon the class was over, he raced out the door and across the Washington Street pedestrian bridge. It was still raining but just a drizzle. He found James in the New Riverside Cafe, eating lunch alone.

Arthur stood outside the window for a moment, looking in at him. He was sitting on the far side of the cafe, legs crossed on a booth as he picked at a sandwich and flipped through a book. And the sight, just this normal, everyday thing, filled Arthur with this sense of possessiveness, and of secret power, that this magnificently cool guy could be his.

Arthur walked into the cafe and when James looked at him, smile slashing, Arthur's brain sort of ... turned to mush. He stumbled over to James' table and sat down. He couldn't stop smiling. He must have looked like a fool, but he really couldn't stop.

"Hey," James said, his mouth a wry smile, his eyes warm and playful.

"Hi," Arthur replied stupidly. And then didn't say anything else. He should probably say something else. Sound even remotely cool instead of just sitting and staring like some lovestruck puppy. "What're you reading?"

James shrugged. "Nietzsche."

"Sorry?"

"Doesn't matter," James said, rolling his eyes and closing the book self-consciously, then smirking a bit at it before he looked up at Arthur. "You hungry?"

"For food?"

James laughed and his cheeks pinked, and Arthur puffed up a bit in the chest. That flush was for him. Delicious. That kind of thing alone could sustain him for days.

"Yeah, I could eat."

They ordered another sandwich from the cafe counter, along with two cups of coffee. Arthur reclaimed his seat in the booth and blew on the steam wafting from his mug.

"Wow, I feel like an ass," Arthur said suddenly. "I don't think I ever asked you if you were a student or not."

James chuckled. "I am. Technically."

"What does that mean?"

"To be entirely honest, I'm enrolled to dodge the draft." James avoided his gaze for a moment. "Does that bother you?"

"Not at all," Arthur replied, focusing hard on his sandwich. "My cousin died out there. My parents couldn't scramble fast enough for me to enroll here once I turned eighteen."

"Sorry to hear that."

"Did you lose anyone?"

"No. I just didn't want to cut my hair." James quipped, taking a sip of coffee.

"That would be a tragedy. For all of us," Arthur said and though he said it lightheartedly, he wasn't actually kidding. "What are you studying?"

"Philosophy," James replied, with a gesture at the book. "It's fine."

"You don't like it?"

"No, it's not that. It's pretty inspiring for lyrics." He shrugged. "I liked it more last year but this year, it's gotten pretty dreary. Too much Nietzsche, I think."

"What are you going to do with it?"

James laughed derisively. "Oh, absolutely nothing. I'm not sure I'll even finish the degree, if the war ends."

"It's supposed to, isn't it?"

"Yeah, but forgive me if I don't really trust the word of politicians." James shrugged. "What kind of engineering do you study?"

"Structural," Arthur replied around a bite of ham and cheese. He swallowed. "I'm going to systematically dash the dreams of a thousand architects."

"A noble life goal. I'll get you a jar for their tears when you graduate. How much do you have left?"

"This year and next." Arthur replied. He noticed how he flinched from looking to the future. It was a strange sensation, and a puzzling one. "What about you?"

"I'll earn enough credits for a bachelor's at the end of this semester," James replied. "But I plan to fail at least one class."

"Won't that piss off your parents?"

James shrugged again. "Who knows. They don't pay for it. My grandparents left me money for school, so I'm using it."

Arthur sensed something there. It felt so rude to ask. But it felt—well, it felt important. "Do you not talk to your parents or something?"

James sighed and scratched at his forehead. "Not really. Not since I broke up with Eve."

Arthur frowned.

"I know it's weird," James jumped in before Arthur could say anything. He lowered his voice. "Our parents are good friends. We all grew up in this tight-knit neighborhood in Highland to-gether. And so when we broke up, they couldn't stop asking me why, trying to convince me that I was making a huge mistake. So I..."

"You told them?"

"Yeah. I knew it wouldn't go well, but I lost my temper. I couldn't have really done it more provocatively." He winced.

"They're Catholics. It was a doomed endeavor from the beginning."

Arthur tried to offer the comfort of his palm over James' hand. But it also would be a lie to say the story didn't sort of break that warm shroud of specialness they'd shared since he sat down. Like they shared this beautiful secret. Because secrets never really stayed secret and at the end of the day, there wasn't space in the world for people like them. That much had been made abundantly clear. For generations.

"I'm assuming your parents don't know," James said, looking up.

Arthur sank a bit into his shoulders. "My mom knows about the cross-dressing. But we don't talk about it."

"Don't. It's not worth it." James looked tired as he pushed crumbs around his plate.

Arthur set his mug down. It was still mostly full, which was the only thing that made him hesitate. He didn't want to seem too eager (even though he absolutely was). "Do you wanna go upstairs?"

James looked up at him and his mouth cracked into a smile. "God, I thought you'd never ask."

The apartment seemed eerily quiet without Eve or Deb or the band of misfits who frequented their parties. James seemed to agree, because as soon as he dropped his keys and coat on the pony wall, he crossed the living room and put on a record.

"Ooh, nice," Arthur said, walking over as The Velvet Underground & Nico's "Sunday Morning" drifted out of the console speakers.

James turned and leaned back against the console. "You had this record on the turntable that night you invited us all up."

"Not surprising," Arthur shrugged. He was drifting towards James like he was being pulled into his gravitational field.

"I've wanted to listen to it with you ever since." James bit his lower lip endearingly.

"Listen?" Arthur teased. He was close enough to touch now, so he did, pushing his hands over James' chest, feeling warm skin and the spring of chest hair just beneath his t-shirt.

"Fine," James replied, lacing his arms around Arthur's waist. "Make-out."

Arthur's hands gripped James' head. Their mouths pressed together, soft and hard and wet and eager, and it repaired the cracks and plugged up all the drafts of reality that had seeped in from outside. He felt like he could understand why John Lennon and Yoko Ono chose their bed for their sit-in for peace publicity stunt. If he and James didn't leave this apartment for a month, he probably wouldn't even notice.

James tumbled him back onto the couch. Climbed over him, pressing his lips to jaw and neck and that tender spot on Arthur's throat just beneath his chin. James' hands yanked Arthur's shirt out of his waistband, worked buttons free and pushed his undershirt up till calloused fingertips met bare skin. They kissed and groped and frotted and it was the sweet stuff of teenage dreams, listening to the record that had opened Arthur's eyes to the knowledge that he wasn't the only freak in the world. It was perfect.

"Femme Fatale" was playing when James surfaced with a gasp and said, "I love this one. It reminds me of—"

"—Eve?" Arthur smiled. He'd be lying if he said he'd never thought about that before, too.

"No. You."

Arthur stilled. James' curling smile was so close, it blurred a bit, even with Arthur's glasses on. "...What?"

"*See the way she walks,*" James murmured. He swiped his thumb over Arthur's lower lip. "*See the way she talks.*"

"Are you calling me a tease?" Arthur demanded, to cover the fact that his eyes had decided this utterly arbitrary compliment was a singular reason to prickle. (Which wasn't even particularly flattering, considering how bitter the lyrics to that song were.

None of this seemed to matter, however, to his stupid tear ducts.)

"Definitely." Teeth nipped at Arthur's earlobes. *Fuck*. That made him prickle in an entirely different way.

"What on earth did I do to tease you?" It would have sounded more accusing if Arthur hadn't gasped it.

James' hand cascaded down his chest. "Let me count the ways."

"I feel like teasing is more your *modus operandi*," Arthur pointed out, bucking his hips needily towards James' hand, which was low but not low enough, dammit.

"Turn around is fair play," James whispered in his ear, stroking his thumb firmly along the denim hollow where Arthur's thigh met his hip. So close. Not close enough.

"You still haven't told me," Arthur had to take a breath and it made him sound wanton, like Marilyn or Jane Mansfield or something, "even one thing I did to tease you."

"You wore my clothes," James murmured. His knuckles brushed the tender skin on the inside of Arthur's thigh through his jeans.

"Nghh," Arthur replied eloquently, then clarified, "I could do that again."

James pushed himself up suddenly, and looked down at Arthur. His eyes were so intent, his lips parted in wanting. *Yes, fuck yes*. His *words* did that to James. Fucking *bombshell* energy. "Would you?"

"Now?"

"Yes."

Arthur nodded, he hoped not so eagerly that it moved over the boundary between sexy and embarrassing. Oh god, the song had ended and the viola was yelping the intro to "Venus in Furs." How did the Velvets manage to compose the soundtrack of Arthur's life?

James sat up, his knees still on either side of Arthur's hips. "Go and pick what you want."

"Don't you want to come with me?" Arthur was so urgently aroused, he didn't think a handie in the midst of dressing would be amiss.

"No," James hedged and the drum and tambourine beat out the rhythm of Arthur's heart. "I don't want to spoil the reveal."

Arthur swallowed. Fuck, no pressure. "Okay."

James sat back on the couch to let Arthur get up. As he rose, James reached out and delivered one more brief but searing kiss. Arthur hesitated for a moment. James' jeans bulged and his neck was flushed and his nipples were pointing through his thin t-shirt. Maybe just a quick one, to take the edge off?

"Please," James murmured, looking up at him under hazy lids. "I want to see you."

And it was a simple enough statement, but it really wasn't. Because Arthur was pretty confident he didn't mean he wanted to see Arthur's body. He wanted to see ... Arthur. Like, the person Arthur was when he was alone. The careless adornment, the loose-limbed elegance he enjoyed draping himself in, the things that made him feel whole. And that was fucking scary. To show that to someone else. To show James something that made him feel so pure, and risk that it would grow stale and sad through his eyes.

Arthur bit his lip. Dithered. James must have seen it in his eyes.

"Please, Arthur," he pleaded. He shifted uncomfortably and he adjusted himself, but it wasn't meant provocatively this time. Fuck, those jeans were tight. "You know ... like *ermine furs adorn imperious*." Lou Reed's lyrics echoed him from the record player. "I just. It's safe here. You're safe with me. *I'll be your mirror*, you know? Please?"

More Velvet Underground lyrics. What eighteen-year-old Arthur would have given to hear a lover whisper lyrics to him like that. Lightning struck down Arthur's spine. What *was* he scared of? James knew. He understood this. It would be okay. Besides, the way James was crumpled on the couch, looking so urgent and supplicant—it was potent stuff. Like a heady mixture of bombshell energy and something stronger. Something hard and husky and pulsing along with this particular song.

"Okay," Arthur decided firmly, then turned and walked back into the bedroom before he could chicken out.

He shucked his clothes and stood in front of Eve's mirror as "Run, Run, Run" played faintly from the living room. Arthur was all flat planes, narrow waist and broad shoulders. He wasn't the curvy, beguiling figure Eve cut. But, he reminded himself, that wasn't what James wanted. Arthur straightened his shoulders, then pushed his shorts off too. His cock was hard and jutting, rude and crass with wanting. This. This was what James wanted. And Arthur would do well not to forget that again.

So Arthur went to the wardrobe and pulled the pink silk gown from its hanger. He inspected the modesty panels—they were attached with just a few threads at each corner—and in a fit of sexual aggression ripped them off. (Carefully. Like, so they could be reattached. If James was pissed, he'd sew them back on. The bombshell energy pulsing through his veins didn't make him a monster.)

Arthur let the silk slide over him, caress his skin like a weightless, soft sigh. It was satin and when Arthur turned to look in the mirror, the shining slip of it clearly outlined his erection. *Yes.* The plunging v-neck in the front and back went down past his sternum. The straps wanted to slip wide on his shoulders, giving a wider swath of hairless, flat chest, teasing the possibility of his nipples that were also visible under the shine of the satin. *Yes yes yes.*

Arthur felt like sex incarnate as he put on a chain of sparkling rhinestones from Eve's pile of costume jewelry. It was long, accentuating the deep dive of the neckline. *More.*

He twisted one of Eve's lipstick tubes and swiped his lips velvety red. He removed his glasses and lined his eyes with an eyeliner pencil. Used the same to make his eyebrows more a beguiling arch than a caterpillar splotch. He smoothed his hair back, held his head high and the figure staring back at him from the mirror was the most formidable cast of elegant eroticism, he could scarcely breath. Soft lips and bobbing Adam's apple. He was Anna May Wong. He was Louise Brooks. He was *Lola*. Androgyny was indeed the point. *Perfect*.

Arthur wished he could just saunter out to the living room and say something so irresistible that James would veritably collapse with wanting, but try as he might, he couldn't shake his nerves when he walked out of the bedroom. With each step, he felt his resolve waver. The slip slide of silk over his skin reminded him that it wasn't made for someone like him. What if he was an imposter, a parody of beauty and elegance? Arthur peeked around the corner, where the hall met the living room, his bare toes curling under the hem.

James was standing at the record console, flipping the Velvets to side B. He stood with his weight on one leg, his hip jutting to one side, cigarette hanging from his lips as he dropped the needle.[2] Guitar strummed, a slow bass drum thumping lazy whole notes. Viola started to drone. James turned, leaned on the console. Dragged on his cigarette. Tousled curls and tight t-shirt. Arthur's skin felt hyper-sensitive. Every rustle of silk lit him up. Or maybe it was James. Just the sight of him. He gave Arthur courage. Enough to slip out into the living room. He wasn't sauntering in like a bombshell, but he wasn't cowering, and that was something to be proud of.

When James saw him, his face went slack.

His cigarette fell out of his mouth and onto the floor, and he had to spring to grab it before it singed the carpet too badly. "Shit!"

James crouched to retrieve the cigarette and rubbed at the burn with his thumb, but his eyes were on Arthur. Wide and limitless. Open and wanting and—did Arthur dare to name

---

2. "Heroin" The Velvet Underground

vulnerable? Arthur's heart matched the increasingly rapid tempo of the drum coming from the console.

"I pulled out the modesty panels," Arthur confessed, gesturing at his wide swath of chest. "I can put them back in after—"

"Don't you dare," James murmured. He left the cigarette in the ashtray without looking, floating towards him, almost dreamlike. "You're stunning."

Arthur's mouth twitched up. James approached, moving into soft focus. Ran his hands lightly over Arthur's bare arms, over the pink satin. His callus caught slightly on the fabric. The ghosts of touches lit Arthur's skin on fire. James wrapped a hand around the back of Arthur's neck and kissed him, long and deep. Soundly and surely, one hand at the nape, the other at the waist. Arthur's hands floated on James' biceps as he drank the wanting in like water from a firehose. It filled him, straightened his spine, reignited that bombshell energy that had quavered only moments ago.

When James pulled back for breath, he had lipstick smeared over his mouth.

"You've got a little..." Arthur murmured, unable to help the smile play over his lips as he gestured to the streaks of red.

"Good," James replied and kissed him again with a heat that took the strength out of Arthur's knees. His hands dragged over the satin, up and down until Arthur was quite certain the outline of his cock in the satin had turned into a fully-pitched tent.

"Fuck," James breathed, holding Arthur at arm's length and tucking his chin to take in the dress some more. His chin jutted forward as he nodded. "This is it, man."

"What?"

"The thing. The thing I wanted. I've been wearing some of this stuff for a year or two, but it's never been me I wanted to see them on. It was someone like you. I was looking for you."

Arthur felt those words in his skin, like a tattoo upon his heart.

"I…" James started, but trailed off absently as he stepped back further to admire Arthur's very apparent, satin-draped interest. "Oh, shit, *yes.*"

He looked up at Arthur and paused, nostrils flaring. In that split second, Arthur felt his heart jump into his throat, fluttering wildly for fear that the helplessness in James' eyes was hesitation. That in a moment or two, he'd realize this was freaky.

"I don't know what to call you," James said sheepishly. "No offense to your parents, but Arthur doesn't exactly have the right *joie de vivre.*"

Arthur felt a laugh erupt. "I've never thought about that. How about … oh I dunno … L-l-l-l-lola?"

James threw his head back and laughed. "I can't call you *that*!"

Arthur laughed until another of James' kisses took his breath away. His lips pressed kisses to the corner of Arthur's mouth, his chin, his jaw, his ear, before he said, "Though you do certainly make me want to get on my knees."

Arthur's breath hitched on the back of his tongue, and he managed a nod through his fluster. *Yes, do it, yes.* And James did. He fell to his knees smoothly before Arthur, supplicant and eager. His face smeared with lipstick. It was enough to make Arthur tremble. It was just as he'd imagined it, except it was better because it was *real.* Arthur gathered up the satin skirt in his hands. Pulled it up. Showed James exactly where to put those lipstick smeared lips. And James trembled too. Reached forward, his hands reverent on Arthur's hips. James pressed kisses over Arthur's thighs, nuzzled his nose in the bundled silk before he pressed his lips to the underside of Arthur's cock. He kissed and licked and touched, as though there were a thousand years to spare. As though Arthur were some sort of oracle, worthy of the most reverent worship. Every touch sent shocks of sensation sizzling through his nerves, tightening muscles and bringing his body slowly to a rising crest of tension and pleasure. He couldn't help the sounds that escaped his lips as he tried to breathe as steadily as he could manage. His breaths were shallow and gasping despite the effort.

James let Arthur's cockhead drag over the roof of his mouth, tongue pressing, cheeks hollowing, and Arthur felt his legs shudder and shake. He bellowed and creased the satin in his clenched fists as James pulled his hips, welcoming the barely restrained thrusts as Arthur spent.

Take the edge off indeed.

James pulled off panting, his lips glistening and swollen and still smeared with lipstick. His eyes were shining, and he looked so fierce and electric with his hair wild around his shoulders.

"C'mere," Arthur growled, releasing his hem and curling his fist in James' collar. James got to his feet, hand pushing at the bulge in his jeans as he let Arthur yank him in and kiss him wildly. Arthur couldn't stop thinking about James' face when he'd fucked Eve. His uncertain memories were lust-clouded, and now all he could think of was James looking down at him with that fierce expression, face tight and severe and zeroed in on him. What would it feel like if he were to actually fuck him like that?

Arthur shivered as James placed his hands on Arthur's ass and pulled his hips in, grinding provocatively against him.

"Fuck, Arthur, I can't stand it," he whined into Arthur's ear, breath hot and desperate.

"You're gonna have to," Arthur breathed. "Because I want you to fuck me."

It had to have been the dress to give him the balls to say something like that. And in a husky Marlena Dietrich voice as well. Jesus. The sound James made in response was worth it though. It sounded like a sob. His hips seized against Arthur's again.

"Come on," Arthur murmured. James' eyes looked wild and drunk as Arthur pulled him towards the bedroom.

24

The next morning, Arthur was sore and tired and stupidly happy. He and James spent hours in bed, murmuring and teasing and kissing and frotting and all of the things of lovers' dreams. Their attempt at sodomy the previous afternoon had been a hard-won success, at once awkward, tentative, desperate, and overwhelming in every sense of the word. They'd had a false start trying to face one another. James was big and it took a bit longer than either of them had hoped to get Arthur open enough for it to feel good. Arthur had ended up on his hands and knees, the silk dress rucked up under his armpits, and once they'd got going, oh fucking hell, it had been ... euphoric. While there'd been a moment early on when Arthur had had to face the possibility that it might not be for him, he found he'd been most assuredly mistaken once they changed positions.[1]

For the next week, James would pop out for coffees that he brought back up from the New Riverside in the mornings and the pair of them would sip from styrofoam cups draped in two of James' silk robes, their legs tangled together on the couch. They listened to records or talked about James' philosophy degree, or lyrics, or poetry, or even a little bit about the structural integrity of reinforced steel beams. They pulled the Rhodes

---

1. "I'll Be Your Mirror" The Velvet Underground

into the living room and jammed. Wrote scraps and fragments of new songs. They went to class, waiting for one another to return. On Thursday, James had tried to make a show of giving Arthur a space to study, but the motivational shoulder rub quickly devolved into something one hundred percent more interesting than structural engineering.

Arthur enjoyed the power he had with James. The way he could capture James' attention with a bite to his lower lip or the turn of a glance. The way he could pull something out of the wardrobe, a mere suggestion of seduction devolving into fulfilled sexual fantasies in a matter of minutes. James made him feel beautiful and enigmatic and irresistible, and fact was, Arthur was beginning to love him for it.

It wasn't until noon on the following Sunday that they finally got dressed and made their way into the chill November air together. Arthur commented on how John and Yoko would be proud of them for staying in bed so long as they walked to the west bank of the Mississippi River. They watched the water churn for a long while in companionable silence, then turned back to have lunch at the New Riverside.

"Are we gonna have any rehearsals while Eve's gone?" Arthur asked absently as he squeezed his sandwich bun tight around the crispy bacon they couldn't get at the Extemp.

James shrugged and pulled his hair back into a band so it wouldn't drag into the chicken soup he'd ordered. "I dunno. I haven't heard from Deb since we got back."

Arthur considered this for a moment. "Wow. I think I might be a terrible person."

"What makes you say that?" James replied, eyes somewhat wary.

"Because not only did I not notice I haven't seen Deb all week, but I don't even know where she lives. Or what her major is in. Or really anything about her, other than that she works at the Electric Fetus."

James sighed. "She likes to keep people at arm's length."

"So it's not my fault?"

"I mean, it's partially your fault," James smiled to transform the harshness of his words into a tease. "For as much as Deb doesn't like talking about herself, you're almost her equal in not wanting to engage in any simple questions, like 'what's your major' or 'which library do you like best?'"

"I don't really care what library Deb likes best. I don't think I care which library anyone likes best."

"It's an arbitrary question, too, because of course the law students will like the law library best, because it's most useful to them."

"I think I like Walter Library best, because it has those cool green desk lamps on all the tables that make me feel like I'm in the New York Public Library."

"How would you know what the New York Public Library is like? You've only left Minnesota once."

"Twice now! Chicago also counts," Arthur corrected imperiously. "I seen pictures of it, though. Or maybe I read about it. But it felt so real I could imagine I was there. And Walter Library assists me with my fantasy."

"Would you ever want to go to New York?" James asked, seemingly idly but with a sideways glance that suggested there might be a correct answer as far as he was concerned.

"Hell yes," Arthur asserted, his eyes steady on James'. "I'd go to Christopher Street and Studio 54, if I could get in, and even if I couldn't, I'd stand outside of it and stare up and know that pop icons were being made just on the other side of that wall."

"I wish we could have seen the Velvets," James lamented.

"Oh my god, don't remind me, I'm still verklempt." Arthur put his hand on his heart. "Who's going to sing to us about drag queens and hard drugs now?"

"Mick Jagger and the Kinks, apparently," James replied as he lit his cigarette like an after-dinner mint.

"Roger Davies can stay. Mick Jagger, though. He's on probation."

"Probation?"

"I mean after Altamont, I'd written all the Stones off, but he does look very nice in lipstick."

James chuckled, his smile crooked and boyish and filling Arthur up just right. "True." James looked up, then, over Arthur's shoulder, and puzzlement seized his expression.

"Arthur Ohashi, doko ni itta no?"

Arthur froze. *Please please please let it be Tomiko,* he thought. But he knew better. Tomiko didn't speak enough Japanese to demand quite so passive-aggressively where he'd been. There was only one person who would speak to him in Japanese in public, and she only did that when she wanted to admonish him publicly in a private language. Arthur turned his head and looked over his shoulder.

"Okaasan," he squeaked. "What are you doing here?"

His mother stood behind his chair with her hands on her hips, her sharp polyester pantsuit and hardshell bouffant in harsh contrast to the hippie floral ephemera wafting through the cafe. Her mouth was drawn like she was plagued by a bad smell—which, he supposed she was, because she hated the smell of cigarettes and this place was hazy with smoke.

"For all I knew, you were lying in a ditch somewhere overdosed on heroin or something," Okaasan sniffed, her Minnesota-accented English in stark contrast to the Japanese she'd spoken moments before. "But Tomiko said you'd been hanging around here quite a bit. Something about a band...?"

"Uh," Arthur squirmed to his feet before she could continue, self-conscious that he was wearing jeans and one of James' flouncy blouses under his coat. "How rude of me. Okaasan, allow me to introduce my, um, friend, James Novak. James, this is my mother. Mrs. Fumiko Ohashi."

Okaasan lifted her brow slightly at James as he scrambled to his feet and leaned forward to offer his hand. She shook it gracefully in spite of maintaining an impressively guarded expression. James seemed very flustered. Arthur would be flattered that meeting his mother caused James to worry about what she thought of him, if he weren't so abjectly terrified himself.

"Mr. Novak," Okaasan murmured. "I assume you know the reason behind Arthur's disappearance?"

Arthur blushed hot red. It took everything he had to not push his face into his hands. James' eyebrows shot up. Okaasan was not being subtle with her suspicion. Whatever happened to the discretion of the tatemae, the public face? Arthur felt panic claw at his rib cage.

James flicked his head and shrugged. "I'm real sorry, Mrs. Ohashi. I didn't know he was supposed to be somewhere, otherwise I woulda reminded him." He smacked Arthur in the shoulder. "Hey, what kind of guy stands up his own mother?"

It was delivered so casually, so playfully, that he might have carried it off if Okaasan didn't already know Arthur so well. Arthur rubbed his forehead and looked repentantly up at her. "Sorry, Okaasan, I know, I said I was coming to visit this weekend."

"Can you believe him, Mr. Novak?" Okaasan said over Arthur, almost as though he weren't there. "We only live in West St. Paul. It's not even an hour by bus."

"It's indefensible, ma'am," James agreed dutifully. "I'd tell him he should go, but he doesn't listen to me."

Arthur shot James a nasty glare. *Judas.*

"It's enough to make a mother wonder whether she's even wanted," Okaasan simpered to the ceiling, as if the nicotine-stained plaster could help her reform her careless son.

"Mom, I'm sorry, I'll come tomorrow—" Anything to make this mortification end.

"Oh, I can't, sweetheart, I'm going to be at the Church for the winter clothing drive." Okaasan dismissed him with the flap of a red-manicured hand. "But I expect you'll be home for Thanksgiving next weekend." It wasn't a question so much as a command.

Arthur nodded his head obsequiously. The corners of Okaasan's mouth turned up slightly in triumph. She nodded curtly at him then redirected her scrutiny onto James, who paled considerably under her singular focus.

"Does your family gather for Thanksgiving, Mr. Novak?"

James blinked. "Uh, yes, but ... I'm not able to be there."

"Live too far?" Okaasan sympathized. "That is so hard." Arthur wondered how much she really could infer. Could she know that James was close to home, but that he simply wasn't welcome there? Could she deduce why? She clapped her hands together, startling Arthur. "I know. Why don't you come to ours? Yes, Arthur, you simply must bring your friend to Thanksgiving. It won't be the same without you, Mr. Novak."

The look she gave Arthur as she said this made Arthur freeze in place. It wasn't that she was being icy, or trying to trap him, or somehow punish him for ignoring her by letting him know she understood James wasn't just a friend. But she *was* letting him know she knew. And that felt ... petrifying. Like his flesh was flayed, and she was looking at his bare muscle. But ... she didn't seem to find him wanting. She knew Arthur well enough by this point to not be surprised, at least.

"Mom," Arthur managed. "I'm sure James has better things—"

"—Thanks, Mrs. Ohashi," James interrupted. "I'd love to."

The long look that passed between Arthur's mother and his lover in that moment was ... well, it was unbearable, really, but not because he didn't want them to know the other existed and now they did. Not that at all. Perhaps the opposite, actually. Arthur found himself terrified by how much he wanted them to like one another, and how much he feared they wouldn't.

"Wonderful," Okaasan said and graciously offered her hand to James again. She pulled out the smile she used to get people to pull out their wallets during the offering at church. Arthur had a moment of discongruity when he realized how short she was compared to James, who grasped her hand with a small, private smile. She was only five feet tall, but she always seemed taller.

"I'm looking forward to it, Mrs. Ohashi," James said politely. And then he uttered the exact correct question, the most perfect one to spark the hope that Okaasan might like him, which was a hope Arthur hadn't even realized he'd been harboring. "What can I bring?"

Okaasan glanced sidelong at Arthur with an impressed little smirk. "Oh, just bring yourself, Mr. Novak. That's more than enough." Her small smile was imminently pleased.

When she turned back on Arthur, that smile dropped like a ton of bricks. "I expect you home early next weekend. I'm going to need your help with the baking."

"Yes, Okaasan," Arthur nodded with the most filial piety he could muster. Which was quite a lot, given the circumstances. He basically bowed.

"Now, walk me to my car, Atchan," she commanded. "This neighborhood is teeming with lowlifes."

Arthur nodded and tripped over his bell bottoms trying to get out from behind his chair. When he was stable, Okaasan placed her hand in the crook of his elbow and let him lead her out of the New Riverside cafe.

On the street, she carefully didn't look at him as she murmured, "You're being cautious?"

Arthur blinked. "Of course."

"Not everyone understands all the faces of love, my darling," she said, her eyes fixed on the red light at the intersection of Cedar and Riverside. "Just tell me you're not going to do anything stupid. That you'll stay safe."

Arthur nodded. "I know. I won't."

The light turned green. Arthur walked his mother across the street, toward her Lincoln parked on the far side of Cedar.

"You..." he started. "You won't tell Otosan, will you?"

"Of course I will," she dismissed. "Family holidays are already exhausting enough without having to keep track of who knows what secrets." She looked up at Arthur and seemed to sense his anxiety. "Arthur, he's your father. He knows you and he loves you. It's not like you've murdered someone or something. Besides, we know well enough the injustice of being targeted for something about yourself you can't change." Arthur tried to nod. "You don't have to talk to him about it if you don't want to."

He didn't. Otosan was brisk and sure. And as much as he tried to hide it, Otosan had seen some very intense action in the war, probably killed a bunch of people, and this tacit knowledge had always put Otosan on an unreachable and slightly terrifying pedestal for Arthur. He wasn't ready to see what a man like that might think of Arthur's life choices. Wasn't ready for the pedestal to come down. "Is anyone else coming?"

"No, just the four of us." Okaasan put her key in the car door and turned the lock. Then she turned and looked back up into Arthur's face for a long moment. Her expression was implacable.

"You look happy, honey." The corners of her mouth twitched up wistfully. "When did you get so grown up?"

Arthur smiled and dipped his chin. "I am. Happy." He hesitated. "He, um, he makes me happy."

Okaasan nodded and patted his cheek. "That's what it's all about, isn't it?"

Arthur nodded and tried to blink back the prickle in his eyes.

"Now," she said businesslike as she climbed into the driver's seat, "no more disappearing on your mother. I can't stand another two weeks not knowing where you are or what you're doing."

"Yes, Okaasan," Arthur nodded. He couldn't stop smiling.

"Good. You need a haircut." She eyed him suspiciously for a moment. "And don't you dare start smoking. Arthur nodded and she abruptly shut the door. She cracked the window a bit as she turned the engine over. "Ki o tsukete ne."

Arthur nodded again as she drove away. He felt some-what detached from his body, and he stood on the corner long enough that the light changed. He waited until the light changed back, then jogged back to the cafe.

James was smoking anxiously, his knee jiggling under the table. When Arthur approached, James stood up.

"Are you okay?" he entreated as Arthur resumed his seat, prompting James to do the same. "What happened?"

Arthur shrugged. "Nothing. She, uh, she said I seemed happy. And I said I was. That you, uh, you make me happy."

James' eyes widened into two stunned circles. They contained a desperate question, one he didn't seem able to articulate.

"She said that's what it's all about," Arthur added, hoping he could convey to James that it was okay. That his mother wasn't so different from him in that society's rules were more to be navigated than obeyed.

James blinked. "So..." he started, then cleared his throat. "So we have Thanksgiving plans, then?"

Arthur nodded. "Yeah, if you still want to go."

"Of course I want to go!" James exclaimed, gesticulating with his cigarette. "Your mom is fucking amazing. I've never seen someone so passive aggressively grill anyone like that. Beyond fucking reproach. She could snap my mom in two with a couple of sentences."

"She liked you too, I think," Arthur said with a grin. Then, with only the barest covert glance to see if anyone was looking, he reached out and clasped James' hand. "I'm sorry she sort of bull-rushed us, but I'm also really glad you, well, liked each other."

James laughed and squeezed Arthur's hand. His smile didn't quite reach his eyes.

"Actually," Arthur quipped, "I'm actually a little concerned that if we break up, she'll choose you over me." He cut himself off abruptly as he realized what he'd just said. They hadn't talked about this. Not really.

"Are we together, then?" James asked quietly. His eyes looked up at Arthur through gilded lashes as he exhaled tobacco smoke into the ambient haze.

Arthur bit his lower lip. "Yes? I mean, I'd like to be if you—"

"—I would. Like to, that is." James leaned forward, smiling in that boyish, hopeful way that made Arthur's heart just soar.

"Good." Arthur nodded and tried not to grin like an idiot. "Good."

25

Arthur was in West St. Paul the Wednesday before Thanksgiving, and he barely slept for nerves about James coming the next day. He was up early with Okaasan, rolling out pie dough and doing all the things *Good Housekeeping* prescribed for a perfect Thanksgiving dinner. By eleven, it became abundantly clear that there was going to be more leftovers than food consumed.

The doorbell rang at 12:30, right on time, but Arthur still almost dropped a serving dish.

"Atchan, watch out with that! It's Corningware!"

Arthur nodded as he set the dish carefully on the trivet shaped like a rooster and grappled with his apron as he sped to the door.

"Don't look too eager," Otosan advised from his seat in his armchair. He was reading the paper and not helping at all. "Fellas hate that."

Arthur froze in horror for a moment at that piece of disturbing romantic advice from his father. How his parents had become the poster parents for gay youth was completely beyond him. As far as he knew, the Methodists were not particularly open-minded towards gays and lesbians. He'd never heard it discussed one way or the other, he supposed. It wasn't desirable, as far as he knew, for Japanese men to behave effeminately either. So where was this coming from? (Not that he was complaining, of course. He knew most people wouldn't even dare to hope for such a family reception to the news their son was dating a man. Still, it bore the question: *why?*)

The bell rang again, shorter this time, like James was embarrassed to call attention to himself. Arthur shook himself and smoothed his hair as he grasped the doorknob. Just before he opened the door, he turned to Otosan and hissed, "Don't embarrass me."

Otosan raised his hands in surrender and chuckled as Arthur swung the front door to the rambler wide.[1]

There was something special about seeing one's partner for the first time after being separated. Hell, it had only been one day and one night, but when Arthur opened the door, he felt like he was seeing James in Technicolor. Maybe it was in contrast to the snow that had been falling all morning, covering everything in a swath of white, but his eyes were bluer, his hair was bigger, his face was realer than Arthur remembered it. It was like putting his glasses on and seeing in focus.

"Hi," Arthur said stupidly.

"Hey," James grinned and shifted from one foot to the other. "I thought I had the wrong place for a second."

"Sorry, I was helping my mom get the casserole out of the oven." Arthur held up the pink gingham apron in his hand and shrugged. He probably looked like a love-lorn puppy dog, but he didn't care. Thank God his mom and dad knew what was going on. It wasn't like he and James would hold hands or kiss or anything, but it was nice to know they wouldn't have to pretend to be just friends all afternoon. Arthur wasn't sure he had the wherewithal to even attempt such a performance.

"You must be James."

Arthur jumped as Otosan materialized over his left shoulder.

"Please excuse Arthur, he's a terrible host. Come in out of the snow!"

---

1. "Soul Love" David Bowie

"Hey—"

"I'm sure you're a great host," James reassured as he stepped in and Arthur closed the door behind him. "Here. I brought a bottle of wine."

"Oh, how thoughtful!" Okaasan gushed as she rolled in from the kitchen, wiping her hands on her Ric-Racked apron. "You shouldn't have."

He should have, and Arthur had made sure he did. Fumiko Ohashi had never once meant it when she said "Your gift is your presence." It was just something Minnesotans said when pretending like they didn't expect a hostess gift when they actually did. Refusing an offer of graciousness was mere protocol, nothing more.

"How were the buses running in this weather?" Otosan asked, walking back to his chair.

"Fine, just a little slow," James replied politely. "Would you like shoes off, then? I don't want to track anything in."

"Arthur, get him some slippers," Otosan called, and Arthur stooped to grab a pair of slippers from the front closet, setting them out for James.

"I think these will fit," Arthur muttered, straightening, and took James' coat, shaking the snowflakes from it. He paused for a brief moment to admire the nice figure his boyfriend cut in a suit. He hadn't even known James owned a suit. It was an understated plaid jacket with black slacks and a printed button-up underneath. If it weren't for the wild hair, Arthur could have brought this version of James home to Mrs. Cleaver. Shit, he was staring. Both of his parents exchanged a look, and Arthur felt his cheeks heat.

"I'm going to give James the tour," Arthur announced and handed his apron to his mother before confidently leading James down the hall to show him where the bathroom was.

Sitting in the living room and making stilted conversation with Otosan was not as awkward as Arthur had anticipated. James thanked him for his service in the war, and Otosan gave

James and Arthur tumblers of Scotch before Okaasan called them all to the dinner table. The table had both leaves in it, even though there were only four diners, because it needed every inch it could get to hold the massive array of food Okaasan had prepared. Turkey, multiple casseroles, cranberry sauce, salad—everything just as *Good Housekeeping* had prescribed. If Arthur knew his mother, he'd think she was trying to impress James. This made Arthur sit a little taller.

James did a good job talking around the band and discussing his major at the university like he cared about it. He masked so well, Arthur found himself wondering if he'd assigned a measure of cynicism to James that he didn't deserve. When the dessert course came, the men all protested that they were too full, but accepted a slice of pie anyway. James even tried one of the mochi Okaasan had made in honor of her late mother.

"This," James said around a mouthful, chewing thoughtfully, "is a texture I've never experienced before."

Arthur laughed along with his parents and felt his heart grow fonder and fonder. It was probably about 3 pm, in the middle of washing dishes while James rinsed, that he realized he was in love.

"So where do you keep all your stuff?" James asked as they were drying their hands on the little printed towel his mom crocheted to hang from the cabinet drawer pull.

"In the basement," Arthur replied with a smile. "Okaa, Oto, I'm gonna go show James the basement!"

"Are you sure?" Okaasan replied. "I don't think James wants to see your mess, honey."

"Leave the door open," Otosan called over her.

"Oh my god, Dad, stop!" Arthur cut him off and, grabbing James' hand, yanked him down the stairs.

"Sorry about them," Arthur said when they got to the bottom of the wooden steps. "I've never brought anyone home before, and I think they want to say all the things they hear on TV sitcoms."

James was laughing. "No older siblings or anything to take the edge off?"

"Ugh, no, I wish," Arthur replied and then led James to the old couch in the main room. The basement was sort of an amalgamation of a storage room, utilities room, and everything else Arthur had set up to make it his own. There was a large boiler in the far back, partially obscured by a sheet Arthur had hung from the unfinished ceiling. The rest was hidden by a large screen, originally for family photo slideshows but now appropriated for films. A threadbare sofa and a 1940s cabinet record player stood nearby. The floor was poured and the walls were block cement, so it was cold, but Arthur had done his best to make the room cozy with blankets, lamps, and anything else he could find. A string of large-bulbed Christmas lights were hung across the far wall, and Arthur crossed to plug those in and turn on the lamp.

"Wow, this is really cool," James said as Arthur ushered him to sit on the couch. "Are you gonna show me your baby pictures now, or something?"

Arthur shook his head vehemently. "No, oh god, they'd love that wouldn't they? No, I have a film projector, so I'd use the screen to watch films."

James' eyes widened. "Really?"

"Yeah, I worked at the movie theater in high school and when they updated their projector, they let me take the old one, and some of the old films they were storing too. I'm pretty confident it was not at all allowed, but my supervisor was a hippie stoner and I don't think he really cared."

James turned and looked at the film reel projector that was set up behind the couch. "That's so fucking cool. What films do you have?"

Arthur preened. "Lots of old silent ones, mostly. My favorites star Louise Brooks."

"You like films, then?"

"Oh yeah, I love them. I wish I could watch the more modern musical ones here but I couldn't smuggle those ones out if I tried. And I did once."

"Which film?"

"*Some Like it Hot.*"

"Marilyn fan?"

"Absolutely. But I got caught by the manager and he threatened to fire me. Apparently the copyright is pretty strict. Ah well." The memory still embarrassed him.

"Who was more inspiring—Marilyn or Tony Curtis?"

"God, both. It's taken a long time to figure out, but I think I wanted him, and I wanted to be her." Arthur threw himself against the back of the couch and looked up at the rafters. "Like Eve. She's so beautiful. I wish I looked like that."

"I don't," James said pointedly. His fingers twitched near his mouth like he was longing for a cigarette.

"Do you need to smoke?" Arthur asked, sitting up.

"No, I'm okay," James said. "I'd much rather be here in your lair, collecting all the clues to what makes you tick."

"And what clues have you found so far?"

"Marilyn, of course."

"Come on, that can't be a surprise."

"It's not, really. You know, there are some guys out there who say that they feel like a woman trapped in a man's body..." James' question went unasked, but Arthur heard it nonetheless.

Arthur furrowed his brow in thought. "I don't think that's how I feel."

"If it was, it wouldn't change how I feel about you," James whispered, turning to face Arthur. "I didn't mean that earlier. If you looked like Marilyn, I'd think you were sexy."

Arthur nodded. "My body isn't part of my, you know, armor. It feels like mine. But I also don't feel how I look in the mirror. At least not most days."

James' voice was low. "What about when you wore my dress? Did you look how you felt then?"

"God, yes."

"I'm not convinced it has to be all one or the other, man or woman and that's it." James said. "There's this researcher from Germany at the turn of the century—I can't remember his name—who said homosexuals were like a third sex unto ourselves and one that is discriminated against unfairly."

"Wait, like the early 1900s?"

"Yeah, before the Nazis came after him."

"Jeez. I didn't know that."

"There's another researcher—American guy named Kinsey—who says that sexuality is a spectrum and human beings exist all along it. That's why there's all sorts of straight guys who have had sex with men."

"I'm sorry, what?"

"Yeah, like in the military and stuff."

Arthur goggled. "I ... did not know that either."

"It's much more common than they'd like us to believe."

"I think, in an ideal world," Arthur said slowly. "I'd want to be something both male and female. The best of both worlds."

"You already are that, Arthur," James murmured. "There's just so few places you can show it."

"It's *really* not what people want," Arthur replied. "I don't even know what it looks like without trial and error, because I've never seen anything like it. Except maybe in silent films."

"I've never seen a silent film," James said, stretching back and splaying his long legs out. "Aren't they all just slap-stick comedy and over-acting? I like some of the stuff coming through now that they finally got Hollywood out from under that studio system. Like, I want to see the whole gamut of humanity reflected on screen, even if it's dirty and ugly and naked."

Arthur kept himself honest and didn't crawl into the nook made between James' arm and side when he draped his arm over the back of the couch. "It wasn't always like that, though, all regulated and stuff. I've got a few silent films with gratuitous nudity in them."

James started with surprise. "For real?"

"Yeah. And there's a whole bunch with cross-dressing—both men and women. The guys all wear makeup and the girls all have their hair short. They're really subversive. In *Pandora's Box*, Louise Brooks is infatuated with a tuxedo-wearing Countess. I have that one, actually." Arthur got up and started rummaging through one of his film boxes.

"I have no idea what you're talking about but that sounds unreal. I'm not sure I believe you. I mean, there are definitely movies with gay undertones, but even now, no one is brave enough to say it out loud." James shifted, peering into the box Arthur was flipping through. "Have you seen *Butch Cassidy and the Sundance Kid*?"

Arthur paused his search so he could adequately scoff with his whole body. "Ugh, yes. What a slog that was."

"I loved the beginning, but once they got to Mexico, I was snoring."

"*Raindrops keep falling on my head*," Arthur sang with mocking precision, dancing his fingers in the air.

"The tandem bicycle!" James groaned like he'd been kneed in the gut.

"Torture," Arthur agreed as he alighted on the reel labeled *Pandora's Box*. "Aha!"

"It was weird that they didn't kiss," James added.

"Who, the girlfriend and Cassidy?" Arthur wove behind the couch and took the film out of its tin.

"No!" James twisted around on the couch and crossed his arms over the back of it. "*Sundance* and Cassidy! What was even the point of the girlfriend?"

Arthur grinned as he imagined a film where Paul Newman and Robert Redford had an onscreen kiss. "To put us to sleep, apparently." He threaded the old, delicate film through the machine. "She did have pretty great costumes, though."

The projector whirred to life and a flicker of frames cast their shadow on the screen. James nodded and said, "I would have paid fifty bucks to see Paul Newman in one of those getups."

Arthur snorted as he rounded the couch and sat next to James. It was strange to not touch, but exciting too. There was a fission in the space that remained between them that felt almost as electric as touch itself.

"Have you seen *Midnight Cowboy*?" James murmured as Louise Brooks swept on screen in the most stunning flutter dress, silk crepe cascading at the edge of the plunging v-neckline.

"The X-rated one that won the Oscar?" Arthur clarified a little too loudly, earning a 'Shh' from James. "I would have if I could have found playing anywhere. Have you?"

"I saw it at one of the theaters downtown," James replied at a much lower volume. "There are gay guys in that one. They were all pretty pathetically portrayed, but they were there."

Arthur didn't reply for a minute. "I don't know that Hollywood can really be trusted to show us what love between men actually looks like. Everything I've ever seen or heard whispers about ends in tragedy."

James sighed. "You're probably right."

They watched for a bit. Louise Brooks danced, swishing her silk dress this way and that, wielding her smile to significant effect. It was weird it was silent at points like these. All the title cards were in German, too, which made it challenging to know what was going on, unless of course, you'd seen it a hundred times. Which Arthur had.

"Sorry I don't have any music," Arthur said abruptly. "I wanted to get a piano down here, so I could play to the movies, but my mom said we'd never get one down the stairs."

"She shoulda bought you a Rhodes," James smiled, his lips stretching in that crooked, boyish grin that Arthur couldn't resist.

Arthur stared. He clenched and unclenched his fingers.

"I want to kiss you right now," he whispered. "I can't. But I wish I could."

James' smile softened to something wistful and dear, something Arthur wanted to capture on film so he could watch it over and over again. Maybe he wasn't the only one who'd found the name of this sensation in his chest this afternoon.

The moment came to its natural conclusion when James reached out and squeezed Arthur's knee. He didn't linger long, but long enough for Arthur to know he wasn't the only one thinking maybe they should call it a night and go where they could be themselves together.

"How did you know?" James asked as Louise Brooks swept around her apartment, artfully charming her monocled lover with her incandescent smile.

"Mm?"

"That you were different?"

Arthur lifted his eyebrows in thought. "Oh, I dunno, always? Being Japanese made sure different was my natural state. I always liked to put on shows for my mom when I was a kid. Until one time I dressed up in the kimono and sang Marilyn Monroe and she smacked me a good one. She taught me to hide it, to keep it down here where no one would see. So I knew it wasn't normal to want to wear dresses and things like that."

James nodded. "I'm glad you're finally getting to see how bullshit that is."

"I really don't blame her. She was just trying to protect me. I mean, you've seen how open she is when she knows it's safe."

"Yeah, but neither of us should have to be our family's secret." James sighed. "For me, I was always as normal as they came. In fact, I thought I was *too* normal and could afford to be more different. I think that's why I was so drawn to music. For a long time, I thought I was in control of all the ways I subverted the status quo. But I was lying to myself."

Arthur turned towards James on the couch. "What do you mean?" he asked gently.[2]

"Turned out I was different all along. I wasn't better with girls than other boys. I wasn't more enlightened, like Eve always told me I was, because I wasn't driven by this teenage urge to fuck her all the time. I was gay. I guess I'm lucky, in a way, that I didn't get dragged into the football team or prom royalty or all those other heteronormative traps, but I didn't even realize that love and sex could feel different than it did with Eve until we were at the U."

James was looking at his hands as he spoke. Arthur suspected he was about to hear something important.

"Eve is, well, you know, she looks like she does, so she was always getting hassled by guys. That was actually part of why we ended up together. I thought I could protect her. She loved anything to do with gender subversion because she hated how guys just got to do that all the time, so when we got to the U, she signed us up for this grassroots class at the Extemp called 'The Homosexual Revolution.' And we went together and thought it'd be a gas, but there were ... Arthur, there were couples there. There was this guy and his boyfriend holding hands and they seemed so happy and I ... I'd never considered that as a possibility before. Especially not in public. And since I'd just taken this class, and I had all these definitions and clear understandings of what it meant to be gay and how it all went down—I just ... I started seeing it everywhere.

"Like, in high school, in different connections I'd felt with other guys. In hindsight, I could easily name, without even thinking about it, which ones I'd had crushes on. I always felt awkward hanging out with guys I liked. It felt like a big deal to be alone with them, so I avoided them. I felt much more comfortable with Eve. We liked all the same things. The same music,

---

2. "The Bewlay Brothers" David Bowie

the same fashion, the same guys, too. Ha. I was so invested in the guys who liked her, which ones deserved her attention. It wasn't any surprise she understood that to mean I wanted her. But I was jealous. I was jealous all along. She could move through the world in pretty dresses and long hair and flirt with guys, and all I could do was to live vicariously through her. And all these memories came bubbling up after I took that class. It was like opening Pandora's Box." James cracked a smile as he gestured wistfully at the screen.

Arthur glanced up at Louise Brook's descent into hedonism and laughed, then started to rest his head on James' increasingly hunching shoulder, but thought better of it halfway, so it ended up more like a little forehead bop to the bicep. "What happened with Eve when you told her?"

James snorted. "Well, I didn't tell her at first. I kicked it all off by lying to her. I went to FREE meetings saying I was going to the Mobe, because I knew she wouldn't want to come along. I'd lurk in the back and trade glances with Tom Boroughs till he asked me to one of their FREE dances in the Coffman Union Basement, and I had to say no because I had a girlfriend."

James winced. His shoulders were curled up near his ears, and he sat on the couch like he was hoping to sink into it. Arthur thought about when they'd run into Tom Boroughs at the Extemp and how cold he'd been toward James. He didn't have a good feeling about where this story was going. He decided it was more important to hold James' hand than to adhere to what his parents were likely to deem appropriate. He laced his fingers between James'.

"I knew I was going to hurt Eve really bad. It was just a matter of whether or not I'd hurt her by telling her the truth, or get caught cheating on her. So I decided to come clean. But I'll tell you what, Arthur, never start a conversation with Eve by saying, 'I think I might'."

"Did she try to talk you out of it?" Arthur guessed.

"Oh, hell yes. She almost did, too."

"She ought to be a lawyer or something."

"Damn right. She talked me in circles all night long and we finally settled on needing more proof." James frowned. "So she..."

"Oh jeez, what kind of proof?"

James took a deep breath and his neck bobbed as he tipped his head back against the couch, gold hair cascading. "I went to the Hennepin Baths."

"Like a public bathhouse? I didn't know those were even still around."

"Yeah, but it's basically just a front for gay hustlers." James wrinkled his nose and looked in his lap.

"What's so terrible about that?"

"It made me feel disgusting. Not that people do that, I guess, but that I was there to consume it, with Eve's monthly allowance in my pocket like proof of my damnation, my perversion. I got as far as the locker room, saw the glances flying around, felt myself be tempted. And I realized I was like those desperate Johns in *Midnight Cowboy*. I saw my future in that locker room—some sad, middle-aged closet-case getting his rocks off on the sly with a hustler, while Eve and our kids were at home. And I just ... I freaked out and I left. And as I was walking back, I got so angry. Why did I need proof? Did I not know myself well enough to know what I wanted? Straight people can be virgins and still know they're straight.

"So I went back to her and I lied. I told her what I thought she expected to hear. That some guy sucked me off, and I loved it. She asked me a thousand questions. She wanted every fucking detail, like she was my shrink or something. And finally, I just told her that she'd wanted proof, I gave her proof, what more did she fucking want? And she decided all calm that she was okay if we had sex with other people. So we could stay together."

Arthur winced.

"That lasted maybe a week. Next time I saw Tom Boroughs, I asked him out. I was so scared, heart in my throat, just terrified I wouldn't, you know, be gay enough for him or something. And he asked if I still had a girlfriend. Well, I had to say yes, so he turned me down. And when I went back to Eve that night, I realized that it was impossible. It wasn't fair, not to her, not to me, not to Tom Boroughs or whatever guy I ended up with. So I went to the apartment, told her it was over, and left before she could say anything else."

"Where did you go?"

"Home. I tried to dodge my parents' questions, but they had heard from Eve's parents that we'd broken up, so they were on my case, telling me I was being stupid, that I should get back together with her, stop breaking that poor girl's heart. And Eve was all messed up, and she told her mom the story I'd made up about the bathhouse, and her mom told my parents, and—Arthur, it was horrible. They confronted me, and I, I dunno, I was just sick and tired and heartbroken, so I doubled down. It didn't matter whether I went to a dance with a guy in the Coffman Union basement or paid for a blowjob in a bathhouse—it was all the same to them. Long story short, they kicked me out."

That sank in like a nightmare Arthur had dreamed for years but had never come to pass. He squeezed James' hand hard.

"I didn't have anywhere left to go, so I went back to the apartment. And Eve showed up for me. She told me they were wrong, that she'd never give up on me, that she loved me no matter what. And I'm sure I don't have to tell you how fucking good it feels to hear that." James exhaled shakily and gripped the Arthur's hand with his.

Arthur wanted to kiss that line between James' eyebrows away. He wanted to do anything that could help James unfold himself from the weight of this terrible story. "So what made Eve change her mind?"

"I don't know," James replied. "Guilt, probably, for letting that story get back to my parents. She encouraged me to date Tom, and it was really good for a while, but then he didn't like that she and I were still living together, so he ended things. She was always a little jealous, but I thought that was normal considering everything that had happened. And she never crossed the line."

"Except in Chicago," Arthur murmured. He wasn't sure if he was supposed to say that but, well, there it was, already out of his mouth.

"Except in Chicago," James agreed. "God, what a mess. I'm so sorry to have dragged you into it. I've been so fucking selfish."

"No, it's okay," Arthur said, and he meant it. "It's hard to find a way when there's no path to follow. I haven't been at my best either. I feel awful about everything that happened with Eve."

"Eve is good," James said resolutely. "She'll be cool with you when she's had some time to cool off, I know it. Even when I left her high and dry, she didn't ever talk shit about me. Everyone else did, but she didn't. I disappointed her, but she valued our friendship higher than any romance, and she prioritized that. She's made some hard choices to stand by me. Man, I consider myself lucky to count her as my friend. My only family left, really."

Arthur regarded James for a moment. He placed his other hand on top of James', so that all four of their hands clasped together. He briefly entertained telling James that he was in love with him, but chickened out. Instead, he said, "You don't need to share DNA to be family."

James returned his gaze, and Arthur suddenly understood how people could just spend hours looking into each other's eyes like ninnies.

"God, I want to kiss you," James murmured.

Arthur leaned forward a bit before he got hold of his senses and said, "Let's go back to the apartment."

"What about the movie?"

"I don't care."

"Won't your mom be put out?"

"I *really* don't care."

James grinned and Arthur couldn't help himself. He leaned forward, putting a hand to either side of James' face, and kissed him. It was brief and chaste, but it just hammered home how imperative it was that they get out of his parents' house before he lost any more of his mind to this earnest, vulnerable, goddamn perfect man.

26

"What time is Deb coming?" Arthur asked, then resumed his lazy kisses across James' clavicle. It was the Sunday after Thanksgiving, and James had managed to track Deb down at the Electric Fetus the day before. She'd begrudgingly agreed to a rehearsal, on the condition that they refrain from PDA in front of her. Seemed she was still angry about the whole *menage a tois* before the recording session that went to hell in a hand-basket.[1]

"Mmm, soon," James hummed, setting his guitar aside and reclining back on the bed. Arthur leveraged the leg he'd hooked over James and pushed himself up and over him.

"That is terrible news," Arthur murmured into James' neck. His hand slid down James' bare stomach, smoothing golden curls as he reached the denim waistband. "What is she going to say about this?" Arthur's palm pressed against the crotch of James' jeans.

"You're the worst," James whined, his hips twitching up to greet Arthur's hand. As if they hadn't just done this before breakfast.

"You love it," Arthur breathed into James' ear and then worried the lobe with his teeth. He was rewarded with a strong buck of James' hips into his hands.

---

1. "Miss X" MC5

"I do," James replied and turned to capture Arthur's mouth. "I really fucking do."

This was of course the opportune moment when the apartment door slammed and Deb's voice rang loudly from the living room.

"You know, you assholes could get the mail once in a while. I know you're shacked up, but honestly, this is ridiculous."

Arthur buried his nose in James' hair and groaned.

"Are you guys here? Are you decent?" Deb called again, louder and more insinuating.

James sighed and sat up straight. "We're here! Give us a minute, Deb."

There was a very loud wolf whistle, then the sound of some rummaging in the fridge. Arthur whined as James stood, leaving his arms very empty. James pulled a t-shirt over his head and grumbled as he adjusted his jeans. He glanced down to regard Arthur.

"Are you going to get dressed?"

Arthur regarded the robe of James' that he was wearing, which was significantly askew at the moment. "Do I have to?"

"If you don't want Deb to pretend to throw up into a wastebasket, then yeah, probably."

Arthur sighed sulkily and sat up, putting his glasses back on. "That sounds like her problem."

"You know, I've been thinking," James said as Arthur stood. "About your name."

"What's wrong with my name?" Arthur shrugged the robe to the floor and looked over his shoulder to see if James noticed. He had.

James cleared his throat. "Arthur feels like a helmet. I mean, your name when you're dressed and adorned."

"I thought it was Lola?" Arthur said with a wink over his shoulder. He felt heady with his bombshell power as he strode elegantly to his discarded jeans slung over the vanity mirror.

"I thought Pandora would suit you well."

The word washed over Arthur as he regarded his reflection in the mirror. His hair had grown long enough to give him more of a Louise Brooks look than a Davy Jones. His lips twitched at the corners. He'd never felt as tall as he had these weeks with James.

"I like that," he said. The mirror reflection afforded him the opportunity to see James standing behind him with wolf eyes.

"You're ruthless," James accused.

Arthur met his gaze in the mirror and gave a little laugh. "I'm not the one who scheduled band practice." Then he bent as provocatively as he could to pull his shorts and jeans on.

Needless to say, it took them ten more minutes to make their way out into the living room. The Who "Live at Leeds" was on the record player.

"Fucking *finally*," Deb declared when they appeared, pushing the kitchen chair out and standing with a squeal of wood skidding over linoleum. Deb had already finished a beer and there were sandwich crusts left on two plates. Noting the plates, Arthur craned his neck to see into the kitchenette.

"Tomiko!?" he exclaimed with a start. His friend was leaning on the counter and sipping a beer, looking like it was very difficult for her to hold in her laugh. "What are you doing here?"

Tomiko gave a small, secret sort of smile and shrugged. "Deb invited me."

"How do you know Deb?" Arthur looked back and forth between the two for a long moment.

"Oh, man, Arthur, you really are self-centered," Tomiko complained, pushing herself off the counter. "I met her at your show. When I was trying and failing to talk to you."

Arthur blinked stupidly. "Oh." He had a lot of questions, but Deb was glaring at him so he shut his mouth.

"Tomiko, is it?" James asked. Arthur winced when he mispronounced it, like Tommy-coh. "I remember you from the Halloween party. I'm James."

"Yes, Tomiko," she corrected gently, crossing to shake James' outstretched hand.

"You do?" Arthur interrogated James. "From when?"

"When I went to change my clothes before walking you home. She was in the bedroom with Deb."

Arthur's mouth dropped open. He couldn't help himself. "Are you two...?" He gestured uselessly.

Deb's eyebrows raised. "Fucking? What do you think?"

Arthur flushed "I don't know." Arthur looked at Tomiko imploringly. "My mom said you had a new boyfriend."

Tomiko raised a brow and rolled her eyes.

"Tomi, is *Deb* the new boyfriend?"

"Maybe." She gave a shrug with a little smile on her face. Holy shit, he couldn't be more angry at her. All this time, they could have been honest with each other? He could have had someone he didn't have to hide from? What a waste.

She seemed to read that from him and, glancing up at James, countered, "Well, what about you? Are you two together?"

Arthur exchanged a glance with James. And he told the truth. "Yeah."

"Well, it's about damn time," Deb concluded impatiently, sifting through the pile of mail she'd dumped on the kitchen table. "You should have seen them, Tomi. Pining like idiotic turtle-doves for a month while Eve played them both like a fiddle. Oh, speak of the devil."

Deb held up a postcard between two fingers. James leaned over and grabbed it. "Oh, god. What is she gonna think of all this when she gets back?"

Deb sighed. "I could really not give a fraction of a fuck after that drama she pulled in the studio."

"Have you heard anything back from them yet?" Arthur asked her, his heart giving a little flip of nerves.

"No," Deb replied, flipping through several envelopes before alighting on a copy of Rolling Stone. "Ooh, Grace Slick—But I'm gonna call him tomorrow and see what's going on. I mean, beggars can't be choosers, but I would hope we'd have an EP in hand before Christmas."

James gasped. Arthur turned and saw him staring at the postcard with his mouth open.

"What is it?" Arthur asked.

James cleared his throat. "Um ... shit, wow. She's moving out there."

"Holy shit!" Deb exclaimed.

"She's staying at her grandma's," James continued. "And she's coming back to get her stuff on Friday."

"For winter break?" Arthur asked. He felt guilty for being glad, given the circumstances, but if Eve wasn't coming back until January, he could enjoy a much longer stay in the apartment with James.

"No. I think she's dropping out." He was lingering over the postcard in a way that made Arthur feel weird.

"Holy *shit*," Deb reiterated, standing and craning to see the postcard. "What does that mean for The Tarts?"

"I don't know." James looked back at the postcard and rubbed a hand through his hair. There was something else there. Arthur wanted to crane and read the postcard too, but Deb snatched it from James' hands. It had a photograph of the London Bridge on it. Her eyes skittered over the words. "For fuck's sake."

Arthur studied her. "What? Is it so surprising? I mean, I'm sure I'm not the only one who wondered why she stayed here."

Deb looked up at James with a flat look. "Just read it, Arthur."

Arthur looked between the two of them as he accepted the postcard.

Hello Darlings, it began. *Must be brief. Granny's house is cleaned up. I've convinced Dad to let me stay. I'm coming back to collect my things Friday. We're going to London, Jimmy! XOXO Eve*

"'We're going to London'?" Arthur repeated. "James, what does that mean?"

James smiled, but it soured on his face as Deb continued to regard him. When he looked at Arthur, his eyes shuttered. Deb looked over at Tomiko awkwardly.

"I guess," James said slowly, "it means that she wants me to go with her?"

The floor felt really far away. Arthur reached across himself, held tight to his opposite arm. "Over winter break, you mean?"

James shrugged. "Maybe. I don't know. Arthur, she's been dangling this trip in front of me for as long as I've known her. I never thought she'd actually bring me."

The words hollowed Arthur out from the inside. He felt his lip curl and he tried to stop it. He opened his mouth, but the only thing that came out was, "Um." A hundred questions, embarrassing and angry and desolate, flew around in his head. For how long? What would he do there? What about school? What about the apartment? What about *them*?

"Fucking Eve, dropping bombshells on people even across the Atlantic," Deb gritted out. "Maybe now isn't the greatest time for rehearsal."

"Arthur," James implored. Arthur couldn't think now. The questions had taken over. Was James going to leave him? To go to London with Eve? Why? He didn't want her. Wasn't that what he'd said? He wouldn't leave him for her. They'd resolved that.

"I'm not just bailing," James said. "I don't even know what the plan is, and I won't until Eve gets back. Don't be upset."

He would leave him for London, though. Where the music scene was full of subversive people doing innovative things. Like Warhol's Factory, but for songwriters. Hell. Fucking *hell*.

Deb awkwardly got to her feet and edged toward the door.

"It was nice to meet you," Tomiko said with strained pleasantry.

Arthur took a deep breath. He was making this weird. He'd do well to remember he'd only known James for a couple of months, that he couldn't expect him to drop a lifetime of ambitions and dreams for a guy who didn't even have the courage to tell him he loved him. "No, it's fine. I'm sorry, I'm just being silly. Of course you should go. You'll regret it forever if you don't."

Eve was James' only family. Of course he wasn't going to pass up a chance to go to London just to get his rocks off with a brand new boyfriend. They had a great connection, yeah, but how could he compete with the London music scene? If David Bowie's picture sleeve was any indication, boys in dresses were not a rarity. God, why did that thought make him want to sob?

"You should come too!" James insisted. He looked up at Deb. "We should all go, as a band. Make it a kind of tour."

Deb regarded him incredulously from the threshold, where she and Tomiko were putting on their coats. "Don't pull me into this."

"No, it's okay," Arthur assured, surprised at how his voice steadied. "I wouldn't ask a stranger to put me up in a foreign country. I have my degree to finish, and anyway, my mother would kill me if I asked for airfare anywhere, much less across the Atlantic."

Deb and Tomiko slipped out the door. The intervening silence swept in with the draft they left in their wake. Arthur swallowed the feelings that were competing for his attention and making his throat feel tight. "It's fine, James. You can't throw away your dream. Neither of us know where this is going. I'm not going to make you choose, or have you resent me for it. I understand. It's okay."

And he did understand. It didn't make it hurt less.

☯

27

If Arthur was smart, he would have taken some time away to think. He would have gone back to his dorm room, which had lain vacant for several weeks, and got his head on straight. Arthur wasn't smart.

He stayed at the apartment with James for the rest of the week. He drank in every piercing glance, every heated kiss, every sweat-slick thrust like it was going to be the last. Because it probably was. And maybe it was stupid to do this to himself, but he couldn't bear the thought of wasting one precious minute. The sex was somehow more intense, more impassioned, because the end was in sight. Unlike before, when it felt like they had all the time in the world to learn each other, it was more frequent and urgent, like some sort of drug neither of them could get enough of.[1]

In spite of the increasing intensity of their physical relationship, James became more reserved, his previous openness curbed by hesitancy. While he still turned to Arthur with the lightest touch or glance, the feeling of connection was stifled by the weight of Eve's imminent arrival. They didn't talk about themselves. The songs they'd started writing languished. They certainly didn't talk about Eve or London again. Arthur just

---

1. "Shoulda Woulda Coulda" Lamont Cranston Band

held onto James like a life-line, and James held him back. They used sex to mask anything that felt vulnerable until something mundane required attention, like meals or classes. And it hurt, so exquisitely, because every touch just reminded Arthur how stupidly in love he was.

No. Arthur refused to be lame about this. He refused to be clingy or entitled. James was his own man, and Eve was his best friend. If he wanted to write music, London was the place for him. Arthur had no right to stand in the way of that. He should have had an easier time being cool about it. They'd barely been together a month, but the past two months had been so intense for Arthur, so eye-opening, that he felt an attachment to James far beyond what was reasonable. Embarrassed, he kept that to himself.

Band practice rescheduled for Wednesday, and they had a genuinely good time jamming and talking about what kinds of music Eve would bring back. They didn't talk about what would happen after Eve and James left, though Deb was certainly fumbling in her effort not to. Arthur wondered if she might like to keep playing after they'd gone. Maybe he could write a sad song, the kind that made people cry in the record store when they heard it. Then Deb could play it at the Electric Fetus while she was working.

Friday came. Arthur had class. He didn't talk about it, but he packed his toothbrush and other toiletries in his bag as he got ready to leave. He intended to go back to the dorm with his dignity, at least for the night, and let whatever was going to play out with Eve and James happen without him.

When he was pulling his coat on in the entry, James came up behind him, still in his boxer shorts, and squeezed him so tight it almost hurt. Arthur reached up and grasped his forearms. James burrowed his face into Arthur's neck.

"Come to London with us," James pleaded in his ear. "Please."

Arthur's heart constricted, and he shrugged uncomfortably, even though he still held James' arms fast around him. "We don't know what that question even means yet."

"I know," James murmured against his neck. "I just know I don't want this to end."

Arthur swallowed with some difficulty around the lump in his throat. "Then stay." Dammit. He really didn't mean to say that aloud. "I'm sorry—that's not fair to ask."

"It's not fair for me to ask you to go either, but I'm damn well doing it anyway," James mumbled into his neck.

Arthur turned in the circle of his arms, resting his hands on James' chest. "That's the kind of thing people in the movies say." He looked up into James' blue eyes, searching for something there. He wasn't sure what, anything really.

"Honey! I'm home!"

The door flung open and sort of rammed into Arthur's backside. He and James stumbled apart as Eve, looking radiant in a big fox fur coat, reeled in surprise at being so greeted and dropped her suitcase on the threshold.

"Oh," she said, her glossy lips in a perfect O as she took in the scene. She looked Arthur up and down in his coat and jeans, his bag over one shoulder, then James, naked but for his boxer shorts. "*Oh.*"

Arthur's eyes darted between James and Eve. Her expression was amused, her eyes alight with mischief. James, meanwhile, was guarded. "So you took my advice to heart, huh, Arthur?"

Arthur blinked at her.

"What advice?" James asked.

"I told him not to do anything I wouldn't do," Eve grinned, then turned to Arthur. "I must say, you have excellent taste, darling."

James' brow furrowed. Arthur wondered if there was a catch somewhere.

"Well, isn't anyone going to welcome me back?" Eve exclaimed and sashayed into the living room, rounding the

Rhodes to throw her bag on the couch. "Goodness, you settled in quite nicely while I was away. Say! Maybe Arthur can take the flat once we're gone! Then it'll stay in the family."

She gave Arthur a friendly little wink. He felt his shoulders start to hitch up towards his ears and his stomach start to turn. He decided to cut his losses before things got too awkward.

"Sorry to rush, but I have to get to class," Arthur said and made for the door.

"Arthur, wait—" James said, but Arthur didn't. He just shut the door and hurried down the steps two at a time.

"What's got his knickers in a twist?" Eve's voice drifted into the stairwell.

The frigid December air was just the sucker punch he needed. He huffed all the way to the East Bank and his ears and nose were red and half-numb by the time he slipped into the lecture hall. He didn't absorb anything the professor said. All he could think about was Eve winking at him like that. He couldn't put his finger on why, but it felt humiliating. Like his heart was breaking.

Arthur was very proud that he didn't tear up once through the whole class. On the way out of the lecture hall, as he turned his feet toward his dorm and huddled into his scarf against the light snow whipping around the quad, a classmate tapped him on the shoulder.

"Hey, Ohashi," the classmate—Arthur thought his name might be Ernie—said with a grin. He pronounced Arthur's name Oh-HASH-ee, like some sort of eclectic nickname for marijuana. "You coming to the lab this afternoon?"

"Oh yeah, of course." Arthur had forgotten about that.

"Oh good," Probably-Ernie said. "The reading was brutal, wasn't it? Sounds like the TA is gonna help us break it down."

"That's good." Arthur hadn't done the reading last night. He'd meant to, but he ended up too busy getting fucked out of his mind over the kitchen table.

"Don't forget your book again!" Ernie called as he dashed down the quad, winking and grinning helpfully.

It took Arthur a minute to remember what book it even was. When he did, he swore so loud, a group of Freshman coeds walking nearby gave him sideways looks.

Fundamentals of Structural Analysis. He'd left it at James' *goddammit.* There was nothing left to do but go back and get it before the lab this afternoon. Arthur clenched his fists in his hair and swore aloud, squatting down like being closer to the ground would somehow make it better.

Arthur stood on the quad for several minutes, trying to figure out a way to avoid this. He didn't want to see Eve. Her flippant way of taking credit for James and Arthur hooking up, like she were their puppet master, left him with a sour taste in his mouth. Of course at no point did it occur to her that they might want to stay together, or that her plan to whisk James off to London for an indefinite amount of time was sabotaging them worse than anything else she could contrive. Arthur was so angry with her, but what could he do? If he tried to pull James back, tried to get him to stay, when he *knew* how much he dreamed of going—he'd be just as manipulative as Eve if he did that. And he didn't have the advantage of years of friendship and loyalty to back him up. Expecting someone to give up a lifelong dream in favor of a romance only three weeks old was completely unreasonable.

Didn't stop him from wanting it, though.

None of this changed the fact that the longer he avoided going to grab his book, the harder it would be. So Arthur pointed his feet back across the Washington Street pedestrian bridge, turned down Cedar, rounded the New Riverside, and went right back up to the apartment door. As he walked, Arthur tried to manage his expectations. He was just going to grab his book. It wasn't like he'd get roped into London, or staying for lunch, much less the night. Sleeping in the same bed with James was over, regardless of anything else. Eve would want her spot back. The thought made him miserable.

He was coming up the stairs when he realized he could hear Eve and James talking on the other side of the apartment door.[2]

"Oh stop, that can't be! Jim, it's *London*. What we always dreamed of."

Shit, was it this easy to eavesdrop? Because that implicated humiliating potential for some key things to have been overheard by other tenants in the building. God, how had they never had the cops called for playing music so loud during practices? Arthur's mortification helpfully eclipsed his obligatory guilt about eavesdropping.

"I know, I know. But ... Eve, I want to ask Arthur to come too."

Arthur stilled on the top stair when he heard James say his name. Oh god, was he serious?

"What? Why?" Eve's voice laughed. "Come on, James. There will be plenty of closeted boys with cock-sucking lips to choose from in London."

Oh god, oh hell, this is why people shouldn't eavesdrop. Things that seemed funny suddenly became cruel when the object of the joke was listening. Arthur was cowed by the gibe, retreating a step. *But the goddamned book*. Arthur grimaced. He needed to make an entrance before things got too messy. He climbed the last step up to the threshold and listened for a change of subject so he could stumble in.

"Eve." James' tone was admonishing. Then, quieter, so that Arthur had to question whether he'd heard him right: "I think I might be in love with him."

The words felt like a painful unfurling inside his chest, like his ribcage was being opened up. Arthur's eyes started to prickle as he lost all semblance of self-respect and sagged against the door,

---

2. "Some Kinda Love" The Velvet Underground

pressing his ear unabashedly to the wood. *Please, say it again. Just the last four words this time, maybe, without the qualifiers.*

"That's impossible," Eve laughed. "You barely know him. Does he even want to go?"

"Well, I don't know. He hasn't said."

Did he? James had expressed his desire that Arthur come too, but he hadn't seriously considered it. Going to Chicago had already been quite a lot.

"And what *has* he said?"

"That he doesn't want me to stay and resent him for asking me to. He hasn't really asked me to. But I know I'm not the only one who wishes we had more time together."

Yes, oh please. Anything for more time.

"God, really? Okay. Jim. Listen to me. Arthur is nice. He's really cute, his lips look like two soft pillows I'd like to sleep on—I get it, okay? But you barely know him. You can't just bully him into going to London with us and leave us all trapped together if you break up." God, she was right. "Besides, Frank was difficult enough to convince about you. I don't really think he's going to be keen to add a pianist to his band on top of a vocalist and guitar player sight unseen. I spent all my familial currency to get him to agree to bring you with me."

Arthur scrambled to make sense of this. Frank must have been her cousin. It sounded like she was joining an established English band, and bending over backward to afford the opportunity to James too. How could Arthur even begin to hope that James would choose to stay home with such an enticing offer in opposition?

"What are you gonna do, Jim?" Eve continued. "Declare your love and ask him to give up his degree and his family and everything he knows to roll the dice on maybe playing keys for a band in London with strangers? He's not like you and I. He's not a musician."

Arthur winced.

"I know," James murmured, so quiet Arthur could scarcely make it out. "That's why I think I might just not go."

"James!" Eve exclaimed. "Are you mad?"

"London's not going anywhere..."

"But the music scene is a mile-a-minute over there. You snap your fingers and everyone's on to the next big thing. Jim, you can't just pass up a chance to move to London—something we have been dreaming of for *almost a decade*—because of some boy you just met!"

"Well, no, when you put it that way—"

"I'm not twisting it, Jim. I'm very accurately describing what's happening." Eve sighed. "Jimmy, you know I love you. You're my *person*. And you know I like Arthur too. I have nothing against him—I fucked him first, for heaven's sake—but I don't like what he's doing to you."

Arthur stepped back from the door. His cheeks were wet, so he wiped the heels of his hands under his glasses. This was not worth a textbook. Arthur shook his head and stumbled toward the steps. This wasn't worth passing the damned class. He'd rather fail than listen to another minute of this.

"You have this nasty tendency to go after boys who go too hard, too fast, Jim. I just don't want to see you get hurt," Eve added sympathetically.

The door to the apartment down the hall opened and a cloud of marijuana smoke billowed into the hallway. "Hey, man, didja lose your key?"

Arthur's face snapped up to face the bearded face of the hippie who lived next door. Eyes wide, he said in a hushed voice, "Uh, no, sorry—don't mind me. I was just leaving."

"Is there someone out there?" Eve called from the other side of the apartment door. "Jimmy, go see who it is."

"They're there, man, so they can probably let you in," the hippie pointed out helpfully. "Are you okay, man?"

Holy shit. This was the most mortifying thing that had ever happened. Arthur nodded and took the steps downstairs two at a time.

The door to the apartment opened as Arthur gained the downstairs exit.

"I think you might be getting cased, man," the hippie said, just as James called out, "Hello? Arthur?"

Arthur pushed the door open tear-blind and stumbled onto the sidewalk. His heart was pumping with hurt and anger. And shame for eavesdropping; humiliation for getting caught. He ran around the New Riverside and made for Washington Avenue, but James caught his arm before he ever reached the end of the block.

"Arthur, wait, what the hell was that?" James said breathlessly. The snow had stopped, but it was still freezing cold. His arms were getting goosebumps in the cold air without a jacket.

Arthur turned to face him. He tried to compose himself and then blurted out, "Are you going then?"

James' face went still. He nodded.

Arthur winced. "When?"

"I'm not sure yet. Eve is getting the tickets booked, and I'm going to pay her back."

"You're not even going to finish the semester?" His voice sounded small and desperate.

"I don't know. Maybe. But it's like I told you, the credits aren't really important," James replied, shifting one foot to the other in the cold.

Arthurr swallowed around something hard, probably the broken pieces of his stupid heart. He wanted to ask what was important, if there was anything important enough to delay for. If he could be that important. But he was too scared of the answer.

"What were you doing up there, Arthur?"

Arthur cringed and looked down at his feet on the cold pavement. There was a big crack splitting through the slab. "I needed my textbook for my lab."

"...How much did you overhear?"

"Enough," Arthur answered. He paused. He'd heard James' hesitance when he was talking to Eve. He was already caught out anyway, it didn't matter if he asked James about it. If there was even a minuscule chance, he had to ask. "Look, James, I don't want to be the thing that separates you from London. But I can't help myself. I want more time."

James' face was slashed with despondency. "Me too," he said at length, "I just ... if Eve goes, I don't have anyone left. And I don't want to put that on you. But ... I mean, is it really that outrageous for me to ask you to come with...?"

Arthur pushed his chin out to keep his face composed. He shook his head, looking anywhere but at James, taking a deep breath to steady his voice. "It would be the same for me if I went with you. I wouldn't have anyone but you and Eve. I'd hold you back."

James squirmed, shoving his hands in his pockets. "I really don't think you would. God, why is everyone I know such a fucking nihilist? Everything doesn't have to be a disaster. Sometimes really wonderful things happen, too. I see how you light up when you play, what music does for you. It's a big change, but it could be the start of something incredible."

Arthur tried to imagine moving to London. He couldn't do it. He couldn't even imagine going to the airport. The mere thought of throwing himself into a completely new place, with no guarantees for a place to sleep or money to eat, no one to turn to if things went sour—the very thought made him nauseous. "Everything I've ever known is here."

"That doesn't mean you have to stay."

"I know. But Eve is right. This is a lot of pressure to put on a new relationship." Arthur sighed. Someone had to say it. "Seems to me, we're stuck. Either we choose to stay together and resent each other for the things we gave up and break up, or we just break up now. At least if we break up now, we don't burn the bridge later. I mean, if either of us ever changed our minds—"

"I can't ask you to wait for me." James' voice took on a tight, desperate tone. "I don't want that, Arthur. I don't want to wait—"

"I don't either," Arthur replied. "But I don't see another way."

James shook his head. "No."

"I'm sorry. James..." Arthur stopped himself from reaching out to touch his arm. If he touched James, he'd lose his nerve. "I gotta go, I have a lab."

Arthur turned around and left James standing on the sidewalk. He couldn't look back, because tears filled his eyes, and he couldn't let James see him that way.

28

Arthur skipped the lab. He went straight to Comstock, shucked off his coat, curled up in his kimono, and sobbed into his pillow. He only surfaced to flip the Janis Joplin record. He wanted to just scream with her, but he was too tired or too worried about disturbing his neighbors to do it. He'd probably played the *I Got Dem Ol' Kozmic Blues Again Mama!* album six times when someone banged on his door and demanded he shut it off already. He finally fell asleep to the sound of early winter wind and sleet battering his window.

In the morning on Saturday, he found his *Fundamentals of Structural Analysis* textbook on the floor outside his door. Its presence felt so final, he'd collapsed back into his bed. James clearly dropped it off but hadn't bothered to knock or try to speak to him. Any delusion Arthur had of James changing his mind was crushed. Arthur willed himself back into unconsciousness just so he didn't have to feel so fucking terrible.

By Sunday, he'd made an art of wallowing. A routine of sorts. Wake up. Check coast was clear. Visit restroom. Get back into kimono. Play record. Eat bag of potato chips. Wallow in self pity. Take nap. Repeat.

It was late Sunday night when a knock came to his door.

"Arthur, are you in there?" Shit. It was Tomiko. Arthur felt a wave of shame crash over him. If he let her see him like this, any remaining impressions she had of his dignity or competency would be crushed into smithereens. So he pretended he wasn't there.

"Arthur, open the goddamn door, we know you're in there," Deb's voice joined in. "Your needle is scratching on the album label, you're clearly in crisis."

Arthur peeked out from under his pillow. "I'm fine. I'm sleeping."

"Sleeping people don't report on their condition, you twit." Deb again. "Open the door or I'm gonna bust it down."

Arthur sat straight up. She wouldn't ... would she?

"Alright, Tomi, stand aside!"

"Hey, you, what do you think you're doing?" a muffled voice down the hall called.

"Jesus, Deb, stop it!" Arthur shouted as he sprang off the bed and dashed across the room. He unlocked and opened the door a sliver and peered out to see if anyone was with Tomi and Deb. "What do you want?"

"I talked to Jim and Eve," Deb said simply, as Tomi said, "We just wanted to see if you're okay."

"Oh," Arthur said. "I'm fine."

"Bullshit," Deb replied and shoved her way past the door before Arthur could stop her. Tomiko followed and shut it securely behind her. Then her eyes alighted on Arthur and she said, "Arthur! You look like—"

Arthur braced himself, pulling the edges of the kimono together and crossing his arms. "I know, don't tell my mom, okay?"

"What do you mean? You look like a beautiful tortured artist, but Kabuki. I love it." Tomiko's grin faltered. "Except for the part where you are actually tortured. That's not cool."

Deb was at the record player. She stopped the needle and picked up the record. "Got the blues, have you now? Sounds like you're really doing fine."

"I am fine," Arthur doubled down. "Thanks for checking on me, guys, but I'm fine."

Deb gave him a penetrating sidelong look. Arthur squirmed.

"I know Eve's back," he said. "I was there when she came through the door."

"So you know she's packing up the whole apartment, Jim with it?" Deb's look was relentless. Arthur couldn't help but wince.

"Yeah. We broke up." Arthur's voice cracked miserably.

Deb shook her head slowly at him and rolled her eyes.

"He's going to London," Arthur explained defensively. He was quite proud of his measured delivery. "I'm not gonna go with him, so there's no point. I'm not gonna try and make him choose."

Deb exchanged a glance with Tomi. "Artie, let us take you somewhere."

Arthur grimaced. "What? No, it's late. I just want to listen to music and be left alone."

"See, that's your problem," Deb retorted, jabbing her index finger into his chest. "You think you're alone."

Arthur looked between her and Tomi for a moment. Deb had clearly run out of patience, but Tomi—Tomi looked a little hurt, almost. Arthur felt another nauseating swell of shame, but this time it was for being so worried that Tomi would see past his shell that he'd pushed her away entirely. Hell. He'd never even given her the opportunity to show him she could be trusted. He'd performed for her, just like he did for everyone else, and assumed her expectations were just like the rest of them. It had never occurred to him before that this had hurt her. That she could have been trusted, if he'd given her half the chance.[1]

"Come on," Deb sighed, stooping to carefully pluck his jeans from the floor by the waistband. "Get dressed. I'll prove to you you're not nearly as big a freak as you think you are."

---

1. "Desperation" Steppenwolf

Arthur caught the jeans she tossed at him but couldn't manage much else. Just the word 'freak' made him feel like his whole body had been frozen in stasis.

"Look," Tomi said softly, approaching him like he was some sort of injured animal. "She's not being very nice about it," Tomi tossed an annoyed look over her shoulder at Deb, "but she's not wrong. She wants to take you to the Club. It's a really cool place for people like us."

Like us. Arthur felt the tears coming, but he couldn't stop them. They'd been flowing free for days; the dam was breached. Tomi scooped him up in her arms, hugging him tightly around the ribs as he sniveled into her shoulder.

"Oh, for Chrissakes," Deb muttered. "And they say women are too emotional."

"Deb, stop it, come on," Tomi said as she stroked Arthur's back. "He's got a big heart. And it just got broken."

A fresh wave of tears swept over Arthur. He just gave in to it. His shell was long cracked open, leaving him exposed and vulnerable. Tomi was still here. Deb was still here (despite her completely caustic attitude). And he didn't have the strength to try and cover anymore. So he let them get him dressed (Deb was completely verklempt and still did it, which was the true testament of her loyalty) and led him out of Comstock Hall to the bus stop.

The bus took them downtown, to Hennepin Avenue. Arthur's mom had always warned him to avoid this area, especially the Gateway District, because it was full of "bums and drunks." As the bus trundled west on Hennepin Avenue, past the monolith of the dingy stone Lumber Exchange building, Arthur caught a glimpse of a discreet sign for the "Hennepin Baths." He started to shrink in his seat.

"Where is it that we're going again?" he squeaked to Tomi.

"It's just called the Club," Tomi whispered. Deb, who sat in the seat in front of them, turned and glared. There weren't a lot of people on the bus, but enough that they could be overheard.

Arthur curled his toes inside his sneakers and tried to turn invisible.

They got off the bus at 8th Street, and Arthur tried not to hide behind Deb, who was significantly shorter, as they walked down the sidewalk. Late-night city dwellers were smoking outside the bars and theaters that flanked the street despite the freezing temperatures. Arthur tried to assume they weren't all muggers waiting for an opportunity, but it was hard. Deb led them past the Orpheum Theater, then to a nondescript black door that said 916 on it. How the hell was anyone supposed to know this was here? Deb pulled the door open and paused in the dim entry.

"Tomi," she hissed, "put some lipstick on the nerd, would you?"

Tomiko raised her eyebrows and then looked up at Arthur.

"I can do it myself," Arthur said, and Tomi handed the tube to him from her purse.

"Dang, that's pretty good for no mirror," Tomiko remarked. "You're showing me all sorts of sides I wish I'd known about earlier."

Arthur withered apologetically and followed Deb up a narrow staircase that felt like a firetrap. At the top of the steps, there was a small booth with a window and a hippie sitting behind it, reading a paperback.

"Hey Deb," the guy said, setting his book down and leaning forward. "Who you got with you tonight?"

"This is my girl," Deb said and fried Arthur's mind with the ease that she said it. "And this is my bandmate."

The guy raised an eyebrow at Arthur. Deb turned and silently mouthed "Glasses!" Arthur fumbled them into his breast pocket. Deb looked back at the guy with a considerable amount of swagger. "She plays keys. That a problem?"

"Nah," the guy replied. "It's a dollar to go in. They're showing 'Some Like it Hot' tonight."

Arthur's ears perked, and he paid his dollar and followed Deb and Tomi inside. The room was small and dim. There were windows but they'd been painted black. It was like the Extemp in a lot of ways; the first room was a cafe with food, then behind it, another room where the movie was playing. Except it wasn't like the Extemp at all because the patrons were ... he didn't even know how to describe them. They were couples. Men, with other men. Women with other women. And a large proportion of the clientele appeared to be female impersonators. But not performers, like the place they'd gone to in Chicago. They were in everyday dress, made up beautifully to be sure, but more for a date with their boyfriends than for a lavish, glittering show.

There was a couple sitting at a table on the far side of the room, eating sandwiches and laughing, their heads tucked close together. She was wearing a go-go dress, pantyhose and a bouffant hair-do, with her long legs tucked to the side, ankles crossed. Her boyfriend hung on her every word. Arthur swallowed hard and sort of stood uselessly in the doorway.

Deb turned around and grabbed his hand, dragging him into the room. "What did I tell you?"

Arthur pulled her back. "Why didn't you tell me there was a place like this?" His voice sounded harsh and cracked.

"I just did," Deb replied levelly. "Come on, let's go watch the movie."

Arthur pushed the heel of his other hand harshly over his cheeks as a wave of laughter erupted from the next room. Deb let go of his hand as she and Tomi entered the room. At the doorway, a tall female impersonator put a well-manicured hand on Arthur's shoulder.

"Oh, honey," she said in a rich, smooth voice. "This your first time?"

Arthur just nodded. Tears were streaming down his face like he was a child. After the weekend he'd had, after the two months he had, he couldn't stop it. He didn't even care to try anymore.

"Well, welcome, then," she replied, wrapping one thick arm around him and pulling him into a quick, tight hug. "You're home." She kissed the top of his head and just like that, he felt anointed.

A while later, Arthur was seated along the side of the room, next to Tomiko and Deb, his glasses back on, watching Jack Lemmon being seduced by an elderly millionaire to great hilarity. He was laughing. He was feeling the most immense relief—he hadn't realized how much armor he'd been carrying. He hadn't realized that it was possible to be in a public place like this, where people could just let down their guard, dress the way that felt best, and be themselves.

He wished he'd known. If he'd known, he'd figured out a way to dress for this place. He'd have brought Pandora here. He'd ... he'd be Pandora here. There was an upright piano, draped in a cloth and stored on the stage where they'd set up the movie screen. There were posters in the bathroom for bands that played here on the weekends. Pandora could play this room. Pandora fucking deserved to play anywhere he wanted.

Arthur was going to miss James when he went to London. So much. His heart still ached for him. But he didn't need James to be truly seen. James had helped him. Eve too, in her way. Without them, he'd still be cowering inside his shell, pretending that hiding alone was enough. James had given him so much. Passion, devotion, inspiration. A name that felt right. God, he wished for a world where he could keep James too. But he didn't need James to feel like he belonged. There was a whole community of people who could understand him. A critical mass, even. Besides, and this was a fresh revelation, he didn't need anyone to save him from his shell. He could climb out whenever he wanted, all on his own.

☯

29

On Tuesday, the EP came in the mail, and Tomi and Arthur dropped all their finals prep to run to the Electric Fetus, where Deb was working, to hear it. They huddled together in a listening room, trying to share the headphones. Arthur couldn't help but smile as it played. He sounded ... good. Deb played it three times before she nodded her head and grinned.

"Fuck, man," she said around her cigarette. "I'm so glad we did 'Hammer Your Heart' instead of 'I've Been Here.'"

Tomi looked at Arthur with round eyes. "You're so talented, Arthur. How have you been keeping all this from me? I could just kill you!" She swatted him with the non-descript record sleeve.

Deb had the headphones on and was listening again, dragging so hard her cigarette crackled as her eyebrows furrowed in thought. "If we could get some copies made, I bet we could get it played on the radio. At least KFAI."

Arthur's heart leapt for a moment, before reality crashed down on him. "We can't do that without the whole band on board, though."

"Eve's not on this recording," Deb shrugged. "Ugh, but Jim is, and he's going off to London to complete his course in bastardry." She paused for a moment, then sighed and begrudgingly said, "But I guess we should probably ask Jim."

Arthur didn't ask the question. He couldn't. So with a glance his way, Tomi did instead. "When are they leaving?"

Deb shrugged again. "Eve is throwing a farewell party on Friday. She actually came by here and tried to get me to play a farewell show at the Extemp."

"And you said no?" Tomi clarified with surprise.

"Fuck if I'm going to go along with her stupid plan to break up the band just for one more chance to play. Hell no. I'm fucking pissed at her. Serves her fucking right to not be able to play one last rocking show before she fucks off to her fucking stupid band of British bozos."

Arthur winced. He felt like an asshole, but he was still stuck on being asked to play one last show. And how he hadn't been asked. But of course he hadn't been. It made sense. He'd dumped Eve's best friend, for goodness sake. Why would she go out of her way to include him?

It still stung.

"You know, there's a part of me that wants to go to that party and play the demo in front of everyone," Deb said, a mean smile curling at the edges of her mouth. "Then she'll have to sit there knowing we played that well without her and pretend like it was her bass and her idea all along."

Tomiko gave Deb a flat look and shook her head. "And what would that accomplish?"

"I dunno, it would make me feel better," Deb sighed.

"We should go to the party though," Arthur said, surprising himself.

"Wait—you want to go to the party?" Deb clarified. If she'd been wearing sunglasses, she would have looked at him over the rims.

Arthur grimaced. "No, not really. But if we want to see if we can get any radio play with this, we need James' permission."

"And you're willing to ask him?"

"Well, yeah, I mean, if you and Tomi come with me."

"I'm not sure Tomi and I are going to have any impact on Jim saying yes. If you ask him, he'll give us his whole-hearted blessing."

"Why would you think that?"

"Because he feels like a supreme asshole for leaving, and it'll make him feel better to know he wasn't standing in your way from halfway around the world."

Arthur's brow furrowed incredulously.

"Oh, come on, Artie. Jim's a total sucker for you. He'll do whatever you tell him to do."

"Except stay," Arthur muttered and immediately wished he hadn't. It made him feel sad.

"Well, I mean, did you try asking him to stay?" Tomi asked.

"No," Arthur said with increasing distress. "I mean, I don't think I did. I suggested he stay once, but then I doubled back and told him I was sorry and that it's not fair for me to try and make him do anything on my account."

"But don't you want him to stay?" Tomiko asked.

"Well, yes, but I don't want him to do it for me," Arthur replied. "If that makes sense."

"It does not," Tomiko said forbearingly.

"For fuck's sake, Arthur," Deb cried, throwing up her hands. "Why would it be so bad if he stayed for you? This is so completely stupid. The two of you are seriously taking years off my life with your complete emotional constipation."

Arthur crossed his arms. This was already hard enough without his friends telling him he was being stupid for not demanding his boyfriend—ex-boyfriend—give up his dreams to stay with him. "Well, I don't know what you expect. We've only been together for a few weeks. That certainly isn't enough time to be giving up life-changing opportunities just to be together."

Deb rolled her eyes. "Come on, three weeks is like three years in lesbian time. What would Marilyn do?"

Arthur gave a long-winded sigh. "Marilyn would sit in a perfectly curvaceous slump and sing 'I'm Through with Love.'"

"Fine, what would Josephine do, then?"

"Josephine would sucker punch a bitch," Tomi pointed out. "Or Daphne? I couldn't keep the two of them straight."

"Daphne would just find a rich dude to marry and live happily ever after."

Deb and Tomiko evaporated into laughter.

Arthur shook his head dismissively, but another question rang in his ears. *What would Pandora do?* He tried to imagine being dressed and adorned, slinging up the stairs to the apartment with the single-minded determination of Louise Brooks or Anna May Wong. Filled to the brim with bombshell energy. Eve would open the door and back away in awe. James would throw his packed suitcase out on the floor and turn to Eve and say, "I can't do this. I'm staying." He'd bundle Arthur into his arms as Eve stormed off and the credits would roll over the swelling music as he and James kissed in a tight embrace.

"No way," Arthur said aloud. "He's already going. It's too late."

Deb rolled her eyes at him. "It's never too late."

30

Arthur spent the rest of the week hitting his books hard in preparation for finals. He had a lot of catching up to do, and it was a good distraction from the impending farewell party that threatened to rip his heart out again and put it on display for everyone to see. But when he thought about not going, that somehow felt worse, so on Wednesday, he carved out time to go to Daytons with Tomiko so he could at least pretend to be confident. A silk scarf or at least a pair of jeans that fit well. If the clothes made the man, Arthur felt ready to expand his options beyond the parade of turtle shells he'd cultivated so far. He wanted some things that made him feel like Pandora (but that also wouldn't get him arrested).

Tomi helped him spend the money his mother had given him to make himself presentable at Christmas on a very tight red turtleneck, a fitted paisley vest, a pair of jeans that were too small (Tomi promised they could get them to fit if he wore them while they were still damp from the wash), and a beautiful turquoise silk ascot. Tomi also acquired a few tubes of lipstick and an eyeliner pencil for him from the makeup counter.

He was supposed to get his hair cut, but he ran out of money. Instead, he waited until after midnight and cut his own hair in the mirror of the dorm bathroom. It was a risk, but he was careful, and besides, he only trimmed up the back and cut his bangs into a pageboy style that made him feel half silent film star, half early-sixties Paul McCartney. Regardless, it was a style that would keep him out of the doghouse with his mother while still giving himself options.

On Friday night, he squeezed into his new jeans and dressed one of his less-drab button-up shirts with the ascot. He left the top three buttons unbuttoned and the ascot draped over his bare chest in a way that gave him a buzz of swagger. Tomi and Deb swung by to pick him up, and the three of them walked across the Washington Avenue pedestrian bridge in the light snow.

When they rounded the New Riverside, Arthur pulled out a tube of maroon-colored lipstick and dabbed it on the center of his lips before they went inside. Arthur was so apprehensive, the staircase looked like it was three stories tall. One of the FREE people let them in, gushing when she saw Deb. Arthur stood awkwardly to one side of the threshold, furtively assessing the packed room of well-wishers.

James caught his eye almost immediately. He was leaning against the record player with a beer between his fingers, presiding over the dancing with his deep, blue eyes. He seemed to sense Arthur's gaze on him and he looked up, meeting his eyes across the room. He still made Arthur's heart thump. Made him want all sorts of things he couldn't have. He felt Tomi squeeze his hand and like that, he looked away and was swept into the kitchen for drinks. They had brought wine, but it seemed most of the other guests had similar notions, because the kitchen table was groaning with bottles.

"Darlings!" Eve descended upon them in a flurry of fringed poncho and generous thigh. "Oh, I'm so glad to see you both!"

She seized Deb and pressed a kiss to her lips, which Deb received with about as much grace as a child would receiving a kiss from his great aunt. Undeterred, Eve turned to Arthur and delivered the same, a brief, soft press of lips to lips. She pulled back and gave Arthur a deeply fond smile.

"You look so gorgeous, darling. You're going to need to tell me that lipstick shade. Oh, I can't bear how much I'm going to miss you two and the Tarts," Eve confessed. "I'm getting a little teary-eyed! Oh, golly, I think I've had too much wine, I'm terribly sorry."

Arthur would be lying if he said he didn't find this somewhat off-putting. It was a little difficult to sympathize when the whole leaving-for-London endeavor was entirely her scheme. However, Fumiko Ohashi didn't raise an oaf, so he said, "It's alright. We're going to miss you too. A lot."

Eve petted the scarf knotted at Arthur's throat fondly and said, "You simply must come and visit us once we're settled. I know it's a long trip, but Arthur!—Deb! Both of you!—You would be in your *element*, I tell you. You'll never want to leave."

Arthur shrugged awkwardly and tried to glance over Eve's shoulder towards James and the record player. There were too many people milling around, dancing in the middle of the living room. A fluff of blonde hair was all he could see. "I have to earn my degree and get a job before I tackle any big trips."

"I don't fly," Deb said seriously. "Not after what happened to the Big Bopper."

Eve giggled. "Deb, come on. It's more likely that you get hit by lightning than die in a plane crash."

"Exactly why I'm also afraid of thunderstorms," Deb retorted, her expression a perfect dignified composure. "This is my girlfriend, Tomiko. Tomiko, this is our former lead singer, Eve."

Tomi gamely put her hand out. "It's nice to meet you, finally. I really enjoyed your shows."

Eve gave Tomiko a blubbery face and then hugged her tightly. "Thank you for saying that!"

Arthur looked up again for James and began to edge away with his wine cup towards the record player.

"Arthur!" Eve's voice called him back towards the little eat-in kitchen. "Please tell me you'll come visit us."

Arthur stalled. "I mean, I really don't have the funds and won't until I start working. Though by then, I might end up drafted."

"Oh, all the more reason to come to London! You could build things for the British, I'm sure of it," Eve exclaimed resolutely. She leaned in close, her hand on his chest again. "It's just, James has been sort of a mess since you two broke up. I'm sure that if you had a visit planned, it wouldn't be so difficult for him."

Arthur failed to understand why he would want to make it easier for James to move away from him, or why he should be expected to travel half-way across the world to soothe James' broken heart. That was Eve-grade bullshit, right there. He gave her a very noncommittal shrug and pressed himself into the crowd.

He squeezed into the group of dancers and spun and shimmied his way to the record player. God, what he would give to go back in time and be able to simply lean against the console and talk with James about music. He tried one last time regardless, slipping out of the group of dancers from the side and inching along the console until he was at James' side.

"Who's this?" Arthur ventured.

James passed the picture sleeve to him. "Some skinheads, I guess? I don't know what that means, but Eve brought it back. They're called Slade."

"I like the vocalist," Arthur said. "He sounds rough, kind of desperate. Raw."

The song rocked intensely, heavy with electric guitar and a driving beat. Arthur flipped the album and tried to determine where they were in the playlist as the vocalist ripped out the chorus, "Nothing can change the shape of things to come." Well fuck. That was not a good omen.

The song ended and so did the side. James turned and occupied himself with flipping the record. A driving swung bass launched Side B. James settled back against the console and lit a cigarette.[1]

"You came," he said after a moment, his voice quiet.

"Of course I came."

"I didn't think you would, after last Friday."

Arthur shrugged. "I guess I didn't either, to be honest. But Deb convinced me I'd regret it if I didn't."

"Oh." James seemed downtrodden. And it wasn't just the way Arthur's words had come out all wrong and demoralizing.

"I, uh," Arthur didn't know what to say, so he launched directly into the purpose he'd come with. "I had a favor to ask you before you go?"

"Yeah?" James replied, but it was muffled by a flurry of fringe pressing herself full length up to James.

"Oh, you have a favor to ask, do you?" Eve said, her arms around James' waist and her eyebrows waggling. "You two, I tell you. You look so very fine together. I do wish we could have found a way to work it all out between us. I think it could have been really good." Her lascivious grin brought to bear the kind of good she was imagining. God, that night in Chicago felt like a hundred years ago. And since when had Eve become so fucking tone deaf? Had this sort of thing lit Arthur up before?

James sort of wriggled out of her arms. "I'm sure it's not that kind of favor, Eve, god."

Arthur regarded Eve warily. He could not let it slide in front of her that they hadn't ended up getting a recording that had her on it. While lying about it didn't sit quite right either, it did feel very necessary. And in its way, generous. It would be a cold, cruel way to send her off.

"Um, maybe we can go somewhere a little quieter to talk about it?" Arthur said cryptically. Eve's eyes went wide and she dropped her mouth open in a wide grin.

---

1. "Know Who You Are" Slade

"*Oh!*" she said significantly. "In that case, I'll make myself scarce. Bedroom should be open," she grinned at James, then set a hand on Arthur's forearm. "Unless you want me to come with…?"

Arthur slipped his arm away. She wasn't trying to be seedy or spiteful—in fact, she was more the Eve he had fallen for than ever. But after the weeks he'd spent with James, weeks that had felt realer than anything he'd ever known, her flirtatious affectation fell flat and stale. He shook his head and gave a small apologetic shrug.

"It'll just take a minute," Arthur said. James nodded and tamped his cigarette out in the ashtray. They squeezed through the dancing guests one after the other, making their way toward the hall. Eve grinned and threw herself into dancing to the brutal guitar wails of Slade.

When they got to the bedroom, Arthur waited for James to enter first, then shut the door behind him. He opened his mouth to begin, but it hung open there for a moment as he took in the bedroom.

He'd never seen it so tidy before. The furniture was bare and dusted. There were no clothes strewn everywhere, nor really any signs that someone lived there apart from a pile of three suitcases in one corner.

"Oh," Arthur said dumbly.

"Yeah," James agreed, looking at the not-wreckage, which existed in strange opposition to the complete wreckage of him leaving. "Packing has been a real challenge. It's hard to decide what to bring when you're limited to one bag."

"What happened to your collection?" Arthur asked, crossing rather absently to the wardrobe and pulling it open. Columns of silk greeted him from the other side like old friends.

"Nothing," James answered unnecessarily, scratching the back of his neck awkwardly. "I was hoping you might want it."

Arthur did want it. But not without James. So he shrugged and said nothing.

"What was it you wanted to ask me, then?" James inquired, his voice tight with tension.

"Oh," Arthur was an idiot. He was staring at James' similarly unbuttoned shirt and the swath of chest hair peeking out that Arthur wasn't going to get to push his fingers through ever again. What an weird, arbitrary thing to make one's eyes sting with tears. "It's the demo. It came in the mail."

James shook his head in surprise. "Oh, that's good news. How does it sound?"

Arthur shrugged. "Pretty good. Deb wants to get copies made and send them to some radio stations. I'm wondering if we can still do that even if you're out of the country."

James sank onto the edge of the mattress with a shrug. "Sure. Whatever you want."

"Oh," Arthur said again, feeling like a broken record. "Great. We were hoping you'd give your permission."

"Of course, you have it," James replied. He didn't sound particularly enthusiastic, but the words were right. "I certainly don't have the money or desire to sue you for it. So have at it."

Arthur nodded. "Okay. Thank you."

He turned and his hand was only halfway to the doorknob when James pleaded, "Arthur, wait."

And just like that, James' hand was on Arthur's forearm, and Arthur was turning, lifting his chin to greet James' seeking mouth with his own. They kissed. Even though they shouldn't, even though it made Arthur's heart feel like it was being squeezed in a vice. Not an ounce of self preservation remained to stop him from pushing his fingers into James' hair, pulling him closer and setting him in motion to press Arthur up against the door. James' hands came up to Arthur's face and cupped his jaw reverently. He kissed Arthur in the same manner, like he was drinking water. Like he was parched.

James pulled back and pressed his forehead to Arthur's. "Please. Won't you come?"

Arthur let out a long sigh. "I can't," he agonized. "I wish I could tell you yes. But I really can't. Even if I had the courage, I don't have the means."

James nodded. "I get it. I understand why you want to stay. You have your family, and Deb and Tomiko, and your degree. I wouldn't want to drop everything and leave if I had those things too."

Arthur stared at him for a moment. "Christ, James, you *do* have those things. Deb is your friend, and I'm pretty sure Tomiko could give you a run for your money in any ethics discussion. And I know we were only together for maybe a month, but I love you, James, and I'll miss you when you're gone. A lot."

He pushed back all of the other things he wanted to say. Things that were unfair, like *When will you be back to visit?* and *Stay.* He was so distracted with keeping these thoughts to himself that it took him a moment to realize what he had let slip. He met James' eyes and swallowed hard.

"You what?"

"I, uh, I love you. I'm in love with you, actually. I'm sorry, I didn't mean to tell you that. I'm not saying it to try and get you to change your mind or anything. I just ... it's true, and I ... Actually, I'm not sorry. Just because it's ending doesn't mean that you didn't make me supremely happy when we were together. You should know that."

Arthur's heart was racing so fast it was making him feel a little dizzy. James' brow was furrowed so tight, only his blue eyes peeked out from beneath. Arthur wasn't sure what to make of his fierce expression until James reached out and pulled Arthur to his chest, wrapping his arms around him. Arthur squeezed him back around the waist, burying his nose in James' shoulder, drawing in the scent memory of his hair.

"God dammit," James muttered tightly. His shoulders were drawn and tight. If Arthur didn't know better, he might think he was crying.

"It's okay," Arthur said, and for the first time since that stupid postcard had arrived, he believed it would be. Perhaps the truth really did set you free. "You're going to live out your rockstar dreams. Play music in a place where there's more than a couple cover bands and venues that only book Top 40 touring groups. Even though we won't be together, I'm still going to be rooting for you."

This did not seem to help. James' hands clutched Arthur's shirt so tight, he thought he might tear it. Arthur could feel that the scarf at his neck was wet.

"Why can't we have both?" James whimpered into Arthur's neck.

"I can't ask you to wait for me," Arthur replied, stroking his hair and wondering how on earth the tables had turned to make him feel like he was the one leaving James and not the other way around. "I dunno, life is long and everything is always changing. I refuse to believe this is goodbye forever."

James pulled back then. His cheeks were wet, but his eyes were searching and intent, his chin working to wrest back control. He opened his mouth, and Arthur remembered his overheard confession of love to Eve. *Come on, James,* he thought. *Say it. Let me have this one thing before you go.*

"No," James said. His hands grasped Arthur at the back of his neck. James pressed their lips together, breathing him in, then turned his face so that his stubble-rough cheek nestled against Arthur's. "No. I can't—I don't know. Arthur, I don't know what I want. I just know that every time I remember I'm leaving you behind, I lock up. My whole body rejects it. And I think I love you, because this whole thing physically hurts. But I also can't just pass it up, this chance I've been waiting for since high school. I can't put that on you. That would be crazy—Fuck, man!"

James pressed his face back into Arthur's neck. Arthur moved his hand over James' back and tried desperately to think of what to say. He felt strange, like he shouldn't be there. He didn't deserve to be witnessing James this way, especially not after he'd dumped him. Maybe he should go get Eve? As soon as the thought occurred to him, he rejected it outright. If James had even the barest notion of staying, Eve would stamp it out of him. And maybe it was selfish, but Arthur wanted to know what was there. Eve didn't know the difference between what she wanted for James and what James himself wanted. And she was so confident and certain in her notions, it was no wonder James was so confused.

"Who says it's crazy?" Arthur asked quietly.

"It's just the kind of stupid shit that happens in movies but never works out in real life."

"Why not?" Arthur frowned. "Why can't people take a chance on each other in the name of love? Who made the rule that love is always punished?"

"The church, politicians, police, general homophobic culture?" James offered miserably.

"Okay, fine, yes, you're right," Arthur sighed. "Jeez, are you sure you're not doing pre-law?"

James snorted, and Arthur felt an abiding satisfaction at making him laugh, even a little bit. Arthur pressed a kiss to his hair and gently pushed his shoulders so they could look each other in the eye again.

"I..." Arthur started, then shook his head and restarted. "I really want to tell you what I want you to do, but I can't. You have to decide. On your own. Only you know what's right for you. If you stayed, I'd be overjoyed. But I don't want you to do it if your heart will always be longing for what could have been in London."

James swiped his cheeks with his hands and sniffed as manfully as he could manage. "No one has ever said that to me before."

"What?"

"That only I know what's right for me." James turned and slumped half against the door, half against Arthur's left shoulder, like his own weight had become too much. "Everyone—my parents, my teachers, Eve—always have to put in their two cents, like I'm too stupid to be trusted with my own decisions." He sighed and tilted his head. "Thanks for trusting me, even though I have given you literally zero reasons to."

Arthur shrugged and looked at the floor. James reached up and tucked Arthur's short, black hair behind his ear.

"I like your haircut," James murmured.

"Thanks," Arthur replied, unable to help but fuss with it. James reached up and pushed his fingers into the hair behind Arthur's ear, turning his face gently towards James'. He pressed a kiss to Arthur's lips. It was soft and chaste, but Arthur could taste its promise. He sensed he could have as much of James as he wanted right now, if he was willing to take it. Part of him wanted to. One last time.

"I should go," Arthur murmured into James' mouth.

"Don't."

"I can't, James," Arthur said, and pulled back this time. If he stayed, if he had sex with James, it would color everything that happened afterward. And even though it was ridiculous, he didn't want to wonder in spite of himself if James would have stayed if only he'd given better head or something. "I've got to go."

James slumped back against the door. His eyes were impossibly sad wells of despairing blue tinged red from crying. "Yeah, okay. I know."

Arthur pulled away, even though it was the last thing he wanted to do. James straightened and stepped back as Arthur opened the door and paused to look back at him.

Everything he thought of saying felt wrong, so he just reached out for James' hand. James offered it, lacing his fingers between Arthur's. They squeezed and it felt like a strange kind of pact, a seal of love that, even if it ended, would still be stamped upon their lives forever. A memory of a time and a person and an intimacy against which others would be measured. And it wasn't the resolution that Arthur wanted, but it was something and it was enough to get him to walk out the door.

31

The plane left early the next day. Arthur woke up in his dorm room feeling the emptiness of his future spreading out before him like oil across the surface of a lake, empty and foul. But Arthur didn't want to wallow, so he packed up his books and hitched a ride with Tomiko to St. Paul.

Tomi dropped him outside his parents' house in West St. Paul, and he picked his way over the driveway slick with black ice to the door. The air was thick with low-hanging clouds that promised snow. When Okaasan opened the door and saw his face, she frowned and said, "What happened?"

It was such a relief that he could tell her the truth.

Okaasan made hot tea for them both and shook her head and sucked her teeth at all the right places as Arthur talked. When his dad returned from the grocery store, he offered to knock some sense into James, which Arthur felt was a nice gesture of support. He watched the first fifteen minutes of some new soap opera called *All My Children* with his mom before he couldn't take it anymore and went to the basement.

He put *Pandora's Box* on the projector and bundled himself under blankets on the couch. Now this was his brand of melodrama. At the part when Lulu was caught in her revealing costume with Schön backstage, he pulled out a notebook and started sketching.

Arthur was not an artist, by any means, but he had enough experience with drafting to cobble together a figure, albeit a very geometric one. He kept an eye on the film as it progressed, marking his favorite moments from memory, as he sketched and tried very hard not to feel sorry for himself. There were many things he still had going for him. For heaven's sake, now that Mick Jagger was wearing lipstick, perhaps in a year or two it would be socially acceptable for guys to wear makeup, regardless of their sexual interests. There were other guys out there who were gay, who appreciated androgyny, right here in the Twin Cities. He was not, as Deb so helpfully pointed out, alone. It wasn't ideal—he wasn't sure it would ever be easy—but it was bearable. He'd survive.

He didn't really track the sound of the front door opening until he heard his mother's voice calling him in Japanese. That was really strange, and it took him a minute to focus enough to understand her with his rudimentary fluency.

Arthur frowned. Someone was here. He didn't know the word (words?) she was using for them, though. Arthur stood from the couch as his mother ducked into the stairwell.

"Atchan," she hissed urgently.

"Who's here?" Arthur asked. "I couldn't understand you."

"Taisetsu na hito wa—oh, for heaven's sake, your boyfriend's here, baka, isoide!" Okaasan flapped her hand at him urgently.

Arthur stood there dumbly (he deserved baka). "James?"

"Yes, James, come on! Hurry up before your father kills him."

Arthur's mouth dropped open. What the hell was James doing here? He was supposed to be on a plane. He couldn't even entertain the possibility of hoping for what that meant. But he also couldn't come up with a disappointing explanation to prepare himself for either. Arthur dashed up the stairs two at a time and skidded through the kitchen.[1]

The cacophony of feelings hammering Arthur's insides escalated to a riot. James was standing awkwardly on the front stoop, in the light, swirling snow, while Otosan glowered at him through the open door with his arms crossed across his chest. James looked tired, like he hadn't slept, and his face and shoulders were tense and angular, making him look like a Picasso painting of himself. Otosan was not helping.

"Otosan, it's okay," Arthur said, touching his shoulder to try and nudge his father out of the way.

Otosan grunted. Then, he tipped his head so he was looking down his nose at James and said, "Do you know what a man sounds like when he dies?"

Arthur's eyes widened in mortification. James shrank even farther into his shoulders as he shook his head slightly and said, "No?"

Otosan blinked slowly at James. "I do." Then he turned and stalked back to his armchair. He gave James another nasty glare as he shook his paper open and disappeared behind it.

James regarded Arthur with a harrowed expression. Arthur grimaced. "Ignore him." Reaching out to pull James into the house by his sleeve, he added, "I think he's been waiting his whole life to use that line. Is that why you always wanted a daughter, Dad?"

Otosan replied in Japanese, and Arthur managed to catch something about how he'd got exactly what he wanted. While threatening his boyfriend was not ideal behavior, the sentiment did warm Arthur's heart. Oh god, his boyfriend.

James was toeing his boots off in the entry, and Arthur ducked into the front closet to grab slippers for him. It was the most ridiculous ritual to have to go through when Arthur's

---

1. "Is It Love?" T. Rex

heart was trying to hammer out of his chest, and he kept blinking to try and figure out if he was dreaming. Arthur straightened and grabbed James' hand to lead him to the basement, but Okaasan stood in the kitchen entry with her arms crossed over her chest.

"Okaa, we're just going to go down to the basement," Arthur said when it became evident that she wasn't going to move.

"Doesn't James want something to drink?" his mother asked, her face hard and unwelcoming. "I wouldn't want him to think we were bad hosts."

"Mom! No!"

"Uh, no thank you, Mrs. Ohashi," James replied at the same time.

"Okaasan, *yamete*," Arthur hissed. While he understood a lot more than he could say, he certainly knew enough Japanese to say 'Quit it.' Okaasan glowered, but she did step aside. Arthur hustled James through the kitchen and down the stairs to the basement. He was probably going to get grief for it later, but he closed the door securely behind him. James was at the bottom of the steps as Arthur descended two at a time and deposited himself straight into James' arms. He wrapped his arms tight around James' waist and pressed his face into the hair over his shoulders. There were still flakes of snow caught in the golden mess of curls.

The only sounds were the whirr of the projector, and the two of them breathing.

"I can't believe you're here," Arthur whispered into his neck. His eyes stung with tears, but he couldn't force himself to care.

"Really?" James replied. His arms were tight around Arthur's shoulders. One of his hands grasped the back of Arthur's neck, and his lips spoke quietly into Arthur's hair. "Coming here has been the most natural thing I've done all week. Well, not here really. I've been all over campus looking for you. But you know."

Arthur tipped his face towards James'. "So you're not going?"

"Not yet anyway," James replied, pressing his forehead to Arthur's. He smiled.

Arthur did not feel like smiling yet. "What does that mean?"

"It means I talked to Eve last night and, well, in hindsight, I probably should have waited until she sobered up a bit, but I told her I wanted to stay. And Eve said all that shit about loyalty and our dreams and protecting me again, and I lapped it all up like I usually do. But then I woke up this morning, and I thought, 'Well, if I'm so excited about going to London, why do I feel like shit?'"

Arthur squeezed his eyes shut and pressed his face back into James' neck. God, James was here. There was nothing to cry about now. He was right here. Stop.

"What did Eve say?"

"Nothing, really. She's pissed, she thinks I'm making a huge mistake, etcetera." James' voice was placid, but his tense shoulders gave away his apprehension. "Here's the thing, Arthur." James pushed Arthur gently to arm's length. His keen blue eyes trapped Arthur's gaze. "When we talked last night, I realized something. Love doesn't look like someone pushing you and forcing you towards what they think is best for you. It looks like trust. *You* put your trust in me."

"I didn't do it to make you stay, though," Arthur protested.

"I know, that's what I'm saying," James replied. His brows were knit together fervently, and it was intense to hold his gaze, but Arthur did not dare look away. "You trusted me to choose, and I freely choose you. I choose to see what we have together. I choose to see that through before I go off to London and see if my guitar-playing is actually any good. I love you, Arthur."

The words sank into Arthur's skin, permeated in his blood, became a part of him and it lifted him higher than any music ever could. James blinked after a moment.

"Is that alright?" he asked falteringly. "I guess maybe I should have asked you what you wanted first."

"No!" Arthur immediately protested. "No, I love you too! All I ever wanted was more time. I want you to stay. I just didn't want you to do it for me. I wanted you to do it because it was what *you* wanted most."

"It is what I want most," James replied. "You are what I want most."

Arthur's hands came up to James' chest as he pulled Arthur in. He tipped his head and parted his lips. James met him halfway with a fierce kiss. The heat of it flooded Arthur's senses, sweeping away the doubts and fears that were fighting for survival. He used one hand to pull James in by his neck.

After indulging for a few long moments, Arthur pulled back. "Sorry." He gasped breathlessly. "My parents already want to kill you, I don't want to give them any other ammunition."

"Did you tell them what's going on?" James asked.

"Yes!" Arthur exclaimed. "Of course I did. I was upset. I missed you. I needed someone to tell me it was okay."

James wrapped him up in a tight hug. "You won the parent jackpot, you know that right?"

"I know," Arthur replied, "which is why we are currently needing to take precautions for your safety, because my dad threatened to kill you."

"Yeah," James said quietly. "That was chilling."

Arthur's hands still clutched at James' t-shirt and shoulder, in spite of the very logical knowledge that Okaasan was likely to make her presence known in a few minutes. "You said you're not going to London yet. What does that mean?"

James pressed his lips together thoughtfully. "It means ... it means I still want to go. But it's more important for me to see where things are going with you first."

"So I'm a greater priority than London?" Arthur clarified, not at all letting this resounding compliment go to his head.

"Well, yeah," James confirmed. Arthur couldn't help but kiss him for that. James tipped his head back to say, "When I go, I'll be bringing you with me or the broken pieces of my heart."

"I have no intention of breaking your heart," Arthur chided. He pressed a beloved kiss to James' jaw.

"No one ever does."

"I would argue Eve might take some enjoyment from breaking hearts."

"Okay, yes, but she's an anomaly."

"The exception that proves the rule?"

"That's it."

"What about Eve?" Arthur asked, more seriously. "I know how important she is to you. The last thing I want to do is pit myself in some sort of weird competition against her for your attention."

James nodded abashedly. "Okay, I guess that's fair." He sighed. "I'll tell you the same thing I told her. I have been friends with Eve since I was ten years old. I ... honestly, I really don't know who I am when she's not around. But we've been ruining each other. Jealous posturing, manipulative competition—the shit we put you through was so selfish and unfair, and I'm ashamed that I participated in it when I could have just talked to you and told you how I felt. Through it all, you've been so open and kind. Even though I don't deserve it, I'm so grateful. Fact is, it's been a while since I've liked who I've become around her. Taking a break, going our separate ways—it maybe isn't what we want, but it's what Eve and I need, if we're going to continue to be friends in the long run."

Arthur nodded. "You're a good man, James," he said, because it was true, and because James looked like he really needed to hear it. "I love you. And I'm *so fucking relieved* you're staying. Holy shit." He pressed his face into James' chest and heard the rumble of his laugh through his t-shirt. God, love felt good. It blossomed, opening his chest and his throat and releasing tension across his whole body. Arthur had never felt more at ease in his own skin. It gave him the reckless confidence to think aloud.

"James."

"Hm?"

"I know I'm not Eve. And I'm probably not enough on my own—"

"Ho, whoa, you're more than enough, don't say that—"

"—Thank you, I'm sorry, that came out wrong." Arthur straightened and looked up into James' limitless eyes. "What I mean is I don't think there's anyone who can be everything to someone else. We need lots of people—friends and family and neighbors—together, and all that maybe makes enough. You've already lost a lot of those things, but I don't know... We aren't the only gay people in Minneapolis."

James' brow was still furrowed, but his lips pursed in curiosity. "No, we certainly aren't."

"There are places where we can find others like us, make our own way," Arthur said. "I don't think there's any reason why we should have to live in the shadows."

James blinked at him with surprise. "This coming from the guy who is freaked out by protests?"

Arthur shrugged. "I dunno. There's a reason why my parents are cautious. They know too well what it's like to be brought under the law for something about yourself you can't change. But..." He took a moment to put his thoughts together. "But I don't want to live in fear. Not anymore. I don't want to be scared that who I am isn't good enough for someone else, or that they're going to treat me like a threat. I've wasted too much of my life already twisting into everyone else's boxes."

"Ain't that the truth."

The basement door clicked abruptly open.

"Arthur?" Okaasan's sharp voice cut through the quiet whirr of the projector as James and Arthur jumped apart. "Is James staying for dinner?"

Arthur looked back at James as a smile played on his lips. James nodded, his crooked smile a slash across his beloved features.

"Yeah, if that's okay," Arthur called back.

Okaasan ducked her head down so she could see them. She lifted an eyebrow at the scant space between them and said curtly, "If you want him here, so do I."

She popped up the stairs again. "And leave the door open! No funny business in my house!"

Arthur and James exchanged glances.

"This is not going to surprise you," James said, "but I think I love your mom."

Arthur couldn't stop himself from laughing.

Epilogue

"Okay, Mrs. Ohashi," Tomiko said as she opened the nondescript black door marked 916. "You have to promise—*promise me*—you're gonna be cool about this."

"What do you mean? Of course I'm going to be 'cool,'" Mrs. Ohashi pressed her hands to the sides of her bouffant to check for fly-aways. "You told me what to expect. Why would I be embarrassing? Just because I'm over forty doesn't mean I'm dead. Although if we linger around in this neighborhood any longer, I might be."

"It's just..." Tomi replied. "This place is very private. So just don't freak anyone out by being too..."

"...What?"

"I dunno, Methodist?"

At the top of the staircase, Rick raised his eyebrows at Tomi from behind the glass window. "Who's this?"

"It's Pandora's mom," Tomi said. "And yes, he knows she's coming."

"Pandora, huh?"

"I told you to be cool, Mrs. Ohashi." Tomi muttered out the side of her mouth.

Rick's eyebrow did not lower, but he took their cover money and let Tomi take Mrs. Ohashi through.

"Don't make me regret this!" he called after them as they went into the cafe.

"Oh," Mrs. Ohashi said, clutching her purse with both hands as a willowy drag queen walked past her in enormous platform heels. "It's very..." She caught Tomi giving her a withering look. "It's very smoky in here. I hope Arthur hasn't taken up the cigarettes. I've noticed James does more than his fair share of that."

Tomiko shh-ed her and led Arthur's mother into the back room, where the band was just getting started. Deb was seated behind her drum kit, sleeves rolled up to her shoulders and hair slicked back like a biker. She flicked a wave at Tomi as she settled Mrs. Ohashi at a back table.

"Oh my," Mrs. Ohashi said. "Does James know he's not wearing a shirt?" James stood opposite the piano with his guitar, tight jeans and a silky smoking jacket open to his bare chest.

"Yeah," Tomi replied. "I'm pretty sure he does. Are you *sure* you're gonna be cool?"

"Stop that already."

"I just want to make sure you're not going to be uncomfortable when you see Arthur," Tomi said gently. "He looks really different when he's Pandora."

"Oh for heaven's sake, I helped make Arthur's dress. Just because he's given himself a new name doesn't mean I don't know my child. I'm going to be quite cool, okay, Tomichan?"

"Sorry."

James struck a loud chord on his guitar that rang throughout the room, calling the attention of the group made up of mostly young college students. Those standing moved eagerly towards the stage. Deb played a few drum fills, the guitar and rhythm together building a fanfare. From stage right, the curtain swept aside, and Arthur—well, Pandora—stepped out from behind it. The crowd's applause overwhelmed the guitar vamping, which was saying something considering James had a Marshall tube amp.

Tomiko felt a rush every time she saw this. Pandora, all bedecked and adorned, was stunning. Hair sleek in a tight bob, lipstick gleaming in stark contrast to his pale skin. The gown tonight was truly impressive, and Tomi didn't hesitate to lean in to say so to Mrs. Ohashi. It was a cascade of gleaming silver lamé, fastened only to the shining cut-glass pendant of a necklace nestled against his clavicle. Unlike many of the other drag queens in the cafe, Pandora did not attempt any facsimile of breasts or hips. The dress seemed made for his geometric shape, cutting complementary triangular angles down his ribs.

Pandora swept his skirt to the side as he seated himself at the piano bench and looked up at the crowd from under his eyelashes, a small, secret smile on his lips.[1]

He played a few chords on the piano. Mrs. Ohashi sucked her teeth and said, "I knew I should have talked him into sleeves."

Tomi shook her head and smiled.

Pandora sang. The song was a ballad, something that sounded like a vampy, end-of-the-night tune for the regulars to sing along with. And the crowd did. They sang right along with the band, swaying, a few of them holding lighters aloft. When Tomi looked down at Mrs. Ohashi, she caught Arthur's mom smiling in satisfaction.

"You know, Tomichan," she said as the song ended in a long chord, "I never thought there'd be a place for him, where he could be whole. It scared me every day. I'm so glad to be proven wrong."

James' guitar chugged right into the next song. This one was upbeat, pushing the blues form and riffing off the top notes as Pandora stood and slammed against the keys like he was James Brown. The guitar squealed and the crowd jumped to life, mov-

---

1. "Lady Stardust" David Bowie

ing and dancing and creating an energy that was effervescent, suffusing the whole room.

"The world won't know what hit it," Tomi replied.

Footnotes

I love learning about what is based in historical evidence in a work of historical fiction. That's why I provide readers with this footnotes section, for those who are really interested in insurance maps and toilets and stuff. The research for this book taught me a lot about resilience, culture, identity, and love, and I think it's so important to lift up the rich queer history of the Midwest, because you don't have the live on the coast to have queer ancestors.

When Stonewall was going on in New York, students at the University of Minnesota were gathering under the moniker of FREE (Fight Repression of Erotic Expression). The organization was founded by Koreen Phelps and Stephen Ihrig, and it started with an offering of a free course at the Coffeehouse Extempore called The Homosexual Revolution. It grew into a full-fledged student group in May 1969 that hosted picnics, dances, and political action for gay and lesbian students. Former president of the group and University of Minnesota student body president Jack Baker is the most famous member, as a law student and filer in *Baker v. Nelson*, the first same-sex marriage case to make it to the Supreme Court (it was rejected and their marriage license was rejected by the lower courts, but a landmark nonetheless). The story goes that Jack came to the University's law program with the express desire to learn what he needed to do to marry his longtime partner, Michael Mc-

Connell, and to support and defend the legal rights of other queer people in the community. They're still married today.

The Club was also a real place, where queer people (particularly drag queens) gathered after hours in a safe place for food, music, and community. Skogie and the Flaming Pachukos (an early punk band) played there in 1972, presented by FREE, which shows how the layers of queer and musical counter-culture were overlapping in Minneapolis.

Cyn Collins' oral history of punk and indie rock in Minneapolis was really helpful, even though her stories started in 1974. It gave me a good idea of where a proto-glam rock band might show up, and set into stark relief how important the London and New York music scenes were to the growth of the sub-genre. Minneapolis wasn't a place where local glam rock thrived (unless you count Prince?), but it definitely was a hotbed for punk bands in the late 1970s. The Coffeehouse Extempore, in addition to being a safe-haven for queer and counter-culture people, also was a music venue. However, it is unlikely that a rock band like the Tarts would have played there, because as far as I can tell, they mostly hosted folk music.

A lot of this research made me super nostalgic, because even though I'm not old enough to have been at the University of Minnesota in the 1970s, I was there in the early aughts and frequented many of the same venues, even if they were under different names. The New Riverside became the Acadia, and the Red Sea Bar, the 400 Bar, the Nomad, and the Cedar Cultural Center were/are all on the same two block stretch where my friends and I stomped around looking for something better than Jock Jams. The musical legacy of the Cedar Riverside neighborhood is remarkable, and I'm curious how it will play out, since the pandemic closed down a lot of venues. We might be back into a desert of touring groups and Top 40 cover bands, but the innovation that comes out of that kind of status quo can be promising!

The road trip to Chicago represents the first scenes I've written that take place outside of Minnesota, but most of the places I featured, I have visited. I thank you for indulging me with the Meyer's Ace Hardware Store—it's closed now and everyone needs to know that the stage is still there. I got to go back there and commune with the jazz gods circa 2015 and it was awesome. There's a wonderful history of balls in Chicago, especially in and around Bronzeville. There would have been an annual Halloween ball around 1970, though it likely would have taken place the same night as the bacchanal in my story, rather than the next weekend.

One of the things that I think about a lot when I'm writing is how to convey that my characters exist not just in a historical context, but in cultural, racial, and ethnic contexts too. The Military Intelligence Service Language School was a program during World War II to recruit Japanese-Americans who had been incarcerated in Japanese internment camps to join the war effort by learning Japanese and doing intelligence work and code-breaking for the US. The school was housed at Fort Snelling and planted the seeds for the Japanese-American community that grew in the Twin Cities directly after the war.

Unrelated but similarly important to the context of the characters I built, South St. Paul and the West Side of St. Paul was host to a growing Mexican-American community. We didn't get much of Deb's backstory in this book (more to come), but she comes out of that community. It is important that my characters reflect the actual racial and ethnic diversity of the Twin Cities in 1970, rather than white-wash it. The ethnic studies movement had already come to the University of Minnesota campus in 1969 with the Morrill Hall takeover, and the FREE movement doesn't make sense or exist without the context of the civil rights and anti-war movements that came before it. I am so grateful to all of the help I received in making these characters ethnically, racially, and culturally whole. Any errors are entirely my own.

Eve Clark as a character has been an exercise in processing internalized misogyny. She sort of ended up a villain in this story, which makes me feel a bit icky, because I'm actually sort of in love with her. (I mean, that's her vibe, of course, but still.) She reflects the many double-edged swords women had to walk during the free-love movement, swords we still walk today. Her hedonistic nihilism and flagrant free-love contrast with how she curates herself, from the way she looks right down to her fake English accent. Her paradox of freedom and control is just one of her many paradoxes that have basically guaranteed she'll be back in a future book. Body autonomy and the commodification of women's bodies are issues about which I have a lot more to say, and Eve will live rent-free in my head until we finish teaching each other how to stop being such bitches.

Finally, I wanted to address Arthur's pronouns. Non-binary pronouns were not common circa 1970. They existed, but they were not often used, especially in the beginning of the Gay Liberation movement when respectability politics ruled. Therefore, I used he/him pronouns for Arthur because given his context, it's unlikely he'd have access to non-binary pronouns to identify with. Additionally, despite the Kinsey studies having been published and available and discussed in queer communities, there was still a lot of bi erasure going around. I tried to convey this in how James and Arthur both think about and process their sexuality in a binary way, despite both more likely falling somewhere along the spectrum rather than at one end or the other.

The way gender plays into their sexuality and their understanding of themselves also exists in a space that's sort of liminal for the period. In a time where pride parades were protests and it was dangerous to come out because you could easily be fired or evicted, coming together under the clear umbrellas of gay and lesbian was important for solidarity. There was a ton of tension within the Gay Liberation Movement between gay men, lesbians, and trans people, as evidenced by Sylvia Rivera's speech at the 1973 Christopher Street Liberation Day rally. I can't say I'm finished with exploring this period, or these characters within this context. There's so much more to learn!

"Armed with Language." *Minnesota Experience*, TPT Twin Cities PBS. Aired 5/17/2021.

Collins, Cyn. *Complicated Fun: The Birth of Minneapolis Punk and Indie Rock, 1974-1984*. Minnesota Historical Society Press: St. Paul, 2017.

DeCarlo, Peter. "Military Intelligence Service Language School (MISLS)." *MNopedia*, Minnesota Historical Society.

Ehrenhalt, Lizzie. "Over the Rainbow: Queer and Trans History in Minnesota." *MNopedia*, Minnesota Historical Society.

Edited by Jenkins, Andrea, John Medeiros, and Lisa Marie Brimmer. *Queer Voices: Poetry, Prose, and Pride*. Minnesota Historical Society Press: St. Paul, 2019.

Friedan, Betty. *The Feminine Mystique*. W. W. Norton & Company; 50th Anniversary edition, 2013.

Johansen, Bruce. "Out of Silence: FREE, Minnesota's First Gay Rights Organization." *Minnesota History*, Vol. 66, Issue 5 (Spring 2019).

"Out North: MNLGBTQ History." *Minnesota Experience*, TPT Twin Cities PBS. Aired 10/16/2017.

Shaw, Julia. *Bi: The Hidden Culture, History, and Science of Bisexuality*. Harry N. Abrams, 2022.

Shirey, Sarah. "Baker v. Nelson." *MNopedia*, Minnesota Historical Society.

Van Cleve, Stewart. *Land of 10,000 Loves*. University of Minnesota Press: Minneapolis, 2012.

Acknowledgements

Thanks to Louise Mayberry, ML Nolan, and Heather Hallman for beta-reading. My absolute favorite thing about the writing community is connecting with so many other incredible indie authors whose wisdom and guidance inspire me. Reading your comments on this book helped me believe I can be a writer. This story wouldn't be what it is without your help.

Thanks to Moondoggy for entertaining my absolutely bonkers hyper fixation with David Bowie and for driving all the way to Rochester to see the David Bowie documentary with me. Thank you to Kat9y for the help with the cover design and for showing me *Velvet Goldmine* at a formative age. And *Rocky Horror*. And *Hedwig and the Angry Inch*. I wouldn't be me without you.

Thank you to my son for writing and drawing with me and reminding me that you can't get good at anything without practice. Thanks to my daughter for challenging me to think about gender roles in endless new ways. Always a thousand thank yous to my spouse for being my first reader, answering all my questions about music gear, teaching me how to talk about how music sounds, and for helping me write "Hammer Your Heart." You're my muse.

Finally, thank you, Dear Reader, for reading this book. Writing is a lonely endeavor, and your feedback is the fuel that keeps indie authors like me going. Leave a rating and review on whatever platform you like—they form a trail of breadcrumbs for other like-minded readers to find my work.

Excerpt from
Can't Hardly Wait

The first time Patti Cooper saw Eve Clark, it was Halloween 1970, during her first (and only) year at the University of Minnesota. She'd been at the Cafe Extempore looking for sad folk music, and she found The Tarts, a wild, screaming mess of a band with the most salacious lead singer Patti had ever seen. It was worlds away from what she'd been looking for, and a thousand times better. It sparked things Patti hadn't been allowing herself to feel—anger and recklessness and lust and all the things the stay at the State Hospital in Anoka had supposedly cured Patti of. The band broke up shortly after that performance. The night lived in Patti's mind as the purest musical experience of her life, until 1975, when she saw The Suicide Commandos at the Blitz Bar. She'd kissed Gloria that night in the filthy dive bathroom and never looked back.

So the first time Patti Cooper actually met Eve Clark, it was significantly less transformative. Inflation was rampant, gas was prohibitively expensive, and Patti'd wrecked her car and therefore her job, so she'd begrudgingly accepted a gig no one else wanted—working as her Uncle Bruce's secretary. Eve Clark's presence was actually due to the precise reason that no one wanted the secretary job. Uncle Bruce was a philandering piece of shit, and he made his secretary do all the dirty work of balancing his multiple mistresses and his estranged wife. Eve Clark was her uncle's latest lunch date in the early spring of 1980 and Patti recognized her immediately when she walked into the office on that cold, clear day.

It was like Patti had time travelled. She was sitting at the desk in her tired polyester suit jacket, trying to figure out how to placate Bruce's wife while he bailed on his son's 8th birthday to do cocaine with Shelley Duvall (it wasn't actually Shelley Duvall, but she had to have a system to keep track of all of them, and this woman had serious front teeth). Then the door to the office opened, and Patti saw through the doorway a window to a past life, a curvy, slippery brunette with pouty lips playing a bass guitar like she was fucking it, only now her brown hair was feathered like Farah Fawcett and she was wearing a plaid miniskirt and a turtleneck, instead of a silk scarf. Oh, and she had a handbag instead of a bass guitar.[1]

Eve Clark's platform heels clacked on the parquet floor, and she looked towards Bruce's closed office door as she hitched her handbag under her arm. She didn't look at Patti until she was directly in front of her desk and only then, it was the barest glance.

"I'm meeting Mr. Hanson for lunch," Eve murmured with a soft English accent, her eyes back on the office door like Patti didn't really exist beyond her immediate function as gatekeeper of Bruce Hanson's calendar.

"What's your name?" Patti droned, even though she knew it. Because how could she not, after that performance all those years ago? She'd asked around, she'd found the band's name and met friends of its members. Actually, now that she thought about it, she might not have found FREE if she hadn't been at that show, which meant she wouldn't have found a Woman's

---

1. "Cherry Bomb" The Runaways

Coffeehouse and Amazon Books and Gloria. No. That was giving this woman far too much credit.

"Miss Clark," Eve said and her fingers went up to the neck of her shirt and adjusted it. Then, as if just realizing she was talking to a human who might have an iota of impact on her day, she looked at Patti and delivered a devastating smile like was a tip.

It was too late. Patti was already devastated. Eve Clark had been a goddess of her memory. A wild and free woman who stuck it to the man like she was fucking the status quo with a strap-on. A gay awakening that marked the beginning of Patti's becoming. To see her now, in Bruce's office, coinciding with a scrawled note on the calendar reading "Tits" underlined twice, was the most disappointing ending to the story Patti could possibly imagine. Hell, Patti had already lost most of her own self-respect just working for the bastard. A woman who was willing to take a lunch date with Bruce was not a woman Patti could regard with any modicum of respect. Bruce's mistresses weren't scarcely women at all; more ventriloquist dolls that Bruce carried around like Olympic medals.

"I see you right here," Patti said, closing the schedule diary before Clark could see what her entry was. Patti stood and smoothed the pencil skirt that made her feel better about her job because it was a horrible costume and represented nothing even close to who Patti was. She couldn't very well page Bruce on the phone and tell him Tits was here, so she walked to the closed office door and knocked gently.

Bruce liked things just so. It was easy to figure it out, because he'd get belligerent if you got it wrong. God, the second Patti could find any other job that paid the bills, she would, but a resume full of six-month stints clerking at record stores or waiting tables at queer bars didn't really get a lot of knocks on her door in these lean times. And as much as her grandmother disapproved of her "deviant lifestyle," she seemed to think that a lesbian was the perfect person to work for her horrible son. Patti was about the only person on planet earth that Bruce would never hit on.

However awful it was, she owed Gloria this much. Gloria had supported Patti through all the years she'd spent trying to get the Meltdowns off the ground, years of one calamity after another as she churned through three bassists and a drummer before ever even getting a show. Though the band was now defunct, she owed it to Gloria to support her through law school. She wouldn't fuck this up for Gloria, even if it meant working a job that drove a lance through everything Patti stood for.

"Bruce," Patti said as she clicked the office door behind her. "Your 12:00 is here."

"Lunch date?" Bruce said, looking up from his account book. Bruce was the CEO of a chain of Midwest grocery stores called the Red Squirrel. He was fucking obsessed with his account book and harassed countless franchise managers every week. He made big, sloppy money and believed deeply that Minneapolitans would starve without him. Like there weren't co-ops and corner shops in every neighborhood.

"Yes," Patti confirmed.

"Which one is it again? Denise?"

Patti's jaw firmed and it hurt a bit. She did it so often, she was starting to grind her teeth in her sleep. "You just wrote 'Tits' in the diary."

Bruce lit up like a forty-five year old child in a candy store. Only his favorite candy store was the third floor of Sex World. "Yes! Tits. She had some man's name like Irving or Curtis or—"

"Clark," Patti supplied without thinking, then regretted it. She would have loved to watch him struggle to figure out her name.

Bruce snapped his fingers. "Yes! Clark." He leveled Patti with a conspiratorial grin. He seemed to think having a gay secretary allowed him the privilege of objectifying women with her like they were in a men's locker room. "She's got a great rack, though, right? Met her at the bar of the Radisson. She's British or something. Bet she gives great head with a mouth like that."

Patti had to quit this job. She had to find something—any-thing—else. "Well, she's waiting just outside."

Bruce rubbed his hands together as he stood and said, "Great—where'd you make reservations?"

Patti grimaced. "Manny's Steakhouse."

"Mm, Pat, can you do something a little cheaper next time? It's only lunch."

Patti rolled her eyes and mumbled something that sounded like agreement. Bruce grasped her manfully by the shoulder and burst out the office door.

"Clark, baby!" he crooned, and Patti refused to look and see how Eve Clark regarded being received thus. "We've got reservations at Manny's."

"Oh, that sounds wonderful," Eve said, her words cut-glass posh despite the sleazy circumstances.

"Only the best for you, babe," Bruce said. Patti turned and saw him sling an arm around Eve as he ushered her out of the office.

For the next hour, Patti drafted her resignation on the type-writer and folded it to save for when she could finally afford to give it.

After work was finished and Bruce was sent off to his cocktail hour with a call-girl Patti'd been forced to engage for him, Patti took the bus back to Uptown feeling like so much shit scraped off the bottom of Bruce's shoe. She wasn't going to be able to go to the Amazon again until she got out of this job. She couldn't look any other feminists in the eye until she stopped being a traitor to all woman-kind.

Gloria was at home when Patti returned, buried in her Mitchell Law School books. She barely hummed a greeting as Patti came in through the door. That was all very well, be-cause Patti had no interest in telling her about her day. She went through the living room of their apartment to the only bedroom and stripped off her secretary costume. She hung the polyester suit up in the closet next to the other three Gloria had bought her. She pulled on jeans and a black t-shirt like she was climbing back into her own skin. She stood there with the closet door open for a minute, staring at her reflection. She'd cut her hair in the bathroom mirror to look like Joan Jett, but it was still ash brown because she didn't want to waste money trying to maintain a black dye job.

Her skin was still crawling, so she smeared her eyes with black liner. The person looking back at her through the mirror looked like someone who didn't give a flying fuck what anyone thought. It was a fraud, though, because if anyone found out what Patti did all day, she'd die of shame. The only comfort she could offer herself was that at least she wasn't the kind of woman who'd actually fuck Bruce Hanson. At least she wasn't Eve Clark.

Eve Clark will return in Can't Hardly Wait, *a punk rock romance.*

Visit <u>janehadleywrites.com</u> and subscribe to the newsletter for updates.

Also by

Jane Hadley

<u>Secret Soldier Series</u>
Fort Snelling, Minnesota. 1861.
A woman dresses as a man to enlist in the Union Army only to
fall in infuriating infatuation with her strapping bunkie.
<u>A Fine Looking Soldier: Volume 1</u>
<u>A Right Honorable Soldier: Volume 2</u>
Out now.

———

<u>Mrs. Milner Gets a Kitchen</u>
St. Paul, Minnesota. 1955.
A divorced mother contracts the installation of a new electric
kitchen and falls for her contractor under the nose of their
conformist 1950s immigrant community.
Free to newsletter subscribers on janehadleywrites.com

———

<u>Mr. Milner Gets Divorced</u>
St. Paul, Minnesota. 1954.
An upstanding husband, father, and city official reignites an
old high school friendship at the 1954 Winter Carnival and
proceeds to blow up his life.
Prequel to <u>Mrs. Milner Gets a Kitchen</u>*. Out now.*

About the Author

Jane Hadley writes historical romance teeming with footnotes and feels. She lives under seven layers of blankets where she can comfortably survey the cold tundra of Minnesota through wavy glass windows which she refuses to replace because old things are inherently valuable.

jane@janehadleywrites.com
On Instagram @janehadleywrites